I0527012

BATTLE'S LEGACY

DARIAN SMITH

Copyright © 2020 Darian Smith
All rights reserved.
ISBN: 978-0-473-54625-0

All rights reserved. No part of this book may be reproduced or transmitted in
any form or by any means, electronic or mechanical, including photocopying,
recording, or any information storage and retrieval system without prior
written permission of the Author. Your support of Author's rights is
appreciated.
Cover by Miblart.
This book is a work of fiction and any similarity to anyone, alive or dead, is
purely coincidental.

ACKNOWLEDGEMENTS

Once again, I need to thank my wife, Adrienne, for putting up with my weirdness and encouraging me to follow my passion.

I'd like to acknowledge Wilfred Berkhof, who won a charity auction put on by myself and other finalists in the SPFBO 5 competition to raise money to help fight bushfires in Australia.

Also, all the finalists in the SPFBO5 competition for their encouragement and support. We're terrible at being nemeses but great at being friends.

Most of all, to the fans and readers who buy, enjoy, and review my books. Your support means the world to me. Thank you for your patience with this one!
I hope it was worth the wait.

PROLOGUE

Master Jordell dipped his fingers into the basin and watched tendrils of blood swirl off in the water like smoke in the wind. The action was familiar and yet also strange. They were old hands now, wrinkled and spotted with age. They'd been smooth when he'd first learned his craft but the years caught up with everyone but the dead. He preferred old age to the alternative.

The clear liquid quickly darkened to the color of diluted wine. Jordell lifted his hands and shook the remaining droplets loose then moved to a second, clean basin. The physician college building was old as well, much of it built when plumbing was yet to be developed properly. The basins were a necessary evil when the beds were full and surgeries had to take place away from the rooms with running water. It reminded him of the medical tents during the war - conditions here were better by far and the patients...well, even in a city like Alapra, it was rare to get more than a few serious traumas at a time. Medical treatment in a war zone was another thing entirely.

The water in the second basin absorbed the barest tinge of color that quickly diffused to nothing. He reached for a towel to dry off. There was something therapeutic about washing off blood after a surgery. Successful or not, cutting into a fellow human being was an action that required cleansing - both emotionally and physically. No matter how long he'd been doing it and how many lives he'd saved, he still had moments where the cutting of flesh gave him pause. He valued those moments. Every good physician had to weigh up the benefits and costs of the treatment they provided. Necessity was his friend and his guide.

He smiled to himself. They'd done good work today, he and necessity. Barring infection, a woman who would otherwise have died of a burst appendix now had a good chance to live. Definitely a better day than back in the war.

"Master Jordell?" One of the student physicians called softly from the doorway. She'd recently cropped her hair short to keep from having to tie it up as she worked. It suited her. "He's doing it again."

Jordell frowned and ran through a list of patients in his head. "Who's doing what again?"

"The man who calls himself the General. He's...foraging."

"Ah. I see." Jordell sighed. He wasn't the only one with bad memories of the war. "Thank you for letting me know. I'll deal with it."

"Thank you, sir."

"And he doesn't 'call himself' a General. He is a General. A Hooded fine one too. That doesn't change because he's fallen on hard times. If it weren't for people like him, we wouldn't be here today. Remember that."

Her face flushed almost as red as the basin water. "Yes, Master Jordell. Sorry."

How quickly they forget, he thought to himself as he made his way through the labyrinth of hallways toward the alley behind the hospital. Youth was society's blank page - all new opportunities and none of the old lessons at all.

The huge garbage bin behind the Physician college hospital had always been a temptation for the homeless and hungry. Sick people often struggled to eat and left plenty of scraps. While hospital food wasn't the tastiest, it was healthy enough and, when thrown away, free. Most potential scavengers lost their appetite quickly when faced with the reality of hospital waste, however. Most, but not all.

As Master Jordell stepped out into the alley, he saw the General climb the wheel spokes of the carriage-sized bin and lift the lid. Flies buzzed past his face in a swarm and the smell of feces, vomit, and blood hit Jordell even at a distance.

The General huffed his breath out through his nostrils, trying to drive away the stench. He still wore the remains of his military uniform. The fabric was worn through at the knees and elbows, covered in dirt, and he no longer had any weapons, but every pin of rank was still present and medals hung at his chest. Jordell often wondered if the man had been tempted to sell them to metal merchants but it seemed there were lines the General would not cross.

"General?" Jordell called. "Are you hungry?"

The General shook his head and edged to the right of the bin. That side was closest to the kitchens and, thanks to the inherent laziness of human nature, more likely to hold food.

Jordell moved closer and touched the man's elbow. "How have you been?"

In the bin, old bandages lay tangled like noodles among abandoned dressings and other hospital debris. They were mostly to the left and separate from the food scraps...mostly.

"Not taking anything important," he muttered. "It's thrown away. All thrown away. Nobody wants it but me." He grinned at Jordell, his teeth brown and broken. "No feet today."

"No," Jordell agreed. "No feet." They'd found the General scavenging after an amputation some weeks back and the gangrenous foot had stuck in his mind but not, apparently, dulled his appetite. "Plenty of other nasties though." He reached for the homeless man's shoulder.

The general dodged and leaned over the side of the bin to scoop up a chunk of dried meat and a slice of bread. He jumped down from the wheel and held the food close to his chest like a precious treasure.

"Put them back," Jordell said. "They're filthy."

"No!" The general pulled a dagger from somewhere in the filthy rags that remained of his uniform and held it out in front of him with one hand while he kept a close grip on the pilfered food with the other. "It's mine. Mine!"

"Come on." Jordell raised his hands to show they were empty and non-threatening. "You know I'm a physician. I'm trying to help you. I really wouldn't eat anything from this bin. It's potentially infectious. How about I take you to the Alapran Third Monastery? They provide food for the homeless and it'll be much safer to eat." He knew as soon as the words were out of his mouth that he'd made a mistake mentioning it.

The General's eyes darkened. "I don't go near the church. I'll never go back there. You can't make me." He waved the knife at Jordell.

The old physician sighed. "I won't make you. I just...I want you to have food that's safe to eat and it's part of the priests' role to take care of people. Ahpra is a nurturing goddess, after all. You're giving the priests an opportunity to show their piety."

"The Hooded One can have Ahpra. She didn't help me in the war."

The old man's eyes and nose crinkled. "Well, she's his sister, so I doubt he will. But you survived, didn't you? So perhaps she had her eye on you after all."

"Others didn't," the general said, then lowered his voice to a whisper. "It's not safe there. The fire finds me." He looked around, searching for an unseen threat. "I hear screaming."

Jordell kept his voice soft. Many soldiers had suffered like this after the war. For some, the things they'd seen lived on in their minds no matter how long Kalanon was at peace. "There's no fire here, General. No screams. No danger. It's just your memories. Just your dreams."

The general shuddered and his eyes narrowed. "You're part of it? Are you one of them? Why do you want to take me back there?"

"I..." Jordell let his voice trail off. Was there anything he could say that could pull the man far enough out of his mixed memories and delusion to be reasoned with? After all these years it seemed the guilt and trauma had eaten whatever was left of his mind. The best he could do was make sure he didn't starve or catch a disease from eating contaminated food. "Okay, General. We won't go anywhere. Just...let me get you something fresh from the kitchens."

The homeless man looked at him for a long moment then, slowly, lowered the knife. "Something nice."

Jordell smiled. "Okay. Something nice." He held out his hand. "Let me throw away that old, rotted stuff and then we'll go to the kitchen."

He stepped closer and his fingers brushed the hard crust of the stale bread but before he could close them, the general dropped it and grasped his wrist in bone-bruising grip. The ex-soldier twisted his arm and pulled him in, hard against his chest. Jordell felt the sharp edge of the general's blade against his throat. The smell of old sweat and soiled clothes filled his nostrils.

The general shuddered against Jordell's back. "I can't go back to the church. I can't see them die. Not again."

Jordell swallowed and the blade cut into his skin. "You don't have to do this. We won't go anywhere you don't want." His voice quavered but he held his body perfectly still.

"You can't make me," the general hissed. "Save

him another way!"

"Save who?"

The dagger pressed harder. "You can't trick me again."

"I don't want to trick you, General. I want to help." If only he could help himself! His old limbs seemed frozen. Despite all that time with the army, he'd never learned the skills of combat. His focus had always been on saving lives. There were always so many more that needed saving and so little time to do the work.

"Master Jordell!" The young apprentice stepped from the doorway, her eyes wide.

"Stay back!" He put all the authority he could into that command. He could save one last life by keeping her out of harm's way. That would be enough. One more would have to be enough. Blood trickled down his neck. "Stay safe. Run."

The general's voice muttered in his ear. "Safe, not safe, safe, not safe."

The tip of the blade twisted, drilling into the soft flesh of Jordell's neck. He ran through the anatomy of it in his mind. An inch or two from the jugular. A little deeper for the windpipe. Death was close.

"Safe, not safe. Save the king. Must stop it. Have to..." The general's words broke off in a scream and a spasm ran through the man's body.

The knife moved away from Jordell's neck just

a fraction. The old physician lunged to the side and downward. The blade scored across the side of his face as he fell but he broke free of the general's hold. He hit the hard cobblestones and rolled, putting as much distance between him and his attacker as he could.

The general kept screaming, a high pitched, desperate shriek.

Jordell struck the wall of the college with a thud that jarred him and sent a burst of pain through his shoulder. Heat poured over his face in waves.

The general was on fire. Flames licked over his limbs, and roared up to his face, casting his features in a weird alien light. His fingers clenched around the metal of his dagger even as the steel glowed red hot. His mouth opened but his screams were smothered by fire dancing on his tongue.

Horror gripped Jordell more tightly than any attacker ever could but he couldn't take his eyes from what was happening before him. "Blood and Tears!"

The general's skin blistered and turned black. His knees gave way and his burning corpse fell to the ground. The smell of cooked meat was overpowering.

Jordell turned away and vomited.

CHAPTER ONE

The king's private audience chamber was an oasis of quiet in a palace overrun with activity. Late afternoon light poured through high windows and gilded the room with gold. In lieu of a throne, a wide couch, piled high with cushions, dominated one side of the room. Smaller chairs were arranged round it like flowers facing the sun. Life-sized paintings of past kings and queens hung on the walls, giving visitors the impression of having stumbled into a strange sort of royal family reunion. The sounds of bustling servants, kitchen staff, and rowdy courtiers were muffled by the closed door, providing an intimacy one didn't often get with the king.

King Aldan sat on the couch, one arm resting across the back, the other hand fiddling with the edge of a cushion. Brannon noticed the dark circles under his friend's eyes. He hadn't seen Aldan so obviously tired in a long time. Not since the first year after the war. Back then, they'd all had trouble finding sleep. The memories of those who had died were always noisiest in the darkest hours of a peaceful night. Every soldier had to find their own way of quieting those memories over time. He had no doubt that royal responsibility weighed heavily in times of peace as well but decisions at court were easier to sleep with than those made in the battlefield.

In the chair to Brannon's right, Ula Lanok sat cross-legged, her leather smock riding high on her thighs, exposing the purple skin of her legs all the way to her bare feet. Tattooed runes twined down her body like dark vines of power, protecting her from the kaluki she used to make Risen.

To the left, a scowling bearded man in rough woolen garb shot glares across at the Djin woman, so caught in his anger that he almost forgot to show proper deference to the king.

"Firstly, I'd like to thank you for meeting today," King Aldan said. "Farmer Kerdic, this is my Champion and Master of Investigations, Sir Brannon Kesh, and the Prioress Ula Lanok. I want to assure you that you all have my respect and my ear. I trust we can resolve any misunderstandings quickly. We wouldn't want an international incident to come out of a simple mistake, after all." He gave a warm, disarming smile.

"There was no misunderstanding, your majesty," Kerdic insisted. "I saw that purple wench with my own eyes. No mistake. I want..." His voice trailed off when the king's jaw hardened and one eyebrow raised. "I saw her," he finished lamely.

Brannon narrowed his eyes. "Prioress Ula has been an invaluable ally to Kalanon. In return she's been promised safe haven here."

Ula herself simply sat still, her gaze on a beam of sunlight that dappled the floor.

Aldan held up his hand. "No one is suggesting anything different, Brannon. But we have to admit, some people find certain Djinan customs unnerving."

Brannon folded his arms. Unnerving was perhaps the kindest description for Ula's ability to command a dark version of the Earth spirits to inhabit and reanimate a corpse into a creature that was immensely strong and difficult to kill. The Risen were dangerous to anyone but the one who controlled them. "Fear of the unknown isn't a good reason to stir up trouble."

"But theft is." The farmer lifted his chin defiantly. "I've a family to feed."

"Ula stole something? Are you sure?" Brannon found it difficult to believe. Ula was possibly the least materialistic person he'd ever met. She had no use for money - her culture traded entirely by barter and gathering what resources they needed from the land and the sea around their islands.

"And her monster tried to kill me." He tilted his head and pointed to a mark on his cheekbone where a split in the skin was scabbed over and surrounded by an angry bruise.

Brannon glanced at Ula.

She shrugged. "If Risen try to kill him, he be dead. When you attack a woman who commands Risen, you get hit. Maybe gentle, maybe not. It risky. Not smart thing to do."

"Attack?" Brannon frowned.

"Perhaps we should hear the whole story from both sides," King Aldan interrupted. "Kerdic, tell us what you saw. From the beginning."

The farmer settled into his chair, swallowed, and nodded. "I was fixing a fence on my far paddock and heard the cattle making a fuss. They were upset like there was a predator in the herd. We don't usually get wolves this close to the city, but we get thieves. A lot of farmers have been talking about their stock going missing lately. When I got there..." He swallowed. "Her undead monster had killed one of my cows. And she was performing some evil ritual over it. Summoning who knows what Hooded demon to kill me next!"

"I be putting Risen back in the ground," Ula grumbled. "Cow for leather to make new clothes. And I send meat to castle kitchen to help feed all the people here."

"But they're *my* cows."

Ula held her hands out, palms exposed. "I not know this. I sorry. In my country animals be for everyone. All people fish and hunt and share what we catch. Is responsibility of everyone to not take too much." She shrugged and shook her head. "I do not understand how a person may own living animals. Is much to learn about Kalan ways."

"There is much about your ways that we Kalans don't understand as well," King Aldan said gently. "I'm sure any of us would be likely to make similar errors if we were transplanted to the Djinan islands. Don't you agree, Brannon?"

Brannon nodded. "Definitely. Poor Ula would have to watch me day and night."

Kerdic huffed and folded his arms.

"The crown will reimburse you for your lost cow, Farmer Kerdic. And at a rate I'm sure you'll find more than generous." Aldan took a coin purse from his pocket and let the contents jingle as he toyed with it.

Kerdic's arms unfolded.

Brannon leaned forward. "I'd say the crown owes the Prioress for services rendered, wouldn't you, Your Majesty?"

Aldan narrowed his eyes and Brannon had to hide a grin. "Quite," Aldan agreed. "The reimbursement comes from Ula's own payment for the work she has done on our behalf. I trust that will be the end of the matter. I would hate to hear word of this misunderstanding spreading now that we've cleared it up that she bought your cow at such a good price."

The farmer nodded and reached for the gold.

Aldan kept hold of the purse and looked the man in the eye.

Kerdic dropped his gaze first. "Of course, Your Majesty. I understand."

Aldan let go of the purse and smiled. "Excellent. Then I'd say we're done. Thank you for your time. I'll have the palace kitchens talk to you about our milk requirements. It's always good to have such a reliable supplier."

Kerdic bowed. "Thank you, Your Majesty."

When the door closed behind the man, Aldan turned to Brannon and Ula. "Can I trust that there will be no further instances of culture clash in my kingdom?"

"I learn more about Kalans every day," said Ula. "Not make same mistake twice."

"Very good." The king turned to Brannon. "Perhaps you could have some discussions about when and where a Risen should be deployed? I don't want the populace terrorized. Especially with the masquerade coming up. The last thing we need at this point is another international incident."

"Of course." Brannon hesitated. "How are you

doing?"

"Fine."

"Really? Because you look exhausted," Brannon said.

Aldan laughed. "I can always count on you to be an antidote to court flattery."

"You know what I mean."

The laugh faded. "It's Claydan. He's having difficulty adjusting to life back here."

"He not be the only one," Ula muttered. At a look from Brannon she fell silent.

Aldan rubbed a hand over his face. "I'm grateful to have my boy back but he's changed so much. Been through so much."

"He's a man now," Brannon said.

"Still my boy." The king shook his head. "I've taken to watching over him while he sleeps. He has night terrors about that place and nothing I do seems to soothe him. I wake him up and he still screams." He took a deep breath and let it out in a long, slow sigh.

"I'm sorry Aldan." Brannon reached out to touch his friend's arm. "You should have said something."

"It's not an enemy to fight and he's not sick. What could you do other than worry with me? And I'm doing more than enough of that on my own."

Brannon gave a wry chuckle. "Well, much as I'd enjoy that, perhaps I could mix up something to help him sleep more peacefully. And something for you as well. You're no use to him or the kingdom if you're exhausted."

The king blinked at him. "Ahpra's Tears. I still forget you have those kinds of skills now."

Brannon grinned. "Well, you've seen me working with a sword much more often. Actually, I might have Taran do it. Medicines are his specialty and it would probably be good for Claydan to have someone to talk to who has been there and understands. After all, Taran had to learn about living away from the Children of Starlight as well." The priest might not have nailed every social nicety, but he'd come a long way since escaping from the assassins. His experience had to be of help to the struggling prince.

"Good idea. Taran visits to deliver the stardust elixir anyway. They can -" A knock on the door interrupted. "Come in."

A guard stepped in and saluted. "Sorry for the interruption, Your Majesty. There's a messenger from the Master Jordell at the Physician College for the Master of Investigations. There's been a murder."

CHAPTER TWO

Brannon and Ula followed the messenger, an anxious apprentice physician, through the castle grounds and out into the city. Though it was still early evening, the air was much cooler than it had been in the audience chamber and Brannon wished he'd brought a coat. The streets were quiet, with most shops closed and many of the houses in this upmarket part of the city sealed up against the night as their inhabitants enjoyed light and warmth within. Their footsteps were loud on the cobblestones and flickering shadows loomed, shifting this way and that as moonlight and lamplight battled in the street. Brannon found his hand resting on the hilt of his sword. It was hard not to wonder if a murderer was hiding in those shadows. He was glad when they found a rental carriage and climbed aboard.

As the carriage started moving, he spoke to the apprentice physician. "What happened?" He asked her. "This murder has to be strange for Master Jordell to send for me. What are we walking into?"

She shook her head. "It's better you see it for yourself. We'll be there soon." She swallowed and turned to watch the street through the window.

Brannon opened his mouth to press for information but then closed it again. She was right. Seeing the evidence with his own eyes was always best, but he couldn't help being disturbed by her reticence. People were usually keen to gossip about what they'd seen and only became silent when it upset them deeply. Physicians were used to injury and death. What could have shocked one into silence?

He took a deep breath and let his mind turn elsewhere. The discussion with Aldan reminded him how difficult the crown prince's life had been with his captors. Kidnapped as a child and addicted to the drug the Assassin House used to control its members, tormented and mutilated, all in an attempt to control Kalanon - no wonder he still had nightmares. Brannon remembered how difficult his own adjustment to regular peace-time life had been after the war. Presumably, it was a similar experience for Prince Claydan. Coming home after such an ordeal was like entering an entirely new world.

He looked across at the tattooed prioress. Prince Claydan was not the only one experiencing a culture shock. "I'm sorry about the difficulty with that farmer."

Ula gave a little smile. "We not know all each other's ways. Easy to not trust when you do not understand. I be sorry too. I did not mean to take what belongs to someone else or to cause trouble."

"I know." They'd come to an agreement that Ula remain in Kalanon until she could be sure of her welcome back in Djinan. The Priory of Gradinath had been unsettled by what she'd done to keep Kalanon safe. Kalanon and the world. Brannon couldn't help thinking they owed her. "How are you settling into life in Kalanon?"

The Djin woman shrugged. "Is fine. Kalan people stare a lot. They be curious."

"Yeah. I guess they don't see many Djin in Alapra. Technically it's 'they *are* curious.'"

Ula pressed her lips together and took a deep breath. "Kalan *are* a difficult language to learn," she said.

"Is," he corrected. "Kalan *is* a difficult language."

A torrent of fast-paced Djin syllables poured from Ula's mouth.

Brannon, realizing curse words had the same tone in any language, tried to change the subject. "If you want, we could get you some Kalan clothing so you don't stand out as much."

Ula frowned. "Why? I'm not Kalan. A fish doesn't wear feathers to please the birds."

"I suppose not." Brannon blinked. "But then you're a fish that lives in the trees now so...if you want to adjust, there's nothing wrong with that."

She pursed her lips for a moment, then shrugged again and grinned. "I like certain Kalans well enough. But I like my Djin self more."

Brannon grinned back. "Fair enough. We like you too."

The carriage turned a corner into an older part of the city and the apprentice physician rapped on the roof to signal the driver. They were close to the physician college hospital now. The carriage pulled over about a block from the main entrance and the apprentice paid the driver. "This way," she said, and led them into an alleyway around the back of the hospital building. They were met by two young men in grey - more student physicians. Further down the alley, lit lanterns had been placed in a circle. Brannon could see Master Jordell in that circle of light and another shape on the ground.

"This is as far as I go," his guide said. "I don't need to see that again." She turned away.

As Brannon drew closer, the smell of garbage and burnt meat filled his nostrils and crammed its way into his lungs. In the lamplight, Master Jordell looked older and more tired than Brannon had ever seen him. Shadows played in the lines on his face, turning them into deep crevices into which hope had fallen and been lost. In the darkest moments of the war, Jordell had been the hope of many a wounded soldier. It was hard to see the deep sadness in his eyes. A sadness that came not from losing a battle with illness or even an enemy in war, but from losing a patient in a senseless, needless death. Murder killed not only the victim, but sometimes the hope for a better world - for humanity - in living witnesses as well.

Brannon embraced his teacher. "I'm sorry. I came as soon as I could."

Jordell shook himself free and waved him away. "Please. I've seen plenty of death in my time."

"I know."

The old man sighed. "Nothing like this, though. Not since the war. Hardly even then."

"What happened?"

"He just...burned." Master Jordell pointed to the shape on the ground.

Brannon looked closer. This was the source of the burnt meat smell. At first, his mind wouldn't recognize it as human. The shape was bent and wrong and there was no skin, little flesh, and what remained was charred black. There was nothing recognizable in what was left, not at first glance anyway. "Who is he?"

"I don't know his actual name," Master Jordell admitted. "He only ever introduced himself as General. He never adjusted after the war. He's homeless. He sometimes scavenges here for scraps. Scavenged."

It had happened more than most people wanted to admit. Soldiers of all ranks were haunted by what they'd seen and what they'd done during the time they served. Brannon himself still had nightmares. For some, the transition back to a normal life in peacetime was too wide a gap when the ghosts of those they'd seen dead were clawing at their backs. The past was dead and gone but the Wolf of memory could be relentless.

"Did he have any enemies?"

"No idea." Jordell shrugged. "I didn't know him well. I think he usually slept down by the docks."

Brannon raised an eyebrow. "He didn't stay at the church sanctuary?"

"He didn't like the church for some reason. Seemed scared of them."

"Really?" Brannon raised an eyebrow. "I wonder why." He knelt next to the corpse and gently lifted the blackened shape that was the victim's head. The underside was a little less damaged, but most of the skin and muscle were gone, exposing teeth and bone turned brown and grey by exposure to heat. There was no sign of a pyre or any kind of fuel under the body. He laid the head down gently. This had been a person...but it was hard to see that now.

"So, he was dumped here?" Twisted by fire as it was, the size and shape of the skeletal structure - once Brannon looked past the charred flesh - suggested a male, which matched Jordell's identification. "Do you know how long ago?"

Master Jordell shook his head. "He wasn't dumped. He burned here. We've changed nothing since ascertaining we couldn't save him."

"But..." For the first time, Brannon noticed the bandages on the old man's hands. He'd tried to save the victim despite the flames. "You're hurt. You were here when it happened."

"I'm fine."

"How badly burned are you?"

"I'm fine," Master Jordell repeated. "I've an entire hospital full of physicians, Brannon. Do you think you're the only one who can treat a simple burn?"

"Okay, okay." Brannon held up his hands in surrender. "Did you see where he originally caught fire? There's no indication of a bonfire. No wood ash or any sign of restraints. Could he have spilled lamp oil on himself?" He couldn't pick up the scent of oil but it was hard to smell anything but the burned flesh. Brannon kept his breathing shallow and tried not to think about that smell and what it meant. It had been a long time since he'd felt sick at the sight of an injury but this...this would turn his stomach if he let it. He stood up and took a step away to separate himself from the smell.

"No. That's why I sent for you." Master Jordell gave a long, slow sigh. "There was nothing. No candle, no bonfire, no lamp. No one nearby but me and Rachela." He gestured toward the alley entrance where the woman who had brought them stood hugging herself and staring out into the night. "The poor man just...burst into flames."

Brannon frowned. "What, from nothing?"

"From nothing." Master Jordell lifted a trembling hand to cover his face. "Ahpra's Tears, Brannon. He screamed like you wouldn't believe. We tried to save him but the flames wouldn't go out. He screamed for such a long time. And...and then he stopped."

A shudder ran across Brannon's skin as his mind played an echo of the man's suffering. To be alive and burning... He'd seen it happen in the war, as a result of burning pitch thrown from city walls. He never wanted to see it again. It had to be one of the worst ways to die.

He blocked out the memories and focused on the task at hand. The night would require more unpleasantness yet. "How well do you know Rachela?"

Jordell lowered his hand and folded his arms.

"What do you mean? She studies at the college and works in the hospital."

"Mmm." Brannon nodded. "And she was the only other person here when it happened? Is there a chance that she could be responsible?"

"What? That she poured oil on him when I wasn't looking and set him alight?"

"Or..." Brannon waggled his fingers. "Magic or Ahpra knows what else. Has there been anything strange about her at all?"

The old man considered it. "She's from a local family. Moderately skilled. Nothing obviously suspicious."

"Of course." Brannon sighed. "It couldn't be that easy."

Ula crouched on the other side of the corpse, silent but for the clacking of the beads in her hair as she moved. She ran her hands over the length of the charred body as if feeling for heat, not quite touching.

"What is she doing?" Master Jordell frowned.

"Helping." Brannon held up his hand to quiet his mentor. "She'll make him a Risen and get access to his memories. We can get an idea of who he was and maybe even who his enemies were."

Ula looked up and shook her head. "Hard to make Risen. Body is much burned. Even very strong kaluki struggle to repair."

Brannon scratched his scar and looked up and

down the alley. There was little in the way of evidence. Whatever the victim had been carrying had burned up along with his flesh. "Can you try?"

The beads in her hair clacked again as she nodded. "I try."

"Let's get a couple of samples first. Taran might be able to identify a compound that explains why he burned." Human beings didn't just catch fire. Not without help.

Brannon took a dagger from his belt and cut a small piece of charred flesh away from the corpse. It smelled like burnt meat. His throat closed up and he gagged.

"Don't throw up on the victim, Brannon," a familiar voice called out. "It's disrespectful."

Brannon looked up to see Magus Draeson strolling towards them. The mage was dressed impeccably, as usual. His coat hung down to his knees, trimmed with embroidery in a thread that sparkled in the lamp-light. He stepped carefully to avoid getting rubbish on his boots.

Ula clapped her hands. "The wizard is here."

"Not wizard," Draeson snapped. "Mage."

Her lips twitched upward. "Is not same?"

"You know it isn't."

Brannon wrapped the sample in a cloth and tucked it into his pocket. "Good to see you, Draeson. How did you know we'd be here?"

"Aldan sent me. He seemed to think you might

require my expertise." The mage gestured around the scene. "Seems like he might have been right."

Brannon nodded. "It sure looks like magic was involved. What can you tell us?"

Draeson looked over the scene, wrinkling his nose as he inspected the victim. "Magic could have done it, certainly. It's hard to say for sure."

"Can't you...I don't know, sense it or something when another mage does their thing?"

Draeson's eyes narrowed. "Can you *sense* when another warrior has used a sword? Or when another physician has given out medicine?"

Brannon sighed. "No. Of course not."

"Well then." The mage folded his arms. "There are limits to what I can do, you know. And even if magic was used, it's long finished now. The man's a barbeque."

"Draeson!"

"Well he is." Draeson huffed. "But I'll look around and see if I can detect any active spells. If I get close enough to an illusion, I might be able to tell."

Brannon clenched his fingers into a fist. An illusion would mean someone was hiding in the alley. Watching them. It was a disquieting thought. "Will Ula's magic influence your search?"

"No. What she does is...different." Draeson wrinkled his nose.

Ula nodded, the beads in her hair clacking as

she did. "Making Risen is not a thing a wizard can do."

"Mage," Draeson growled.

Ula grinned and began taking small jars of earth from a leather bag she had strapped around her waist. She placed them around the body, followed by a candle, and a small sheaf of straw. Brannon had seen her perform the ritual to make a Risen a few times before but still felt as if invisible insects crawled over his skin as he watched her burn the straw and smudge ash on the already charred body. She drooled saliva onto the ground next to the corpse and then blew gently across it. An unnatural wind blew through the alley, stirring the dust and loose garbage into swirling eddies.

Master Jordell took three steps back from the Djin woman and her ritual. His eyes were wide and though his mouth opened, his voice remained silent.

Another voice, however, did not. "Wow. Is that a dead person? What are you doing with it?"

The mystical wind faded as Ula lifted her head and frowned. "Who?"

Brannon looked past her to see a girl of about ten years of age standing just at the edge of the lamp light. "Shalyn? What are you doing here?" He hadn't seen the cobbler's daughter since they'd rescued her and several other kidnapped children from a slaver some weeks ago. With no remaining family, she'd moved into Lady Magda's Orphanage, now being managed by the church.

"Um...I followed Draeson." Shalyn stared at the dead man until Master Jordell shuffled forward and blocked her vision.

"Rachela, you can't just let anyone through," the old man called to the apprentice physicians at the ally entrance. "This is no place for a child."

"She said she's with the mage," the short haired woman replied.

Brannon, Ula, and Jordell all turned to look at Draeson.

"Oh, Ahpra's Tears. You again?" The mage rolled his eyes. "She's been following me everywhere." He flapped his hand at Shalyn. "Go back to the orphanage, girl. You're not my puppy."

Brannon shot the mage a glare. "She lost her father. Try to show a little compassion." He joined Jordell in trying to shield the girl's view and usher her away. "This isn't the place for a child, Shalyn. We don't want you having nightmares. Why don't we have someone take you home? They'll be worried about you."

She shrugged. "They won't have noticed I'm gone."

"I'm sure that's not true," Brannon said. He started to say more but felt the tug of spirit wind running through him again. He turned to see Ula crouched over the body once more.

Ula chanted in her own language, the sounds

sharp to Brannon's ears. The wind swirled around her, kicking up dead leaves, dust, and ash.

The burned corpse at her feet twitched. Brannon watched, waiting to see how much of the damage the Kaluki Ula had summoned would heal as it animated the body. He'd seen Ula make Risen before and knew some of the rules. A kaluki would always try to heal the body it inhabited but the amount of repair depended on the strength of the kaluki and the freshness of the body in which it was placed. Once healed to the best of its ability and fully inhabiting the Risen, the kaluki could access the more established memories of the person whose body it was using. Memories immediately preceding death were too damaged but there were likely clues in the General's mind that could help shed light on who might have plotted his murder.

A tremor ran though the burned body as the incinerated muscles spasmed. The damage did not heal. The body jerked again and its mouth opened, silent and gasping at first, then it emitted a rasp that became gradually louder.

Ula's hands were clenched into fists, her shoulders tight. "Body too much burned," she ground out through gritted teeth.

Brannon's stomach dropped. He shoved his mentor toward Shalyn. "Get her out of here. Something's wrong."

The wind around Ula and the Risen whipped

harder, a precise tornado, encapsulating the two of them. The Risen raised a hand, its fingers fused into claws. The rasping in its throat gained voice. It became a scream. The kaluki in the burned shell of a man was screaming.

A moment later, Ula screamed too.

CHAPTER THREE

U la felt the kaluki slip into the burned flesh and its grip falter. She pushed harder. The kaluki she'd summoned was strong and if any could repair a body so severely burned, it would be this one. She willed it on. She was stronger now. Surely she could push the kaluki to do more. The body need not be perfect. Just good enough to speak and access memories. The body twitched, wind moving around it as the kaluki sank deeper, but then the connection crumbled like ash.

The kaluki struggled in her grip, forcing itself back, out of the body and into Ula. She swore and focused her power, holding the incorporeal form like a terrified cat trying to escape, and pushed it back. "You must do as I command, kaluki! You must."

She felt it bond once more with the body and then, terrifyingly, the burned flesh released its pain. The kaluki, caught half in and half out of the process of becoming a Risen, was flooded with fire. It screamed a bloodcurdling shriek of agony directly into Ula's mind. She gasped and almost lost her hold. She couldn't allow the kaluki to flee - not without the proper ritual to return it to its realm. Unbound, there was no telling what such a powerful creature would do in this world.

It screamed again and she could sense the agony burning along the tether that bound a Risen to its master. The power swirled between them, uncontrolled but trapped. Then the pain hit her too and her body dissolved in fire.

She didn't know how long she spent lost in pain but, when she woke, her body was numb. Her arms and legs seemed frozen in place, her sense of touch sheared off or encased in ice. As her vision returned, she felt a shock of fear in her gut. She was no longer in the alleyway in Alapra. The hard stone of the cavern of the Gatuul Naah surrounded her. She faced the reflective waters of the tidal pool that had once threatened to take her life.

She struggled but her body was held fast.

"Ssshh." A multitude of voices came to her from the pool. Her own reflection stared back at her but with glowing beads in her hair and eyes that were solid agate with no whites in them at all. "Wait."

The water in the pool rippled and her reflection broke into glimmering fragments of light, only to reassemble into a new image: the alley in which her own body stood over a screaming burned corpse.

She saw Master Jordell and Shalyn running to the safety of the building, keeping clear of the spill of kaluki power that swirled around her. Brannon faced her, his sword drawn and his jaw tight. Ula felt for him. He knew the challenge of an unbound Risen. No matter what extra strength the Earth Spirits had given him against Risen, he wouldn't be able to hold one off forever and he had no way to return a kaluki to its own realm. Opposite Brannon, Magus Draeson held a ball of lightning in the palm of his hand. She hoped the mage intended it for the screaming kaluki and not for her but...her own screams were terrifying.

"Ula? Are you okay?" She saw Brannon take a tentative step forward.

The screaming stopped and the Risen jerked and fell still.

Ula saw the version of herself in the water turn to face him and tilt her head to the side. Her eyes had no whites in them at all, just solid glistening agate. The beads in her hair glowed like a swarm of fireflies. When she spoke, it was with a multitude of voices. "Ula is safe. For now."

The real Ula struggled against her bonds. "That's my body," she hissed. "Mine!"

Brannon swallowed. "You're the Avatar. What happened?"

The Ula in the water spoke. "All Djin know that a cremated body cannot become Risen, but this body is not fully ash. Ula hoped there was enough for a strong kaluki to mend but the kaluki became trapped. It was both Risen and not Risen - partly caught in the body and partly in the bond to its summoner. Ula was being pulled along with it. We could not allow this."

"Because she's still your avatar?"

"Because she is ours. Like you and the other."

The other being Ambassador Ylani, the only other person present when they'd first made a pact with the Earth Spirits. A pact that the elemental creatures seemed unlikely to forget. Ula frowned. The spirits were possessive. It worried her but at the same time, they were correct that she'd been out of her depth. Had they not stepped in, she would still be screaming with the kaluki in an endless cycle of fire.

Brannon took a deep breath. "And now?"

Avatar Ula shrugged. "We have returned the kaluki to its own realm and untangled your friend. You must protect her. Remind her that even her new powers are not limitless."

Ula swore. Why would they mention her newfound strengths to Brannon? She didn't yet understand them herself!

Brannon's eyebrows raised. "New powers?"

"We go," said the voices. The light faded from the Avatar's hair beads, the whites returned to her eyes, and she slumped to the ground.

Ula gasped as a something hooked deep in her gut and yanked her into the pool and back into her body. The hard alley floor struck her skin and her nerves flared into full sensitivity as breath was shoved from her lungs. The smell of burned flesh and garbage rushed into her nostrils and mouth as she gulped for air. Her entire body ached with fatigue.

Brannon and Draeson both raced to her side. "Ula? Are you okay?"

"Garuul tuk nae." Ula rubbed her face with her hands but the ache in her head remained. "I...I be fine. Just...need to rest." She stared at the limp burned corpse. "I'm sorry."

Brannon shook his head. "Don't be sorry. I'm just glad you're okay."

"All magics can be dangerous if taken to extreme," Draeson said. He patted her hand. "You need to be careful."

Ula looked at the hand and then looked at him. Even when trying to be kind, the man couldn't help being patronizing. She made her face as innocent as possible. "Does the wizard worry about me?"

Draeson huffed and pulled his hand back. "Mage. Not wizard."

Ula smothered a smile and winced as the effort hurt her head. She could never resist needling Draeson and the man made it far too easy.

Brannon chuckled and helped her to her feet. "Let's get you inside and check you out."

She tried to wave him off but swayed unsteadily so was grateful to lean on his arm for the few steps to the hospital door. She glanced around and saw Master Jordell passing young Shalyn off to Rachela, presumably with instructions to take the girl home. The old man hurried back to join them as they reached the door of the hospital.

"I take it that's not how that usually goes?" he said, with a wave toward the corpse.

"No." Ula shook her head and swayed again as the motion caused dizziness to swell up within her.

Jordell led them inside and Draeson stayed in the alley, continuing his checks for active magic. They found the nearest examination room, a small space with stone walls on three sides and a curtain to seal it off from prying eyes. A shelf on one wall held bandages and scalpels. Along the other wall was a hard, wooden bench that was uncomfortable to sit on but, Ula assumed, would be easy to clean should the patient leak bodily fluids.

Brannon patted the bench. "Sit down while we

examine you."

Ula remained standing. "I be fine. You think you can do something the Earth Spirits cannot? You know they heal if they want."

"Yeah," Brannon said. "But they don't always do what we expect, do they?"

A smile flickered over her lips. "They do not."

"Well then."

She hesitated, uncertain of what they might find. No one had ever become an Avatar for the Earth Spirits in the way she had done - without the full force of the Priory of Gradinath for back up in the ritual. No one could say for certain how much it had changed her.

"Perhaps just a quick physical check to be certain," Master Jordell said gently. "It would be bad for business if you were to leave my hospital with an injury and I hadn't made an effort to help."

"I..." She cursed her limited knowledge of the Kalan language. It was frustrating being so stifled in how she expressed herself. "I do not want to delay finding murderer."

"It's fine," Brannon began.

Master Jordell flapped his hand. "Sir Brannon can continue the investigation without you, I'm sure. If you're needed, they can send for you."

"But," Brannon began.

"I taught you everything you know about medicine," the old man continued. "I'm sure I can handle this. Go find your fire demon or whatever it was."

Brannon nodded. "Of course."

When he'd gone, Ula let herself sink onto the bench, leaned back against the wall, and folded her arms.

Master Jordell pulled a stool up and sat in front of her. He peered into her eyes and laid the back of a hand on her forehead. His skin was cool and dry like wrinkled leaves just before winter. He took her wrist and pressed his fingers to her pulse. He murmured softly to himself while she waited and then released her. "Any dizziness? Nausea?"

Ula shrugged. "A little. But it be passing."

"Has this happened before?"

"No."

"Do you know of anyone of your people it has happened to?"

"No one fool enough to make cremated person Risen." She gave a wry smile. She'd known she was walking a thin line with the attempt, hoping that there was enough unburned for the kaluki to work with. She'd grown overconfident. Knowing she was stronger now than she'd been before becoming an Avatar had made her careless. She could work without many of the protections most shamans needed to keep them safe, but it was still unwise to do so. That path led to dangers she'd been warned against all her life. She shook her head. "You do not know how Djin magic works. The danger be not physical."

"Is that why you didn't want Brannon here to examine you?" The old man's voice was soft.

Ula jerked her gaze up and her headache throbbed in protest. "I be new to this country and I must remain here for some time." She again cursed the lack of eloquence in Kalan speech that made it difficult to articulate just how she felt after running from her homeland for fear the Priory of Gradinath - her Priory, her friends - would take action against her. She was a stranger in this strange land and had little chance of return for the time being. "Sir Brannon be kind to me. I not want him to think...". She trailed off.

"You don't want him thinking you might have lost control of your powers," Master Jordell finished for her.

"I want to remain useful," she said. "That's all."

Jordell smiled and patted her hand. "Well, I don't see any reason you wouldn't be. As far as I can tell, you're in excellent health. Just a bit over-exerted right now. As you thought, you need rest."

Ula nodded. "Thank you."

"So why don't you rest up and I'll see to moving our victim's body to the morgue. I'm sure Brannon will want to do an autopsy. Not that there's much left to examine."

She shook her head. "I can help. Useful,

remember?"

"Very well. But then home to bed. You've done more than your share tonight." He held out a hand to help her up, but Ula stood on her own, her strength returning quickly.

She followed the older man back out into the alley. It was deserted now. Brannon and Draeson were both gone, presumably investigating some lead they'd found without her help. Someone had draped a sheet over the body - either as a kindness to those who saw it or to provide some form of dignity to the deceased.

"I'll get the young ones to bring a stretcher," Master Jordell said and moved off toward his trainee physicians who still stood guard.

Ula crouched down next to the figure under the sheet. It had been a long time since she'd last failed to make a Risen. Back in her earliest days of training. Even stretching her powers as she'd done a few times of late had always been reliable.

She touched a corner of the sheet, hesitated, then lifted the fabric to see the burned body beneath. She looked at it with less proud eyes now. It was a charred husk. She shook her head at her own hubris in trying to force a kaluki into such a thing. Decomposition was slow and natural and a kaluki's power could reverse it. The total immolation of dead flesh was another thing entirely.

She stared at the burned body and her eyes

widened. There was a gaping hole in the dead man's chest that had not been there before. A chunk of the burned flesh was missing. "Master Jordell!" she called. "You must seal this area and search it again."

Someone - or something - had stolen a piece of the corpse.

CHAPTER FOUR

Taran sat at his workbench and stared across at the two princes: one, a boy with a serious face and blond hair, the other a man a few years older than himself with eyes haunted by abuse. Taran ran his hand along the underside of the workbench, letting his fingertips brush the hilt of the dagger he kept strapped there - not because he thought he would need it but because it gave him a sense of security knowing it was there. Comfort was in short supply and touching the hidden weapon gave him a small taste of it, at least.

He took a deep breath. It was still strange seeing Claydan alive and well. No matter how often his childhood friend assured him that he didn't harbor any grudge for Taran having left him behind with the Children of Starlight, Taran couldn't help the surge of guilt that rose in him every time he saw the prince. And he saw him regularly as he synthesized the stardust elixir that kept Claydan and him from going mad. "I would have brought the new batch to the palace," he said. "You didn't have to come down here."

Claydan smiled. "I know," he said. His voice was a higher pitch than average. His body had not completed puberty when he'd chosen castration over allowing the Father of Starlight to use him as breeding stock. "But the boy wanted to come see you. He loves all the strange things in your lab."

Tomidan made his way past the vials and tubes filled with various colored liquids and lifted the cloth covering the large glass container that housed the creagor spiders. The boy watched, fascinated, as one of the creatures hunted a helpless beetle that had been released into the enclosure earlier in the day. The spider pounced and Tommy's eyes widened as the beetle struggled and died.

"How have you been settling in?" Taran asked.

Claydan shrugged. "It's strange. Things aren't exactly the way I remember them. I got lost a couple times in the palace grounds."

"Does it feel like home though?"

"Yeah. I guess." The prince smiled. "I like the freedom to come and go as I please."

Taran chuckled. "Yeah, that takes getting used to." He handed Claydan a freshly brewed flask of stardust elixir.

The prince slipped it into his pocket. "Thank you for this. I never thought we'd have the chance to live normal lives again. I can't believe you managed to piece together the recipe. Kreegin never knew what he was in for when he took you."

Taran pushed his smile to stay in place. Leaving the Father of Starlight had been a huge accomplishment but a difficult one. He only wished he could have helped others escape his influence. "Um...well...we don't have to worry about him anymore."

"Yeah." Claydan's gaze dropped to the floor. He took a long slow breath. "Yeah."

"And we got Tommy away from him. You helped with that." Taran gestured to the young prince who was still staring at the spiders. They'd saved one innocent person. Surely that had to be enough.

"You still think it was soon enough?"

"It seems like it. Have you seen any signs otherwise?"

Claydan shook his head. "No. Not yet."

Taran nodded slowly. It was difficult to spot the early signs. He remembered his conversation with the king about the dangers of this experiment. About what it could do to the boy if they were wrong. They'd been debriefing in the King's private audience room at the palace.

"Is there a chance Tommy can go without further doses of the drug?" Aldan had asked as soon as they'd returned from the Assassin House.

Taran had hedged and stammered, but the truth was he didn't know. Children were resilient but...he'd never seen anyone stop taking Stardust once they'd started and stay intact. Exactly how many doses were required before the dependence was permanent was something maybe not even Kreegin had known. "Darnec and Prince Tomidan both insist he only took one dose. We've held off giving him more. It's possible he might escape the effects of withdrawal. But...he might not."

The king had stared out the window for a long time. "I understand that my son can never stop taking the drug and I know he can live a normal life if he manages this - if you help him manage it." The king turned to Taran. "I've seen how you survive well enough. But I worry about the risks to the royal line - and to the kingdom - if both my heirs are reliant on your elixir. It would take very little for someone to exploit such a thing. It would be best if at least one of them was free of it."

"Your Majesty, I can monitor Prince Tomidan regularly and begin treatment if he shows signs of madness." Taran swallowed. "But if he is addicted already and we take too long to treat him, the damage to his mind could be permanent."

Aldan nodded and sighed. "I understand the

risks. It must be done."

Taran walked across to the spider enclosure and crouched next to the young prince. "Good to see you, Tommy. How have you been?"

The boy shrugged. "I'm okay."

Taran reached out to touch his shoulder. "Any of the things we talked about? Voices other people can't hear or strange feelings about things?"

"Wait!" Claydan held out his hand and hissed for silence. "There's somebody listening at the door."

Taran cocked his head but heard nothing. "Are you sure?" He pitched his voice low, just as the prince had done. Their training with the Children of Starlight was deeply ingrained. If Claydan heard someone approach, then there was definitely someone at the door.

The prince nodded and gestured to the sword at his side.

Taran shook his head. Best to avoid violence if possible, especially from the newly returned crown prince. His own daggers were hidden in the sleeves of his cowled robe. He held his finger to his lips and nudged Tomidan toward his cousin. The boy stayed quiet - even at such a young age, he had enough experience with danger to know how to behave.

Taran crept to the door and listened, his ear close to the ancient wood. The slow steady intake of breath was almost imperceptible...but it was there and out of time with his own. There was someone on the other side of the door, sure enough.

Taran slipped one of the daggers from his sleeve, then reached for the handle with his other hand and yanked it open.

Bishop Narayan jerked back, his face turning a brief but violent crimson. "I...er...I..." he stammered.

Taran stood in the doorway and released his grip on the dagger, letting it slip into his pocket. Narayan was nosy and a source of difficulty for him within the church hierarchy, but Taran didn't consider him physically dangerous. "Did you want something, Bishop? You can always send an acolyte to ask. I know you don't feel comfortable in my workshop." Narayan had once described Taran's lab and all that went on within it as an abomination against nature. A comment Taran found particularly amusing given that science was, in fact, the study of nature.

Bishop Narayan drew himself up, hiding his surprise at being caught eavesdropping behind bluster, and pushed his way into the room. "Don't be ridiculous. I've no reason to feel uncomfortable around your peculiar deviances." His eyes widened when he saw the princes. "I'd heard you had guests." He bowed. "Your highnesses. If you're seeking a private blessing from the gods, please let me guide you to the upper levels of our cathedral.

Any of the bishops will be pleased to see you."

Taran felt his jaw tighten. His position as a priest might have begun as a cover identity for his own safety and not as a true calling to the church, but he was aware of the slight Narayan was dealing him. The bishop clearly considered Taran not good enough for princes.

Claydan also noticed. He lifted his chin and looked down his nose. "My father, the king, greatly admires Brother Taran and suggested we seek him out. We are more than happy with his work here."

Taran pulled the cowl around his face, hoping the shadows would hide his smile.

Small bursts of red appeared in Bishop Narayan's cheeks but he was not so easily deterred. "May I ask what it is that you and the king enjoy in Brother Taran? Perhaps we can extend it to the rest of our clergy."

Taran and Claydan's eyes met. They'd not yet considered a cover story for their frequent meetings and the crown prince's addiction to stardust could never become public knowledge for fear of being used against him, just as Taran's own history with the Children of Starlight could be a danger to him. Taran stammered but another strong voice overrode him.

"No, Bishop Narayan, you may not ask." Sir Brannon strode into the lab, tall and imposing, with Magus Draeson on his heels. "Taran consults for me on matters relating to my role as Master of Investigations and with the royal family on matters as they see fit. Those matters are often of a confidential nature and have nothing to do with the church. Your discretion is greatly appreciated by me and by His Majesty." Brannon smiled but his eyes were like steel. "As you know, the king and I speak regularly and he is always pleased to hear my reports about his subjects."

Taran hid his smile again.

Narayan swallowed and bowed again. "Of course, Bloodhawk - er, Sir Brannon. I merely offer myself to ensure all is well here in the monastery."

"The bishop is a source of inspiration to us all," Taran murmured.

Magus Draeson shot him a glance with a raised eyebrow. "I'm sure he is."

Sir Brannon nodded. "Perhaps you could help me with my current case, Bishop Narayan. The church provides food for the homeless in Alapra, correct?"

"Yes, Sir Brannon. Ahpra is a caring goddess and we take inspiration from her."

"Excellent. Could you talk to your people and make me a list of all the places our homeless citizens tend to sleep? Draeson and I need to find someone."

Narayan nodded. "Certainly, I'll talk to the others in the morning and put together a list."

"Now, please." Brannon put a hand on the bishop's shoulder and nudged him toward the door. "We need to find them tonight. The king will be grateful for your assistance."

"Oh. Of course, sir. Right away."

As the bishop's footsteps disappeared up the stairs, Taran closed the door behind him and turned to face those still in the room. "Um...was that just to get rid of him for us or was it real?"

"Sadly, all too real." Brannon pulled a cloth-wrapped package from his pocket and laid it on the workbench. "I brought you a sample to test. Someone was burned to death this evening and I need to know how it was done."

"A murder?" Prince Claydan moved closer and peered at the package. "I'd heard my father had you working with the Bloodhawk investigating crimes now. I didn't quite believe it."

"Mmmm." Taran fought the urge to look away. His life had changed so much while Claydan's had been nothing but torture and servitude but there was little he could do to change that. Clinging to guilt did nothing to help either of them. The best he could do was try to help Claydan adjust to his new life. Although, technically, it was his old life but one that had moved on without him.

"Taran is a huge help," Sir Brannon said. "We would never have found you without his assistance, for example."

"It took long enough even with it," Claydan muttered.

The room fell awkwardly silent. Red faced and with nothing else he could think to say, Taran leaned over the packet and used his hand to waft the scent closer to his nose. Death was nothing new to him. He'd seen less of it in his time as a priest than he had as a Child of Starlight, but he would never be shocked by it the way some in the church continued to be. "Burned flesh. I don't smell an accelerant though." He began gathering equipment, a glass flask, tweezers, and scalpel. "I'll run some tests just in case there's something that didn't leave a smell. There are some chemicals that burn off very quickly. Did anyone see him before it happened? Did his clothes look wet?"

Sir Brannon shook his head. "Witnesses said there was nothing suspicious. No strange smell or anything like that."

Taran nodded thoughtfully. "Where did you cut the sample from?"

There was a small gasp from the direction of the spider enclosure. Prince Tomidan's eyes were wide as he stared at the packet on the bench.

"Oh," said Taran. The prince had seen a lot of death and trauma in his short life. Taran had intended to try to shield him from more. "Um...perhaps..."

Claydan nodded, the understanding they'd

shared in childhood still present. "I'll take Tommy home now. It's getting late anyway and you three obviously need to work."

"Thanks," Taran said. He pointed to the flask on the bench. "Don't forget your elixir."

Sir Brannon's head tilted up. "That reminds me, Claydan. Your father said you're having trouble sleeping. Perhaps Taran can give you something to help with that as well."

Taran could see Claydan's jaw tighten and his spine became very straight. "That won't be necessary," the prince said in careful, clipped tones. "I'm not sure why my father would think that. I'm perfectly fine. But thank you for your concern."

Brannon's eyebrows drew closer in puzzlement and concern but Claydan was already ushering Tommy out the door.

Taran sighed and watched them go. Different as his life and Claydan's had been for the last several years, he still recognized one thing in his friend. No matter what Claydan said, he was anything but fine.

CHAPTER FIVE

The third sanctuary for the homeless on Bishop Narayan's list was the burned-out shell of a warehouse near the docks. Brannon and Draeson spent a couple of hours of exploring the riskier parts of the city and talking to those who lived there before they reached this place. The facade of the building was intact but the inside had been hollowed out, first by a fire and then by scavengers. The owners had made no attempt to rebuild - no doubt having lost a fortune in whatever stock had been stored there at the time of the fire - and so, over time, it had become a haven for those who had nowhere else to go. A kind of city within the city. A walled community of those who lived on the streets.

What was left of the door had been reinforced by nailing random offcuts of wood across it, but a gentle tug proved it worked well enough and they slipped inside.

The interior of the warehouse was a mass of lean-tos and cobbled together tents. Fire pits were scattered here and there in the mess with people warming themselves at the flames and drinking. The smell of unwashed clothes and urine was strong. Empty wine bottles and flasks lay strewn around like fallen leaves in a forest. Many of the rough shelters were occupied by figures bundled in threadbare coats and dirty blankets. Others had people sitting or standing outside them. Brannon recognized the remnants of army tents and uniforms in the mix.

Faces turned to eye the newcomers warily. Several of them ducked into their shelters, hiding from the strangers in their midst. A few whispered "Bloodhawk" as they stared at Brannon. One or two saluted.

"Ahpra's Tears, what a mess," Draeson muttered.

"I didn't realize there were so many," Brannon said. He turned slowly, trying to estimate how many shelters, how many people. Every city had homeless but the war had left too many displaced or broken. That they were still living like this was disturbing. "We should talk to the church. To Aldan. Something should be done."

"You think he doesn't know?" Draeson said. "There are no easy answers. Never have been."

Brannon sighed. A problem for another day. One that required more resources than he had alone but that needed to be addressed just the same. He approached the nearest fire pit where four people huddled around the flames. "Can you help me?" he said. "I'm looking for someone."

Three of them turned their backs.

The fourth was a woman with scraggly dark hair and missing teeth. "What are you doing here, Bloodhawk? Most of us haven't seen you since the war."

"I'm looking for people who know a man who called himself the General. We were told he was staying here."

She frowned at him. "Was?"

"He was killed tonight." Draeson stepped up. "Murdered. We're trying to find out why."

A murmur ran through the homeless folk within ear shot. The woman with the missing teeth glanced around at her companions. "People like us die all the time. No one ever cares why."

"We care." Brannon met her eyes. "Whoever killed him will be brought to justice."

She watched his face for a long moment, then nodded. "I'll help you. Follow me."

She led the way through a tangle of stone, wood, thatch, blankets, and canvas that created the patchwork of shelters within the walls of the old warehouse. The roof of the place was long gone so those who slept there had to create what protection from rain they could. Most of the occupants turned away at their approach or ignored them completely. None challenged them though. They seemed to recognize their guide.

"I don't know his real name," she said. "So don't ask. As far as I know, everyone just called him the General. I don't even think that was really his rank in the war but that's what everyone calls him."

"You didn't tell us your name," Brannon said, sidestepping a pile of excrement as he hurried to keep up. "I'm Brannon and this is Draeson."

"I'm none of your concern," the woman replied. "I don't want your charity or even to see you here again but I do want you to do right by the General. He was kind to most of us."

"We'll do what we can," Brannon said. Away from the fire, the night air was cold. He didn't like to think how it would be to sleep in such poor shelter every night, with little trust in those around you. "When you say he was kind to most of you. Does that mean there were those he didn't get along with?"

She paused next to a lean-to about the height of Brannon's shoulders, made of stacked stone, broken planks, and canvas. She pursed her lips as she looked at them both before answering. "Look, a lot of people are here because they have trouble letting go of the war. The General is one of those." She frowned and shook her head. "*Was* one of those. People get stuck in their memories or get obsessed with strange ideas. With that stuff there's always going to be something or someone that sets it off. Sounds or sights just send you right back to it, you know?" She closed her eyes with a grimace. "You can't avoid it."

Brannon knew all too well. He'd seen that face - he'd made that face. He could guess some of the things she was trying not to see. "What was the General's obsession?"

Her eyes opened again as she latched onto the distraction. "Nilarians. He saw spies everywhere. Always thought he was in danger. He didn't trust many people. He wouldn't even take food from the church. Most of us couldn't get by without that."

"Surely that meant more for everyone else," Draeson said. "Why would that get anyone annoyed at him?"

"It wasn't that so much as his being scared all the time got exhausting for some people."

"Anyone in particular?"

"Yeah." A large man in a filthy coat and a floppy brimmed hat stepped out of the shadows. "That would be me."

Brannon raised an eyebrow. "And you are?"

"Gerrad." The man stuck out his hand. "Good to meet you, Sir Bloodhawk. You're a good man. I remember seeing you at the battle of Lineen."

"Just Brannon is fine." Brannon shook his hand. "You must have done good work yourself if you got out of Lineen."

Gerrad smiled. "Thank you, sir."

"You and the General had issues?"

The smile faded. "He was no General. And he had issues, all right. What's he done now?"

"He's dead," the woman said quietly.

"Well, I won't miss him." Gerrad folded his arms.

"That seems harsh," Brannon said. "Why do you say that?"

"The man thought I was a Nilarian spy. What Hooded good would it do to be spying in this dump? I ask you!"

"You do wear a hat," Draeson pointed out. "Nilarians always wear hats."

Gerrad snorted. "That they do. Unless they're Hooded spying because that'd be a dead giveaway, wouldn't it?" He pulled the hat from his head and rubbed a scalp that was bald as an egg but mottled in color. "I wear it so the sun doesn't burn me. It's the only cover my poor head gets these days. I'm not going to fry because some idiot is scared of a hat."

Brannon and Draeson exchanged a glance. Hats were not entirely unheard of in Kalanon. Just because Nilarians wore them, didn't mean everyone who wore one was Nilarian.

"Where were you earlier this evening?" Brannon asked.

"Here." Gerrad frowned. "Why? How did he die?"

"He was murdered," Brannon said. "By magic."

Gerrad shoved the hat back on his head. "Blood and Tears. So you're asking me about it? I'm supposed to be a Nilarian spy and a mage as well? By the Wolf, everyone's gone mad. Ask around. I've been here all day. And if I could magic people dead, I would've done it a long time ago." He pushed his way past a hanging sheet that served as a doorway to a makeshift tent and huffed, clearly done talking.

"Was he here all day?" Brannon asked their guide.

She shrugged. "I think so. I don't exactly keep tabs on people. We're all free to come and go as we please."

Brannon looked around the crowded, filthy space with its bundles of displaced humanity. It was a miracle they came together at all. Keeping track of each other in the midst of just trying to survive would be near impossible. If the General had not died in such a strange way with a witness who knew the Master of Investigations personally, would anyone have even realized who had died? Would anyone have cared? Worse - what if others had been murdered already and no one had reported it? How many vulnerable, homeless Kalans were at risk or had already died at the hands of some depraved force?

"Can you show us where the General slept?" he asked. "Did he have a regular spot?"

"This one." She tapped the structure they'd stopped beside.

"What, right opposite Gerrad?" The incredulity in Draeson's voice matched Brannon's own feeling.

"Yeah. They knocked each other's shelter down a couple times but neither of them was willing to shift. Stubborn old coots." Their guide shrugged. "I guess you're welcome to it now. Until someone else needs it."

Brannon crouched and pulled the door covering aside. He edged slowly into the darkness within. There was little room inside the shack, barely enough length for a man to lay down. The ground had the soft feel of a blanket or clothing but there was little else he could tell. "Draeson can you pass me a lantern?"

"Okay. Hang on." Footsteps led back toward the fire pit.

There was a sudden scrabbling noise from the darkness ahead of him and the flap at the other end of the shelter flew open. A figure ran out into the night.

"Who's that?" Brannon scrambled after the fleeing figure. He banged his shin on something hard, swore, and exited the shelter just a moment later. The moonlight and fire pits scattered shadows this way and that. There was no way to tell which direction the person who'd been in the General's shelter had gone. "Blood and Tears!"

"What's wrong?"

Brannon turned to see Draeson and the guide approaching with a small tallow candle. "There was someone inside. They ran off. Did you see them?"

Draeson shook his head. "Wasn't that annoying kid again, was it?"

"No. Far too big for a child and...well she's a child. How would she have followed us here this late at night?"

Their guide shrugged. "Someone probably just saw it was empty and wanted to stay warm. You would have scared them more than they scared you."

"Maybe." Brannon squinted at the shadows. Nothing moved. "Okay. Bring the candle inside. Let's see what we can find out about our victim."

As he crawled back into the shelter, Draeson did the same from the other side, candle in hand. They stared around. A few food scraps were wrapped in paper in one corner, and the blankets and clothing Brannon had first encountered were on the floor. The sloping planks that formed both wall and roof were covered in large, crude letters. It looked to have been done with a charred stick from the fire pit. "Save the king," it said, over and over.

"Save the king. Save the king. Save the king."

Brannon swallowed. His skin crawled. These could be the written ravings of a mad man who saw spies wherever he looked. Or was it possible the General had stumbled onto something serious and been killed for it?

Draeson gave a deep sigh. "Well, that's ominous." He leaned forward and poked at something tucked into the edge where the wooden covering met the ground. It came away in his hand and he lifted it into the light. It was an elaborate masquerade mask with a polished green lacquer beak and peacock feathers splayed out around the eyes. "What do you suppose he has this for?"

Brannon's stomach sank. "Ahpra's Tears," he said. "I think I know."

CHAPTER SIX

The moon was smothered by cloud when Brannon reached his apartment, having decided it was too late to investigate further. He wrapped himself in blankets and fell into a fitful sleep, full of dreams about the war, death, and fire-blackened corpses. When he finally woke enough to give up on rest, the morning was crisp and sunny - the exact opposite of Brannon's own fuzzy-headed state. He ate a quick breakfast and went to meet Draeson in the courtyard.

"You look even more tired than I feel," the mage grumbled. "Next time we question people, let's do it in daylight."

They made their way to Ambassador Ylani's apartment on the palace grounds, the masquerade mask in hand. The door was opened by a servant who ushered them into the greeting room with its soft cushioned chairs and silk panels decorating the walls.

Ylani joined them a moment later. She wore a sleeveless dress of green silk and a hat with black and white patterning around the base and a green feather to match the dress. Her hair was swept up on one side and tumbled down to her shoulder on the other in a mass of dark curls. Brannon couldn't help but notice the scent of spice and vanilla that seemed to accompany her everywhere. He nodded a greeting and smiled.

The servant glanced toward Brannon and then said something in Nilarian.

The corner of Ylani's lips twitched. "Please speak Kalan in front of our guests. We wouldn't want them to think we're plotting something in front of them."

"Very well, Ambassador." The woman nodded. There was a twinkle in her eye. "Would you like me to repeat what I said in Kalan?"

Ylani pursed her lips. "No. That won't be necessary. You may leave us for now."

"Should I ask?" Brannon raised an eyebrow.

"Not really. She has some strange ideas about our friendship." Ylani settled herself into a chair and arranged her silk skirt. "What can I do for you, Brannon?"

"I'm hoping you might be able to help us with a case." He leaned forward in his seat and outlined the strange murder at the hospital and their findings from the night before. When he got to the part about the General's belief in Nilarian spies, Ylani held up her hand to stop him.

"So, you want to know if Nilar has spies embedded in your homeless population?" The pitch of her voice rose incredulously. "What would be the point?"

"Nilarians have done stranger things," Draeson muttered.

Brannon spread his hands, palms up. "I don't see what good it would do either," he said. "But we had to ask. Is there a chance he was right?"

Ylani frowned. "You know I couldn't tell you if he was. But to my knowledge, no, there are no official operatives active in that area."

"That's a cagey politician's response," Draeson said.

Ylani wrinkled her nose at him. "But I *am* a politician. And an ex spy. Did you really expect any different?"

"Do you think there's a chance a Nilarian is involved?"

She sighed, folded her arms, and leaned back in her chair. "There are very few Nilarians here in Alapra. Until a couple of days ago, my staff and I were pretty much it. Given that you're holding a masquerade mask, I'm sure you know that a new envoy arrived recently and there's a welcome event planned at the palace in two days. Is it possible one of them was involved? About as possible as anyone else in this city. But you're saying the man died by magic and there's one obvious suspect if that's the case."

"Nycol." Brannon's chest tightened. The mage had been involved with a Nilarian criminal before and had kidnapped Draeson and kept him in a magically induced coma. It wouldn't be much of a leap to consider him the prime suspect in a new magical murder.

"Exactly," Ylani agreed. "We never found him. He could have hidden somewhere or just snuck back in. Either way, I don't think he's done with his plans for our own charming mage."

"He won't catch me off guard again," Draeson growled.

Brannon noticed Ylani was chewing her lower lip. "You're worried," he said. "What about?"

She hesitated, then unfolded her arms and sat forward on the seat. "I've had an uneasy feeling about the masquerade ball your king is throwing to welcome the envoy. A sense of danger. To be honest, I thought it was with regard to my position here after I helped you uncover the slave trade but what if it's something worse? Something about Nycol? Given that your murder victim had a masquerade mask with his things, what if he knew something or was involved in something that will happen at the ball?"

Brannon felt a chill in the room. "How strong of a feeling?"

"Can I see the mask?" She reached out her hand. When her fingers touched it, they trembled. "There's definitely danger. Exactly what, I don't know."

Draeson snorted. "The man who owned it is dead. That's danger enough."

Brannon and Ylani both shot him a narrow-eyed look and he fell silent.

"The masquerade," Ylani said. "Will you both be there?"

Brannon nodded. "I'm still technically the King's Champion. And there will be other palace guards as security."

"Perhaps you'd be better blended in with the guests. Would you consider going as my escort?"

He blinked. "I...um...I'm not sure how much we'd blend in if we went together. The Nilarian Ambassador and the King's Champion? People will talk."

She smiled her charming, slightly lopsided smile. "That's the point of a masquerade, Brannon." She lifted the mask in front of her face. "To get away with things people would normally talk about."

Brannon grinned. "I suppose you're right."

"Of course I am," Ylani said. "So it's a date."

CHAPTER SEVEN

The bell over the door rang as Brannon and Draeson entered the shop. Bolts of fabric lined the walls and shelves, creating a labyrinth of color. As they made their way through the aisles, they passed mannequins in elaborate gowns sporting necklaces, earrings and bracelets that sparkled in the lamplight. At the far end of the shop was a huge cabinet filled with yet more jewelry and elaborate masquerade masks. A small woman with short dark hair stepped around the cabinet and strode toward them. She wore a series of different sized rings on a chain around her neck and had a tape measure tucked into her belt.

"Welcome to Stitch and Stone," she greeted them. "I'm Alissa. Are you looking for clothing or accessories today?"

"Both," said Draeson.

"Neither," said Brannon.

Alissa smiled. "Perhaps if you tell me what brought you into the store?"

"My friend here is going to the masquerade ball at the palace and needs an entire new outfit," Draeson said. "He has a date and shouldn't show up looking like himself."

"Ah, it's not a date," Brannon said. "Not really."

"But it could be." Alissa gave him a wink. "Those are the best kind. I had several of those with Karlin before we ended up married and running this place. So you never know how it'll turn out."

Draeson chuckled. "She called it a date."

Brannon swallowed. This was not at all what he had in mind. "Alissa, could you give us a moment?"

The small woman nodded and moved a few steps away.

"Getting cold feet?" Draeson said.

Brannon grabbed the mage's arm. "Stop it. You know full well that it would be ridiculous to think the Nilarian Ambassador and I could actually go on a date."

Draeson shrugged. "And yet you're apparently going to a masquerade at the palace together."

"That's a mission," Brannon hissed. He pulled the mask they'd found in the homeless compound from his pocket. "If we hadn't found this and if we didn't suspect Magus Nycol might show up, Ylani would never have suggested we go together."

"Perhaps. But no friend of mine is going on anything resembling a date without dressing the part." Draeson waved at the fabric around them. "You always manage to make civilian clothes look like you're still in uniform. For once I'd like to see you with some style."

Brannon narrowed his eyes. "Really? Are my clothing choices the most important thing for us to focus on right now? We're investigating a murder."

"Fine. Fine." Draeson raised his hands in surrender. "If you don't want to look good for your not-a-date, who am I to argue? But there's no reason we can't do both."

Brannon sighed. He did enjoy Ylani's company and the attraction was impossible to deny but even if he overlooked the political implications of the King's Champion embarking on anything more than friendship with the Nilarian Ambassador, it was very unlikely she would. Ylani was a politician. She understood how court life worked. Or was that why she was okay with it? Would her government see this as an ex spy using her wiles to get closer to the foreign leaders? The envoy would be present at the masquerade. Was this a friendship evolving into something more or a carefully constructed play by Ylani to improve her standing back home?

Part of him couldn't blame her if it was. She'd certainly proven her worth to Kalanon and to Brannon himself in the past and potentially damaged her standing back home by doing so. If he needed to play the dupe in front of the envoy to help her regain some of that standing, he'd be willing to do so. But he hoped that wasn't the case. If he was honest, he hoped it wasn't even about Nycol or the mystery they were trying to solve. Deny it as much as he could, part of him hoped it was a date.

Either way, it would be useful to look the part.

He waved Alissa over. "Actually, I would like a new outfit and a mask for the ball tomorrow night. Is that too short notice?"

"Not at all. But we will have to charge a little extra for the rush." She turned and called toward the back of the shop. "Karlin, honey! When you have a moment, these customers will need to talk to you."

"Glad you came to your senses." Draeson smirked. "I assume you want my input after all?"

Brannon rolled his eyes. "I imagine I'll be getting it either way."

Alissa turned back to Brannon and pulled the tape measure from her belt. "My husband does the sewing and I make the accessories. As you can imagine, we've both been very busy with the ball coming up and he's making some alterations at the moment. Fortunately necklaces and masks still fit even if you sneak a few extra desserts before the event so that's less work for me." She gave them a wink. "Have you seen any fabric you like? Do you have an idea of what your date will be wearing?

You'll want to tie in with that, of course."

"Um..." Brannon floundered. "I don't..."

"Yes," Draeson interrupted. "I have some ideas."

Alissa beamed at them both. "Excellent. We'll have you looking amazing in no time." She gestured to the mask in Brannon's hand. "Is this what your date will be wearing?"

"Oh, no." Brannon held it up so she could get a better view. "Actually, there was another reason we came in today."

Alissa paled. "Where did you get that?"

"You recognize it?"

She nodded. "I made it. For an old friend."

"Then I'm sorry," Brannon said, putting as much kindness into his voice as he could. "But we need to talk."

They found chairs next to the cabinet of jewelry and Alissa and Brannon sat facing each other while Draeson perched on the edge of a desk. Alissa fidgeted, picking at her fingernails. "How did you get that mask? Is he all right?"

"I'm sorry, Alissa," Brannon said. "But if your friend is the homeless man known as the General, he was killed last night."

"Oh no." She covered her mouth with her hands. "Ahpra's Tears. The poor poor man." Her shoulders shook as she took long ragged breaths. "What happened?"

"That's what we're trying to find out," Draeson said.

She sniffed. "I'll help however I can but...we hadn't been in contact for a long time until just recently."

"So it is the General that you know? He's the one you made the mask for?"

Alissa nodded.

"His name wasn't General," a deeper voice said as a tall, thin man appeared from the back room. He had a pin cushion strapped to his left wrist and scissors in a sheath on his belt the way many men would wear a dagger or a sword. He hurried to Alissa's side and laid a hand on her shoulder. "I don't even think it was his rank in the war. His name was Jemiren. My wife and he were friends in their youth."

"Close friends?" Brannon asked.

Alissa nodded. "We were to be married at one point. But the war changed him. He was never the same and we...weren't compatible after that."

"And you knew this?" Draeson raised an eyebrow at the woman's husband.

"I did."

"Karlin has always known our history," Alissa said. "And he has encouraged me to help Jemiren where I can."

"Generous," muttered Draeson.

Karlin shrugged. "If you'd known the man you

would understand. I don't mean to speak ill of the dead but he was a very lost soul." He gazed lovingly at his wife and she reached up to pat his hand. "I've never had anything to be jealous of."

Brannon scratched at his scar. They seemed genuine. So if a love triangle wasn't the motive, what was? "You gave him the mask, I assume? I can't imagine he could have afforded to shop in a place like this. So why did he want it?"

Karlin and Alissa exchanged a glance. "We don't want to get into trouble," Karlin said.

"Just tell us. It'll only be worse if you don't help," said Brannon.

Alissa swallowed then spoke. "The thing you have to know is he wasn't always like this. He was a good man. A fine soldier. King Raldan himself appointed him to a special church-based division. I don't know exactly what they did - he never talked about it - but it was an important job. He was trusted. Reliable. Not like...not like what he was later."

Brannon felt the hairs on his arm raise. "Why did he want the mask, Alissa?"

She looked at the floor. "He wanted to sneak into the masquerade. He believed there was a danger coming that no one knew about. He wanted to warn the king."

CHAPTER EIGHT

B rannon followed an usher into one of the King's private audience chambers at the palace to find his friend hovering over a selection of platters, each with tiny portions of finger foods and baked goods displayed like gemstones on velvet. Kitchen staff lined the wall watching, but barely breathing, while he sampled their offerings.

"Good timing, Brannon," the king said. "You can help me pick out the menu for tomorrow's ball."

"Actually, Your Majesty, you may want to reconsider that." Brannon crossed the room to stand close to his friend. He lowered his voice. "I need to update you on our investigation and it seems there's a threat to your safety."

Aldan hesitated, his fingers hovering over a puffed extravagance of pastry and blended fruits. "How serious?"

Brannon shrugged.

The king sighed. "One day, my friend, it would be nice to have you just visit for fun"

"You're usually too busy, Your Majesty. And with the appointments you've given me, so am I."

Aldan chuckled. "Oh, so it's my fault, is it?"

"I would never suggest such a thing," said Brannon and winked.

"Fine. Fine." Aldan waved his hand at the collected kitchen staff. "Clear the room. You've all done well. I'll inform you of my decisions shortly."

Once they'd filed out of the room, Brannon outlined what they'd discovered so far about Jemiren, the man many had known as the General, and his belief in Nilarian spies and a threat to the king's safety. He showed him the mask they'd found and explained that Jemiren had intended on sneaking into the masquerade.

Aldan picked at the foods arrayed in front of him as he listened. As he tasted each one he shifted the plate it came from to one side of the table or the other. When Brannon finished his report, the king frowned. "But what exactly are you supposed to be warning me about? You haven't brought me anything but the secondhand ravings of a mad man who lived on the street. It doesn't seem reliable, Brannon."

"A man who wound up murdered, Your Majesty," Brannon pointed out. "Which could have been someone's way of keeping him quiet."

"Or it could have been because he had a fight with another homeless person over a half empty wine skin. We don't know anything at this point." The king handed him a pastry bird with delicate flaked wings. "Try this. The filling is delicious."

"It's unlikely that another homeless person could have set him on fire with magic." Brannon took the pastry bird and held it in his hand, untasted.

"And you're sure this was magic then?"

"Taran's tests found nothing to suggest flammable chemicals. Magic is the best explanation for what the witnesses saw."

Aldan popped a tiny meringue in his mouth and chewed thoughtfully.

Brannon ran his thumbnail over the pastry bird in his hand as if petting it and waited.

Aldan swallowed. "Okay. Here's the thing: I'm not cancelling the ball."

"But-"

The king held up his hand. "No, Brannon. I know you only have my safety at heart but there's not enough here to consider it a credible threat and this is the first significant event including the Nilarians since Ambassador Ylani's arrival. Not to mention the careful negotiations we've had to go through to get our people who were captured in the war returned. I'm not throwing all that way on a maybe."

Brannon sighed. "Will you at least allow me to put some extra precautions in place?"

"I don't want our guests to feel like prisoners. It shows weakness if we don't feel safe in our own palace."

"You were planning to have guards present though, surely?"

"Some."

"Aldan!"

The king frowned. "I thought you wanted me to be nicer to the Nilarians. You seem to be getting chummy with their ambassador."

"I do." Brannon felt his face grow hot. The last thing he wanted to do was try to define his relationship with Ylani to the king. "And I trust Ylani but we don't know anything about the envoy. And it's the rogue mage I'm most worried about."

"You think this Nycol is back again? You think your team can catch him this time?"

Brannon looked at his hand and discovered he'd crushed the pastry bird. "We'll do our best."

"From anyone but you, I'd be concerned by that." Aldan popped a tiny horse and carriage carved out of melon into his mouth and chewed slowly. "Okay, I'll have Darnec and a few extra guards in the room in plain clothes. But if a mage shows up, you and your team will be the only ones with a chance of stopping him. And last time he was here, it wasn't me he was after, Brannon. You tell your people to watch out for themselves because if he's back, it's probably for revenge."

CHAPTER NINE

The faded sign above the door still named it Lady Magda's Orphanage, despite the fact it was now run entirely by the church after Magda's untimely passing. Brannon hadn't been back since she'd died. He was glad the children who lived here hadn't seen the bloodshed that had occurred in their home that night. They had enough to deal with after having been kidnapped and nearly sold into slavery. As he and Draeson approached the entrance, the sound of those children's voices could be heard even in the street. A ball and a spinning top were abandoned on the steps and a small group of children skipped rope nearby. Brannon smiled. Perhaps they were more resilient than he thought.

Draeson wrinkled his nose. "Are you sure we couldn't just wait for him to get back to the church?

It'd be easier to talk without children fighting us for his attention."

"If Aldan won't cancel the masquerade then we need to find out as much as we can as quickly as possible," Brannon said. "I'm not waiting around for the bishop to finish whatever duties he has here at the orphanage. We need answers." He took the steps in a single bound and knocked on the door.

A clatter of small footprints cascaded toward them and the door was flung open. "I knew you'd come!" Shalyn bounced on her toes.

Brannon smiled. "Good to see you Shalyn. I hope you're staying away from crime scenes from now on." Despite his concern for the girl when she'd showed up at the scene of Jemiren's death, it was nice to see her. She was a reminder that sometimes victims could be saved. He'd seen a lot of deaths in his short tenure as Master of Investigations.

As they entered the house, Shalyn pushed past Brannon and wrapped her arms around Magus Draeson. "You're here."

Draeson's eyes widened and he raised his arms as if touching the child would somehow contaminate him. He looked across at Brannon. "Get her off me," he mouthed silently. He might have been four hundred years old, but Draeson was not experienced in dealing with children.

Brannon grinned and slapped the mage on the shoulder. "Enjoy the gratitude," he said. Draeson had been the one to wake Shalyn and the other children from a spell-induced sleep when they'd been kidnapped and it seemed she considered him solely responsible for her rescue.

The other children crowded around as well but at a distance, hesitant to come too close. The Bloodhawk and the mage were intimidating figures for children who had not had easy lives.

"We're looking for Bishop Narayan," Brannon told them. "Do you know where he is?"

Some of the children stepped back and a few drifted away. Even Shalyn pulled away from Draeson and frowned.

An older boy held his ground and nodded. "I'll tell him you're here." He bounded down the hallway and up the stairs, all long legs and dangling arms.

"Why do you want him?" Shalyn asked. She pointed at the sword at Brannon's side. "Will you kill him?"

"No," Brannon assured her. "Of course not. I would only draw my sword on someone who deserved it."

"Oh."

She turned back to Draeson. "The Djin lady came to visit us too. She's so pretty and purple. She said we should call you a wizard."

Draeson scowled. "You should not! I'm a mage."

"What's the difference?"

"More than I can explain in the time available," Draeson said. "Go and see what's keeping your bishop."

Shalyn stomped away. "He's not my bishop," she said over her shoulder and slammed the door into the playroom.

The other children dispersed quickly, leaving Brannon and Draeson to wait on their own.

"Well, I guess we could go into the lounge," Brannon said quietly. The last time they'd been in that room the carpet had been soaked with blood.

"Let's not," said Draeson.

"Yeah. Here is fine." Brannon didn't want anything triggering those horrible memories either. He paced the length of the hallway and back again. Bishop Narayan was nowhere to be seen and the children didn't return. It was hard not to feel the ghosts of the place now that the living inhabitants were out of the room.

Draeson leaned against the wall, arms crossed.

From the other room, a child's voice shouted, "Wizard!" And several children laughed.

Draeson scowled. "That Hooded Ula thinks she's hilarious."

Brannon chuckled. "To be honest, I think she just likes to wind you up. You gave her a hard time about her kind of magic when we first met her."

"Because she messes with elementals and death magic. It's not the same as real magic at all!"

"And that's the attitude that encourages her to needle you when she can," Brannon told him. "Why do you let it bother you so much? What do you care if she calls you a wizard or a mage?"

Draeson stared at the wall and took a long, slow breath. "Mages have an understanding of the different types of magic. Ours is the purest. The most difficult and powerful. I'm not saying that to malign Ula and her elementals. It's just the truth. It's why we take so long to study it and why there are so few of us around. Most who try to become a mage die before they learn enough to master the true power."

"I remember," Brannon said softly, thinking of the fight they'd had on the journey to Sandilar on their first murder case together. "You said mages lose their youth in study because one lifetime is not enough to learn magic. You spend the first lifetime figuring out how to live longer so you can learn the rest." It had been the first time he'd seen true human pain in the mage - the suffering of his lost youth and living almost four hundred years in an old and aching body. He'd only found a way to recreate his youth somehow after the war had ended. He'd never told Brannon how.

"So there you go." Draeson glanced at Brannon before looking away again. "Makes sense that we're protective of the title."

"Sure." Brannon licked his lips before speaking

again. "But is there something else that bothers you? Something about the name wizard? It just seems like that particular name bothers you."

This time when Draeson met Brannon's eyes, he didn't look away. There was something haunted in his gaze. "The term wizard usually means a charlatan in mage circles - someone who pretends magic and rips off vulnerable people. But there is another kind of wizard. They are the ones who steal power."

Brannon frowned, leaning closer. "What do you mean?"

Draeson unfolded his arms and gestured vaguely in the air. "A mage uses his own power or sometimes comes to an agreement with another entity to bolster it."

"Like your dragon tattoo?"

"Exactly. But there are those that steal the life force of others and use it or store it. They're also known as wizards. It can create spectres - dangerous side effects - and it's not something a true mage would ever want to be associated with."

"Oh." Brannon's eyes widened. He'd lived for years with the knowledge that someone could take his life with the point of a sword - there was no escaping mortality in a war - but to think of your life force being stolen and used supernaturally...it sent a chill over his skin. "How?" he asked. "How do they steal it?"

Draeson opened his mouth to reply, but then his eyes flicked to the staircase above Brannon's head. "We have company."

Bishop Narayan stood on the landing in dark blue robes with the hood thrown back and a large-linked gold chain of office hanging down to the middle of his chest. "Sir Brannon, Magus Draeson." He nodded and descended the stairs to join them on the ground floor. "An unexpected pleasure. What brings you here today?"

Brannon watched the bishop closely. He knew Taran had experienced difficulties with Narayan in the past. The bishop was suspicious of the young priest's scientific tendencies and mysterious past. Without the king's protection, Brannon suspected the bishop might have posed even more of a problem. He'd seen the type before - people with power in their circle of influence who couldn't handle anything different within their little kingdom. He kept his expression genial. "We're hoping you can help us with some information on church history."

"Of course." The bishop smiled. "Anything to help the great Bloodhawk."

Brannon hid his distaste for the name. His exploits in the war were a necessary evil in his mind but he knew many Kalans respected and even revered him for it. If that respect meant getting answers more easily, he could put up with being called their name for him.

"It relates to the war," Brannon said. "We need to know about a special force that was attached to the church during that time. They had special duties beyond what most of the army knew about. I need to know what."

Bishop Narayan leaned against the banister. He licked his lips before he replied. "I'm not sure what use the church would have for an army unit. Fighting isn't what we do."

"And yet there was one," Draeson said. "So how about you tell us what you know?"

Narayan scowled.

"This is essential to our current murder investigation," Brannon said. "Anything you tell us will be treated with the utmost discretion but we need to know."

"I..." Narayan shrugged.

"The king would want you to tell us."

"There's nothing to tell. The church is not in the habit of running secret ops for the military. And if we did, no doubt you would already know about it, Sir Brannon. As you say, the king gives you high level clearance for your work."

Brannon's eyes narrowed as he studied the bishop's face. There was a twitch in his eyelid. His eyes flicked to the left, almost too quickly to see. The man was lying, Brannon was sure of it. But why?

Draeson opened his mouth to speak but Brannon lifted a hand to stop him.

"Here's the thing, Bishop Narayan," he said. "We know such a force existed. Our victim was one of the soldiers in it. He was haunted by his time in the war. I want to know why."

"Many people are haunted by the war, Sir Brannon." Narayan shrugged. "I see it all the time. They come to church to seek absolution or charity because they struggle with the things they did. Some make up fantasies to make themselves feel better about what happened. Maybe that's what your man did. But if he's dead, it seems neither of us can question him about it." He turned away and headed back up the stairs. "I'm sorry I can't help you further."

"I think you can," Brannon said. "Talk to us."

Draeson pushed off from the wall he'd been leaning against. "If we find out you're keeping something from us..." He let the threat hang in the air.

"You both know your way out," Bishop Narayan said. "I'm busy."

Brannon sighed and gestured to Draeson to follow him. They weren't going to get anything more out of the Bishop. He was hiding something and Brannon didn't know why. He could guess though. He had plenty of things from the war he didn't like to talk about. If the priesthood had taken part in the fighting, they were even more likely to want to forget about it.

As they headed back to the front door, Shalyn stepped out of a side room. She glanced toward the staircase where the bishop had disappeared from sight and lifted a finger to her lips.

Brannon frowned. "What is it?" He whispered.

Shalyn pointed upwards. "Look upstairs," she mouthed silently. "See what he does." She slipped back into the other room and closed the door.

Brannon exchanged a look with Draeson. "I guess we're looking upstairs."

He and Draeson made their way back to the stairwell and began to climb. Brannon kept his footsteps as soft as possible, silent on the old worn carpet.

At the top of the stairs, Draeson tapped his shoulder and pointed in both directions, a silent but clear question, "Which way?"

There was no sign of Narayan. At the end of the hall, a gate sealed off the last few feet that included the door to the final room. The gate was closed but the door was ajar. "That way," Brannon mouthed. If Narayan was up to something that frightened Shalyn, it would be in that room. The room with the chains.

They moved quietly to the gate and unlatched it before slipping through. As he passed the wheel set into the wall which adjusted the length of chains inside, he remembered the last time he'd seen this room - the prison cell of a madwoman, who'd gotten free at last. It was hard to believe anything good could happen in this room.

The door swung open before his outstretched hand could touch it and Bishop Narayan stood framed in the empty space. "Our discussion is over, gentlemen. What are you doing up here? This is private property."

"Sorry to disturb you, Bishop, but I need to see what you have in that room."

Narayan's eyes narrowed. "Nothing that concerns you, Sir Brannon. This is a church facility now and I've asked you to leave."

"I'm afraid I'm going to have to insist." Brannon rested his hand on the hilt of his sword. He had little to base his unease on but this was a house filled with children. If Narayan was harming them, he would do more than imply a threat.

Behind him, Draeson summoned a crackle of energy to dance on his palm. Brannon wasn't the only one willing to force the issue.

Narayan's gaze flicked from Brannon to Draeson and back again. "Fine." His voice was flat and his words clipped. "Look all you want." He moved out of the way and waved his hand at the inside of the room.

Brannon pushed past and circled, taking everything in. The walls had a fresh coat of paint, covering the filth that had been smeared on the walls by the previous inhabitant but the star-shaped etchings she'd made were still visible as impressions in the paint. The carpet had been replaced and the bedding was fresh and clean. The manacles were still in place, hanging over the end of the bedhead, a strange and out of place sight in this newly sanitized room. There was nobody here. No sign of anything other than decorating improvement.

"Satisfied?" Bishop Narayan folded his arms, and a smug smirk turned up the edge of his lips. "In the future I'd ask you not to overstep your jurisdiction based on unfounded suspicion. This is a church facility now and we do not take kindly to false accusations or whimsical searches. You are no longer welcome here, Sir Brannon. I will assist you with your murder investigation in any way I can but I can't have the children in this orphanage being scared by your bullying tactics or your pet mage. Please leave."

With nothing more to go on, Brannon had no choice but to do as he was asked. When they reached the alley, the door slammed behind them. The sunlight was harshly bright compared to the shadowy inside of the orphanage.

"He's up to something," Draeson grumbled. "But I'm a Hooded Wolf if I know what it is."

"Yeah. He is." Brannon forced himself to unclench his fists. "He's hiding something now and he's hiding something about there being a church military unit. I want to know why." His jaw tightened. One way or another, he would keep an eye on Bishop Narayan.

CHAPTER TEN

Donal Gifson peered out the window at the street below. The lamps were dim and shadows edged the cobblestoned road. A few figures scurried down the footpath and a horse and carriage rattled past but there was no sign of the face he'd hoped to see. The moon had already risen. His son should have been home hours since. As the night got darker, the street outside became less and less visible until at last he was staring at his own reflection in the glass - grey hair, thick arms, workman's tunic and his war medal on a chain around his neck.

He paced the room, clenching and unclenching his hand on an off cut of stone he'd been carving and polishing into a paperweight. "Where is he? He should be home by now."

His wife rubbed at an invisible mark on the dining table with the cloth she'd been using to polish every item of spotless furniture in the room. Her dark hair had streaks of silver in it now and was gathered at the back of her neck with a clip before reaching half way down her spine like an elegant mane. "Ahpra knows. The boy's unreliable. You know that."

"He promised, Lira. You heard him."

Lira stopped scrubbing and stared at the cloth in her hand. "And you believed him. Because you always believe him. When will you understand that he's not a little boy anymore? He's a grown man and he makes his own choices and they are always the same ones."

Donal sighed. They'd had this conversation more than once. "I just think he's fallen in with the wrong crowd. He just needs to focus on his work and settle down."

"It's the work that's the problem," Lisa said. "And you know it."

Donal stared at the window. Ren had inherited his own skill with stone but combined it with a creativity all of his own. It was part of the reason they'd been able to do well here in Alapra instead of moving across the Tilal to where most of the construction work was, rebuilding from the destruction of the war.

There was something so satisfying and simple about working with stone. Cutting, shaping, slotting the pieces together. Masonry had given him the ability to create - to build and contribute to the world. He'd always loved that part of the job. Then the war came and his stones were used not to build but to destroy. Hurled from the top of castle walls, they crushed the Nilarian soldiers below. It was an image that still haunted his dreams and the reason he'd refused to return. Even helping to rebuild broken homes and cities could do nothing to wring the blood from his memories. Here in Alapra, there was building work too but most of the stonemasonry was in decorative, creative work. Statues, gargoyles, and building facings. Things of beauty to cast out the ugly thoughts.

"He's good at it," he said. Ren's skill at carving and cutting any kind of stone was at least as good as his own and had been from a young age and his sculptures were much better.

"I know," Lira said. "But he seeks challenge. And money."

The stone paperweight seemed overly heavy in Donal's hand. Ren had been spending a lot of time in the workshop alone lately working on the sculpture of the prow of a boat, complete with mermaid figurehead, for one of the more upmarket sailor bars. They'd brought in the stone over a month ago but, if he was honest, the progress had been slow. Donal slammed the paperweight on the table. "I'm searching his room."

"Don't look for what you're not willing to find,

Donal," Lira said. "You have our boy on a pedestal. What if you find something you don't want to see?"

Donal strode to the door. "I'm done putting my head in the sand. I need to know what he's up to."

The entire downstairs was devoted to workshop space and mostly used for the smaller, artistic commissions - carvings and decorative stonework. Ren worked alone often. Donal himself did most of the building blocks on site to avoid the effort of shifting the stone too many times.

The floor was covered in dust and stone chips. Sheets of fabric were draped over three large works in progress. Donal lifted the edge of the biggest one and peered beneath. The rough shape of the sculpture was in place but only barely. There was none of the form and detail that should have been there after so much time working on it.

"What's he been doing down here all this time?" He ran to the next cloth and lifted it. The block of stone beneath was completely untouched. The third cloth revealed a stone block with a design sketched out on the surface in dark wax. Sketched but not carved. "He should have done more than this. Much more. These are for paying customers!" He turned to Lira. "Did you know he's been mucking around?"

His wife shook his head. "He's down here when he's not out doing whatever he does in the city. You know that."

Donal looked around the workshop. What else

could his son have been up to down here? Why wouldn't he have gotten further along with his commissions? "We won't get paid on time if he doesn't finish them on time." There was a careful balance to the construction and artistic works. If they got out of sync then the cashflow fell behind. "If we don't get paid then our suppliers don't get paid, Lira. Then what?"

"I don't know." Lira touched his shoulder. "You shouldn't have trusted him to work unsupervised. We'll get onto him when he gets back."

"He has to learn at some point." Donal stared at the uncut stone. Unformed. Still trying to find its shape. It could become anything. Anyone. Just like his son. He'd believed he'd shaped Ren into a good man but lately...lately the boy was as unformed as this stone. Or perhaps, even worse, he'd carved himself into another shape entirely.

"What's that?" Lira pointed to a shape tucked under the corner of the sheet.

Donal flicked the fabric out of the way. He frowned. "It's the cash box. Why's the cash box down here?"

He lifted it onto a work bench and opened the lid. A collection of colored stones and chunks of glass reflected the lamplight back at him. There were no coins in the box. None at all.

"Blood and Tears," Lira swore. "Where's the money?"

Donal stumbled back, trembling.

"Donal!" Lira's voice was shrill. "Where's all our money?"

Donal's chest constricted, crushing the air out of him. This box was supposed to contain their entire cashflow. No cashflow meant no credit, no materials. He would lose all his construction work and the penalties for non-completion would be crippling. The weight of that responsibility bore down on him - his family would be homeless, starving, helpless.

It was like those poor soldiers crushed beneath his stones during the war. Nothing they could do to save themselves. Crushed. Bleeding. Destroyed.

His chest felt tighter. How could he have been so stupid? How could he have trusted so much when they'd seen Ren make bad decisions over and over? They would be crushed by debt all because of that stupidity. He couldn't breathe. He was an invading soldier and the stone was crushing the life out of him. This was his comeuppance. He'd somehow known it would happen as soon as he'd begun letting his skills be used for killing instead of for creation. The death he'd dished out was coming back for him.

He turned and reached for Lira, his eyes bulging with the lack of air.

Lira's skull burst like a soldier struck by a falling rock. Her body crumpled to the floor.

Donal tried to scream but his rib cage shattered and he could breathe no more.

CHAPTER ELEVEN

Brannon had been in the palace ballroom many times. As the King's Champion he'd been required to attend formal events and sat through them all with whatever fortitude he could muster for the sake of duty and his friendship with King Aldan, but he was not a man who enjoyed state affairs or politics. They made him feel out of place - a curiosity on display for courtiers who wanted to gawk at the Bloodhawk and imagine how he had been in battle.

Never once had he expected the arrival of Nilarians in the ballroom.

Never once had he brought one as a date.

The ballroom was decorated with colored lanterns and the guests were even more elaborately festooned. The nobles of Kalanon had embraced the masquerade concept with passion. Bright gowns and coats were embroidered in colorful thread and stitched with crystals. Masks were crusted with gems and peacock feathers. With faces hidden, the guests were especially risqué in their flirting and dancing, giving the entire spectacle the air of a mating display in an aviary of the gods. Musicians played from a corner of the room and many guests had already taken to the dance floor.

"Do you think he'll show up?" Ylani's voice was soft, pitched just low enough to reach his ears and no further. Her hand was on his arm, a light touch with heavy meaning - a public intimacy despite the privacy of the masks.

Where the other women present wore large skirted ballgowns - in some cases as wide as they were tall - Ylani's gown was sleek, gold silk that left her arms bare and clung to her curves all the way to the floor. Beneath the embroidered hem peeked one-of-a-kind jeweled shoes made by a recently deceased cobbler whose creations had fashionable courtiers raving. Strings of gems hung in loops across her shoulders, a sparkling spiderweb that hinted at sleeves. The same gems, strung on wire to mimic feathers, rose from her hat, which curved down over her face, transforming into a gold filigree mask.

Brannon was glad Draeson had insisted on dressing him for the event. He would have felt horribly out of place in his usual attire. The mage was right - Brannon did usually dress as if in uniform. The end result was steel grey trousers and matching vest over a crisp white linen shirt. The vest was embroidered in black thread with a hawk - a nod to his identity behind the grey mask he wore. The mask was beaten steel in a more masculine filigree than Ylani's, meaning their outfits complimented without matching. They looked good together, like two equal pieces from the opposite sides of the chess board.

Ylani's hand squeezed gently on Brannon's arm, reminding him of her question.

He cleared his throat. "Draeson thinks he will."

"And do we entirely trust Magus Draeson?" Ylani glanced toward the drinks table where the mage was helping himself to a third or possibly fourth goblet. The mage was dressed as stylishly as usual but with much more vibrant color. He stood out even in this crowd, a flamboyant confection who was hard to miss. Exactly like what he was: bait.

"When it comes to magical matters, we do." Brannon said. The corner of his mouth turned up wryly and he shrugged. "Mostly. And I trust your Instinct. You said it felt like something important would happen tonight."

"True." Ylani chewed her lower lip a moment. "Let's hope we spot him quickly if he does arrive then. If this goes awry..." Her head tilted towards the crowd of courtiers.

"Yeah," Brannon said. "This could be a bloodbath." He scratched at his cheek where the edge of the metal mask rubbed against his scar. Compared to some of the masks in the room, his intricately worked piece was almost dull, but he felt the natural grey of the steel suited his nature. For most of this life he'd been considered a weapon. Tonight, even with his newly crafted Nilarian steel sword at his side, his wits and awareness of their surroundings were his strongest weapons in keeping his king and their guests safe.

Ylani wrinkled her nose. "It somewhat detracts from the point of the mask if you keep drawing attention to your identifying characteristics."

Brannon pulled his eyes from searching the crowd to smile at her. "Says the only woman in the room wearing a hat."

Her laughter was like a waterfall over bells. "You have me there. For now." The Nilarian contingent had yet to arrive so her hat was a dead giveaway as to her culture, and thus her identity. Only the ambassador from Nilar would be wearing such a thing here. And the two of them together drew more than their share of stares. She touched his cheek where the scar ended. "You scratch it when you're stressed, do you realize that? You'd be wonderful at a tiles table. I'd have you penniless in a heartbeat."

"I'm sure you would."

"Perhaps we should dance instead?"

Brannon took her hand and placed his other in the small of her back, suddenly aware of how warm she was and that his movements on the dance floor were likely even more military in nature than his clothing choices. His steps led them around the floor with precision but, he suspected, a certain lack of musicality. Ylani let her chin rest on his shoulder.

"I see Ula has gathered some admirers," she said.

Brannon turned his head to look. Sure enough, the Djin woman was surrounded by fascinated courtiers, all eager to be seen with her. She'd refused the offer of Kalan clothing and wore a dress similar to her usual leather garb but embellished with woven flax, coral beads, and painted designs. She was showing no sign of her collapse a few days earlier and had assured the team that she'd bounced back to full strength.

"What's the bet she's telling them she doesn't speak Kalan?"

Ylani chuckled. "Pretty high. I told her to signal us if she needs a rescue."

Brannon thought that was unlikely. "As long as she doesn't call a Risen in to chase them off."

They reached the corner of the dance floor and

turned to face the other way. As he scanned the crowd, a male figure caught Brannon's eye. The upper part of the man's face was hidden by a mask designed to look like an emerald eagle, with dyed feathers and a hooked beak over the nose. The man's jaw line looked familiar but Brannon couldn't be sure.

As he watched, the eagle-headed man reached into the pocket of his coat and moved close to one of the other guests. When he withdrew his hand, he kept it closed in a fist as if to contain something from his pocket.

"This could be it." Brannon let go of Ylani and reached for his sword even as he took his first steps towards the man.

The eagle masked man raised the closed fist to his mouth as if to blow the contents.

"Blood and Tears, it's him."

Ylani caught his wrist. "Wait," she said. "He's the wrong body type."

"Are you sure?"

The man coughed onto his closed fist. His fingers stayed closed and no sparkling powder flew. He coughed again, thumped his chest, and then pushed up his mask.

The tension left Brannon in a rush of breath. "You're right. It's not him."

She squeezed his wrist. "We'll keep watching. If he shows up, we'll get him."

Brannon was saved from having to agree or not by the king's attendants ringing a bell for attention. The music ceased.

King Aldan stood to address his guests. He wore gold, almost the same color as his hair and beard, and the crown on his head shone with reflected light. To his left sat young Tomidan Sandilar, until recently the only heir to the throne. On his right, the newly returned Prince Claydan. "It's been almost eight years since our war with Nilar ended and, in many ways, Kalanon is thriving again. But the legacy of that war has persisted for many of us. We've had a hole in our hearts and in our lives where our missing loved ones once were." He gestured to Claydan and smiled. "I'm grateful to my Champion...my Master of Investigations...and his team for returning my son to me and giving back a piece of my heart I thought was gone forever."

The audience broke into applause.

Claydan gave an awkward half bow in his seat.

Aldan beamed. "Tonight, I hope to see many more Kalans have their loved ones restored to them. But first, let me introduce the other children rescued by Sir Brannon's special investigations team." He waved his hand and a door to an antechamber opened.

An unmasked woman led a train of children into the hall. They were a range of ages, dressed in simple but clean clothes. Brannon recognized

Shalyn, the murdered cobbler's daughter, and a few others he'd last seen pulled from crates. They were the children who'd been taken and almost sold in Nilar as slaves.

Ylani stiffened.

Brannon leaned in. "I'm sorry," he said. "I asked him not to do this." The visiting Nilarian dignitaries were about to arrive and this was a pointed way to embarrass them.

"He wants to make a point," she said. "I get it. And it helps establish your team's value. I just wish..."

Brannon squeezed her hand.

The children arrayed themselves to either side of the king and then, at a signal from the woman leading them, sat on the floor with crossed legs. Many of them were only little Duke Tomidan's age, making him seem somehow even smaller and younger perched on a semi-throne behind them.

"Sadly, these children have no parents to return to, but every effort is being made to see to their care," King Aldan said. "In Kalanon, we take care of each other. Today, we continue to do that and we embrace the change peace brings. With that in mind, I'd like to invite our honored guests from Nilar to join us and help us in the healing of old wounds."

The large double doors at the end of the hall opened and the Nilarian visitors streamed into the ballroom like a colorful links in a chain. They weren't wearing masks like the other guests, but each one wore a large hat decorated with ribbons and feathers. A murmur went through the gathered courtiers. Few had seen so many Nilarians in one place since the war. Or in some cases any Nilarians at all, other than Ambassador Ylani. After fighting so hard to keep Nilar's soldiers from the Kalan capital, it was odd to have them here as invited guests. Odder still that only the first few were truly dressed for the occasion. The rest were in clothes and hats of lesser quality and their hands were bound in a long strip of silk, connecting them one to the next like beads threaded on a child's necklace. Those with bound hands were a variety of ages and many showed signs of hard labor or poor nutrition with callouses on their hands and faces weathered like leather by the sun. These were not, Brannon realized, Nilarians at all.

The leader of the party bowed in greeting to King Aldan. She was a woman in a burnt orange silk gown, straight auburn hair to her shoulders and an enormous hat. Whereas Brannon had seen Ylani often make concessions for the sake of diplomacy to her traditional attire and keep her head gear smaller for Kalan eyes, this woman seemed to want to emphasize her Nilarianness. The hat was easily three times the size of any Brannon had seen a Nilarian wear before. She handed Aldan a large bundle of folded silk. "A gift with my thanks," she said in a voice designed to carry throughout the room, "to the Kalan king and all his people for the gracious welcome we have received." She reached up and tapped the brim of her hat in an unconscious gesture.

"It's a painting of Aldan," Ylani whispered. "Probably about the size of a small house. The bigger the portrait, the more respect or contrition it represents."

"And why's she fiddling with her hat?"

"She wants to make sure the gods don't lose track of her among her enemies." The corner of Ylani's mouth twitched.

"You think so?"

"Oh yes. This is seriously awkward for her."

"My name is Alyra Jalin and I have been sent here because the Nilarian government wishes to continue to foster peace with Kalanon in good faith and to right a wrong that was left over from a time when our great countries were not such good friends." She gave a wry little shrug as if the war that had nearly overrun Kalanon could be considered a small disagreement. "As you know, the effects of that dark time have been lasting for both our countries and it has been a struggle to rebuild what was lost. There have been moments of desperation for citizens of both countries and, in desperate moments, people sometimes do foolish things. Terrible things."

The room was silent as Alyra paused. Brannon noticed that Draeson had moved closer, the mage's lips a thin tight line against angry words.

Alyra sighed. "At first, we eschewed the old ways but, over time, we began to justify it. We turned to the soldiers we had captured in our desperate need to rebuild. It seemed a reasonable use of a resource and a way for them to earn their food and shelter. They were prisoners of war and we had lost so many of our own able-bodied men and women when your River Tilal flooded."

Flooded. It was an interesting choice of words. There had been no natural flooding involved. The river had been dammed and weaponized with the intention of drowning as many of the invading army as possible. Brannon had been instrumental in the mission. He and Draeson, back when the Magus had been an old man rather than the restored youth he was today.

"But it was slavery, and our people had thought to abandon that practice a long time ago. So when those of us in positions of power learned that some of our countrymen had taken it upon themselves to capture new slaves, and children at that, these actions held a mirror up to Nilarian society and we saw what we had allowed to happen. We could not, in good conscience, continue to keep our Kalan neighbors as slaves-"

"Easy to say when you've been caught," Draeson muttered.

"Ssh," Brannon hissed.

"-and in the spirit of the new friendship and healing between our countries, we return to Kalanon all those who were taken." The Nilarian woman raised her arms to take in the people who were bound in silk. At her gesture, the other Nilarians in the party cut the bonds and they fell to the floor in short ribbons. "These are but the first of those we return to you. We hope you will see that they have not been ill-treated. Over the years, many have become part of our families, but we know they are truly part of yours."

A murmur rippled through the guests and the crowd seemed to surge forward as people craned their heads to examine the group. It was a rare Kalan who hadn't lost someone in the war and many times the bodies had not been able to be returned to their families. For these people, the hope that their loved one would simply show up one day was hard to deny. Especially when that was exactly what had happened with the crown prince.

A few of the freed Kalan prisoners pulled the hats from their heads and threw them to the ground, quick to cast off the Nilarian custom. Others stood silent, bewildered and unsure of themselves. One man with an eye patch simply sat on the floor and stared at his hands.

"Callum?" a voice cried out from the crowd. " Ahpra's Tears, it is you! I thought you'd died!"

One of the released men jerked his head up. "Mother?"

An elderly woman elbowed her way to the front and pulled off her mask. Her eyes streamed with tears but her face was filled with radiant joy. Her son broke free of the rank of slaves and she flung herself into his arms. They clung to each other, sobbing and laughing as the surrounding courtiers broke into spontaneous applause.

Brannon couldn't keep a grin from his own face. It had been a rare thing for him to see a happy reunion during the war and rarer still since its end. He'd thought bringing Claydan back for his friend the king had been an impossible miracle. Now he'd been lucky enough to see another. He wondered how many more would occur as Nilar returned their prisoners of war.

An elbow nudged him.

"Don't get distracted," Draeson said. "He could still show up."

Brannon flicked his gaze around the room. "I know."

"And I hope you're watching closely," Draeson murmured to Ylani. "You and I are the ones most likely to recognize the Hooded man."

"Believe me," she returned. "I've been seeing his face in my nightmares ever since my brother was exiled. I want him caught as much as you do."

"Keep an eye on the Nilarians," Draeson said. "We can't trust any of them."

Ylani raised an eyebrow.

Brannon's eyes narrowed. "You recall Ambassador Ylani is Nilarian."

Draeson shrugged. "I'm aware."

The reunited mother and son pulled back from their embrace but the elderly woman couldn't seem to make herself let go of his tunic sleeve. She clung to it as if afraid that, if she let it go for even an instant, he would disappear again.

King Aldan raised his hands and the murmuring of the crowd quietened but the air of excitement still buzzed throughout the room. "This is one of many families we hope to see reunited as a result of a stronger bond between Kalanon and Nilar. It's a new step in the healing of our great nations." He nodded to Alyra and her companions. "Our guests will be with us for a few weeks and help manage the logistics of returning our lost countrymen to their families. When they return to Nilar we will, of course, continue to have a relationship with that country through Ambassador Ylani."

Several faces turned to stare. It seemed the filigree mask had done little to truly hide who she was. Brannon stood a little taller at her side, daring anyone to challenge. No one did.

"But now," Aldan continued, "it feels right to deepen our new friendship with Nilar. So I have chosen to send two of my most prized citizens to Nilar as ambassadors of our own. Please welcome Lord and Lady Kesh."

Brannon's eyes widened and his jaw dropped. "What?"

Ylani frowned. "Is that...?"

The doors at the end of the hall opened again to reveal a regal couple in their late sixties.

Brannon swallowed. "My parents."

CHAPTER TWELVE

The gathered courtiers applauded loudly as Brannon's parents walked the length of the room. Draeson sidled up to Brannon, half full goblet still in hand. "Were you expecting that?"

Brannon shook his head.

"Do I sense a family drama?" The mage pursed his lips and raised his eyebrows.

"Shut up."

Draeson shrugged. "As long as they don't get in the way of our plan."

"Go circulate, Draeson. It does none of us any good to be all in one place." Brannon took Ylani's elbow and moved them a little way from the mage. "You were talking to Aldan about this earlier. Arranging all this with your government."

"I was," Ylani said. "But I didn't know it was

going to be your parents. He didn't tell me who he'd chosen. I would have told you if I'd known. I'm surprised Aldan didn't."

Brannon sighed. "Well, he's the king. He doesn't tell me everything." He watched as his mother and father approached the throne and bowed. They both looked older than he remembered. Kesh was a long way from Alapra and he didn't visit much. There was no reason to. Now, as he noted the extra lines, sagging jowls and grey hair, he wondered if he'd been foolish. Not even parents lived forever and if they were to spend much of their remaining years in Nilar there would be little opportunity to see them again.

Lost as he was in his thoughts, he hardly noticed as another figure entered the room and quickly crossed the crowd to stand beside him.

"Little brother! You're looking handsome for once. It must be the mask covering your face!"

He turned, startled. "Reanna?"

His sister grinned. "How can you be the legendary Bloodhawk when you're this easy to sneak up on?" She wrapped her arms around him in a tight hug. "It's good to see you again, Brannon."

He pushed the mask up onto the top of his head and stared. Reanna still had the dark hair they'd always shared but hers was long and wavy whereas Brannon kept his in the short military style. She wore the Kesh colors of red and orange. She'd opted for wide flowing trousers rather than a gown, which didn't surprise him. Reanna had always been more comfortable on the farm than at court. The only jewelry she wore was the signet ring of Kesh on a chain around her neck. He raised an eyebrow at it.

"You know I'm the heir, Brannon," she said.

"Yes, but our parents aren't dead."

"They're going to Nilar," Reanna said. "They might as well be." She looked at Brannon's date. "And who is this lovely lady? I didn't know you were seeing anyone."

Brannon gestured between the two women. "Ambassador Ylani Shaylar of Nilar, this is my sister, Reanna, soon to be Lady of Kesh."

Ylani nodded and smiled. "It's a pleasure to meet you, Reanna." She held out her hand but Reanna did not take it.

"Really?" Brannon's sister looked at Brannon, her eyes narrowed. "Your judgement hasn't changed much."

His jaw tightened. "Yours either, apparently."

Ylani dropped her hand to her side.

Reanna shrugged. "I should catch up with our parents before the next announcement. Come say hi later. Or don't." With that, she walked off toward the throne where the king and his new ambassadors stood.

"So the daughter of the new ambassadors to Nilar doesn't like Nilarians," muttered Ylani.

"Great. I hope I didn't cause trouble for you with your family."

"You didn't." Brannon tugged the mask back over his face. "That wasn't about you or even about Nilar. It was about me."

Ylani chewed her lip as she watched him, searching for something behind the mask he wore. "It's okay if we decide we should classify this as just a mission and not a date," she said at last. "I get that it could make things difficult for you with your family to be seen with me."

"No, that's not-" he began.

She gestured between them. "We don't have to take this...whatever this is...too fast or serious, you know."

Brannon shook his head again. "My family, much as they might think otherwise, do not dictate who I spend my time with." He heard the clipped tone of his voice and fought to relax it, despite the burning sensation in his chest. "Not now. Not for a long time. I choose my own companions and I don't care what others think of them. And you, Ylani Shaylar, are well worth spending time with."

She smiled and it brought light to her face even through the mask. "Careful. You'll make me want to kiss you in front of all your disapproving countrymen."

The burning in his chest evaporated and was replaced with an entirely different heat in his face, warm against the cool metal mask. "You've kissed me before," he reminded her.

She shrugged. "True. But I thought you were about to die at the time so...I'm not sure it counts."

Brannon chuckled. "It counts. And your countrymen are here as well and they'd be just as disapproving."

"Nah. They'll think I'm getting close to manipulate you." The innocence fairly dripped from her voice. She shifted slightly and suddenly he felt her presence all along his body. She brought her lips closer to his cheek and spoke softly. "I was a spy in the war, you know."

Brannon's grin widened. "I think I heard that somewhere." He leaned in to claim the threatened kiss.

The heat from her lips radiated out to his and just as they were about to touch, Ylani stiffened and stumbled back, eyes wide. She cursed in Nilarian.

"What's wrong?"

"Draeson!" she gasped, searching the crowd. "Something's happening. Where is he?"

Brannon searched the crowd but there was no sign of the mage's colorful clothing. "Blood and Tears. I told him to stay in sight." The guests were milling and chatting, oblivious to the urgency Brannon felt flooding his veins. He caught Ula's eye and the Djin woman pointed toward the side of the room. Brannon glanced across and saw a door closing. "There!"

He and Ylani pushed through the crowd, headed for the door. Ula abandoned her admirers and joined them as Brannon reached for the handle.

The door banged open and Brannon strode into the room, Prioress Ula and Ambassador Ylani at his back. Ula's leather was a contrast to Ylani's gold silk gown but the expression of determination they wore was the same. Brannon's sword was a hard, cold line of death in his hand, the symbol of the Bloodhawk name on the hilt as steely as his resolve to embody it. The women closed the door behind them, protecting the people in the grand hall beyond.

The room was easily as large as Brannon's entire apartment but much more lushly appointed. Carpets and wall hangings covered the stone of the castle structure. The room was a waiting chamber attached to the great hall but tonight, the furniture had been removed or pushed to the side and extra tables brought in to hold catering for the event. The food was in the hall now and just one waiter huddled in a corner, his eyes wide.

In the middle of the room, two figures circled each other warily. Tiny crackles of lightning outlined their fists and the dragon tattoo on Draeson's face hissed.

"Get out of here," the mage growled. "This is my fight."

Brannon snorted. "Not Hooded likely. You didn't do so well last time you faced him."

"This time I'm ready."

"So are we."

Their adversary was a muscular man in his forties, grey-speckled hair and deep blue eyes. He and Draeson had both abandoned their masks. Brannon pulled his own mask from his face and threw it as if skipping a stone on a pond. The metal spun through the air towards the mages. The older looking of the two lashed out and the lightning in his hand struck the mask, shattering with a boom that shook the chandelier overhead and rattled the cutlery piled on the table.

There was no doubting who this was. Brannon swallowed. "Magus Nycol. Nice to meet you at last."

The mage sneered. "I doubt it."

Draeson took advantage of the exchange and flicked the lightning in his own fingers toward the other mage. It struck an invisible shield and skittered around Nycol to crash into the wall behind him. Black scorch marks spread out from the point of impact like branches of a dead tree.

"Nice try." Nycol smirked. "I would have thought you'd remember that trick."

Draeson frowned. "Remember...?"

Brannon saw Nycol reach into his pocket and lunged forward. "Look out!" He swung his sword, hoping the invisible shield that deflected lightning was specific enough magic not to block Nilarian steel.

A blast of magic struck Brannon in the chest and hurled him backward. He twisted as he fell, so that when he came down on a tabletop, the impact was spread across his full length, but even so, it pushed the breath from his lungs in a painful rush. He rolled and slid off the edge, landing on his hands and knees.

When Brannon looked up, Nycol had pulled something from his pocket and blew across his palm. A cloud of sparkling dust flew towards Draeson's face.

Draeson moved his hand in a swatting motion and a gust of wind scattered the magic powder harmlessly aside. "Not this time," he growled.

As Brannon scrambled to his feet, Ylani pulled two of her hat pins from her hair, revealing them to be daggers in disguise. She flicked her wrist and sent one of them flying at Nycol's chest.

Nycol thrust his hand out and the dagger stopped mid-air.

Brannon rushed the mage again. There had to be a limit to the number of attacks the man could deflect at once. If they could synchronize their blows, perhaps one would get lucky and strike home.

Draeson seemed to have the same thought,

sending another burst of lightning but it bounced back at him only to be swallowed by the dragon tattoo.

Ula chanted in her own language and Brannon felt the hairs on his arm stand up as her power filled the room. He swung the sword low, aiming for the enemy mage's legs as Ylani sprang onto a chair and then to the table, her split skirt rippling around her in a flow of golden silk. She hurled her second dagger down from above as the mage was focused on the sword below.

Brannon's sword stopped dead, and jarring impact of the power shot up his arm to his shoulder in a jolt of pain. But the attempt to split the mage's attention worked. Ylani's dagger sank into Nycol's bicep.

The mage screamed and released the power holding Brannon's sword. He yanked the dagger from his arm and dropped it to the ground.

Brannon moved in again with the sword, feinting to the injured side.

Nycol jerked back...and into the waiter who was now standing behind him. The waiter wrapped his arms around Nycol, pinning the mage's own arms to his side in a tight and immobile embrace. Nycol struggled to break free, but the waiter's body was solid as stone. Nycol called fire around his fingers and let it burn into the man's body but there was no reaction.

Ula chuckled. "I put Risen throughout the area, just in case," she said. "Good Risen. Not look dead but...he dead. You cannot hurt him. Kaluki heal." Sure enough, the charred flesh of the Risen's body was already healing. Apparently fire was no problem for an established Risen the way it was with a burned body that had not yet become one.

Brannon took Ylani's hand and helped her down from the table, keeping his sword in the other hand with the tip level with Nycol's chest. "It wouldn't take much for that Risen to crush your ribs," he commented. "I don't think your lungs would recover from that."

Nycol stopped struggling. "Very clever. What do you want?"

"That's our question," Brannon said. "Why are you trying to kidnap Draeson? What do you want with him? Why are you here?"

"Technically that's three questions. And shouldn't you be off investigating a mysterious death?" Nycol wrinkled his nose. "I hear the smell was quite...interesting. Or are you up to the second one now?"

Brannon's chest tightened. "What second one?"

"Oh, you haven't heard about it yet?" The trapped mage sounded genuinely surprised. "I assumed your mentor would have told you by now."

"Mentor?" Brannon's thoughts raced. Who would Nycol consider to be his mentor? He'd had many throughout the war but in recent years, there had been only one. His fingers clenched harder on the hilt of his sword until his knuckles were white. "Master Jordell? If you've hurt him..."

Nycol snorted. "If I wanted him dead, he would be. And if I had wanted you dead, do you really think you could stop me?"

It was Ula who answered. She gestured to Risen that held him. "Is strong kaluki in freshly dead body. Can squeeze very hard. Maybe I see a wizard pop today." She mimed crushing something between her thumb and forefinger. "Like berry. Squish."

"Mage," said Draeson. "Not wizard."

Brannon gave him a narrow-eyed, sideways look. "Really? Is this the time for a language lesson?"

Draeson shrugged and averted his eyes.

"He's always been particular about the difference," Nycol muttered. "So quick to look down on other forms of magic."

Brannon frowned. "How long have you known Magus Draeson."

"He doesn't know me," Draeson snapped. "Other than as his kidnap victim."

Nycol smirked. "Speaking of kidnaps...who's this bright young thing joining us?"

Brannon turned to see the door close behind a familiar girl of eleven. She'd had royal stylists at her since he'd seen her last at the orphanage. Her hair was curled to her shoulders and she wore a white dress with a blue sash at the waist. The dress had been chosen by the king's tailors and matched the garb of the other children who had been paraded before the masquerade guests. She tugged at the hem of it as she walked into the room. Her eyes brightened when she saw Draeson. "Mister Magus!" she said, excitedly.

"Go back to the party, Shalyn," Brannon called. "Stay back."

Ylani reached for the girl but Shalyn was too quick and ducked past her, heading for Draeson.

"The king said I could talk to -" She stopped suddenly, her eyes fixed on Nycol, still in the grasp of the Risen. "It's you!"

"He can't hurt you," Brannon told her. He sheathed his sword and laid his hand on the girl's shoulder, drawing her back. "The Risen has him trapped."

Shalyn nodded, the movement frenetic and unconvincing. "Yeah. Okay." She turned face Brannon. "What's a Risen?"

Before he could answer, a movement behind her caught his eye. The Risen had Nycol around the upper arms, leaving his lower arms free to move. Nycol thrust his hands into his pockets and pulled out reagents for his spells. This time he had none of the mesmerizing dust. In one hand he had a simple river stone and in the other, a glass ball, like an oversized marble, glowing with trapped lightning.

"Ula!" Brannon yelled. "Stop him!" He shoved Shalyn aside, hoping to keep her from becoming a target of the lightning, but it was the river stone the mage used first.

Nycol threw the stone to the ground and shattered, releasing a flash of light and a concussive force that boomed through the room like an earthquake, shaking them all from their feet.

Brannon reached for his sword as he stumbled upright, only to see Nycol push the lightning marble into the Risen's mouth and duck his head, muttering. The lighting within exploded, blowing off the back of the Risen's skull, splattering bone and tissue across the wall. The Risen slumped, its arms falling loosely to its sides as it fell backward and away from the mage.

Nycol pointed to Shalyn and crooked his finger.

Brannon watched in horror as magic grasped the girl and pulled her across the room into the mage's arms.

Nycol wrapped one arm around her throat and held his other hand to her temple. A crackle of power danced between his fingers. "Now," he said, his voice low and menacing. "That thing might heal having its brains blown out but I doubt this young lady will. So let's revisit the notion that you have me trapped, shall we?"

"Don't do it, Nycol," Brannon warned. "You kill a child and there won't be anywhere in this city you can hide."

"Then don't make me. I just want to leave. I'll let the girl go as soon as I'm convinced no one is following me. Sound fair?" The mage looked from one to the other until Brannon and his team had each nodded their consent. "Good. Nice to see you all. Let's not do it again soon."

He backed away toward the door that lead to the kitchens, dragging Shalyn with him. The door swung open at a flick of his finger.

Brannon leaned forward, his fingers itching to stick the sword into the mage, but he didn't dare move. There was no way any of them could get close enough to disable Nycol before he could hurt his hostage. He watched helplessly as the mage took the little girl with him.

As they slipped into the doorway, Nycol gave Shalyn a shove and she stumbled into the room, tripped on the body of the Risen, and collided with Brannon. Nycol turned and ran. Draeson hurled a fireball after him but the door slammed shut and the flames smashed into the wood.

Brannon thrust Shalyn toward Ambassador Ylani. "Here." He ran for the scorched and smoking door and jerked it open.

The hallway was empty.

"Ahpra's Tears! Where did he go?" Brannon ran to fork in the corridor and looked both ways. There was no sign of anyone. Nycol was gone.

Brannon swore and sheathed his sword. He turned back and almost bumped into Draeson.

"We had him!" The mage slammed his palm into the stone wall angrily. "Blood and Tears, we had him and the Hooded bastard got away." He turned and stomped back to the others, clenching and unclenching his fists.

Brannon followed. Two guards appeared at the doorway to the ballroom. Behind them, Brannon could hear the King reassuring his guests that everything was fine and to continue dancing. The river stone detonation must have been even louder than Brannon realized. He signaled the guards and they hurried forward, shutting the door behind them. "The man we're looking for is here on the palace grounds. Down there. You'll need to split up. I don't know which way he went."

The guard saluted and hurried off.

Brannon watched them go and leaned against the wall, his stomach twisted in knots. He hoped sending them was the right decision. He had little hope they would find the mage and even less that they could contain him if they did. His magic made him something well beyond what any of the palace guards had dealt with before. Nycol could kill any guard who attempted to apprehend him with ease.

Brannon and his team had gotten lucky so far tonight.

He sighed. There was little chance Nycol would be found now. He let his gaze drift over the antechamber. The room was a shambles. Furniture was broken and tipped over. But it could have been worse. Instead of broken furniture, they could easily be looking at broken bodies.

Ula sat next to the Risen waiter, quietly focused on banishing the kaluki inhabiting it. It had healed some of the damage inflicted by Nycol's attack, but what was left was a charred and bloody mess.

Draeson raged at no one in particular and Ylani held the shaking Shalyn in her arms.

"I'm sorry," the girl sobbed.

Ylani gave Draeson a stern glance. "It couldn't be helped."

Draeson opened his mouth to reply but Brannon cut him off.

"Of course not. We'll get another chance at it. He still seems obsessed with you, Draeson. The fact that he tried to grab you again tonight shows we were right. Worst case scenario, we find another way to put you up as bait."

Draeson snorted. "Assuming he falls for it a second time."

Brannon scratched at his scar. "You're right. We can't wait for him to make another move. We need to find him and contain him."

"Easier said than done."

"Ylani, can you think of anywhere he might go? Any connections he or Marrol had here that we don't already know?"

She shook her head. "I would have told you by now if I knew."

"Yeah." Brannon sighed. He picked up a toppled chair and set it on its feet again, the small gesture giving him at least the tiniest feeling of putting something right. Beneath it, a glint of steel caught his eye. It was one of Ylani's knives. The ones she'd disguised as hat pins. "This is yours, I believe." He bent down to scoop it up.

"Thank you," Ylani said. "Do you see where the other one went? I think I actually cut him with that one."

Brannon chuckled ruefully. "You were the only one to manage it."

"What?" Draeson stopped pacing. "Are you serious? You cut him? Is there blood?"

Ylani frowned. "Assuming mages bleed. Why?"

"Find it. Find it now!"

"Ahpra's Tears." Brannon's eyes widened. "The moth! Your tracking spell..."

"Needs a part of the person I'm tracking. Exactly." Draeson punched the air. "And his blood is the best part of all."

Brannon grinned. "So we find the knife and we

find him. No matter where he's hiding."

"The moth's range is limited," Draeson pointed out. "I'll need to act fast."

They searched quickly. Ula, having finished dealing with the Risen, got up to help and even Shalyn joined in, though she kept as far from the dead man as she could and thus searched the part of the room least likely to hold the knife. They checked under tables, and in the corners and still had no success. The blade was smaller than Brannon was used to but it was difficult to see how it could have been so thoroughly lost. He was beginning to wonder if Nycol had realized the danger his spilled blood represented and somehow found a way to destroy it.

"How far could it have slid?" he muttered, scouring the floor yet again. He lifted a rug on the off chance the blade had slipped beneath it. "It has to be here."

"Even just a few drops spilled blood would help," Draeson muttered. "It doesn't have to be the knife itself."

Brannon ran his gaze along crease where the floor met the wall. Nothing. He came to the door that lead to the servants' entrance and kitchens. He paused. The crack beneath the door was a dark strip, almost two fingers deep. Enough for a slim dagger to slide through. "Here."

He opened the door and came face to face with

a young woman with a magistrate's insignia on her chest. She held Ylani's missing dagger between her thumb and forefinger, letting it dangle as if she found touching it distasteful.

She blinked at him. "Sir Brannon. I was...ah, is this yours?" She held out the dagger. A streak of red colored the edge of the blade.

Brannon took it by the hilt. "Thank you," he said.

She smiled and shrugged. "You're welcome."

He passed the dagger behind him and Draeson took it eagerly. "You're a long way from the courts." He raised an eyebrow, making it a question.

Her smile faded. "Yes. I'm afraid I was sent to find you. There's been another murder."

CHAPTER THIRTEEN

Ylani tucked a loose strand of hair behind her ear and closed the door behind Shalyn as one of the guardians from the orphanage escorted her back to the masquerade where the other children were waiting. Ylani couldn't help wondering how the child would cope with this second kidnapping. The hot ball of shame and anger she'd pushed down in her chest since first discovering her family and country's connection to the stolen children burned with a nauseating intensity.

Things had been simpler when she'd first come to Kalanon. They were the enemy then. A necessary evil. Now, Kalans were her friends and they'd battled true evil together. And Nilar...she loved her country but the return of prisoners of war kept as slaves showed just how far from true justice and morality her people had strayed when faced with the difficulties war had left them with. She watched as Brannon spoke with the messenger who had come to tell them of another magical murder. She knew he hated the things he'd had to do in the war. Things that had earned him the name Bloodhawk and made him a hero to his own people and a figure of nightmares to hers. Perhaps it was a similar emotion. War had made them all do things they weren't proud of. Necessity - or at least the belief of it - was a cruel and twisted guide.

She picked up a fallen chair, set it upright, and smoothed the front of her skirt.

Draeson sat cross-legged on the floor and cradled Ylani's blood-stained dagger in his hands. The mage closed his eyes, his brow furrowed in concentration. For a moment, it seemed nothing would happen. Ylani wondered if they'd delayed too long and Nycol was beyond the range of the mage's spell, but then the blood on the blade began to move. It ran along the metal, condensing and pooling, shaping itself into a small, red moth. The wings of the moth quivered and lifted up from the blade. They fluttered and the creature lifted into the air.

"Open the door please," Draeson whispered.

Ylani crossed the room and did as he asked and the moth flew out of the room and down the corridor after Nycol. Ylani stared after it until the tiny creature had disappeared around the corner, then she brushed her hands on her skirt once more. "That's that then. Now we wait."

She looked around for something useful to do and her eyes were quickly drawn to the fallen Risen Ula had returned to its natural state. She tugged a tablecloth from the nearby table and approached the Djin.

"Perhaps we should cover him up," she suggested. "Just so nobody gets upset."

Ula shrugged. "Kalans have such wet stomachs when it comes to the dead."

"Weak stomachs," Ylani corrected, the corners of her mouth twitching.

"Yes, that." Ula nodded. "Are Nilarians like this also?"

Ylani couldn't hide her chuckle. "Yes, I'm afraid we are."

The two of them draped the cloth over the dead man, shrouding him from immediate view.

Draeson remained seated, all his focus on keeping the spell. "You can all go," he said, his eyes still closed. "This could take a while. I'll send word when I'm sure he's stopped for the night."

Ylani glanced at Brannon and caught her lower lip in her teeth, frowning.

Brannon hesitated. "Don't try to take him on your own."

"I won't."

Brannon scratched at the scar on his cheek,

watching the mage's face for any sign of duplicity.

The messenger hovered nearby, feet twitching, obviously eager to return to the crime scene.

"I'll watch over him," Ylani said quietly. "And there are plenty of guards nearby. Nycol is unlikely to return. You're the Master of Investigations, remember? If this murder is as strange as it sounds, you can't ignore it."

He drew himself up and touched the sword at his side like a talisman. "Okay. I'll go. Just make sure he lets me know as soon as he has a location."

Draeson waved a hand at him. "Get."

"Okay, okay."

Ula stood and brushed herself off. "I come with you. Perhaps help."

"Thank you," Brannon said.

Ylani wondered when they'd all become so used to Ula's ways that leaving the Risen's body to be dealt with later seemed normal.

With Brannon and Ula gone, the room felt strangely quiet and isolated. She could hear the party next door winding down and imagined the guests drifting off to their homes or to private after-parties and secret rendezvous as they made the most of the mystery the masks provided. None of them came through this room. Even the servants had been instructed to find another way to the kitchen. There was nothing but her own footsteps as she paced and, when she paused to lean against a chair back or table edge, Draeson's breathing.

She let a wry smile play on her face at that. A few months ago, neither of them would have considered being in the same room, let alone working together or standing guard for one another. How times had changed.

"Can you tell where he's gone yet?"

The mage frowned. "He stopped for a few minutes but he's on the move again. I think he suspects we're following him. He's being evasive."

Ylani clenched her fists until her fingernails dug into her palms. She'd seen the fear in Shalyn's face. She'd seen what had been planned for Shalyn and the other children Nycol had participated in kidnapping. She couldn't bear the thought of him escaping yet again. "How do we make sure he doesn't get away?"

"Well, for starters, you can keep quiet and let me concentrate." Draeson cracked his eyelids and gave her a hard look through narrowed eyes.

Ylani forced her fingers to uncurl, raised her hands palms outward and backed away. "Fine, fine. I'll leave you to it."

He closed his eyes again and ignored her.

A clock she hadn't even noticed before ticked loudly in the silence.

Standing guard over a meditating mage was a peaceful reprieve from the party - and not just because she'd spent the entire time with the warning bell of the Instinct in her mind, waiting for Nycol to appear. If nothing else, her absence from the festivities gave her an excuse to avoid the expectation of making small talk with the Nilarian envoy. Of all the people from home Ylani had hoped to see, Alyra Jalin had not been on her list. She didn't need the Instinct to tell her that a conversation alone with the woman would not be a good idea.

The door opened and Ylani jumped. Had her thoughts summoned Alyra herself? But it was not the Nilarian woman who stepped into the room. It was Reanna Kesh, Brannon's older sister.

"Hi." Ylani gestured around the mostly empty room. "Brannon's not here."

Reanna nodded and moved closer, the door behind her not quite closed. "I know.

"Then what...?"

"I wanted to talk to you alone." Reanna glanced at the meditating Draeson and then seemed to decide his attention was fixed enough elsewhere. "I have a favor to ask you."

Ylani raised an eyebrow. "A favor? Have we become so close so quickly?"

"Okay, I deserved that." Reanna nodded. "I have a reputation for blurting things out when I shouldn't sometimes. But I'm a big enough person to admit when I was rude and I'm sorry. What I said earlier was not about you. It related to an issue between my brother and our parents."

Ylani shrugged and turned away. "Then it's best I don't get involved."

"Wait." Reanna's hand grasped Ylani's arm, her fingers rough for a noble. "Let me explain. When we were younger, Brannon fell in love with this girl-"

"Stop, Reanna." Ylani pulled her arm out of the woman's grip. The spy in her was intrigued by the potential for illicit knowledge but the part of her that had come to care about Brannon knew letting his sister spill his secrets would only hurt him - and their family relationship - further. She'd seen enough families damaged. "It's not your story to tell. When Sir Brannon wants me to hear about his past relationships, *he* will tell me. Not you."

The other woman gave a rueful grimace. "There I go again. The blurting. You're right, of course. I just..." She sighed. "I've made a bad second impression as well as a bad first one, haven't I?"

Ylani took pity. "What was the favor?"

Reanna shifted uncomfortably. "My parents have been chosen as ambassadors to your country. I...would rather they weren't. I assume you have some influence with your government. Perhaps you could suggest that they're not appropriate for the role for some reason. Who knows the pitfalls of an ambassadorial position better than you? Nobody here would need to know what happened."

"You want me to secretly sabotage your

parents' careers?" Ylani frowned. There were family dynamics here she didn't understand. "Why would you do that?" Brannon had given the impression Reanna and his parents got along well. It was strange to think the child they were closest to was the one throwing obstacles in the Keshs' way.

"I'm sure it seems bad." Reanna's cheeks reddened. "But I have my reasons. My parents and Brannon don't need to know what happened. It can just be an announcement from your government that they're not ready for an ambassador or they'd prefer someone else."

Ylani shook her head. "I'm sorry, that's not something I can do. And even if I could, I don't think I would. Brannon is my friend. I don't want to keep that kind of secret from him and it's not my place to interfere with his family."

"But surely you understand how dangerous-"

"How dangerous my home is?" Ylani's voice was hard even in her own ears. Anger filled her like an overflowing goblet. This woman had insulted Ylani, asked her to betray her friend, and now insulted her homeland. If anyone knew the dangers of being in a hostile country, it was Ylani but she had done it. She had faced her enemies and made friends among them. How dare this woman - in whose blood should flow the same courage and fire that Brannon had shown against supernatural foes no one could have expected to survive - suggest that her family were too feeble to do the same? Ylani drew herself up ready to give Reanna a piece of her mind but a burst of shouting from the other room pulled her attention away from the conversation. Ylani ran to the door and looked into the ballroom.

A small group of remaining guests and servers clustered around the giant portrait on silk that had been Nilar's gift to the king. They spoke in urgent, high pitched voices and pointed.

Prince Claydan hugged himself as he spoke. "Did anyone see what happened? I thought I saw...but it can't have just ripped on its own!"

Heads shook. No one had seen.

Ylani stared at the portrait. The fabric sagged oddly in the middle. Ylani gasped. The silk wasn't just sagging, it had been slashed. Someone had cut the King's throat in his portrait.

She turned away. The Nilarians were going to see the destruction of their gift as a slight against them. The Kalans were going to see it as a threat. This single act of vandalism had the potential to set back relations between the two countries for months, if not years.

She caught Reanna's eye. "You want to talk about dangerous places?" She pointed back at the portrait. "Someone just issued a threat to your king in his own castle. I've got more important things to worry about than your family dramas."

CHAPTER FOURTEEN

Despite the lateness of the evening, neighbors crowded outside the stonemason's house, many in dressing gowns and sleepwear. Brannon and Ula pushed their way through the crowd, receiving odd looks for their party attire and Ula's purple skin, dreadlocks, and swirling runic tattoos. Whispers about who they were and what their presence meant rippled through the gathering like an alarm call in a flock of roosting birds. It was a working middle class part of town where a lot of moderately successful tradesmen, artisans, and merchants lived and worked from the same buildings. A nice neighborhood with respectable people. They didn't expect to see this sort of thing.

The city guard was doing a good job of protecting the scene and they kept the onlookers back from the house but ushered the investigators through with only a curious glance. The doors were huge, multi-paneled things that could be folded back to open almost the entire front wall of the lower level. Two young men stood by that door. One was in guard uniform, the other in civilian clothes, hugging a wooden box. Both had a pale, almost green tinge to their faces and haunted eyes.

"This is Ren," the guard said. "He found the victims. They're his parents."

"I'm sorry for your loss, Ren." Brannon touched the man on the shoulder.

Ren nodded silently.

"Did you move anything inside?"

Both men shook their heads. "There was no chance of saving them," the guard said, his voice quiet.

"I'm sure you did all you could." Brannon glanced at the door panels. Even a young city guard would have seen some things. For him to be this shaken up, what was inside the house must have been disturbing. Brannon wasn't looking forward to it. "Ren, I know this has been hard but we'll have some questions for you once we've had a chance to see for ourselves. If you can think of anything we need to know or people who might have wished your parents harm, be sure to let me know." He glanced at the box in the man's arms. "Is the box from inside?"

Ren blinked as if he'd forgotten what he was carrying. "Oh, yes. It's the cash box. I must have picked it up out of habit. My father never liked it to be left alone."

"Okay. Have a think about whether you touched anything else. It might help us understand what happened. I'll be back out to talk to you soon." He nodded to the guard and the young man cracked open one of the door panels to let them through.

Inside was a large stonemason's workroom. There was a pool of vomit next to the door. Brannon wondered if it was from the young guardsman who had let them in. He certainly seemed in no hurry to return to the scene.

Massive chunks of marble and granite were placed throughout the space, some covered in sheets of fabric, others exposed and in various states of being cut or carved. Light filled the room from lamps burning at regular intervals on the walls and from hanging sconces on the ceiling - they were either still burning from before the inhabitants were killed or lit by Ren and the city guard when they arrived. Knowing which might help them figure out a time of death.

Brannon exchanged a glance with Ula and the two of them moved into the room. The metallic stench of blood and viscera was unavoidable and reached them before they saw the bodies. What was left of the bodies.

The floor was stained red. At first glance, it looked like a carpet but it was slick and shiny and the color was inconsistent. Blood spread out in a crimson lake with pieces of flesh, bone, and internal organs floating like broken boats after a storm.

"Ahpra's Tears," Brannon muttered. He lifted one of the lanterns off the hook by the door and carried it with him for a closer look, stepping carefully in the blood.

The bodies were crushed beyond recognition, more skin sacks in a roughly human shape than people. Whatever had killed them had smashed bone and pulverized organs alike. The skin was split along the sides like a squashed tomato, allowing the broken organs to leak out in a chunky paste.

Brannon had seen injuries like this before. During the war, some of the castles had run out of oil and arrows to defend their walls and had taken to dropping masonry or boulders onto enemy soldiers who got too close. Draeson had even used magic to lob a few huge rocks into enemy formations from time to time. Those unfortunate enough to have been directly underneath such an attack were crushed, much like Donal and Lira Gifson. The difference here, is that someone had already lifted the stone. That meant either a superhuman amount of strength or an intricate system of levers and pulleys. He looked around, seeking the stone and the device used to shift it.

He almost bumped into Ula as he stepped back from the bodies.

The Djin woman shook her head, setting the beads in her hair clacking like windchimes. "This be magic?" she asked. "But why? There must be easier ways to kill."

Brannon took a deep breath to sigh and instantly regretted it. The smell of death was not easy to expel. "It's possible to do without magic," he said. "But not easy. Not here." He looked up. The ceiling was high to make room for large sculptures but even so, there was little room to hoist a heavy enough stone to do this kind of damage to a person. It was possible an obelisk type rock had toppled onto the couple but then he would have expected the splatter pattern to be different. This looked like vertical drop damage to him. "See if you can spot the murder weapon. I'd guess it's a chunk of stone like the ones being carved into statues. It'll have blood on it."

Ula nodded and moved through the workshop, inspecting each item large enough to do the damage.

Brannon circled the bodies, hoping a different perspective might reveal more clues.

A masculine hand had escaped the crushing weight and was oddly intact at the end of an arm like an empty wineskin. Brannon leaned in with his lantern. A metallic glint shone back from between the dead man's fingers. He pried them open and revealed a medal of honor. This victim had been a soldier too. But then, the war had made soldiers of everyone. It was hardly a significant pattern.

"But why is he holding it?" Brannon frowned and looked closer. The bodies were not just side by side. They were overlapped. The woman - he could identify her more from her clothing than what was left of her features - and then the man's shoulder and arm over hers. Could they have been crushed at separate times? Lira first, then Donal as he knelt to check on his wife's corpse?

Again, Brannon glanced overhead, an itch in his mind almost expecting to see the phantom block suspended above him. It would take a lot of time and effort to re-rig the stone to fall again. Could the two have died at different times? Surely neighbors would have heard the thuds as the stone hit the ground. But then, living next to stonemasons, perhaps they were used to it.

Bracing himself, Brannon placed a hand on what he perceived to be the back of each corpse, judging by their blood-soaked clothing. His fingers slipped into the sticky blood and unnaturally soft flesh and broken spines beneath. Even for a physician who was used to blood and gore, this was disturbing. Even for someone called Bloodhawk. But the bodies felt the same temperature. If they'd died a significant time apart, he'd expect one to be colder than the other. So whatever had lifted the stone had been quick. Or perhaps there were two stones.

"There's none," Ula reported. "No stones have blood on them."

"Of course." Brannon sighed. Why would it be that simple? "So the murderer just took a rock large enough to crush two people with him. In his pocket, perhaps."

Ula grinned. "Sound like the wizard."

"I wish he was here. He might have some answers."

"Why not ask them?" Ula pointed to the dead bodies on the floor. "I can make Risen. Not get much information from before they died but perhaps they know about enemies."

Of course. He was still getting used to Ula's ability to access the memories of the dead through her Risen. "Can you do it though? Safely, I mean. They're pretty damaged and I wouldn't want a repeat of last time."

Ula huffed at him. "That body was burned and gone. These are not. It be no trouble. Just need strong kaluki to mend them."

Brannon studied her expression. Ula was one of the strongest, most capable women he knew, but he couldn't help feeling a sense of protectiveness for her. She'd never fully explained the details of why she'd left the Djinan Isles, but it was clear she'd gotten into trouble because of what she'd done here in Kalanon, for Brannon. It was the pact he, Ula, and Ylani had made with the Earth spirits that had changed her - changed all of them - and led to consequences with the Priory of Gradinath that he didn't fully understand. But if she said she could reanimate these smashed and broken bodies, he had to believe her.

"What do you need?"

Ula swung the leather satchel she carried off her shoulder. "Not to be interrupted."

"Deal."

As Ula laid out the bowl, candles, and special dirt for her ritual, Brannon wandered around the site, searching for anything that might give a more mundane explanation for what had crushed the couple than magic. There were certainly a couple of blocks of raw stone that would have been capable of the job, but they seemed undisturbed, their bases surrounded by dust and small chips that built up in the workroom while carving and cutting was done. It seemed sweeping wasn't high on Gifson priorities.

Brannon pulled a stool over to one of the larger blocks and used it to climb on top of the stone and look more closely at the high ceiling. There was a pulley system but it was positioned too far away from the bodies to have been useful. The building structure had been reinforced to support it and it was hard to think the ceiling would have supported the weight of one of these stones without such reinforcement. He sat atop the large cube of rock and sighed. No, if they'd been crushed by rock, magic had to have been used to lift it and then, presumably, remove it entirely since none of the stone here showed signs of being the murder weapon. No matter how carefully someone cleaned, there would have been traces in the stone pores and there were none.

So either the victims had been crushed by a stone lifted and removed by magic or simply crushed by magic itself. Both options suggested the elusive Magus Nycol but he'd been at the masquerade this evening. Had he had time to commit double homicide before crashing the party and attempting a kidnapping?

Brannon sighed. With the bodies so crushed, a level of rigor mortis was impossible to ascertain. If no neighbors had heard the thud of a dropped rock then it would be very difficult to learn the time of death. It could have been anywhere from when Donal and Lira were last seen by customers to when they were discovered by their son.

He looked down over the floor where the dead couple lay.

Candles and a small bowl of dirt surrounded the bodies at compass points. Ula let a strand of drool ooze from her lips and into one of the bowls and then sat back on her heels. She changed in her native tongue, a guttural sound that spoke of passion and nature and darkness, and then leaned forward and to breathe across the bloody remains of Donal and Lira Gifson.

Brannon felt the tug of the unseen wind as it blew past him from the realm of the kaluki, through Ula, and into the corpses she'd prepared for it.

"*Kruul da nook*," Ula intoned, her voice harsh and commanding.

What was left of Donal twitched. The sticky and drying blood pooled on the floor became more liquid and flowed back toward the bodies.

Brannon gritted his teeth. He'd not thought to ask how much making the victims Risen would disturb the scene. It would be near impossible to gather evidence from the bodies now. An autopsy would be irreversibly compromised by the animation process. It was too late to worry about it now. He had to hope that the information in the dead couple's memories would be more valuable than anything left to glean from their blood patterns or physical injuries.

Donal and Lira's bodies puffed up, inflating like a balloon. The broken chunks of bone and internal organs pulled back in through the split skin and writhed beneath the surface like maggots in the sun as the kaluki Ula's power had forced into this world struggled to reassemble their new bodies into a workable order.

A shudder ran through them as they drew a long gasping breath. An answering shudder ran through Brannon. No matter how many times he'd seen Ula do it, the making of a Risen still made his skin crawl.

"*Yool gah doh.*" The remaining wounds healed over and the Risen sat up.

"Speak the language of this land," Ula commanded. "And answer the questions put to you about the people whose bodies you hold."

"We obey, Prioress."

Ula glanced up at Brannon's perch on the stone block. "Will you join us, Sir Master of Investigations?"

He hadn't realized she'd known he was up there. He chuckled. "I obey, Prioress."

He stood up, his head brushing close to the ceiling, and considered simply jumping to the floor. It was a big drop but, in theory, the kaluk or earth spirits had given him extra strength and recovery abilities in the presence of a Risen. In practice, however, it was an unpredictable gift and didn't often kick in until he had taken a beating. He didn't fancy adding a broken ankle to the complications of the evening.

He climbed down carefully and approached the Risen. "Did you see who killed you?"

Ula shook her head before the Risen could

answer. "They do not have memories of their death. Not enough time for them to settle in the mind. Only memories from before."

The Risen nodded at their mistress's words.

"This is true," the Risen that was Donal Gifson said. The dead face twisted into a smirk. "We do not know how these bodies died. Only that they did."

It was strange how well the creatures spoke Kalan compared to Ula's sometimes awkward turn of phrase but Brannon supposed they had the advantage of their host body's knowledge of the language. He'd seen Risen mimic the deceased's mannerisms well enough to fool those who knew them - at least for a short time. It was disconcerting and required power of a kind rarely seen in Kalanon. Risen acted in accordance with a Djin shaman's instructions or whatever amused the kaluki inside them. And kaluki were not kind.

"Well what do you know that could help us figure out how they died? Do they have enemies?"

"Why should we tell you?" the Risen that was Lira said.

"Because I command you to," Ula replied before Brannon could speak.

Lira sneered. "What if we resist? We have heard of your problems. Do you think, if you call them, the Priory will answer?"

Ula's eyes narrowed and the Risen stiffened and groaned in pain. "I have more than enough power to deal with you myself," she said. "I will not need the Priory."

"Stop!" The Risen reached out their hands in a pleading gesture. "We will obey."

"Good," said Ula.

Concern bled into Brannon's chest, making it momentarily hard to breath. He searched Ula's face for any sign of the Avatar entity but her eyes remained free of agate. This was all Ula, strong and in control.

She nodded for him to continue.

"Now that we're clear on who is in charge," he said. "What enemies to Donal and Lira have?"

"A less qualified stonemason who sees himself as competition and a disgruntled customer whose sculpture is late," Donal said. "But neither one seems likely to commit murder over it."

The Risen that was Lira stretched like a cat, her undead joints cracking like popping logs in a fire. "You ask what enemies the parents have," she said. "Better to ask about their son."

"What do you mean?"

"He's fallen in with bad company. This body didn't trust him."

Brannon leaned forward. "Who? What has he been doing?"

Lira shrugged. "She doesn't know. He is secretive. Parents are so often the last to know when their child is up to no good, don't you think?"

Donal tilted his head to the side and held out the medal of honor in his hand. "He wanted his son to have this but...he was waiting for him to prove himself worthy." The Risen's eyes narrowed and he turned in a slow circle, studying the room. "Where is the cash box? It was important somehow."

"It's outside with the guards and Ren." Brannon gestured to the door and his voice caught. "Ren!"

The young man stepped into the doorway, his face grey and eyes wide as he stared at his reanimated parents. Even at this distance, Brannon could see Ren's entire body trembled.

"Ren, wait. This isn't what it seems."

"You...you brought them back." Ren stumbled a step into the house then stopped. "How?"

"They be not your parents," Ula said quickly. "They be Risen."

Ren stared at her, then at Brannon, then at his parents. "What? What do you mean?"

"It's magic," Brannon told him gently. "It's best you don't see this. They'll go back to being dead when the interrogation is done. This isn't them and it won't last."

"There he is," the Risen that was Donal said. "Ren, my boy. Will you wear my medal now I'm gone?"

"I...I..." Ren stammered.

"He pawned that medal, you know," Lira scoffed. "And you didn't even notice."

"Nonsense," Donal said. "It's right here."

"Only because I paid to get it back. You never could see when the boy was misbehaving."

Ren's face crumpled.

Brannon felt for the young man. Bad enough that his parents corpses had been reanimated to play a macabre puppet show of themselves, but now they were arguing about him like the married couple they'd been in life and the last memory Ren would have of his parents would be this kaluki fueled discussion of their disappointment in him. "Stop it," he commanded. "You will answer my questions and leave the boy alone."

"Do as Sir Brannon says," Ula said, her magic giving power to the words.

The Risen straightened up and fell silent.

Brannon turned to the dead couple's son again. "You should leave, Ren. This isn't going to be pleasant for you."

Ren shook his head in a short, fast burst. "I'll stay. If these are the last moments I get to see them, I don't want to miss any."

Brannon took a long deep breath as he studied the young man's face. There was fear there, but also determination. Commitment. Chances were, he'd heard his parents' discussions before and knew they fought about him. Who was Brannon to deny a son a final few moments with his lost parents? Even if it wasn't truly his parents, it was the closest thing he'd ever have again. "Okay."

The Risen stood silent, watching. There was an unnatural stillness to them now that was such a contrast to the way they'd been a moment ago. Brannon wasn't sure which was more frightening - the inhumanness of their true kaluki selves or the ease with which they adopted the guise of the people whose bodies they wore. They were fearsome things, the Risen. Fearsome indeed.

He scratched at his scar. Fear could be the angle he needed. The Risen couldn't access memories close to their deaths and they didn't seem to recall any true enemies but a subconscious fear could tell him more than they thought they knew. Brannon's gut reaction - that instinctive fear response to cues the mind had yet to process - had saved him many times in the war.

"Tell me," he said. "What were you afraid of in life? If you lay awake worrying, what was it you thought about?"

"Money," said Lira quickly. "And Ren."

Donal trembled. "Uh...there was...in the war..." His mouth worked but he seemed to struggle to make words with it. "Stones. Big stones."

Ula frowned. "Speak clearly, Risen. Answer now." Her power pulsed through the room and Donal shuddered and screwed up his face but did not answer.

"What's wrong with him?" Brannon asked. "Do

Risen get fear-frozen?" He'd seen soldiers on the battlefield caught between the desire to fight and the need to run, unable to do either as the enemy cut them down.

Ula shook her head and peered closer at the Risen.

A deep rumble echoed around them, as if a runaway carriage were crashing through the room. The floor vibrated beneath Brannon's feet.

"What's going on?" Brannon searched the room for the source of the sound. It seemed to be coming from the Risen or from somewhere overhead. The rumble sounded again and this time the entire house shook. Stone chips around the carved stone blocks rattled and dust filled the air, both stirred up from the debris on the ground and shaken loose from the ceiling. Brannon swallowed. His hand moved uselessly to his sword hilt. "Ula? Is this you?"

Ula's face was strained. "There be another magic," she said. "It has attached to the kaluki."

Brannon's swept the room with his gaze again, searching for anything suspicious. "From where? Who?"

"I not know," she growled through clenched teeth. "I'm not a wizard!"

"Can you stop it?"

"I'm trying."

He watched as she murmured to herself, fists clenched. The Risen shuddered and flung their heads back, staring upward with their dead eyes. Cracks appeared in the ceiling overhead.

"Ahpra's Tears," Brannon swore. There was a limit to how much damage a building could take. "Do you need to go all...you know?" Brannon pointed to his eyes.

Ula shot him a narrow glare. "Avatar be not the solution for every problem," she said.

The cracks in the ceiling widened.

"That's it. We're getting out of here." Brannon reached for Ula to pull her back toward the door but she held out her hand to stop him.

The whites of Ula's eyes stood out in stark contrast to her purple skin. "Get back!"

A gust of wind hurled Brannon backward. He fell, sliding across the hard floor, and slammed into a partially carved stone block. The house shook again and a section of the ceiling collapsed, obliterating the center of the room in an avalanche of broken wood panels, dust, and debris.

"No!" Brannon yelled.

Ula and the Risen were gone.

CHAPTER FIFTEEN

Stone dust and crumbled plaster filled the air and forced its way into Brannon's lungs in chokingly dry clouds. His back ached from the impact of striking the stone block behind him and he coughed, eyes watering as he peered through the dust. Shapes moved in the clouds, some human, others loose debris still breaking free from the ceiling above. As he watched, a chair from the upstairs part of the house slid on what was now a sagging floor and tumbled through the hole and into this lower room. Brannon flinched as it struck the pile below. It was impossible to know how many more such items could fall onto Ula and her Risen. Or, for that matter, whether the entire building was now unstable enough to collapse on top of them all.

A figure appeared and reached out a hand. "Sir Brannon? Are you all right? What happened?"

A good question. "I'm fine." Brannon blinked

to clear his vision and squinted up at the guard. "You left your post."

The man frowned and waved at the collapsed ceiling. "I needed to see if you're okay."

Brannon nodded. His head was ringing. "Of course. But go back out. I need you to see if there's anyone suspicious around. Someone did this. Someone magical."

"How do I tell if they're magical?"

"I don't know. Just do it." Brannon coughed and scrambled forward through the fallen chunks of ceiling panels and wooden beams. "Ula!" he shouted, his voice hoarse and dry. "Ula! Where are you?"

He felt his way through the haze. Everything was hard edges and soft powder. None of the shapes beneath his fingers made sense. The section of the ceiling that had fallen in was more than enough to seriously injure or kill anyone caught beneath it. His own chest felt constricted by the crushing weight of the urgent fear driving him forward even as his lungs rebelled.

His foot touched something soft and he looked to see a hand poking out from beneath a chunk of ceiling. Blood oozed around it. Whoever it was had been completely crushed.

He looked closer. The service medal still sat in the palm of that hand, miraculously preserved in the midst of the damage. It was Donal.

Brannon tapped the fingers with his own to see if there was a response. He'd seen Risen recover from impossible injuries before but only Ula would know if the kaluki inside this one had enough power to rebuild a crushed body twice. The hand lay still. He picked up the medal and slipped it into his pocket. Donal's son should have it.

With that thought came the question: where was Ren? He looked around and saw the young man leaning against the wall, frozen, eyes wide. "Ren! Come and help me lift this!" If there was any chance of finding Ula alive, they had to move fast.

Ren turned his face to the wall. "I-I can't."

"Blood and Tears." Brannon swore even as he understood. Ren had already found his parents crushed to death once. There was a good chance removing the debris would bring him face to face with that horror again. This time, though, Ula's life was also at risk. There was no time to waste on arguing.

He grabbed the nearest broken piece of ceiling and lifted it off the pile. A few small stones shifted, rolling in a tiny avalanche across the floor. Brannon held his breath as he waited for the rubble to settle. The last thing he wanted to do was cause further injury to his friend.

A groan sounded from deep in the debris.

Hope sparked in Brannon. "Ula? Are you okay?"

There was only silence.

"Don't you Hooded die on me, Djin," Brannon

muttered. He grabbed the edge of a wooden beam and heaved. It shifted about a finger's length before the weight became too much for his arms. "Ren! Get your ass over here. We don't have time for your emotions right now. Get the other end of this!" He gripped it harder, the sharp edge of the wood driving into the pads of flesh on the underside of his fingers. He heaved, calling for the magical strength the Earth spirits had given him against Risen. His muscles screamed in protest and the spirits were silent. "Come on!"

Suddenly the beam lifted. Another man had taken hold of the other end. This man had a soldier's build. Squinting through the settling dust haze, Brannon could see he wore a small, simple hat. Together, they lifted the beam and hurled it aside.

The man paused to give a salute. He had a silk ribbon tied around his wrist like a bracelet. "Brillen Carleen, reporting for duty, Sir Brannon."

There was something familiar about him. "You're one of the people the Nilarians brought back."

Brillen pulled the hat off his head and nodded. "Yes sir. They released us at the masquerade. You were my nearest commanding officer so...I followed you here. I was waiting with the guards outside but then this happened." He gestured to the gaping hole in the ceiling. "The guards said I could help."

Brannon nodded. He was suspicious of anyone

who showed up at the time this spell had taken effect but the man's story checked out. He couldn't have been here and in Nilarian custody at the masquerade at the same time so he couldn't be responsible for the initial attack and, if he'd been in sight of the guards the whole time, it was unlikely he was the source of the second one either. Brannon swallowed. He'd become so suspicious lately. A returned prisoner of war was hardly going to be wielding the kind of magic that collapsed a house and there was no way Brannon could save Ula alone. "Okay. Help me clear this. But carefully. She's still alive." He only hoped that would prove to be true.

They moved smaller chunks of rock and plaster, careful not to shift the underlying layers too much for fear of crushing anyone even further. A large chunk of stone rolled away to reveal the crushed remains of the Risen that was Donal - his face and upper torso were nothing but pulp.

Brillen paused, staring at the mess. "I thought I was hard done by when the Nilarians took me...Ahpra's Tears, that's some perspective."

Brannon clenched his fist, feeling the fingernails cut into his palm. "Ula? I need you to make some noise so we know where you are."

Silence. Then there was a thud and a scattering of pebbles rattled down the pile.

"Ula?"

Thud. Thud.

Relief flooded through Brannon. He let the fingers in his hand relax. Ula was alive. Or at least, a small voice in his mind worried, something was alive. He froze as that thought took hold. What if Ula was dead and the thing that was alive was the remaining Risen? He had no idea how an untethered Risen would react with no Djin shaman available to return it to a properly dead state. Even with the extra strength the earth spirits sometimes gave him against Risen, there would be no way to fully contain one without Djin magic. Releasing this one from the rubble could mean releasing a monster on Alapra.

"It's coming from over here." Brillen pointed to a spot deeper in the rubble.

Brannon shoved his fears aside and stepped over the mess that was Donal. He couldn't risk Ula's life on a maybe. They'd dealt with monsters before and if they had to, they'd find a way to do it again. "Hold on, Ula. We've nearly got you."

He examined the pile. Broken stone, plaster and timber all interlocked like a child's puzzle game. Moving one was almost certain to shift the others. With only two of them to do the lifting, it would be impossible to brace the rest and keep the pile from collapsing further. The trick was to figure out which would be best - to remove the top most chunk of rock and hope that it reduced the pressure of weight enough that any further collapse would be minimal or to remove a piece on the side and hope what remained was supported enough for Ula to scramble out.

"Hurry," a muffled voice said from beneath the debris. "Can't hold much longer."

Brannon took a deep breath. He couldn't afford to wait. He tapped the largest rock chunk on the side. "This one."

Brillen nodded and took hold. Brannon did the same and they heaved. A few small pieces of rubble shook loose but the stone they were lifting hardly budged.

"We're not going to be able to lift it. Let's just try to tip it over."

"That'll land on..." Brillen nodded towards Donal's corpse.

"I know." Brannon avoided eye contact with the young man by the door, still seemingly paralyzed by shock. "I'm sorry, Ren. You'd best look away."

Brannon grasped the edge of the stone but just as he was about to signal to Brillen to push, something touched his ankle. Brannon jerked his foot back.

"Blood and Tears," Brillen swore. The Risen that was Donal clenched its hand, fingers brushing the spot where Brannon's ankle had been. "How is it doing that? He can't still be alive."

Brannon shook his head. "Not alive exactly, no. But useful." He bent down and grasped the Risen's hand and lifted it up to the stone they needed to move. Part of the crushed torso peeled off the ground with a wet suction sound.

The Risen gave a shudder, fingers convulsing.

"Help us pull this down and you help your mistress," Brannon told it, hoping the kaluki within the body could hear and understand despite the body's head being crushed. "You have to do that, right?"

The hand paused, then gripped the stone tighter.

"Pull," Brannon said. He grabbed the stone himself. "Pull!"

The broken slab of ceiling shifted beneath their combined strength, tilted, and then gravity snatched it from Brannon's hands and he jumped out of the way as it crashed to the floor. The pulped parts of Donal's body squelched under the impact, squirting blood across the floor. The Risen's hand lay still.

Brannon crouched over the fallen stone and peered into the gap it had opened up. Lira's undead face peered back at him. She was bent over, her back holding up the weight of the fallen rubble. Her teeth were gritted against the strain of it. Brannon's eyes widened with the sharp horror that he'd released an uncontrolled Risen - then a familiar purple face appeared, crouched under the Risen's chest. "Ula! You're alive. Thank Ahpra."

"I be the Hide and Seek champion, yes?" Ula's voice trembled, despite the humor in her words.

Relief burst from Brannon in a laugh. "Yes. Yes, you are." He reached out to help her scramble clear. She climbed to her feet on unsteady legs, shaky, a little bloodied, but alive.

The Risen shifted and the debris moved alarmingly. There was no way she could get free without the entire thing collapsing. Brannon and Ula moved away from the unstable pile.

"What about my mother?" Ren moved closer, his paralysis apparently wearing off. "She's still alive in there. Help her!"

Brannon touched the young man's shoulder and turned him away. "That's not her, Ren. Remember what I told you? Your mother is gone. That's just something else in her body."

"But..." The young man hugged the cash box to his chest. "I don't understand."

"I know. I'm sorry." He turned to the soldier. " Brillen, could you and Ren step back a moment. Ula and I have to make sure the magic is undone. It's best he doesn't look."

Brillen nodded and moved to Ren's side.

"What's the best way to do this?" Brannon asked Ula quietly.

Ula shrugged. "I return kaluki to its own realm. Will have to dig body out after if you want a funeral."

"Blood and Tears," said Brannon.

"Unless you have way to hold the ceiling up while Risen gets out. But I think she cannot hold it much longer so there be not enough time."

Brannon nodded. "Okay. Do it." He looked around the crumbled room. "I don't know where your things went. Do you need the candles and whatnot?"

Ula shook her head. "It is better with them but I can do without. This one will not fight me, I think." She reached her hand toward the struggling Risen and whispered in her own guttural language.

Lira's body shuddered and Brannon felt the inner tug and mystical wind he'd come to associate with Ula's magic. The Risen sighed and went limp. The entity animating it vanished and the empty body fell, flesh liquified as the damage the kaluki had repaired returned with a vengeance. Lira splattered against the floor, followed by the rubble she'd been holding away from Ula. The stone, beams and plaster crushed what remained of her corpse into paste.

Brannon turned away. His and Ula's actions had taken what remained of that poor woman's dignity, even in death. Now they'd taken what remained of her body as well. His gaze caught on her son. The young man had seen his mother's crushed and lifeless body twice now and his face was grey.

The cash box slipped from Ren's fingers and smashed open on the floor. Colorful stones sprayed out from it like a rainbow of blood.

Ren turned and ran for the door.

CHAPTER SIXTEEN

Brannon gathered up the stones and tipped them back into the cash box. There were no coins. No cash of any kind. He rolled the stones around in the box like dice. They glinted in the lamp light, sparkling on sharp edges, softly glowing in the smoother planes. Brannon frowned and looked around the room. There was no sign of gemstones in any of the carving or cutting work in the shop. What would have convinced this family to branch out into a new form of stonework at this stage of their career? And to the point that all their cash was spent on rough stones?

He looked up as one of the guards came in.

"Ren?"

The guard shook his head. "I'm sorry, Sir Brannon. By the time we realized you wanted us to keep him in the area, he was already out of sight. I've asked the men to keep looking."

"Blood and Tears. We shouldn't have let him stay in here." Brannon sighed. "It's fine. He probably hasn't got anywhere to go. He's just upset about his parents." Seeing them die twice would be enough to send anyone running. Brannon slipped the war medal the dead man had been holding into the cash box with the stones and held it out to the guard. "Leave enough people here to keep the building secure and if he returns, have them bring him to me. I want to talk to him some more. Meanwhile, take this to Alissa the jeweler. Ask her to assess the value of the contents and I'll be by for a report tomorrow afternoon."

"Yes sir."

"And get a receipt."

"Of course, sir." The guard saluted and left.

Brannon turned and surveyed the room. As crime scenes went, this one was messier than most. The victims crushed twice, the ceiling collapsed - the chance of collecting any uncompromised evidence was slim. Not to mention he'd had the guards and a newly returned prisoner of war traipsing through the area.

He turned to his unexpected assistant, a question nagging in his memory. "We've met before, haven't we, Brillen? Before today, I mean."

"Yes, Sir Bloodhawk. I've had that honor."

Brannon hid a wince. So many soldiers still considered Bloodhawk to be an honorable title. They respected him - Ahpra's Tears, they'd hero worshipped him often enough - and didn't understand how he felt about the things he'd done to keep Kalanon safe. They meant the name as a compliment but he felt it as a guilty barb. "Did we serve together?"

"Not exactly. I was in the prince's guard detail when he...when we...were overrun and captured." Brillen stared at his feet. Brannon could see the memories playing behind the man's eyes. "We tried..."

Brannon reached out and squeezed the man's shoulder. "It was war," he said. "Things happened."

Brillen looked up, relief on his face. "Yeah," he said. "Yeah, they did."

"You were taken by different people though?" Ula spoke up. "You be with the Nilarians but the prince be with the Children of Starlight."

Brillen nodded. "We were separated. I had no idea what happened to the prince until recently. I searched for him. Any chance I got in Nilar, I tried to find him but nobody could tell me what had happened to him. I didn't know if he'd gotten away or been killed..." The muscles in Brillen's throat clenched as he swallowed his emotion. "I delayed trying to escape because I knew, if he was captured, I had to take him with me. I've been a slave for so long."

"So has he," Brannon said quietly. "Just not of the Nilarians."

Brillen sniffed and nodded. "I was searching in the wrong country. And my prince suffered because of it."

"You did what you could," said Brannon.

The soldier nodded. "I suppose. I just..." He looked up and his expression was lost. "What do I do now?"

Brannon had seen that hopelessness in many soldiers in the days after the war. With the purpose that had driven them gone, they were lost. They'd all had to find a new way of being in a world of peace. Some never found their way. For Brillen and the other slaves, the war had only truly ended with their return to home and freedom, much as it had for Claydan with his liberation from the Assassin House. For Claydan, been having someone who understood what he was experiencing seemed to be helping him reintegrate into Kalan society. Perhaps Brillen needed the same.

"Come with me," Brannon said. "I have an idea."

The area around the collapsed house was crowded with onlookers but beyond those gathered, the streets were nearly deserted. The trip to the Third Alapran Monastery was quiet and swift. Brannon let the way, lost in his thoughts about the events of the evening. Ula and Brillen followed, both equally silent. Brannon supposed that Ula read his mood and respected it and Brillen...well, Brillen had adopted Brannon as his senior officer and wouldn't question orders now.

The monastery buildings were attached to the large stone cathedral where most of Alapra came to worship. The doors to the cathedral were always open, signaling the nurturing embrace of Ahpra herself. The way into the monastery was through the foyer and to the side of the huge double doors into the cathedral's worship space. The monks mostly lived on the upper levels but Brannon knew the man he sought would almost certainly be in his laboratory in the lower levels of the stone complex. He led the way through the corridors and down the stairs, thinking how like a labyrinth this place must seem to Brillen. The man had likely never been beyond the public areas of the cathedral and even that was years ago. Much of the city had changed during the war and the years afterward. It was likely all of Alapra would feel like an unfamiliar rabbit warren after so long away.

The door to the lab was ajar when they arrived. Brannon knocked and pushed it open.

Brother Taran was bent over a mortar and pestle, grinding the contents with a determined concentration of a hunting dog digging for its prey. He wore his usual cowled tunic over trousers with the hood pushed back and red leather gloves.

Brannon paused halfway across the room and cleared his throat.

Taran looked up and his eyes widened. "Brannon! Ula! And...someone. Um...Welcome. What brings you to visit in the middle of the night?"

"There's been another murder," Brannon told him. "Possibly even stranger than the last one."

Taran blinked. "Stranger than spontaneous combustion?"

"Yeah." Brannon said wryly. "Spontaneous crushing." He pulled the blood-soaked cloth he'd used to collect a sample from the dead couple out of his pocket. "I brought you another sample for testing. I don't suppose you found anything of interest in the samples from the General?"

Taran shook his head. "Nothing so far, I'm sorry. Certainly no accelerants or...crushing agents? I'm not sure how I test for chemicals that crush people."

Brannon chuckled. "Fair point. I doubt there's a compound that would do that - not without magical enhancement anyway. But perhaps they were drugged to make them hold still while it happened? Anything you can find will help us."

"That I can do," the priest said. "But there's no guarantee I'll find anything."

"I understand that." Brannon took a deep breath. "I have other missions for you as well."

"Um..." Taran set the pestle down on the bench.

"The tests do take a bit of time," he said. "What else do you have in mind?"

Brannon ushered Brillen forward. "This is Brillen, one of the people the Nilarians returned to us this evening. I thought you might take him to meet Prince Claydan when you have one of your sessions next. The two of them might find it helpful to share their experiences."

Brillen stepped forward. "Pleased to meet you, Brother Taran." He reached out shake the priest's hand.

Taran backed away, keeping his hands out of reach. "Don't touch me."

"What's wrong? Brillen frowned, confused. "What did I do?"

Even Brannon, familiar with Taran's odd ways though he was, was shocked. Then he saw the yellow powder dusting the fingers of Taran's gloves. "What are you mixing, Taran? Is it safe?"

The priest nodded in short staccato bursts. "Oh yes. Perfectly safe," he said. "Unless you touch it. Then it absorbs into your skin and causes disorientation and night terrors until you throw up and possibly die. Usually from choking on your own vomit though, not from the sutcha powder itself. Well, unless you eat shellfish while it's in your system. Or drink milk."

Brillen's one eye was round as a moon in his face. "It *what*?"

Brannon took his elbow and gently guided him back from Taran's workbench. "Brother Taran has a certain expertise in unusual chemical compounds."

"Poisons, mostly." Taran seemed remarkably cheerful about it. "But sutcha powder is also a useful catalyst when testing for gruncha venom."

"Gruncha? What's a grun...?"

"Don't ask," Brannon said. "We find it best to follow any precautions he recommends and don't take any of it personally."

"I-I won't," Brillen spluttered, shaking his head. "I'd certainly prefer to avoid death by shellfish milk or whatever. We can shake hands another time."

Taran smiled. "Come back tomorrow though and I'll take you to see the prince."

"Sure." Brillen glanced at Brannon, then at the door, seemingly uncertain of where to go.

Brannon wasn't sure what arrangements had been made for the returned slaves. Certainly Brillen would have missed out on any accommodations the others had been provided by following Brannon to the crime scene instead of staying with the group. He didn't want to see another returned soldier go homeless on the streets. "Wait outside," he told the man. "I'll make sure you're given a bed at the barracks. After all, you're technically still a soldier. You might even have some back-pay waiting."

Brillen smiled and gave a salute. "Yes sir."

Ula followed him to the door. "I keep you

company," she said. "I like Kalans who save my life more than poisons and spiders." She gestured to the corner of the room where a glass tank held several large arachnids.

When they were gone, Brannon stood and watched as Taran placed a glass bell jar over the mortar and pestle and peeled off the red leather gloves, placing them carefully in a bucket of some kind of neutralizing solution.

"There's more, isn't there?" Taran said as the solution bubbled and ate the toxic powder from the gloves. "What didn't you want to say in front of our new friend?"

"Old friend, apparently," Brannon said. "But yes. I want you to dig into what's happening at Magda's orphanage. In particular, Bishop Narayan's involvement."

Taran frowned. "The bishop doesn't like me," he said.

"Well, he may not like any of us if we find he's up to no good," Brannon said. It was hardly a surprise that a stuffy bishop found Taran's oddities unpalatable. Charming people was not the young priest's strong suit. "Just...keep an eye on him and maybe ask around if anyone has seen anything strange. Other than you." He gave a wink and a grin so Taran would know he was teasing.

The priest grinned back. "Many of the bishop's friends do seem to think I'm odd. But then..." He held up his arms so the sleeves of his priest's tunic fell back and revealed the daggers in hidden sheaths on his forearms. "They don't know the half of it. I'll let you know what I find out."

At that moment there was a knock and, as Taran let his sleeves fall back into place, the door opened to reveal Ula and, surprisingly, Ylani. It was the ambassador who spoke. "Magus Draeson says his tracking spell shows Nycol has stopped. If we move now, we can catch him."

CHAPTER SEVENTEEN

The first rays of dawn peeked over the horizon like a warning beacon as Brannon, Draeson, Ula, and Ylani approached what Draeson assured them was the final destination of his tracking spell. They'd trekked through most of the city as Draeson followed the path his magical moth had taken as it trailed the rogue mage. Nycol had clearly taken steps to ensure he wasn't followed. The path had doubled back on itself and gone in circles several times - even taking a short detour through the sewers at one point - but Draeson's faithful little moth spell could not be shaken. It took them to the Blue Rose, then to a warehouse full of unspun wool, then to a boarded up empty townhouse, but their quarry had moved on from each potential lair. Now they'd reached the city limits along the riverbank, beyond the docks, where housing and warehouses had spilled out of the city proper and went without some of the protections of a true Alapran residence. The few people lurking in the shadows this far along the canal scattered as their group approached, preferring to remain unseen. They made their way along the edge of the water until the smells of the city faded - even the stench of fish guts dumped by boats - and the early morning air became fresh and crisp.

"Are you sure this is the place?" Brannon asked. There were no buildings ahead. Nothing to suggest a shelter or hiding place where Nycol might be holed up.

Draeson nodded. "He's close."

Brannon turned and spoke to the captain of the group of twenty archers from the city guard who had come with them. Archers who had orders to shoot Nycol if Brannon's party failed to contain him. "Wait here," he said. "If you see us go down or it looks like he's getting away, don't hesitate."

"Yes, Sir Brannon."

They could only hope a lucky arrow would get through. Brannon doubted the mage would be taken down by such mundane means but they needed a back-up plan. He looked over his group and his eyes settled on Ylani. She still wore the golden dress from the masquerade but had thrown a heavy woolen cloak over it to counter the night's chill.

Ylani was an incredibly capable woman but this was likely to be a battle of magic. It was a kind of battle Brannon felt poorly equipped to face.

"I really think you should consider returning to your apartment, Ambassador," Brannon said. "Or at least staying back with the archers. This is going to be far too dangerous for a foreign dignitary to be involved in. We know what he looks like now. You've done your part. More than your part."

Ylani was having none of it. "Nycol originally came here with my countrymen," she pointed out. "It will help international relations to have me present when you apprehend him. It shows that my government does not back his actions and are helping bring a criminal to justice." Her voice softened as she added, "Besides, after what he and my brother did, I need to see this out."

Brannon sighed. "I can understand that. Just...be careful."

"You be careful." She poked her tongue out at him. "I've been taking care of myself perfectly well for years without the legendary Bloodhawk telling me what to do."

He spread his hands helplessly. "True enough."

"So let's go."

Brannon caught Draeson and Ula exchange an amused glance, then the mage led the way forward. They traipsed through the grass until it gave way to hard rock worn by wind and water, then to the point the ground gave way to darkness and the soft sound of water far below.

"Where, exactly, are we going?" Brannon asked.

Draeson shrugged and pointed over the edge of the riverbank. "Down there."

"Really?" Brannon sighed. "Of course it is. Great."

"There be a path," Ula said. She waved the torch she was carrying over the bank and the firelight brought a narrow descending ledge into view.

"Is that a rail?" Ylani said, peering over.

Brannon looked. A rope was nailed into the edge of the cliff, running as far along the path as he could see in the torchlight. "Close enough. We should be able to make it but it'll be risky in the dark."

"He did it," said Draeson. "So we can too."

"Could you levitate us?" Brannon wiggled fingers in what he considered a magical manner. "You've done it to me before."

Draeson shook his head. "Not while I'm keeping a connection to the tracking spell. And I don't want to let go of it just yet."

Brannon nodded. That made sense. They couldn't be sure Nycol would stay put or if he had an exit strategy in place in this hiding spot. Or even where exactly he was. They needed Draeson's magical connection to the moth spell intact. That also meant Draeson, their strongest weapon, needed to be held in reserve. "I'll go first. The rest of you follow close and be ready for anything."

He took a moment to loosen his sword in his scabbard and stepped over the edge onto the narrow path. The stone was smooth and slippery but broken into uneven steps. In the dark it was hard to see where each one ended, forcing Brannon to make his way slowly, feeling the edge of each one with his foot before moving to the next. Further down the cliff, the contrast of cold air on one side and cold earth on the other became more and more noticeable. A single misstep would send him tumbling into nothing until he struck the freezing water of the canal below. He kept one hand on the rope as a gentle reassurance and hoped the spikes that attached it to the cliff face would hold should he or his friends have need of them.

"Watch your step," he whispered behind him. "It'd be easy to slip."

"Thanks. I wouldn't have thought of that." Draeson's face was shadowed by the torch Ula still carried behind him but he could feel, more than see, the mage's sarcastic expression.

A moment later, Brannon's own foot stepped out into empty air.

"Blood and Tears!" His fingers clenched on the rope and he jerked himself back from falling. "The path is gone."

"Gone?" Draeson's voice was colored with irritation. "It can't be gone. The moth spell definitely continued forward."

"The moth can fly," Brannon muttered. "Pass the torch forward. Maybe I can see a way to climb down."

Ula handed the torch to Draeson who passed it to Brannon. He held it out over the gap in the path. A spot of light reflected on the water far below like an artificial moon. The rope continued a little further, attached to the cliff but a wide section of the path had fallen away in a landslide. He squinted along the path's trajectory, hoping to find where it picked up again but saw nothing. This was no simple jump over a missing piece. He leaned over and could see tiny spots of shadow in the rock. "There might be footholds but they're small."

"Let me see." Ula squeezed past Draeson, pushing the mage flat against the cliff face as she reached around to grasp the safety rope again on the other side of him. "Excuse me, wizard."

"Mage," grumbled Draeson, his face pressed into the dirt.

Dawn brightened the morning but cast deep shadows across the missing path. Brannon moved as close to the wall as he could so the Djin woman could look past him and held the torch out to cast as much light as he could. "Do you see the footholds?"

Ula nodded but there was a frown on her face. "I see them but the Earth Spirits do not."

Brannon raised his eyebrows. "What does that mean?"

She gestured down at the foot holds. "I asked the Earth Spirits to make the holes bigger for us but they're confused by my request. They see no foot holds. No rock or earth here at all. It makes no sense."

Brannon stared at the cliff. "Nycol has hidden the cliff from the Earth spirits? How would he do that?"

"Why would he do that?" Ylani added. "How could he have known Ula would be here? Let alone that she would ask her *kaluk* to give us better footholds?"

"He couldn't have," Brannon murmured. So why cast a spell to hide a patch of earth from the Djin Earth spirits? It was odd. Pointless even. Nycol had never done anything pointless, as far as Brannon could tell. The point might have been mysterious and thus far unexplained, but there was definitely a point behind everything the mage did. A plan. Perhaps they were looking at it the wrong way. Brannon ran his fingers over the stone and packed dirt of the cliff face. Nycol had hidden an entire room from them once before. At the Blue Rose, he'd cast an illusion to hide the door and make it look like an unbroken wall. Brannon's fingers clenched, digging into the dirt. "Ahpra's Tears. He's not making stone look like nothing to the Earth Spirits. He's making nothing look like stone to us!"

"What?" Draeson frowned.

"I think there's a cave."

Realization flooded Draeson's features. "Oh! Clever!"

"Am I right?"

The mage's eyes narrowed and he pushed past Brannon and Ula to reach out over the gap and his fingers splayed over the stone, drifting just above its surface. "Hmmm." He lowered his hand and waved it at the fallen rocks and river below. "Oh yes. That's an illusion all right. Watch this." With that he stepped off the ledge.

"Stop!" Brannon lunged forward, reaching for Draeson to pull him back. His fingers brushed fabric but closed on air. The mage dropped below the level of the path and vanished.

Ylani, Ula, and Brannon all crowded as close to the edge as they dared. "Where did he go?"

"Down here," Draeson's voice called from below them. The mage himself was still invisible. "It's not far and there's a ledge. The illusion covers that too. Jump. It's safe."

"Really?" Brannon grumbled under his breath. "It better be."

Ylani touched him on the shoulder. "Are we

sure?"

Brannon sighed. "We never are." He stepped over the edge and dropped into the illusion. A chill and a bright blue light washed over him as he passed through the spell, then he was on the other side and the ground rushed to meet him. He bent his knees as he landed on the stone ledge and looked around. The river was only a few feet away. The wide stone ledge on which he and Draeson stood was worn smooth by erosion. Draeson stood next to an opening in the cliff face - the hidden cave that explained the Earth Spirits' response - the cave entrance rose well over Brannon's head and was wide enough to fit a horse and carriage. The stone changed color at eye level. "This is a high tide mark. We're closer to the water than it looked."

"Yeah," Draeson said, and waved his hand back the way they'd come. The blue light above hid the rest of their group and extended some distance along the cliff. "The illusion extends a lot further back. It's been faking height so people were scared to follow the path. He's hidden this cave entrance well."

"I wonder how long he's been set up here."

Draeson scowled. "Too long."

Ula landed with the grace of a predatory cat and Ylani's golden dress fluttered like a bird as she jumped through the illusion to join them. Sunlight filtered through the illusion as the day came alive but only penetrated a short distance into the cave. Brannon took the torch Ula had been carrying and waved it in the entrance. The cave floor dipped just inside, forming a pool of trapped water left behind by higher river levels and rain. The pool had what looked to be oddly shaped rocks scattered throughout - long, pale sticks and rounded rocks the size of a person's head. Brannon looked closer. They were exactly the size of a head. He reached down and rolled one over, exposing eye sockets and teeth. They were human skulls.

"Ahpra's Tears," Ylani swore.

"Is this the bad wizard's doing?" Ula asked. "His victims?"

Brannon shook his head and turned the skull back over to hide its face. A crab scuttled from behind it and burrowed into one of the piles of bones and debris. "No," he said. "These are some of the soldiers that were drowned at the end of the war. The river still has most of their bodies in her grasp. Sometimes she washes them up on the shores." It was as if the Tilal was making sure he could never forget what they'd done. What had needed to be done to protect Kalanon.

"My countrymen," Ylani whispered. "They never got a proper burial."

Brannon swallowed. How many of the soldiers he'd killed had been people Ylani had known? Maybe people she'd loved. Could she ever truly forgive him for that? "We'll have someone gather them up," he said. "Send them home to Nilar."

"Not much point now." Draeson snorted. "They're not going to know the difference. They're dead."

Brannon glared at him.

Ylani's chin lifted. "They might not know, Magus Draeson, but my people will. Those families whose loved ones never came home will know. They'll have hope that maybe it's their son or husband or daughter finally returned to Nilar and put to rest. It might not be the same as having a prisoner of war returned to you, but it's the best my people can get." Ylani's eyes glistened.

Brannon touched her arm. "We'll treat them with respect, I promise." he said. "For now, let's find this mage." They could only hope Nycol was still unaware of their arrival. He glanced at Draeson. "He's still inside?"

Draeson nodded.

Brannon drew his sword with his right hand and, with the torch in his left, skirted the tidal pool with its collection of captured bones, and led the way into the cave. The early dawn light was lost within just a few steps and the flickering light of the torch created shadow monsters on the walls. The air smelled of damp earth and algae. The ground underfoot was uneven and the walls of the cave closed in at some points to barely enough width for one person at a time before opening out again. Brannon searched for traces that another human had passed this way but found none. Clawed tracks on the ground suggested it had been a den for animals at some stage - he hoped whatever animal made those tracks had moved on.

Brannon moved slowly, his body alert and eyes searching movement in the deeper shadows that could suggest a human in the darkness - the true monster in the cave. Twice they came to branches in the cavern and each time Draeson pointed in the direction the moth spell indicated to go.

"Just how deep can this cave be?" Brannon muttered under his breath.

"A lot of the stone used to build the older parts of Alapra came from near here," Draeson said. "I think we're heading towards the old quarry."

Brannon's fingers clenched harder on the hilt of his sword. If the cave connected to a network of excavations it would provide Nycol with an array of potential escape routes. They couldn't afford to allow him to get away again. "We need to move faster."

He increased the speed of his steps, walking as silently as he could on the hard-packed earth and rock.

He'd barely moved more than a few steps when Ylani lunged forward and grabbed his arm. "Wait!" She pointed at the ground in front of him. Brannon lowered the torch and looked closer. Sharp, thin spikes rose out of the ground like a tiny forest of needles for the next two paces. Each one was tipped with a rusty substance - perhaps blood, perhaps some nefarious poison only Taran could identify.

Brannon bent down and tapped the nearest one. It was strong and metal. There was a good chance it would have pierced the sole of his shoe and into his foot before he'd finished his step. Even if the substance were not poison, an injury from a filthy weapon in a dank cave was a certain recipe for an infection that would be difficult to cure.

He swallowed as he stood. "I think you just saved my life, Ambassador."

Ylani smiled, the firelight lending warmth to her face and her gown. "It's our thing, Sir Brannon. I'm sure we'll save each other again." She winked. "We definitely need to keep an eye out for booby traps. No self-respecting spy - or mage, apparently - would have a secret lair without them."

Ula crowded past to look at the spikes. "I wonder how he gets past them," she said.

Draeson shrugged. "Magic, I should imagine. He doesn't have to hold a tracking spell so he's free to do other things."

Ula shook her head. "Not the mage. The animal." She pointed at the ground where, once again, there were claw marks as if from some great beast. They seemed to leap over the forest of spikes and begin again on the other side. "What is it?"

"I'm not sure." The creature had ventured a long way into the cave. Brannon wondered if it had made a den here or simply used it as a thoroughfare to and from the old quarry. "I'm not keen to find out."

"Well, the longer we stay in this cave the more likely that is," Draeson said. "The tracking spell is on the other side of these spikes. I can't levitate you and hold the spell at the same time but it's not that far. We can jump."

"Yeah." Brannon measured the distance with his eyes. "With a bit of a run up, that should be easy."

"Fine." Draeson waved his hands to indicate they should clear the way and backed up a few steps. "The longer we wait, the more chance he realizes we're coming and gets away."

Brannon hesitated. His gut was tense and the back of his neck prickled as if someone was aiming an arrow at it. Something didn't sit right. The trap was easy to get over once it was seen. Yet, despite missing it himself in the dark, the spikes weren't all that difficult to spot. It seemed strange for a mage who specialized in hiding things with illusions. Why hadn't Nycol hidden his spikes?

"Wait!" Brannon and Ylani spoke at the same time. Brannon looked at the Ambassador. "You're thinking what I'm thinking, then?"

She pointed to a spot just above eye level over the spikes. "That's the real trap."

The tiniest glint of reflected firelight showed a thin wire stretched across the tunnel. Anyone jumping across the spikes would garrot themselves on the wire as they did so.

"Ouch," said Ula, squinting at the near invisible wire.

"Clever though." Brannon leaned forward, stretched out and brought his sword down hard on the wire. The Nilarian blade sliced through the wire and it drifted like spider silk to hang limply on either side of the tunnel. "*Now* we can jump."

"Is long jump," Ula muttered. "Maybe too long."

Brannon took a few steps back, then ran up and leapt over the spikes. He held his sword up in front of him in case of any wires. He sailed safely over the danger and landed on the other side, bending his knees for the impact. He turned back with a smile. "Not too long. Come on over."

Ula slapped Draeson on the shoulder. "If I need a boost, you boost me, wizard?"

"Mage, not wizard," Draeson corrected. "And I need to hold onto the tracking spell. Maybe ask your elementals for help."

Ula's eyes narrowed. She pointed to the spikes. "Boost me!"

"All right, all right. If it looks like you won't make it, I'll boost you."

"You'll be fine, Ula," Ylani said. "Watch." She lifted the golden skirt of her gown, took a few steps to run and sailed over the spikes like a deer.

Ula grumbled and took a few more steps back for an even longer run up. She made the crossing without the need for a magical boost and grinned when she landed. "Come, Wizard. It's easy."

"What did I just say?" Draeson rolled his eyes and jumped as well. "We need to keep quiet now. He's close. Really close. If we're lucky, he'll be sleeping. The moth still hasn't moved."

Brannon nodded, keeping silent and internally crossing his fingers. If the mage was asleep and they caught him by surprise, this plan might go more smoothly than he could have imagined. They'd been up all night and, based on the movements of the moth spell, so had Nycol. Even a mage had to sleep sometime and he probably thought he was safe here. This was going to be their chance to finally bring him to justice - and hopefully survive doing it! Just a little further into the cave and this whole nightmare could be over.

He stepped out and his foot slipped into nothingness. The floor vanished and the world around him pitched like a boat in a storm. "Blood and Tears!" He felt the brush of fingers on his back as someone tried to grab him and pull him back but it was no good. He fell through a wash of chill blue light - an illusion hiding the hole in the floor.

He dropped his sword and torch and flailed for a hand hold. His knuckles scraped on the smooth stone walls of the shaft, helpless. His shoulder slammed into a rock outcrop and his body ricocheted off the wall, tumbling until he no longer knew which way he faced. He heard the metallic clang of his sword striking stone and then the ground slammed into him. Hard.

The air burst from his lungs and his head hit rock and an explosion of pain

He pushed himself up but his arm was numb and he slipped back to the ground. The torch lay a few feet away, sputtering light into his eyes and casting the rest of the room in pitch darkness. His ears filled with ringing. Voices panicked in the distance but he couldn't make out the words.

He crawled toward the torch and his bloodied knuckles finally clenched around the handle. The movement caused his brain to rattle alarmingly in his head. Up ahead was a stone plinth with a small cage on it. Something within the cage fluttered, trying to escape.

It was the moth spell.

Brannon swallowed his rising panic. Nycol had trapped the moth. He knew they were coming.

As the pain in his head darkened his vision, Brannon realized the roar he could hear wasn't a ringing in his ears after all. It was the low, menacing growl of an animal. There was a predator in the room with him.

The moth wasn't the only one in a trap.

CHAPTER EIGHTEEN

Taran hated being in this part of the monastery first thing in the morning. He pushed open the door to the dining hall and peered inside. So many people! The early morning crowd was already building as the monastery's inhabitants prepared for the day. First it was all the priests and acolytes. Soon the homeless and hungry would start to arrive, seeking the kindness of Ahpra to keep them fed. There weren't as many homeless as in the early days after the war but there were those who still hadn't found their feet after losing property, family, or limbs as a result of battle. Those on kitchen duty worked hard to prepare the food. In a few hours, this hall would be teaming with hungry mouths.

Crowds were something Taran avoided if possible. Today though, he had to face this one. A good portion of donated food would be headed to

Lady Magda's orphanage this morning. It was a chance to get inside and see what was going on there.

He spied Bishop Narayan at a table next to the kitchen and made his way over. A dark-haired boy of about thirteen helped Narayan gather containers of food and place them into two large, wheeled baskets.

"Brother Taran." The bishop's eyebrows raised. "We don't usually see you in here at this time of day."

The teen glanced briefly and then continued to pack food into the baskets.

Taran picked up a bowl of porridge. "I stay up late and get food when I need it so I eat at odd times." He shrugged. "Ah...I assume you're taking food to the orphans today? Perhaps I could help you," he said. "I...haven't been there since Marbella left."

"You have an understated way of putting things." The bishop looked him over and then gestured at the boy. "Thank you for your offer, but we have things under control so your help isn't necessary. You can stay with your little gadgets and chemicals, Brother Taran. I'm sure you have something to do for Sir Brannon if you don't have your own experiments to play with."

Taran bit his tongue and nodded. He certainly did have an assignment from Sir Brannon - and it was to find out the truth of Bishop Narayan's involvement at the orphanage. "Of course." Taran took his bowl and headed to the door as if to return to his lab. Once out of sight, he slipped into an alcove containing a statue of Ahpra. He laid the bowl at the goddess's feet and waited. A few moments later, he watched Bishop Narayan and the boy leave the dining hall and make their way toward the foyer of the cathedral and, beyond that, to the street. The wheeled baskets bounced down the stairs behind them.

Taran followed at a distance.

Early vendors were up and about on the streets, selling baked goods and hot drinks to passers-by as they hurried about their business. Taran allowed himself to be waylaid by several of the vendors but didn't tarry long enough to buy anything. He kept Narayan in sight, but only just. He knew where the bishop and his assistant were headed, after all, so there was no risk of losing them. Indeed, he was tempted to let them out of sight entirely but his training would not allow it. A mark could to unexpected things en route to an expected destination. If Bishop Narayan were to pick up goods or payment or engage in any other suspicious activity along the way to the orphanage, Taran wanted to be in a position to see it and report to Sir Brannon.

He continued to follow them through the city

and the pair made no unexpected stops. They briefly fended off a street urchin who made a grab for some of the food in their baskets before directing him toward the cathedral. Taran ducked behind a stand selling woven rugs as Narayan pointed in his direction. No doubt the urchin would make his way to the Alapran Third Monastery for something to eat and add to the morning crowds in the dining hall. Taran pulled at the hanging rugs to make a peephole and waited until the urchin passed and he could be certain Narayan was no longer looking this way before stepping back out into the street. By the time he did so, they'd turned a corner.

Taran hurried to the end of the street just in time to see his quarry turn another corner into a familiar alleyway. He let a family pass by between him and the entrance before making his way to the side of the corner building. Leaning against the cool stone of the wall, he crouched down as if adjusting the buckles on his boot and leaned slightly forward to allow himself to see into the alley. The smell of rubbish and wastewater washed up from the drain that ran the length of the street. In the distance, Bishop Narayan and his young companion climbed the stairs to the orphanage entrance. The faded sign above the door remained as a tribute to the woman who had started this home for children who'd been displaced by the war. It swung gently in the breeze as they disappeared inside.

Taran stood and strode past the alley. He turned at the second building over and climbed a trellis up the side of the house and onto the wooden tile roof. Careful footing and a few short jumps between buildings took him to a position level to the third floor of the orphanage.

He edged along until he was opposite an open window. The glass shone with morning light but he could see just enough through the opening to tell there was no one in the room beyond. Moments later, he was through the window and hidden inside the orphanage. Growing up in an Assassin House did have its advantages.

He'd entered through the window of a playroom. A dollhouse in the corner sat partially open, hinged along one side with a broken latch and a snapped off chimney. Board games were piled on shelves against the wall and a basket next to them contained wooden carved animals. He peered into the hallway, ducking back just in time to avoid the woman who watched over the orphanage at night as she headed for the stairs, a small bag over her shoulder. Taran waited a few more breaths to give her time to get out of sight before he stepped out of the room.

Children's voices and laughter wafted up from downstairs as they set out the food Bishop Narayan had brought and settled into the meal. Taran felt a twinge in his chest. Happy laughter had been in short supply in his own childhood. The Children of Starlight focused on teaching ways to sneak and kill. Happiness and play were not a priority. It wasn't until he'd spent time in Kalanon that he'd understood what a normal childhood should look like. These orphans might not have a traditional normal childhood, but Lady Magda had cared for them in a way Taran hadn't known at the House. It was one of the reasons he wanted to ensure they were still being taken care of properly now Magda was gone. Also one of the reasons he was so committed to ensuring Tomidan was safe from any lasting impact of his time with the Children of Starlight. Taran might not be able to protect these children from all suffering - they'd had enough already with the loss of their parents - but he could help make sure those who cared for them now did not add further abuse.

Mealtime was the perfect opportunity for snooping in the orphanage. It was one of the few times all of the building's inhabitants were gathered in one place, leaving the rest of the house open to investigation. Taran moved silently down the hall, testing each floorboard for creaks before putting his full weight on it. His infiltration training was steeped into his muscle memory. He would never have reached adulthood if he'd been unable to move through a house undetected. The first few doors opened to bedrooms containing bunk beds with bedcovers pulled up tight. One or two of them had threadbare stuffed animals resting on the pillows. That indicated younger children on this level than there'd been when Marbella had been an inhabitant, but that made sense. There was no need to worry about children encountering the madwoman now. A change in sleeping arrangements was nothing he thought Sir Brannon would consider noteworthy.

A glance down the hallway showed the gate that separated the room that had once housed the mad Child of Starlight from the rest of the orphanage was still in place. Brannon had indicated he had concerns about what might currently go on there. Taran had hoped to never see that particular room again but, in light of Sir Brannon's request, investigating it was a priority he couldn't ignore.

He crept toward the gate and through to the closed doorway. The wheel that controlled the length of chain was at its loosest setting. As he opened the door to Marbella's old room, a child's voice called out.

"You can let me out now. I don't have the whatever it is. And I'm hungry! Come on."

Taran blinked. There was a little girl chained with Marbella's old shackles, sitting on the bed. She was maybe eleven years old with brown hair. The length of chain had been left full so she could explore the room but she was unable to leave. Every move she made clanged the metal links. "What's going on here?" Taran stepped into the room. "Why are you chained up?"

The girl looked up, her eyes wide. "You don't know? Oh. You're one of Magus Draeson's friends, aren't you? Are you here to rescue us again?"

Taran shook his head confused. "Rescue you?"

Her face fell and she slumped on the bed, dejected. "Surely he won't let them keep doing this?"

Taran blinked. "Who? Draeson? I don't think he knows what's happening. Who are you?"

The girl lifted her head. "I'm Shalyn. My dad..." She closed her eyes and swallowed. "I live here now. But the Bishop keeps testing us."

Taran looked around the room, frowning. "Us? Are there others chained up?"

Shalyn shook her head. "Not right now. He tests a different one of us every night."

"Test? What kind of test?"

The girl lifted her wrists to display the shackles. "A stupid messed up kind, that's what."

Taran hurried forward, pulling lock picks from his pocket. "Don't worry. I'll get you out of these."

"You can do that?"

"Yeah. I had these shackles made. I know how they work."

Shalyn's eyes widened. "You had them made?"

Taran nodded. "For someone else. Not you."

Shalyn swallowed. "I guess that's okay then.

What happened to him?"

"Her," Taran corrected, slipping two metal picks into the lock on her right wrist. "She's dead now. She um...well, she killed a lot of people so..."

There was a click and the shackle fell from Shalyn's wrist. The girl rubbed at the chaffed skin beneath. "Thanks," she said and held out the other shackle.

Before Taran could slide the tools into the lock, he heard footsteps in the hallway. He slipped the picks into his pocket, held a finger to his lips and stepped back, pressing himself against the wall next to the door. A moment later the young man who had been with Bishop Narayan walked into the room. He passed Taran without a sideways glance and approached Shalyn where she sat on the bed.

His eyes widened when he saw she had a wrist free of chains. "You found it? You found the key! That's wonderful!" He bounced on the balls of his feet. "You're like me!"

Shalyn shook her head. "No, Jecksen. I'm not. I told you that the last time." She held up the still locked shackle. "See? Still locked in."

"But then...how?" He pointed to her free wrist.

Shalyn's eyes flickered to Taran's hiding place before she forced herself to look away. "It wasn't locked properly."

"Yes it was. I-" Jecksen spun around, his gaze unerringly fixing on Taran. "You!"

Taran's fingers twitched for his daggers but he held off. An assassin's instincts weren't needed yet. Not for a child. A bluff would be better. "Bishop Narayan is looking for you," he said. "He wants help tidying up after breakfast."

Jecksen shook his head. "No. That's a lie." He backed away slowly. "You're from the monastery. You have danger in your blood."

"Um...what?" Taran blinked.

The boy started shouting. "Help! Father! He's here!"

"Sssh!" Taran hissed. "There's no danger."

Jecksen kept shouting.

Taran pulled a dagger from one of the hidden sheaths in his sleeves. "Be quiet!"

"Very reassuring," Shalyn said.

Taran looked from one to the other and then to the door leading to the hallway. It wouldn't be long until Bishop Narayan or whoever else was working with him came running to see what all the shouting was about. When he'd still been a Child of Starlight, he would have simply killed them and made his escape but that life was behind him. He needed to find a safer solution. A way to report what was going on here to the appropriate authorities - whoever that might be.

"Go," Shalyn hissed at him. "Go. I'll tell them Jecksen made it up. People think he's crazy anyway."

"But..." Taran waved at the chains.

"They don't hurt us," she said. "They just do this to test us. They want us to prove we can find the key. I'm okay. Don't let them see you here."

He was torn. "Are...are you sure?"

She nodded frantically. "Go. Go."

There were steps on the staircase and a voice called out.

Taran turned and ran.

Chapter Nineteen

Brannon's head ached and the voices around him shredded what was left of the protective blanket of unconsciousness. He forced his eyes open and light stabbed into his brain. The torch he'd dropped burned low but a bright globe of light hung above him, illuminating his surroundings. The room was a wide-open chamber dug out by quarrying that extended beyond the reach of the light. The shaft he'd fallen down was still directly overhead. Draeson, Ula, and Ylani all crouched around him, murmuring in worried voices. They seemed oblivious to the threat.

"Monster," he croaked. "Wild animal."

The creature growled again, menace laced through the sound like alcohol in a fruit punch. Brannon turned, squinting against the pain in his head to seek out the danger. A wolf the size of a small pony glared back at him with eyes that reflected red in the light of Draeson's magical lantern. It had horns above its ears and thin lips pulled back from long fangs as it snarled.

"It's okay," Ylani touched his shoulder. "It's not real."

Brannon blinked, trying to clear his vision. "What?"

"It's a Hooded ward," Draeson said. "Noisy one too."

Brannon looked closer and, sure enough, the wolf was two dimensional, like a painting on the wall that could move. "So Nycol set it to warn him if anyone fell into his trap. Where is he?"

"I don't know." Draeson flicked his hand and a whip of light sliced across the room to crack the wolf ward in two. The creature fell silent, now just a broken static image with no life at all. "He figured out my moth spell and contained it. No one has ever done that."

Brannon pushed himself upright. "How did he know it was following him?"

Draeson's eyes narrowed. "If I knew that, I would've done something to prevent it, wouldn't I?"

Ylani peered at the little cage. The moth fluttered anxiously inside, battering at the sides with its wings. "Nycol wanted us to find it," she said quietly. "He's showing off that he knows you. He knows how you think." She reached out but stopped her hand short of touching the thing. "It's lined with mirrors. Why is it lined with mirrors?"

"What?" Draeson's voice was sharp. "Let me see."

Brannon climbed to his feet and followed the others to the little cage and its magical inhabitant. Sure enough, five small mirrors were placed around the circumference of the cage with only small gaps between them. The light from Draeson's floating globe reflected inside where it caught on the mirrors, bouncing back and forth until the inside of the cage shone like a condensed full moon. The fluttering moth was the only dark spot as it ricocheted between the reflective surfaces. The gaps between the mirrors were small but, Brannon was sure, still large enough for the moth to escape and yet the tiny spell-creature seemed unable to do so.

"Hooded Blood," Draeson swore.

"What is it?"

"It's a quartz mirror spell. Basically a training arena for magic."

Brannon looked from the tiny cage to Draeson and back. "Come again?"

The mage sighed and tapped the top of the cage. "It's a spell used by master mages when they're training a young one. The mirrors reflect magical power. Obviously, it's usually much bigger than this. An apprentice mage goes into a room lined with these special mirrors to practice and whatever they do is contained inside. That way, if things get out of hand, they can't hurt anyone but themselves." He folded his arms and set is jaw. "It's how I was planning to contain Nycol if we caught him."

"Blood and Tears." Brannon stared. "You think he knew?"

Draeson jerked his head toward the cage. "It's one Hooded coincidence if he didn't."

"Does he need to be nearby?" Ula asked. "To maintain the mirror? The magic?"

"No." Draeson shook his head and then turned to look around the room. "It requires the mage who created it to recharge it once a day. He could have cast it at any time from when I first sensed the moth had stopped here and then left. I can't say how much of a head start he's gotten while we wasted time in this cave."

"It depends when he noticed you were tracking him," Brannon said. "And whether he took the time to lay more traps. He obviously knew this place pretty well so I'd say he's stayed here a bit. I doubt he's still here though." He squinted at the tracking spell. "If we release the moth, can it still follow him?"

"No. The trail is too cold and I let go of the spell to get us down to you when you fell." Draeson swept the mirror cage from its pedestal and it smashed on the stone floor. The tiny moth inside flew up and dissipated like smoke. "He's beaten us again."

"For now," agreed Brannon. "But he can't be this lucky forever. Let's get out of here."

Draeson's magic levitated them back up the shaft Brannon had so ungracefully fallen down and over the spikes in the floor. They made their way back to the cave entrance and he levitated them again to get back up to the cliff-side path. When they reached the top of the cliff, the mage swayed a little and stumbled.

"Are you okay?" Brannon grasped Draeson's shoulder to steady him. "You seem tired."

"Well I have been up all night and pumping out magic the entire time," Draeson snapped. "Plus you lot aren't exactly feathers. I'll be fine."

Brannon sighed and withdrew his hand. Draeson had been alive for four hundred years but he'd yet to learn to manage his emotions. Or perhaps he'd just grown too old to bother trying. Of all of them, he was likely to be feeling their failure to catch Nycol the most. The other mage had bested him three times now. It wasn't an experience Draeson was used to.

They turned their feet in the direction of the city and walked back to where they'd left the archers. The sun had risen high enough to burn away the early morning fog and it glared off the water as they went. Brannon shaded his eyes with his hand and squinted ahead. "Where are they?"

"Who?"

"The archers. They might have seen Nycol come through here."

Ula peered into the distance and shook her head. "I cannot see them. They were supposed to stay, yes?"

"Something's wrong," Ylani muttered. "They're hurt."

Brannon glanced at her sharply. "You sure? How can you tell?"

She tapped the side of her head. "Instinct."

"Blood and Tears." Brannon drew his sword and started running.

As he got closer, the glare of sunlight faded and his chest tightened. The guards were there but none of them were standing. They were sprawled on the ground like broken dolls. His mind flashed back to memories of the war - the bodies of soldiers, battered and bloody on the fields of battle. These were very like that except for one vital difference.

"There's no blood. No blood!" The physician part of his mind took a moment to bask in relief before moving on to the many ways a soldier could die without shedding blood. Had they been poisoned? Gassed? Head injury? Nycol was a mage with a range of lethal abilities at his disposal. They knew he'd killed with magic before - turning the hearts of his victims to glass. He'd have no qualms about doing so again in order to escape.

Brannon dropped his sword on the grass and skidded to his knees next to the nearest guard. His fingers found the man's neck and felt for a pulse. *Thud. Thu-thud.* It was there. The man's chest rose and fell in a slow breath. He was alive. Brannon reached for the next. He too was breathing but unconscious.

Draeson, Ylani, and Ula caught up and started checking the others. "What happened? Are they all right?"

"Something's knocked them out," Brannon said. "Roll them onto their sides. We need to figure out what he did to them."

Draeson shrugged. "It'll be the same spell he used on me and those children when he kidnapped us. They'll come around eventually."

"Let's hope you're right." Brannon continued rolling the guards onto their sides anyway. Treating magic might be different to treating head injury or poisoning but best not to risk it. He didn't want any of them to choke if they were to vomit while unconscious. He reached the captain of the guard and touched his shoulder to roll him over.

The man coughed and sat up. His eyes were wide and he looked around fearfully.

"Take it easy," Brannon told him. "You're okay."

"Sir Brannon?" The captain swallowed and

nodded. "Yeah, I'm okay. Did you catch him?"

"No. He was ready for us. What happened here?"

"I...I'm not sure. We saw something moving and then there was a cloud of dust and I don't remember anything after that." He scrambled into a crouch and stared at the fallen archers. "Are they okay?"

"We think so," Brannon reassured him. "We think the mage we were after hit you all with a kind of sleeping spell. We've seen him do it before. Some people find it harder to wake than others."

"That's a relief." The captain nodded thoughtfully. "I can keep an eye on them if you and your team want to go get help from the hospital. Maybe some carriages? If they don't wake up, we'll need to transport everyone somewhere safe."

"Good idea." Brannon stood. "Just keep checking everyone to make sure they're breathing. We'll be back as soon as we can."

"Sir Brannon, can I see you a moment?" Ylani's suddenly formal tone caught his attention.

He walked a few steps towards her.

She nodded at the unconscious guard at her feet. The man had fallen face down when he'd been caught by the sleeping spell but his face was exposed when Ylani gently nudged his shoulder back with her foot. It was the face Brannon had just been conversing with. The captain of the guard.

Eyes wide, Brannon reached for his sword but his scabbard was empty. The blade lay on the grass where he'd dropped it a few moments before. He turned back to the version of the captain who was awake and on his feet.

The man gave a rueful smile. "So close," he said. "You are more of a pest than I anticipated, Sir Brannon." His face and uniform shimmered as the illusion melted way to reveal Magus Nycol. "Probably just as well. I wasn't going to be able to hold that illusion much longer. You're right, by the way. It is a sleeping spell." He gestured to the fallen archers. "They'll be fine as long as you or Magus Draeson don't try anything silly. I'd hate for them to get caught in a crossfire."

Brannon saw Draeson move his hand in the gesture he used to summon lightning and shook his head. The guards were too close and Draeson was already exhausted. The risk was too great.

Nycol sighed. "I honestly didn't want to hurt these guards. They're just doing their jobs, after all. I wasted a lot of time trying to sneak past them but you lot were back so fast I had to get more creative."

"You should have run away from the city," Brannon told him. He reached into his pocket. With his sword out of reach, he would have to use another weapon. "You could have been long gone."

Nycol shrugged. "We've been chasing each

other all night. You'll forgive me if sleeping in the wilderness didn't appeal."

"What was your plan then?" Brannon ran his thumbnail over the vial in his pocket and flicked the lid off. He closed his fingers around the glass, careful to keep it upright to avoid spilling the contents. "Just hide in Alapra and carry on murdering the populace one by one? What does that gain you?"

"Absolutely nothing." Nycol frowned, his head tilted. "I'm not the one murdering people. Why would you think that?"

Brannon blinked. How could they not think that? And yet, it seemed out of character for Nycol not to claim credit.

Draeson snorted. "You're mad if you think we will believe anything that comes out of your lying mouth. You're done."

Nycol's eyes narrowed. "We'll see about that." He swept his hand in a semi-circle, trailing sparkling powder into the air. The magic powder Brannon knew enabled the mage to put people into a trance or knock them out entirely.

"No!" Ula clapped her hands together with a sound like a thunder crack. "*Kaluk hul*!"

A powerful gust of wind slammed down on them all as the air spirits responded to Ula's call. Nycol's powder blasted into the dirt at their feet before it touched them.

Brannon pulled the open vial from his pocket and flung it at Nycol. Yellow sutcha powder sprayed from the opening as it flew. This time the air spirits guided the powder toward its goal.

Yellow smeared over Nycol's face. His eyes widened and he took a sharp breath. He stumbled. "What?" He fell to his knees, swaying as though drunk. "What did you do to me?"

"Used your own trick against you," Brannon said. "Sweet dreams."

Nycol's eyes rolled back and he passed out.

CHAPTER TWENTY

Brannon laid the unconscious body of the captured mage on the floor in the designated cell at the courthouse. The holding wings of the old building housed criminals and accused as they waited for their trails and sentencing and were usually busy. This section had been cleared out in preparation for this specific prisoner. Nycol would be kept in isolation and with a range of special precautions in place - both magical and physical. The room was stone with what was essentially a cage built into the middle of it. The floor around the cage was painted black for an arm's length all the way around, warning visitors of the safe distance to avoid a prisoner's grasp. The bars had been reinforced and large silver-framed mirrors wrapped in gauze circled the cage, ready to be activated into the containment spell Draeson assured them would reflect all magic back inward against the trapped caster.

Nycol's head bumped on the stone floor and Brannon winced as the physician part of him assessed it. That was going to leave a bruise. Still, it was hard to feel sympathy for the likes of Nycol. The mage groaned but remained still, his breathing slow and steady. Brannon reached for the unconscious man's wrist and checked his pulse. It was strong. The powder he'd been dosed with didn't seem to be doing serious harm.

Brannon sat back on his heels and reached into his pocket, feeling for the tiny vial Taran had provided when he'd supplied the sutcha powder. "Should I give him the antidote now?"

"Not unless you want him to escape again." Draeson tugged the fabric cover off the last of the mirrors, exposing the reflective surface to the light. "This cage will take a good hour to activate."

Brannon frowned. "I thought you'd have it ready and waiting. We've been after him for a long time."

Draeson hurled the fabric against the outer stone wall. "And if I'd activated it back then I would have been spending most of my magic each day keeping it active. Did you want me at half strength when we came up against him?"

Brannon raised his hands. "No, no. You made the right choice. I just don't like having any patient under the influence of a drug I don't really understand."

Draeson snorted. "He's not your patient, Brannon. He's our prisoner."

Brannon stared at the unconscious man. "I guess there's no harm in letting him sleep it off - other than the night terrors. I'll roll him onto his side in case he vomits though." He pushed Nycol into position.

"He's a murderer and a kidnapper," Draeson said. "A few nightmares courtesy of Taran's concoction are only the start of what he deserves."

Brannon didn't have it in him to argue with that. "We all need some sleep. Keeping him out to it until we're ready to deal with him again sounds wise."

Draeson shrugged. "I'm a wise man." He stepped up to one of the mirrors and breathed onto the crystal surface, fogging it up. Then he traced symbols in the resultant mist. The dragon tattoo rested on the side of his neck, its head tucked under his chin. As each symbol was completed, it briefly glowed before vanishing. The little dragon huffed as if its sleep was disturbed.

"There's nothing untoward in this magic, is there?" Brannon asked.

"Nothing more than a lot of effort on my part," Draeson grumbled. "It has to be strong enough to reflect anything thrown at it. And if not renewed, it will wear off after precisely one day. I won't be much use for other magics while we're questioning him."

Brannon nodded. "Keeping him contained is our main priority right now. At least the murders will stop now."

"There's that." Draeson nodded, then flapped his hand at Brannon. "Go get some sleep. I don't need you hovering over me like some oversized mother hen. And neither does Nycol. Come back in the morning and we'll interrogate him when we're fresh."

"Wisdom again?" Brannon grinned. "You're making a habit of it."

Draeson paused in his magic to make a rude gesture. "Get out."

Brannon exited the cage and locked the grilled door behind him. As he headed toward the outside world, he paused, lifted the antidote vial as if making a toast and set it down on the small table where a guard would sit on duty, well out of reach of the cell's inhabitant. "Just in case." The physician in him still found it odd to delay treatment and the Master of Investigations wanted to be sure that if Nycol died in custody it was as a result of sentencing, not before it. "Let the guard know that's there if he needs it."

Draeson nodded and flapped his hand at him again.

Brannon stepped out into the street and turned

his feet towards home. The mid-morning city was a hive of people going about their business. Most of them had no idea of the danger that had been in their midst.

He took a deep breath and let the tension that had sustained him throughout the night release. Alapra was safer now as a result of what he and his team had done. All that was left now was to figure out why Nycol had chosen to murder the people he had. The General may have stumbled onto Nycol's plan to attend the masquerade but how a stone carver and his wife could have factored into that scheme eluded Brannon's sleep deprived mind. If the General's concern that the king was in danger was true, it was vital to figure out what the full plan had been. Without knowing the nature of the threat, there was no way of knowing for sure if any danger remained even with Nycol imprisoned.

Brannon sighed. Tired as he was, he knew he'd struggle to truly rest without answers. But getting those answers was going to be difficult. The chances of Nycol revealing his entire plan were slim to say the least and there was little else to go on at this point.

A pebble skittered across the path in front of Brannon's foot, kicked by an unwitting passer-by. Brannon paused and stared at it. Stones. The stones in the cash box at the stonemason's house were an oddity he didn't yet have an explanation for. The missing cash suggested a robbery as well as murder but then why would valuable gems be left behind? Was the stonemason branching out into gem cutting? And how did gemstones play into a plot against the king?

He glanced up at the sun. It was already mid-morning. Alissa the jeweler would be working. Perhaps she'd had a chance to look at the stones and could give him some insight. Any extra information might be the leverage he needed to get answers from Nycol later. He hesitated, weighing the weariness in his muscles with the questioning in his mind. His mind won and his weary muscles made their way to the Stitch and Stone store.

As soon as Brannon turned into the street, it was evident something was wrong. People crowded around the store but city guards at the entrance prevented them from going inside. Muttering in the crowd speculated that Alissa had been arrested or killed. That Karlin had been selected as the king's royal tailor. That they'd both been Nilarian spies all along and every guest at last night's masquerade who had purchased an outfit from them would be deported. That they'd been robbed and the thieves had made off with the royal jewels, secretly brought here for cleaning and repair.

Brannon rolled his eyes. The quickest way to get to a wrong answer was to listen to idle speculation and gossip. He pushed his way through the gathered people and approached the guard closest to the door.

The man snapped to attention when he saw Brannon. "Sir Bloodhawk - er, Sir Brannon. I didn't realize the messenger had found you."

"They didn't." Brannon gestured toward the shop door. "Alissa is helping answer some questions about a case I'm working on. What's going on?"

The young guard swallowed, his Adam's apple bobbing nervously. "Best you go inside, Sir. Your apprentice will be better able to explain."

"My apprentice?"

Brannon pushed open the door and walked into the stop. Little had changed since he'd been here last. The bolts of fabric were undisturbed and the gowns on hangers shone with vibrant color next to matching masks and jewels. Alissa stood at the counter, flanked by Darnec Raldene in his palace guard uniform. Her hair was loose and unbrushed. Her eyes were red and her jaw trembled as she looked up at his approach. The gemstones and war medal Brannon had sent over for evaluation lay scattered on the bench in front of her, a shattered rainbow fortune she and the guards ignored.

Darnec nodded to Brannon. "I'm glad you made it, Sir Brannon. We couldn't find you so I offered to step in but..."

"Of course." Darnec had taken on many of the

duties of King's Champion since Brannon had become Master of Investigations. It was the first time the Champion role had been held by two people at the same time. It was unsurprising that people blurred the lines between them in their other roles as well. "I'm sure you're doing a good job. Can you tell me what's going on?"

Alissa's shoulders shook as she sobbed silently. She covered her face in her hands.

Darnec opened his mouth to speak, then hesitated and closed it again. He turned and pointed into the back room behind the counter. "This."

Brannon shifted to get a better view.

"Up," said Darnec.

Brannon tilted his head and saw it.

Karlin the tailor, Alissa's husband, dangled near the high ceiling as if hanged but with no rope around his neck or any other means of suspension.

"Blood and Tears." There was little else to say. Brannon had seen three magical deaths is as many days but there was something unnerving about the way Karlin's body simply hung in the air. He turned to the city guard. "Has anyone tried to get him down? Checked his pulse?"

"Can't figure out how to get him down," Darnec said. "We didn't check his pulse but he's definitely dead." He leaned forward and shielded his mouth from Alissa's view before adding in an exaggerated whisper, "His face is purple."

Brannon stepped around the counter. "A purple face doesn't equal death, for Ahpra's sake." He pulled a stool over to the body while the guard's face flushed as if to prove his point.

"He's not breathing," Alissa whispered. "I checked."

Brannon climbed on the stool to get a closer look. He waved his hand over the dead man's head in the hope of finding some sign of a rope but his hand passed without encountering anything at all. He placed his fingers on the Karlin's neck, searching for a pulse. There was an indent of force around his throat where the invisible rope should have been, but no sign of the rope and no sign of heartbeat. Karlin's skin was cool to touch but not completely room temperature. Brannon looked down to see Alissa staring up at him, clearly praying she and the city guards were wrong. "I'm sorry," he told her. He climbed down from the stool. "When did you find him?"

Alissa sniffed and rubbed at her eyes. "He was there when I woke up." She waved her hand at the gemstones and magnifying glass on the desk. "I stayed up late looking at the stones you sent over and fell asleep. I don't know how anyone could have gotten in and done that to him while I was sleeping right there. Why didn't I hear anything? Why didn't I wake up?"

"There probably wasn't anyone else," Darnec

said. "Most hangings like this are suicides."

"No!" Fire flashed in Alissa's eyes. "Karlin would never hang himself."

"I don't mean to upset you. Darnec touched her shoulder. "But sometimes people are going through things even those of us who are close to them don't understand."

"No, you don't understand." She shook her head. "I've always been terrified of hanging. He knows that. Even if he wanted to kill himself, he wouldn't have done it like that." There was an earnestness in her eyes that shone like jewels in the sun.

"This was done by magic, Darnec," Brannon pointed out. "Karlin didn't have that ability. However, we just caught someone who does. I'm so sorry, Alissa, but I think Karlin might have been his last victim."

Tears welled up in Alissa's eyes. "Why? Why would anyone want to kill my husband?"

Brannon could feel Alissa's grief like some heavy, tangible thing. "I don't know," he admitted. "I don't know why he did any of it. But I plan on finding out. Is there anything you can tell us that might help? When did you last see Karlin alive?"

"No, nothing. He went to bed before I did. I fell asleep out here a few hours before dawn." Alissa swallowed and rubbed at her eyes as if to scrub away tears. "Do you think...if I'd been in bed beside him that this wouldn't have happened?"

Brannon shook his head. "There's nothing you could have done, Alissa. Nothing." He turned to Darnec. "Have someone take Alissa to a friend's for a while. I'll ask Magus Draeson to see what he can do about getting the body down. When he does, have it taken to the Physician College for examination. We need as much evidence as we can get."

The younger man nodded. "Yes, Sir Brannon." He guided the grieving woman toward the door.

A few steps between the shelves, Alissa stopped and turned back. "Could this be anything to do with the fake jewels?"

Brannon froze. "Fake jewels?"

"Yes. The gemstones you sent through to be assessed. They're all fake. Even the one in the service medal." She looked from Brannon to Darnec to the room where her husband's body was suspended in the air. "Am I in danger?"

Brannon considered it. The gems had been present at two murder scenes now. Was that coincidence? "I don't think so but Darnec and the other guards will keep you safe. As I said, we have the mage in custody so there should be no further danger. I'm so sorry this happened, Alissa. I'll let you know what we find out."

"Thank you." The jeweler nodded and made her way to the door as Darnec trailed behind.

Brannon stood in the abandoned shop,

pondering what she'd said. The gems were fake so why would they be worth killing over? More importantly, how had Nycol gotten to the shop and managed to murder poor Karlin at the same time as he was leading Brannon and his team all over town. The tracking spell hadn't sent them here and as far as Brannon understood that aspect of Draeson's magic, that meant the person being tracked hadn't either. And if, as Alissa had suggested, the deed had been done in the early hours of the morning...the timeline didn't add up.

Unless Karlin had been murdered well in advance of Alissa falling asleep and simply placed there for her to find when she woke up.

There was one way to find out.

Brannon made his way back to the body and gingerly lifted the hem of Karlin's trousers to expose his ankle. There was only the barest hint of darkening of the skin. Lividity had hardly started. If the man had been hanging like this for any length of time, the blood in his body should be pooling at the lowest points and extremely visible by now. Karlin was only a few hours dead at most.

Brannon swore. There was no way Nycol could have committed this murder.

There were two magical murderers in Alapra.

CHAPTER TWENTY-ONE

Ylani's eyelids drooped as she slipped the key into the lock of her apartment and turned it with a smooth click. She paused, leaned her head against the door, took a deep breath in and exhaled slowly. The wood was hard and cool against her forehead. The masquerade seemed an eternity ago. There was mud on her shoes and the hem of her dress, and her hat sat crooked on her loosened curls, but she felt satisfied with what they had achieved. Still, something niggled in the back of her mind - a twinge of instinct she couldn't quite explain. She hugged herself, feeling the silk of her dress beneath her fingertips. Nycol - the last of her countrymen who'd been involved in her brother's slavery scheme to steal Kalan children - was captured and with him went the familial guilt she'd been carrying over Marrol's actions. Her debt to the people of Kalanon, with regard to this, at least, was paid.

What that meant for her relationship with the Kalans she'd come to know and rely on was less clear.

She chuckled to herself at the ambiguousness of that thought. If she was honest, it was the relationship with one particular Kalan she was most concerned about. She had little reason to spend time with Sir Brannon Kesh if they were no longer working together to track down the rogue mage. Whatever the true nature of their fledgling relationship, they would now have to let it fly on its own strength.

She shook her head. If anyone had told her during the war that she'd be considering a relationship with the infamous Bloodhawk, she'd have thought they were mad. Yet somehow, here they were. She respected the man and trusted him. Even if it developed into nothing else, they were friends. And that was miracle enough.

She took a deep breath, straightened her spine, and reached for the door handle. Her fingers barely brushed the metal when the door swung open. Ylani jerked back, startled.

Reanna Kesh stood in the doorway. She smirked when she saw Ylani's stunned expression and disheveled appearance. "Good to see you again, Ambassador."

Ylani forced herself not to frown at the

invasion and raised her eyebrow instead. "An unexpected pleasure, to be sure. What brings you to my apartment?"

"She was here to see me, Ylani." A familiar voice came from inside and Reanna stepped aside to reveal Alyra Jalin, the Nilarian envoy who had been tasked with returning the slaves. "And I'm here to see you."

Myli, Ylani's assistant, peered over Alyra's shoulder and mouthed "I'm sorry." Ylani gave an imperceptible nod in return. Myli had no authority to turn away the envoy when she arrived. And once established in the apartment, Alyra could use the space to meet with Brannon's sister.

"Well then." Ylani forced a smile to her lips. "It would seem we all have much to discuss. "Myli, perhaps you could bring our guests some tea."

"Actually, I was just leaving," Reanna said. She turned and gave a nod to Alyra. "Thank you for your time." She pushed past Ylani and strode away.

Ylani stepped into the apartment and closed the door behind her. She took a moment to breathe in the sanctuary she'd created for herself here in Kalanon. The colorful silk panels that lined the walls of this initial waiting area had inspirational words stitched in Nilarian characters in the center of each one. Words like courage, strength, and patience. Qualities she'd known she would need to exhibit here in the land of her enemies as she struggled to draw her country and this one closer together. Now, it seemed, she would need those qualities as she dealt with one of her own people.

"Reanna Kesh has an ulterior motive for approaching you," she said. "She approached me last night. She wants something and she came to you because I wouldn't give it to her."

Alyra shrugged. "Everyone wants something. Everyone has an ulterior motive. You taught me that."

Ylani bit her lower lip and evaluated the other woman. The Alyra she knew had always appreciated a direct approach. "So what's your ulterior motive for being in Kalanon? I wouldn't have thought delivering cargo was your first choice of mission."

Alyra made a tutting noise with her tongue. "Describing Kalan prisoners of war as cargo, Ylani? What would your new friends say? The Nilarian government doesn't think of human beings that way."

"Clearly they do or they wouldn't have kept them as slaves all this time," Ylani countered. "They're only being returned now because the attempt to capture new slaves during a time of peace was uncovered."

"Perhaps." Alyra shrugged. "Times are rough at home. But you wouldn't know that because you're here getting cozy with the man responsible for killing more of our countrymen than anyone else in the history of the world."

A flash of heat burned across Ylani's face. The image of the bones trapped in a tide pool rose in her mind. Bones of Nilarians killed by the actions of the men she'd been working with. She forced air into her lungs, expanding the tightness in her chest. "We are at peace with Kalanon now. Clinging to what was done during the war helps no one. Our army was in their country. Of course they defended themselves."

Alyra snorted. "You've gone native, Ylani. How can our government trust you to act in Nilar's best interests?"

"I have always acted in Nilar's best interests." Ylani's voice snapped like a whip and her eyes narrowed. "I risked my life behind enemy lines while the likes of you were safe in your beds at home. I did more than you'll ever know for my country and don't you forget it."

"Now who's clinging to what was done in the war?" Alyra sat on one of the cushioned chairs, crossed her legs and spread her arms as if on a throne. "Since you've been here you've acted against your country's interests more than once. The weapons debacle. This slavery thing. What else? People back home have questions."

"Then they should read my reports." Ylani remained standing and folded her arms. "The weapons debacle was an unsanctioned attempt by a rogue element to start a coup in country we have a peace treaty with. My job here is to build and maintain that peace so you bet I did what I could to put a stop to it. As for helping to uncover a plot to murder innocent people and steal their children - I hope any decent person would do the same. I have also built strong relationships within the Kalan court and established trade agreements for our products that guarantee Nilar an ongoing supply of gold. That is the role of an Ambassador."

"And you think that's what was expected when they put the great all-knowing Mistress Mercury into the role?"

Ylani hid a flinch at her old code name. There were likely some who had hoped she would continue as a spy. "I think I have a better understanding of my role than you do, Alyra. That's why it was given to me and not to you. I know you wanted the job but no matter how bitter you are about that decision, it doesn't change the fact that it was made."

"Perhaps." Alyra drummed her fingertips on the arm of the chair and stared at the door to Ylani's office for a several moments. When she finally turned her gaze back to Ylani, her eyes were cold. "Or perhaps I've been sent here to evaluate you." She reached into a pocket in her skirt and pulled out a sheaf of paper. Ylani instantly recognized the

Nilarian government seal at the bottom of the first page. "This gives me authority to take steps if I deem you are no longer an appropriate choice for Ambassador to Kalanon," Alyra said. "You're fired, Ylani. And no matter how bitter you are about the decision, it doesn't change the fact that it's been made."

CHAPTER TWENTY-TWO

The day was too warm and Brannon's mind too concerned to fully give in to sleep so he twisted and kicked at the tangled blankets in a fitful doze. The drapes drawn across the window kept out most of the day's light but could not prevent the noises of chattering courtiers, marching guards, and the normal comings and goings in the apartment building and surrounding palace grounds. A lifetime of sleeping in war camps had taught Brannon to tune out such disturbances but somehow this time it seemed more difficult. What sleep he did manage to get was restless and plagued with dreams.

The sounds mingled with his memories of army camps and his sleeping mind returned him to a place of tents and soldiers beside the River Tilal.

In his dream, Brannon drifted along the bank of the river. The wounded stretched out to his left like a field of cut wheat. Master Jordell and his team of physicians moved from broken body to broken body, doing what they could for each loyal Kalan who had put his or her life on the line for their country. They'd given everything to defend Kalanon and they were losing.

On the other side of the river, the Nilarian army amassed, a swarm of deadly insects in the distance, darkening the shore. When the wind gusted from the East, snatches of sound blew across the water, bursts of harsh Nilarian speech and metal clanging.

"When they cross, we're done for," said the king.

Brannon blinked at Aldan's sudden appearance. The king's golden beard was longer than he usually liked to keep it and his hair hung in dirty strips.

"The river is the only thing that's kept us from being overrun," Brannon admitted. "We're in real trouble."

Aldan nodded. "I'm calling a special council with my most trusted advisors. You, Roydan, the mage, and a few others. Now is the time for your most creative solutions, Bloodhawk. I need you at your berserker best."

Brannon saluted. "My sword is yours, my king."

"And always hungry for enemy blood." Aldan grinned at him. "I know."

Brannon forced the familiar smile in response.

The truth was, he'd long since had his fill of blood but necessity required his blade keep drinking. The Nilarian steel sword he'd taken from a General had ended many Nilarian lives - beginning with the young son of that very General, a lad who had tried to avenge his father. As Aldan turned to lead the way to the command tent, Brannon let himself take a long shuddering breath. Winning was no longer a good outcome in this war. So much damage had been done on both sides. It would be impossible to wash out the stain of this life even if they managed to save Kalanon. And the way things were looking, there was a very good chance they couldn't.

Not without doing something extreme.

Brannon lifted back the entrance flap to the command tent and stepped inside but as it fell back into place, the dream blurred and shifted. He was back at the river now, but further north, at a spot where the grass was less trampled and the water was high on the banks.

Magus Draeson looked up as Brannon approached. His face was crinkled like scrunched up paper, blotted with age spots and skin so thin and papery that Brannon could see every broken capillary beneath the surface. The tattoo of a dragon peeked out from under the wispy white hair tucked behind his ear and extended its neck onto his cheek. He had a puffy cushion on the chair beneath him and he made no effort to stand as Brannon approached. "I'm not getting up so you can just assume I've bowed or saluted or whatever a King's Champion expects these days. At my age, my ass hurts when I sit and everything else hurts when I stand, so I'll take the lesser of the evils."

"That's fine, Magus," Brannon said. "I'm not particularly interested in courtly niceties. Certainly not here."

Draeson huffed. "Good. Now are you ready to get rid of these Nilarians?"

Ready to put their plan into place. To use the river to commit mass murder. Brannon nodded. "Yeah." The guilt was already a heavy stone in his chest. "We have to."

Brannon helped the old mage to his feet and they made their way to the edge of the river. Brannon's soldiers had built walls on either side in an attempt to control the build-up of water that - if all went according to plan - would soon spill out over the surrounding land. "Are you sure you can do this?"

The tattoo on Draeson's neck regarded Brannon with narrowed eyes. "Of course I can," the ancient mage said. "Just because you and your merry band of grunts with sharpened metal sticks have been ineffective, don't assume the rest of us don't know what we're doing."

"That's not what I meant." Brannon swallowed a sharp retort. "Just...this seems like a lot. Even for you."

The mage snorted. "Watch and learn, boy. I was doing magic and protecting this country since before your great grandfather was even a twinkle in his parents' eye." He raised his hand over the river and a jet of fog sprayed out from one side to the other. It hung in the air for a moment, then drifted downward in a long, white curtain.

Brannon reached out toward the mist but the old man slapped his hand away.

"Don't touch it," Draeson snapped. "You'll lose a finger."

"Really?" Brannon frowned. "It doesn't look solid."

"It isn't. It's cold. Cold enough to give you frostbite instantly. You know what that is?"

Brannon shook his head.

"Then you're lucky. Basically this is a blade of coldness that will freeze anything it touches. So stand clear." The mage lowered his arm slowly and the sheet of mist moved with it. The blade of frost sank into the river and hissed as the water touched it, froze, cracked beneath the weight of the current, and froze again. "Here's where it gets tricky." Draeson grumbled through clenched teeth. His eyes narrowed and the curtain of fog thickened. So did the ice.

The cracking stopped as the ice became thick enough to plug the flow of water behind it. The river flowed away on the downward side, leaving a shiny wall of ice, and began to fill the banks on the upper side. The mage kept pushing his magic into the newly formed dam until the ice plug was as wide as a road. Then he closed his hand and slumped.

Brannon caught the old man and tried to help him back to his chair but the old man shook his head and pushed him away.

"Not yet." He stumbled forward and began clambering down the muddy banks of the now empty riverbed. "Must move quickly." He slipped and slid down the wet earth on his knees until he came to a stop on a clump of slimy waterweed. He hunched there, gasping for breath.

"Magus!" Brannon hurried after him. "Are you all right?"

The mage scrambled to his feet and continued on, mud caked onto his clothes like butter on bread. By the time Brannon caught up with him, he was already pulling a wand of ice from the dam wall. A small stream of frigid water poured from the hole left behind, trickling over Brannon. The cold washed through him in a wave and the physical sensation of it shook him from the dream.

He woke up, shivering from the cold, and rolled over in his bed. He squinted at the light leaking in around the tightly drawn curtains. Too soon. He pulled the blanket up over himself and closed his eyes again.

This time, when sleep swallowed him, he found himself back in battle. The smell of blood and mud was all around him, combined with the sound of screams and clashing metal in an overwhelming whirlwind of sensory input. Behind him, the loud thwack of a catapult unleashed a barrel of burning pitch across the river and into the Nilarian army beyond. Smoke and the scent of burning flesh drifted across the enemy soldiers who were wading through the Tilal, muddy water only up to their knees.

"Archers," Brannon yelled. "Archers!!"

A moment later a swarm of Kalan arrows shot into the air and hurled themselves down onto the approaching soldiers. The Nilarians paused in their advance across the river and raised shields. A few men fell into the mud but most remained protected and continued their advance when the arrows ceased.

"Hooded Blood," Brannon muttered.

"Here, take this." Draeson pressed the wand of ice into Brannon's hand. The old mage's warm skin felt like thin paper against the cold of the wand. "When the time comes, break it."

Brannon felt the chill in his fingers spread to his chest. "I'm not a mage, Draeson. I think you should be the one to do it."

"I've my own job to do, Bloodhawk," the magus growled. "It's simple enough. Break the wand and you break the spell. Do as you're told and most of us will go home alive." He shuffled off muttering. "Kalans anyway."

Brannon fought his way toward the river's edge. The low tide was no impediment to the Nilarian army. They flooded across, a wave of superior steel crashing against the wall of Kalans desperate to hold them back. At the edge of the river, the mix of two armies was chaos and death. Slowly, but surely, more and more Nilarians made it to dry land and joined the battle against the Kalan defenders. There was no stopping them without the river to hold them back. Kalanon had lost too many of its people in this war already. If they were overwhelmed here, the country would fall.

Brannon fought hard. The stolen Nilarian steel of his sword clanged against the weapons of its countrymen and drank their blood. But it was not enough. Barely a quarter of the Nilarian army had made it across the river and already the Kalans were being overrun. The rest of the Nilarians were making the crossing.

Brannon felt the bar of cold in his tunic freezing his soul. It had to be done or there would be no Kalanon left to defend. And it had to be now.

He plunged his sword into the ground and pulled the wand of ice from his pocket. It felt small in his hands. Such a tiny thing for the destruction it would wreak. He swallowed his conscience and snapped it in two.

For a long moment, nothing happened. Then, even above the sounds of battle, he heard a distant roar. It grew louder and louder. The fighting paused as soldiers hesitated and glanced around, seeking the source of the sound. The Nilarian soldiers still crossing the river - near half the invading army, began to run for the shore, some falling and being trampled in the rush.

They were not fast enough.

The released waters of the Tilal rushed down the riverbed in a wall of devastation. The flash flood shredded the army like tissue paper and washed them away. Thousands of men, unable to swim in their heavy armor, were drowned in moments.

The horror of what he had done washed through him and Brannon jerked awake, his breath strangled. He coughed, dream-water choking his lungs. He sat up and took large gulps of air, willing the panic to leave his body with each breath. It'd been a long time since he'd had such an intense nightmare about the war.

He pulled back the sheets. They were soaked through, almost as if he'd been drowning himself. He supposed he had been, in a way. Drowning in guilt and memory for a long time. He'd thought he'd left most of those feelings behind but perhaps seeing the Nilarians and their released prisoners of war had brought those memories bubbling back to the surface. There was only one way he knew to fight those memories: to do whatever he could to prevent more killing.

He splashed water on his face, gave himself a quick towel-dry, and pulled on his clothes. He had one murderer in custody but the mystery was not yet solved. And until he truly knew what was going on in this city, there was a risk more people would die. Brannon couldn't let that happen.

CHAPTER TWENTY-THREE

It was late afternoon when Brannon made his way back to the court complex to visit their captive once more. Shalyn, the cobbler's daughter, loitered on the street outside, dressed in mismatched but sturdy clothing. She still had the quality shoes she'd inherited from her father. Brannon made a mental note to check that she'd received any payment from the sale of the man's stock. His wares had been quite popular with the nobility and it seemed wrong if that money had been swallowed up by the orphanage where she now lived.

"Anything I can help you with, Shalyn?"

She stood up straight. "No, Sir Brannon." The girl shuffled her feet. "Only...I wondered if Magus Draeson..."

Brannon chuckled. "He's busy, I'm afraid. Go on home and I'll let him know you'd like a visit, how's that?"

She looked at her feet. "Yes, sir. Thank you."

She trudged down the street and Brannon went inside.

Draeson was already in attendance at the prison cell. Brannon wasn't sure if the magus had stayed the entire time or slept and come back to reinforce the spells in the mirrors around the cage. He sat cross legged, just out of reach beyond the black painted area around the bars, his hands palm up and glowing with light. The small dragon tattoo was curled around his left wrist like a sleeping bracelet. The mage inside the cage of iron and quartz mirrors paced up and down the length of his prison, arms folded across his chest. He had dark circles under his eyes, no doubt from the night terrors Taran's powder had brought on.

Both mages looked up as Brannon walked in.

"You look like shit," Draeson said and climbed to his feet. "Are you sure you didn't get any of that sutcha powder on you?"

Brannon shook his head. "I just slept badly is all. Nightmares aren't new to me." He nodded toward the outside world. "It seems you have a fan."

Draeson scowled. "That girl again? Bother. Tell her to go away."

"It wouldn't hurt you to be nice to her," Brannon said. "Few enough people like you as it is." He waved at the cell. "Will this hold?"

Draeson glanced at their prisoner. "No doubt

he'll test it when we leave, but it'll hold all right."

"I'm sure it will." Nycol snorted and unfolded his arms. "Given who you learned the mirror spell from."

Brannon exchanged a look with Draeson. "What does he mean by that?"

"No idea." Draeson shrugged. "He's been talking cryptic nonsense since he woke up."

"You don't recognize me, Draeson? Ah, well, I suppose that's not surprising." Nycol's voice took on a teasing lilt.

"Oh, I recognize you from when you kidnapped me," Draeson snarled. "That's more than enough recognition for me."

"Enough games," Brannon said. "You're here because of your connection to the kidnapping and slavery attempt and the recent murders. Things will go easier on you if you tell us what we want to know."

Nycol gave a sweet smile and leaned back against the bars on the far side of his cage. "Of course, Sir Brannon. Anything to help exonerate me."

Draeson snorted. "There's no exonerating you. You're guilty as the Hooded One's favorite frost wolf."

Nycol raised an eyebrow. "Is that so?"
"Yes."
"Sir Brannon?" The captured mage smirked.

"Anything to add?"

Draeson whirled to face Brannon. "What's he talking about?"

Brannon sighed and scratched at the scar on his cheek. "There was another murder last night," he said. "When he wasn't in the area."

"What? That's impossible. Was it a magical one?"

The image of the dead man suspended in mid-air flashed into Brannon's mind. "Yeah. Definitely. The tailor at Stitch and Stone."

"Blood and Tears." Draeson stared at the floor for a moment, then shook his head. "That doesn't mean anything. Maybe he had an accomplice."

"Maybe. Either way, we have some questions that need answering." Especially given the apparent threat to the king. Brannon stared at the prisoner.

Nycol met his gaze with a mild expression. "Ask away."

Brannon clenched his fist. Despite having the mage trapped and helpless, he couldn't shake the feeling that he was still at a disadvantage in this interrogation. He needed leverage. He needed a way to pressure the truth out of Nycol. "Why are you here?" he asked quietly. "What is it you actually want?"

Nycol's eyes slid sideways to Draeson and back again. "Well, Sir Brannon, you get straight to the point, don't you?" He pursed his lips thoughtfully. "I came at the request of my friend Marrol Shaylar and remained out of curiosity. Alapra is such a nice city, after all."

"Not that nice," Draeson grumbled. "Not for a Nilarian slaver."

"We know you're part of a plot against the king," Brannon said. "Tell us about it and we can make your life easier here."

Nycol snorted. "I've no interest in your king. Why would I?"

"Why would you do any of what you've done?" Draeson retorted.

"You came to the masquerade. The General knew you were up to something and tried to prevent it so you killed him. How did you meet him?"

"Meet who?" Nycol frowned. "I didn't go anywhere near your king at the masquerade. I had other goals." His eyes flicked toward Draeson again.

"Then why the threat? Why the torn portrait?"

Nycol shrugged. "I have no idea what you're talking about."

"You lying piece of -" Draeson started.

"Really. Your king means nothing to me."

Brannon touched Draeson's shoulder to quiet him. "But you did kill the homeless man known as the General, and the stonemason and his wife."

"I did no such thing."

"These crimes were done by magic," Brannon

said. "Do you really expect us to believe that's a coincidence with you here?"

"I'm not the only mage in the world. Neither are mages the only source of magic - despite what some would have us believe."

"You would know." Draeson muttered.

Brannon raised an eyebrow at the mage. "Oh?"

"I know the signs of someone who dabbles in things they shouldn't," Draeson said. "And I'd wager this one more than dabbles."

Nycol snorted. "Look who's talking."

"Shut your Hooded mouth," Draeson snapped.

Brannon touched his friend's shoulder. "Don't let him rile you. We know you're a good man."

Draeson shrugged him off. "I'm loyal to Kalanon. You know better than most that doesn't always mean 'good'."

The memories that had invaded his dreams flashed briefly in Brannon's mind. Waterlogged bodies had washed up on the riverbanks for weeks after the act that finally ended the war. The stench alone lingered like a stain. The wave of disease that had followed in the wake of those rotting corpses had been a battle of its own. The cheers of citizens relieved that the war was over had done little to wash away the guilt.

All three men were quiet for a long moment.

"Live as long as we do and there's always something we're not proud of," Nycol said. "We do our best with what we have at any given moment. That's all we can do."

Brannon swallowed. "Is that what you've been doing here? The best with what you have?"

"It is." Nycol sighed. "And I'll admit my best isn't much compared to most people's but there it is. Sometimes that has meant killing - as it has for both of you - but I didn't kill the people you've asked me about."

"And the threat against the king?"

"Nothing to do with that either."

Brannon folded his arms. "It'd be easier to believe if you told us what you *are* involved with then. You're Nilarian so there's no family or connections to stay for. You need to tell us what scheme you're involved in. Because nobody stays in a city where they're being hunted by the authorities without a good reason."

Nycol opened his mouth to speak when the door opened and the Nilarian envoy stepped into the room, followed by a harried looking city guard. She wore a grey silk gown and a wide brimmed hat to match. The set of her jaw was hard and she strode across the room toward the cage.

"I'm sorry, Sir Brannon," said the guard. "She insisted."

"It's fine," Brannon said. "You can go." He moved to block Alyra from stepping too close to the bars. "Stay outside the black marks on the floor, please, Envoy. For your own safety."

"Oh please. I've been glared at by almost every Kalan I've encountered since I entered Kalanon, gentlemen. I hardly think a fellow Nilarian will be the worst of the threats I encounter while I'm here." Nevertheless, she stopped shy of the markings, as he'd requested.

"I wouldn't bet on it," Draeson muttered.

Alyra lifted her chin. "I hope you're not badgering my countryman into a false confession."

"There's no need to badger," Brannon said. "We know he's guilty. We're just trying to establish for how many crimes."

"Isn't he entitled to an advocate in your legal system? Or to fight for his honor against the King's Champion?" She nodded toward Brannon. "Or do you just mean to starve, drug, and intimidate him until he confesses to whatever you say?"

"Only Kalan nobility can claim trial by combat," Brannon pointed out. "And as you say, he's Nilarian so that doesn't count. He'll have to be judged on the actual evidence and we have plenty of that."

"Pff," Alyra sniffed. "You have conjecture and circumstance. You think that because there have been killings of a magical nature that it must be the foreign mage who did it. That's lazy investigation at best and simple racism at worst. Surely you wouldn't want to damage the fragile friendship between our two countries with your faulty assumptions."

"He drugged and kidnapped me and was instrumental in making a number of children orphans," Draeson said. The tattoo on his face hissed. "There are no assumptions in that. Since we know he murdered those people, it's hardly a huge leap to think he murdered these recent ones as well."

"But it is a leap just the same." Alyra's finger punctured the air between them. "History is full of miscarriages of justice based on prejudice. There's a similar story in Nilarian history where a small-town wise woman was blamed for crops failing and strange deaths when it turned out to be a curse on a stolen treasure the mayor had found. I don't want to see something like that happen here."

"This isn't some Nilarian backwater," said Draeson. "We're not stupid here."

"He'll be judged fairly." Brannon kept his voice low. "We want the truth. That's how we protect our citizens."

"I would hope so," Alyra said mildly. "And it is my duty protect Nilarian citizens. That includes Magus Nycol so you should remember that I'll be watching everything you do."

Steel crept into Brannon's voice, hard and sharp. His fingers clenched into fists. "Watch as much as you like but don't think for a second that we won't do what needs to be done. Kalanon wants to be friends with Nilar, Envoy, but we haven't forgotten that it was Nilar who attacked us and started the war. We've learned how to defend ourselves in the years that followed and we don't intend to stop now."

CHAPTER TWENTY-FOUR

The palace sitting room allocated to Taran's little group had a single window overlooking the gardens. A fountain depicting the goddess Ahpra weeping the river Tilal was surrounded by trees and flowerbeds. The water trickling from her eyes into the pool below provided a musical tinkle beneath the birdsong. Overstuffed chairs stacked with cushions were placed in a circle around the room. Claydan and Tommy were already seated. Tommy sat cross-legged on the chair, fiddling with a toy horse and soldier.

Taran led Ula and Brillen into the room. Ula took the chair beside Tomidan and crossed her legs in much the same way, her leather smock riding high up her purple thighs. The tattoos on her skin were a pattern of light and shadow. She smiled at Tommy and he handed her the horse but kept the soldier for himself.

"Thank you, young prince," she said and galloped it along her knee.

Brillen, the recently returned prisoner of war, bowed to the two princes.

"Ugh. None of that," Claydan said. "I'm still not used to it. Bad enough people do it in formal settings." He patted the chair next to him. "Have a seat."

"Yes, your highness." Brillen sat as instructed and the entire group turned to face Taran expectantly.

"Um." Taran felt his face go warm. "Welcome to our group. Thank you for coming."

"I wasn't sure I had a choice," Ula said dryly. "King and Brannon say come so I come."

"Wise," said Brillen. "You don't want to piss off the Bloodhawk."

"Right. Right." Taran hurried onward. "Sir Brannon and the king asked for us to do this because each of us has had an experience of being taken by someone and we have to adjust to life now we're home." He hesitated. "Or, I suppose, for Prioress Ula, it is us who are doing the taking and you are getting used to being away from your home. Do...do we still call you prioress?"

The purple woman gestured to her tattoos. "It is permanent."

"Oh. Yes. Of course." He looked around the

group, uncertain where to start. It would be easy enough to teach them assimilation techniques used by the Children of Starlight, but those were intended to imitate fitting in, to infiltrate and avoid detection. Truly feeling like you belonged was something different entirely. Something he'd taken years to work on and, in all honesty, not mastered. Hiding in the church as he had done would not be an option for anyone else in this room. And even Taran himself would never have managed to pull it off without the assistance of the king. He fingered the King's Pass talisman he always wore under his clothes - a gift of gratitude for when he'd saved King Aldan's life. That decision had changed his destiny entirely and, he supposed, that kind of change was what the members of this group were hoping for.

The young prince Tomidan dropped his toy soldier and climbed off the chair to pick it up.

Taran watched him, alert for any signs of the madness that came from withdrawal from stardust elixir. The poor boy's life had already changed so much, what with the murder of both his parents, it hardly seemed fair that he might yet face a lifetime of addiction. Taran remembered all too well the fear that came with stardust and the horror of what it could do to a person once it took hold. He'd grown up in the knowledge the Father of Starlight held the key to his life and sanity at all times. It was a terrible thing to realize someone or something had that power over you. Even more terrible for a child. No one should have to experience a childhood like his.

But it wasn't only the young prince whose childhood was at risk right now. After what Taran had seen in Lady Magda's orphanage, he was worried he'd swapped belonging to one abusive organization for another. Or, rather, swapped one bully for another. Whatever Bishop Narayan was doing at the orphanage had to be stopped and the best solution for that was to go to the top.

"Will the king be joining us?" King Aldan owed Taran his life and had asked him to help his son. Taran was sure he'd help the orphans too.

Claydan shook his head. "I don't think so. But maybe you can tell him how well we're all doing later."

Taran gave him a little smile and nod. "Yes. Of course." He paused, still unsure of how to begin. "Um..."

"Should we start by telling each other our stories?" Brillen suggested. "So we know what brings us here."

"Our feet," Ula said in a wry tone. "And maybe a horse."

"Good idea," Taran said quickly. "Who would like to start?"

Prince Claydan shifted in his chair. "Well, I

suppose everyone already knows most of my story," he said. "Kidnapped as a child during the war and tortured. They took everything. My family, my country - eventually even Taran here, who was the only friend I had at the Assassin House." He stared out the window at the weeping statue. "And the sad truth is, they didn't even really want me. They just wanted someone they could use to breed a branch of the royal line. Anyone from the royal family would have been fine. Anyone. But it was me." His voice grew quieter as he spoke. "I resisted them the only way I could and well, that was that."

Taran reached out to try to comfort him but Claydan shifted uncomfortably in his seat and Taran let his hand drop.

"I've only recently gotten back to Kalanon and things have changed a lot," the prince continued. "Everything has changed, really. My mother is gone, my father is...different. Older. Everything. I guess...obviously I've changed too." He swallowed, blinked, and looked around the room. "So that's me."

"Um...thank you." Taran could find no words to comfort his friend. He'd believed for many years that Claydan had died with the Children of Starlight. Learning he'd been left behind when Taran made his own escape had put a cold weight in his chest that still hadn't lifted, despite helping rescue the prince in the end. Bringing Claydan home had felt good but it hadn't made up for the years he'd been locked up and abused and it hadn't made them friends again. "Thank you for sharing."

Next to him, Ula nodded solemnly. "Life always changes. You stronger now, I think. Like clay baked in fire."

The prince gave her a wry smile. "Hence my name, perhaps. Although I doubt that's what my mother had in mind."

"Perhaps not." The smile Ula returned him held warmth and kindness. She held out the little toy horse Tomidan had given her and nodded her head toward the younger prince. "But you have family that welcomes you still. Even if they have been through a fire of their own."

Claydan took the toy and stared at it. "Maybe," he said quietly. "But it's not something I'm used to."

Brillen leaned forward and spoke. "I don't know if you remember, Your Highness, but I was there with you that day."

Taran blinked.

"What?" The prince straightened up. "What do you mean?"

"I was one of the soldiers in your escort, Your Highness. When we were ambushed, I was sent to get help. We weren't far from a larger force, headed to meet up with the main army. The captain thought our group could hold them off while I went for reinforcements."

"But...what happened?"

"When I reached the camp, they were already packing up. There had been word that the Nilarians had been seen near Cretaine. Your father was there at the time and..." Brillen trailed off for a moment and fiddled with the piece of silk ribbon tied around his wrist. Eventually, he took a deep breath and continued. "The commander in charge made the decision to rescue your father instead of you. He said the king was the priority and sent me back with just a few men to help. By the time we returned, my captain and the others were dead and you were gone. We followed your trail for two days but we ran into a raiding party of Nilarians and were captured ourselves. I'm so sorry, my prince. I tried many times to escape to search for you but...I couldn't."

"Who..." Claydan stopped and swallowed, his hands trembling, white knuckled around the toy horse. "Who was the commander who refused to help?"

Brillen cast his gaze at the floor. "It was Sir Brannon, your highness. He did what he had to do. I understand that, I suppose. I'm sure he loved Your Highness as much as anyone."

Claydan's jaw twitched. "Not as much as he loved my father, it seems. And not enough to find me until Tomidan was also taken." He moved with careful precision, setting the toy horse on the ground before turning to face Brillen again. "You have my thanks, brave soldier. You did what you could for me and you have suffered because of it in much the same way I myself suffered. I'm glad we have met one another again."

Brillen bowed his head. "As am I, Your Highness."

"Call me Clay."

Taran recognized the anger simmering beneath Clay's surface. He'd seen it when they were young. Brillen had given him someone to pin the blame for his frustration and pain on. Taran wished it hadn't been Sir Brannon. His old friend and his new friend seemed likely to clash unless Claydan could be made to understand the difficult decision Brannon had clearly been forced to make in the midst of battle. If only he could think of a way to make Clay understand.

"Duty is very important to Sir Brannon," Ula said. "Duty forces people to make difficult decisions. Sometimes decisions they don't like."

"And decisions other people don't like," Claydan muttered.

"Prioress Ula," Taran hurried to change the subject. "Perhaps you'd like to tell us your story?"

She nodded, the colorful wood and coral beads in her deadlocks clacking together like windchimes.

Taran found it difficult to concentrate on her words. Juggling the emotional needs of his friends was difficult at the best of times - Ahpra knew he had trouble enough with his own - but now he worried that those needs would clash. Perhaps sharing their stories in such an open way would cause more problems than it solved. It was too late to stop the process now. He wondered how Tomidan was coping with what the adults were sharing. Exposing the boy to more trauma seemed cruel given his history but perhaps it would do him good to hear that everyone went through difficulties and managed to come out the other side. He watched as the young prince played with his toy soldier. Tommy seemed oblivious to the discussions of the adults around him. Taran was glad. He needed to keep an eye on Tommy but the last thing he wanted was to become an emotional equivalent of Bishop Narayan chaining up orphans in some bizarre test.

"Earth spirits here but different too," Ula as saying. Brillen and Claydan were focused on each other, but it seemed to help the Djin woman to speak her situation aloud. "Not bad, but different." She sighed and looked at her hands. "I miss home but the Priory of Gradinath do not understand my situation. I think they be scared of me now." She trailed off, watching her fingers flex. A gust of wind blew in through the window, bringing with it the scent of water from the fountain. "Perhaps they are right to fear me. Perhaps I make army of Risen, take over Kalanon, and be queen."

"What?" Claydan sat up straight, his eyes wide.

Taran felt his own breath catch in his chest.

"Oh good. You do listen," Ula said, the corners of her mouth twitching upwards. "It's okay. You keep crown. It looks uncomfortable."

"It is," Tommy piped up. "Uncle Aldan let me try it on one time."

Ula threw back her head and laughed.

Taran saw Claydan frown and was about to speak up when the door swung open with a bang.

Bishop Narayan and Jecksen, the boy from the orphanage, stepped into the room, flanked by Darnec Raldene and three palace guards. The bishop's cowled robe was gathered at the waist by a wide gold chain. The orphan boy wore the same hand-me-down clothes Taran had seen him in the day before. Darnec was in his guard uniform with a badge on the shoulder denoting his place as a King's Champion.

A few steps into the room, Jecksen stopped and pointed at Taran. "That's him."

The bishop gestured and for the palace guard to come forward. "Brother Taran, you are hereby arrested for treason and conspiracy against the king."

"What?" The entire group leapt to their feet.

"That's crazy," Claydan said. "Taran would never." But the conviction in his voice grew softer with every word and Taran was acutely aware that they didn't know each other as well as they once had. The prince knew Taran had betrayed his own people once. Why not again? He'd wondered how long his safe haven here in Kalanon would last. Perhaps this was the day it crumbled.

"I didn't." Taran watched as Bishop Narayan strutted. The man had never liked him. He distrusted science and had found reasons to protest Taran's lab more than once but this was extreme even for him. "Why would you think that?"

It was Jecksen who answered. The boy trembled as he spoke. "Death surrounds you. It surrounds all of you but you most of all." He pointed to Taran again, then swung his finger to point at Ula. "And you! Queen of the Dead!"

"That be enough of fingers," Ula said sharply. "Boys who judge without knowing a person should keep their fingers to themselves. Or maybe a Risen bite them off."

Jecksen jerked his hand back and cradled it to his chest.

"Prioress," Brillen chided softly. "I don't think the child is the problem here."

"True." Her beads clicked as she nodded. "Problem is adults who behave like children."

"I'm sorry about this," Darnec said. "But we have to take any accusation of a threat against the king seriously."

"Oh, of course," Taran agreed. "But, um, maybe not everyone who makes an accusation is serious?" He fingered the daggers hidden up his sleeves and watched the guards. If he acted now, he could incapacitate two of them with his daggers and the element of surprise alone. If he'd brought his poisons, he could easily have deal with all four. But that would only confirm the accusations and Darnec was almost a friend. Certainly, Sir Brannon would not be happy if Darnec were to meet an untimely end as he'd taken over many of the more distasteful duties of King's Champion.

"It would help if you could give us some evidence to back up what you're saying," Darnec said. "Your word carries a lot of weight, Bishop, but you are asking us to arrest a man for treason."

Narayan looked at Jecksen but the boy had nothing more to say. "You just need to trust me. You can't risk the king's safety."

Taran sighed and pulled the medallion out from under his tunic. "Do you know what this means?"

"It doesn't matter what it means," Narayan said. "You're a threat to the king."

"It's the King's Pass." Darnec sighed. "It means we give him the benefit of the doubt."

"It means you call King Aldan and Sir Brannon," Taran said. "And we see what they have to say about what's been going on." He paused and looked Bishop Narayan straight in the eye.

"Everything that's been going on. Like at the orphanage, for example. In Marbella's old room."

Narayan's face paled. "I..." He opened his mouth and then closed it again. His throat moved as he swallowed. "I don't think that will be necessary."

Taran steeled himself. He held the medallion out like a shield. "I think it is." He turned to Darnec. "Call the king. He's going to want to hear this."

Darnec nodded to one of the guards. "Do as he says."

Narayan sneered. "Yeah, do as he says. Everyone always does. No matter how dangerous he is, somehow he always makes the right friends. Always gets people to let him do whatever he wants. Make some dangerous lab in the basement of the church? Fine! Isolate himself from every other person in the monastery? Sure! Lock a madwoman in an orphanage and keep it secret? Why the Hooded Blood not!" He stared around the room and stabbed the air with his finger. "When it all blows up in your faces, when *he* blows up in your faces, don't come crying to me."

He turned on his heel and left the room. The orphan boy ran in his wake and the door closed behind them.

CHAPTER TWENTY-FIVE

Brannon hammered the final nail on an angle through the door of Marbella's old room at the orphanage and into the doorframe. He handed the hammer to the city guard, turned the door handle and pushed. It didn't budge.

"No one is to unseal this room, Is that clear? It will no longer be used for anything, by order of the king."

The guard nodded. "Yes, sir."

"I want someone stationed at the front door at all times and if Bishop Narayan returns at any point, you are to report it immediately." He took a few steps towards the stairs and paused. "Actually, if you notice anything unusual at all, let me know. These are vulnerable children now that they don't have Magda looking out for them. We need to do a better job of protecting them."

"Yes Sir Bloodhaw- I mean, sir Brannon."

Brannon sighed. No matter what else he did in his lifetime, it seemed he would never live down the reputation of the Bloodhawk. He'd saved many lives as a physician and many more as the Master of Investigations, but still it was the killings people admired. He slipped his hand into his pocket and felt the medal that had been retrieved from the murdered stone mason. A medal with a fake emerald, according to Alissa the jeweler and somehow that seemed appropriate. The glory of war was fake. Anyone who had truly seen battle knew that. It was blood, death, and cruel fate but people's memories were short and, of course, they were grateful for the safety those who fought and died had brought them so they made war into some kind of wonderful thing. Perhaps those protective motivations were what his admirer was thinking of when he defaulted to calling Brannon Bloodhawk. The war, for all its horror and killings, had been necessary to protect Kalanon, after all. Brannon had done his best to be a protector then and was trying to be a protector now for the orphan children Magda had left behind. He supposed there was a kind of glory or nobility in that. It was hard to remember it when the memory of thousands of drowning Nilarians was so fresh in his mind.

"Oh, Sir Brannon, I almost forgot." The guard tucked the hammer into his belt next to his sword as he spoke. "The Nilarian ambassador is waiting downstairs. She said you'd asked to meet with her. What should I tell her?"

"Ylani? Yes, of course." Brannon felt the weight of memories lighten. His history with Nilar might be a dark one, but their ambassador was another matter. "Send her up. Actually, no. I'll come down and get her."

As he reached the landing, Brannon saw Ylani waiting at the foot of the stairs. Her hat was an effusion of colorful feathers and netting. Her gown was black silk edged with fuchsia embroidery.

She looked up at him. "First a masquerade, then a cave, now an orphanage. You really know how to show a girl a good time." She smiled, but there was a sadness lurking in her eyes.

Brannon held out his hand. "I have something new to show you."

"How could I possibly say no?"

"What's wrong?" he asked quietly as they climbed the stairs together.

"I...nothing." She gave him the forced smile again. "I'm fine."

When they reached the top floor, Brannon paused in the hallway. "We're alone up here," he said. "The guards did a sweep just in case. You can tell me what's bothering you."

"It's nothing you can help with." Ylani sighed. "It seems I've allowed myself to fall out of favor back home. My government may be replacing me."

"What?" Brannon stared. "Why would you think that? Why would they do it?"

Ylani shrugged. "With what happened with the swords and with my brother. Insisting on the return of the slaves. There's a case to be made that I've helped Kalanon more than Nilar at times."

"But your job is to build the relationship between the countries. And you've only done what's right in each of those cases. You certainly haven't always done what Aldan wanted."

"True, but Alyra and I have a history and she's been determined to make waves for me."

"What does this mean?" Brannon tried to keep his voice light. Whatever this fledgling relationship he had with Ylani was, it relied on her being in Alapra as the Nilarian Ambassador.

"It means I'll have to go home," she said, confirming his worst fears. "And Alyra will take over."

Brannon shook his head. "No. That's crazy. I'll talk to Aldan. I'll talk to your government - tell them what a difference you've made. No one else could have done what you've done here."

This time Ylani's smile was real, even if her eyes still held sadness. "Thank you, but I don't think an endorsement from the Bloodhawk will help. You're still something of a bogyman back home." She patted his shoulder. "I've sent to my government for confirmation. With luck, I'll still have some allies who can help turn this around. If not...well, I'll get to know your parents, I suppose." She gave him a wink.

"Blood and Tears," Brannon said. "I'm not sure how I feel about that!"

She laughed. "Come on. What do you have to show me?"

Brannon pushed his feelings about her job aside and led Ylani through the gate at the end of the hallway to the door of Marbella's old room.

Ylani raised her eyebrows as she took in the metal bars and the nails. "Interesting decor."

"Can you get any sort of impressions from it?" Brannon asked. "You know, with your..." He wiggled his fingers in a mystical gesture.

Ylani chuckled. "The Instinct, you mean? It's not really something that works on command but I can try."

"I just need to know what Narayan was up to in here."

Her smile vanished. "I heard what Taran saw. I'm assuming you have the bishop already in custody."

Brannon sighed. "He's in hiding. But we'll find him." It felt horribly familiar after spending so long chasing Nycol around the city to be now trying to find another person who had hurt the children in this orphanage.

"Have you talked to the children?"

"Not yet. I wanted to get as much context as I can before I make them talk about something traumatic."

She nodded, biting her lower lip thoughtfully. "That makes sense. Let me see what I can get."

Brannon stepped back to give her space to work.

Ylani placed the palm of her hand on the surface of the door and closed her eyes. Her breathing slowed and deepened. An aura of stillness flowed out and from the point at which her skin connected with the wood.

Brannon held his breath as he watched, searching her face for any sign of what she might be sensing. Her eyelids twitched and she tilted her head to the side. Then she took a sharp breath and opened her eyes.

"Anything?" Brannon said.

Ylani shook her head. "There's too much residue of Taran's friend Marbella in that room. Her madness is a curtain in front of anything else. I don't think children have been physically hurt but...I can't tell for sure. I'm sorry."

Brannon's chest tightened. He'd hoped for more confirmation before he spoke to the children themselves. These children had been through enough trauma already in their lives. If he couldn't protect them from being abused further, what was the point of all his efforts? What was the point of the war? To fight off an enemy and then hunt down murderers and yet find danger in the very home he'd returned them to...that was a failure, not just for him personally but for all of Kalanon.

"Are you okay?" Ylani's voice held concern.

Brannon nodded, swallowing past the tightness. "I'm just tired. I didn't sleep well."

The recent nightmare had stirred up memories and emotions he'd thought he'd had under control. He supposed it was only to be expected with the return of so many prisoners and an influx of new Nilarians here in Alapra, but the image of those drowned soldiers had left him feeling raw. Now the thought of these children being at risk was sand scraping at the wound.

Feelings of guilt about Nilarian deaths and children in danger brought up the death of one particular child. The son of a Nilarian General who had been served his father as a squire and attacked Brannon in response to seeing his father cut down. Much as he'd tried to avoid it, Brannon had been forced to kill the young man with his dead father's sword. The blade sinking into the furious, desperate boy's body was an image that had haunted Brannon for years. The warm blood from father and son mixing on his hands was a red stain he'd struggled to wash off. Now that the war was over, there was no way he would allow any child to be hurt if he could avoid it.

A scream pierced through his shield of guilt and struck deep into the memories, scattering them. He jerked his head up. "What? Where did that come from?"

Ylani gestured to the sealed-up room. "Not...?"

Brannon focused. "No. But near." He turned slowly, listening for the sound. "Here!" He led the way back down the hallway, through the grilled gate, to the next door on the left. He turned the handle and opened it carefully.

A whimper came from the room within.

"Hello?" Brannon called. "Are you okay?"

The bedroom had been converted into a storage space, likely because of its proximity to the room that had once housed Marbella during her madness. Shelves, filled with toys, clothes, and bedlinen, lined the walls and ran in a row down the middle of the room. At the far end, an adolescent boy cowered behind a pile of pillows with blood seeping through his shirt. There was no one else in the room.

Brannon ran toward him.

"No! Stay away! Please, no."

Brannon slowed down. "We won't hurt you." He held out his hand, showing they were empty of weapons. The boy looked familiar. "You're Jecksen, aren't you? We met the other day. I'm Brannon. I know Shalyn, remember? Is she with you?"

Jecksen shook his head and pressed himself into the pile of pillows. The red patch on his shirt spread wider. "She's looking for the mage, like always. Please don't hurt me. Where's my father?"

"I won't hurt you," Brannon said. "I just want to help. Let me see that wound."

"You will. You kill everyone," the boy said, his eyes wide.

It hurt to see that fear in a child, but Brannon pushed it aside. It was his legacy, the trouble with being the Bloodhawk. "I won't," he promised. "I'm here to help. That's all." He took the boy's arm gently and examined the cut on his shoulder. It was deep. He frowned and grabbed a wad of pillowcases from a nearby shelf, pressing them onto the wound to staunch the bleeding. "Is this from a sword? Who stabbed you?"

"You," the boy said.

Brannon half laughed, startled. "No, it definitely wasn't me." He put a hand on the boy's forehead, checking temperature. There wasn't enough blood for Jecksen to be hallucinating just yet.

Jecksen frowned at his own words and shook his head, dislodging Brannon's hand. "No, that's not right. It was...no one. I was just waiting for my father to come back and it happened."

"What do you mean?"

The boy shrugged, then yelped as the movement tore at his injury.

"Stay still," Brannon told him. "You're going to

need stitches for this."

"Who's your father?" Ylani asked gently.

Jecksen swallowed. His voice was barely a whisper. "The bishop."

Brannon's eyebrows rose. "Bishop Narayan is your father?"

When Jecksen stayed silent, staring fearfully at Brannon, Ylani touched his hand and prompted. "You can tell us."

The boy nodded.

Brannon exchanged a glance with Ylani. He hadn't been aware Narayan had a child. And if he did, why was the boy living at the orphanage instead of with his father? And who was the boy's mother?

Whatever the answers to those questions, the bleeding from the boy's injured shoulder needed care and there was most likely an attacker somewhere in the orphanage. He turned to Ylani. "I should have the guards do a search. Whoever did this can't have gotten far."

Ylani shook her head. "Far? You heard him, Brannon, he said it was no one."

"He's confused," Brannon pointed out. "He doesn't know."

Ylani gestured around them. "There's only one door in and out of this room and we were standing in the hallway the entire time. We would have seen anyone leave. There was no one."

"Hooded shit." Brannon thumped the shelves and they shook. The pain in his palm was a fraction of his frustration. "This is another magical attack then. It has to be. How? How is he doing this?"

"Who?"

"Nycol, of course. Who else?"

Ylani shook her head. "I'm not sure he is. There's too much going on that we can't piece together properly. He's a bad guy, don't get me wrong, but this...it doesn't feel right."

Brannon sighed. "We need to do a sweep of the house anyway and look for clues. But you're right. Nothing about any of this feels right." How did the murders of a homeless veteran, a stonemason and his wife, and a tailor fit in with fake gemstones and a threat against the king? Nothing was clear and the one suspect he'd been sure of was now locked up and yet magical attacks were still happening. "Can you keep pressure on this cut? I'll talk to the guards and find some supplies to patch him up properly." At least this victim was one he could save. This child was one he'd protected.

Ylani took over holding the wadded fabric against the boy's shoulder but when her fingers touched where the blood had soaked through, she stiffened.

"Ylani? What's wrong?"

"Blood and Tears," she gasped. "That's unexpected."

"What?"

"This boy." Ylani turned to Brannon, her eyes wide. "He has the Instinct."

CHAPTER TWENTY-SIX

The cell was empty when Draeson arrived. The bars and mirrors were all in place and a half-eaten loaf of bread lay on the floor next to a thin blanket but Nycol was nowhere to be seen. Draeson froze, his eyes flicking around the room, searching for tell-tale signs.

The guard assigned to watch over the prisoner stared with wide eyes, his mouth working silently as he struggled to find words. "I don't understand how this happened," he said at last. "I only looked away for a moment. I...I've never had a prisoner escape before."

Draeson gritted his teeth. "Well, I doubt your other prisoners have been mages. Maybe try not to fall asleep on the job next time." He waved his hand. "Go! See if you can find him. He can't have gotten far."

The man gave a startled nod and ran out the

door.

Draeson walked around the room, circling the cage in slow, careful steps. He sent his magical senses into the quartz mirror spell, inspecting the edges of the boundary. All was intact. He pushed a little more power into the spell and the mirrors gleamed brighter for a moment.

He stepped back. "The bread is a nice touch. But you forget, I already know you're good at illusions."

The air in the cell rippled and the bread vanished. In its place was the trapped Nilarian mage. "It was worth a try," he said with a shrug. "I certainly had your little guard fooled."

"Not exactly difficult." Draeson folded his arms. "But what was the point? Surely you didn't think I would deactivate the spell or unlock your cell."

"Why to get you alone, of course." Nycol winked. "It's been far too long since I had you to myself."

Draeson snorted. "The last time I was alone with you, you used magic to put me into a coma. That's not something I'm eager to repeat, even if you could."

"If?" Nycol raised an eyebrow.

"You've used the mirror spell yourself so you know it can't be undone from the inside."

Nycol pursed his lips. "Are you so sure?"

"Yes. I've tried."

"I remember."

Draeson frowned, irritation flickering in his chest. "That's the second time you've implied knowing me from the past. But we'd never met before that day at the Blue Rose. There aren't many mages in the world. I don't forget the ones I know."

"You don't forget but you don't stay in touch either." Nycol chuckled. "Still, time changes us all. Do you really think you're so recognizable looking the way you do?"

Truthfully, he did not. His current youthful state was a very recent occurrence. Anyone who had known him prior to the last few years would remember him as an elderly man. Binding his life force to that of the royal line had kept Draeson alive and given him the time to study magic but it had left him trapped in an aging body for almost four hundred years.

He looked away. "No, I don't suppose they would. But somehow you do."

Nycol shrugged. "Yes, well. I keep tabs. And when I heard you'd become suddenly rejuvenated, I was curious."

Curious and dangerous. Draeson didn't intend to let himself be sweet talked by this man again. "Why are you here, Nycol? Why ally yourself to slave traders and murderers? Why stay when you've been found out?"

Nycol sighed. "You really haven't figured it out yet?"

"Figured what out?"

"I'm here for you, Draeson. To reconnect. The rest of that stuff is meaningless. Just a way to fill in the time. I want us to learn from each other. To be together. We can ease each other's loneliness."

Draeson scowled. "Who said I was lonely?"

"Have you ever met a mage who wasn't?"

An ache pulsed in Draeson's chest as if the hole he carried there expanded. Lonely? Of course he was lonely. He'd spent several lifetimes alone. Attempting to form romantic relationships had only emphasized the gap. Anyone he cared for would have a normal human lifespan. He would not. Death took everyone from him while he was forced to watch and do nothing. It was the sacrifice he had made for the sake of his power. The trade for being able to protect Kalanon. Brief moments of connectedness were all he ever had with lovers because it was all there could ever be. To connect on a deeper level invited grief and pain. Unless...unless the person he connected with was also a mage. Also immortal. "I haven't met any mages at all for decades," he said. "Maybe longer."

"Me neither." A silence grew between them, filling the space until Nycol shifted his feet. "Did you ever try to train any?"

Draeson looked away. "No. You?"

"A few. They never advanced fast enough. You know the first test of a mage."

"Yeah. Immortality." Becoming a mage required intensive study and training - more than one lifetime could contain. Any mage's first task was to discover a way to live beyond a single lifetime. For most, it was a task they failed and death found them unfulfilled. Draeson drew a long shuddering breath and let it out slowly.

Nycol nodded. "You are lonely, aren't you? How can you not be? Our lives are so long and empty because everyone we care for dies. What if we stayed together? Lived together. Combined, we could do anything. Go anywhere."

Draeson looked back at him sharply. Live with a Nilarian who had murdered and enslaved Kalans? The very idea of it was absurd. But then, mages were few and far between and, if he was honest, often difficult to get along with. One didn't live hundreds of years without getting a little set in your ways and making the odd bad decision. That didn't mean they couldn't change. "I wouldn't want to go anywhere. I'm Kalan. I won't leave my country unprotected."

"Fine. We stay in Kalanon. We could rule the Hooded place if you want. Who's going to stop us?"

"I will."

"Fine, fine. We play it your way. You'll be a good influence on me." Nycol grinned. "But think about it. We will be around for a long time, you and I. Why not do it together?"

Draeson watched the other man's eyes, searching for any hint of deceit. In this, at least, Nycol seemed sincere. "Who are you?" he said at last. "If you say we've met in the past, tell me who you are."

The trapped mage spread his hands. "Think hard, Draeson. You're right that I know the quartz mirror spell well. Tell me, who taught it to you?"

"Are you saying we had a teacher in common?" Draeson snorted before he could help himself. The man's claims were getting more and more ridiculous. "I was taught that particular spell by my second master when I was still an apprentice mage. A powerful woman named..." He trailed off as the memory rose, his eyes wide.

"Yes?" Nycol smiled. "And what was her name?"

"Nycola. Her name was Nycola." He frowned. "It's a coincidence. Anyone can take a name that sounds like another."

"True. But, like you, I prefer to keep my own name through the ages."

"You?" Draeson stumbled back, the shock of it hitting him like a wave. "That's impossible. You were a woman."

"What of it? You were older when I knew you and now you're young. We work with magic,

Draeson. Why should we be surprised by impossible things?"

"But how?"

Nycol grinned. "Do you want me to tell you? I'll show you mine if you show me yours."

"You first."

"Really? Are you going to be that petty?"

Draeson shrugged. "Show me a sign of good faith and maybe I'll believe you're serious. So far I haven't heard anything that couldn't be the desperate manipulation of a trapped man." He paused. "Or woman."

The corner of Nycol's lips twitched up. "Okay," he said. "Fine. It's not like you're going to use it anyway. Your method of immortality is obviously much better. Or maybe it's just the same."

"Tell me and we'll see."

"I..." Nycol made abstract circles with his hand. "I switch bodies. Always have. When one body wears out, I'm able to take another as long as it's related to me."

Draeson's jaw dropped. "You steal another person's body? A family member?"

"Yes."

"But what happens to them?"

"They go into the old body and I take care of them for their twilight years."

"*Their* twilight years? Those twilight years are *yours*. You're stealing life from people. Stealing who they are!"

Nycol grimaced. "See, that's the problem. It's not ideal. And I've tried, but I just can't see another way of doing it satisfactorily. I've never wanted to wander around in an old, falling apart body like you did and the only way I could avoid that was to jump into someone else's. But then I hear you're suddenly young again and...how did you do it, Draeson? If I know, then I can stop being this parasite on my family lineage. I can just stay in a body I like. Don't you see? It's best for everyone if you tell me."

Draeson stepped back. After a life as long as he'd had, very little horrified him but this...the theft of someone's body. Of their life and very identity. "You're a monster." How many people had Nycol done this to? How many young lives had lost their vitality and been thrust into old age before their time? He remembered the aches, the pains, the endless difficulties of a body that felt so much older than his inner self. He'd come by his aged body naturally. He'd chosen to give up his youth in pursuit of magic. It was a trade he'd sometimes grieved for but never regretted because the choice had been his. Nycol's victims had been ripped from youth through no fault of their own. Their lives stolen before they'd truly begun. "No." He stepped back from the bars. From Nycol. "No, this time you can feel your true age. You're going to rot in that cage and in that body until you die. I don't care how many centuries it takes. You can feel every wrinkle, every ache, everything you forced those people to bear on your behalf. You've earned many lifetimes of suffering, Nycol. And it's about time you paid."

Nycol sneered. "Oh, come on. You can't tell me you didn't do something a little underhanded to achieve this." He waved his hand up and down Draeson's body. "That power is beyond even your little friend there."

The dragon tattoo on Draeson's neck hissed.

"Come on. We had a deal. What happened to operating in good faith?"

Draeson shook his head. "You proposed a deal. It's not the same thing. Why would I deal with someone I already have trapped? You have no leverage here."

"Other than your concerns about the king."

Draeson's eyes narrowed. "You already claimed you have nothing to do with that. I think I believe you now. I think you're an evil piece of shit but there are things happening in Alapra that you have nothing to do with. If you did, you'd have played those cards by now."

"Are you really willing to take that risk?"

"You're powerless in here. So yeah, I think I am."

Nycol growled and struck at the bars with the palm of his hand. The metal vibrated with the force of it. "I'll get out of here eventually. You have to know that."

Draeson shrugged and gestured to the mirrors. "I don't see how."

"You're still only my student." Nycol's lip curled. He stepped back from the bars and raised his hands. He linked his thumbs together and flapped his fingers like bird wings. Sparks flew from his palms as if from a stoked furnace. He flapped them again and flames flickered over his skin, flaring out from his fingertips, longer and hotter with each movement until they were wide, fiery wings, as broad as a man was tall. A beaked head of fire rose up from Nycol's thumbs and the creature screeched. A flame bird.

A jolt of fear ran through Draeson. Despite his confidence that the mirror spell could contain it, Nycol's magic had proven formidable in the past. "Don't," he said.

Nycol stepped back, trailing flames like streamers, and thrust his hands forward, launching the firebird at Draeson. The creature swelled as it flew, beak wide and flaming wings extended the full width of the cell. Its screech pierced Draeson's ears in a high-pitched stab of burning pain.

Draeson threw himself to one side, dodging the wave of heat. He crouched next to the guard's desk, eyes on Nycol's magic, his own power itching in his fingertips.

The firebird battered at the edge of the cell. The

flames roiled up and down the bars, washing across the mirrors in a bright, churning wave. The fireball swallowed Nycol and the entire cell, giving it the appearance of a captured sun. The roar of flames filled the room.

The mirrors around the cell glowed with cool silver light, rectangles of ice in the orange fire. For a moment, it seemed the mirrors would be overwhelmed. The flames licked over them, attempting to swallow them whole. Then the silver light pulsed brighter and the flames receded, sucked slowly into the reflective surface of the mirrors and extinguished. The roar of the fire quieted and the smell of soot filled the air.

Draeson took a slow, deep breath and stood, facing the cell.

The floor was blackened, as was the ceiling above, but the damage was contained. The mirror spell held.

In the center of the cell, Nycol stood, unsinged and chuckling. "Almost," he said. "You should have seen your face."

Draeson scowled. "You're lucky you didn't kill yourself. Next time you probably will."

Nycol blew him a kiss. "Wait and see."

Draeson snorted and turned away. Unsettled as he'd been, he knew the mirror spell was strong enough to contain whatever Nycol could throw at it. There was no possible way for magic to exit that cell. Powerful as he may be, much of Nycol's magic relied on reagents and he had none of those with him now.

Just the same, as he closed the door behind him, Draeson vowed to return and reinforce the containment magic earlier tomorrow. Better safe than sorry.

CHAPTER TWENTY-SEVEN

The door slammed closed behind Magus Draeson and Shalyn swallowed hard. Her hands and knees trembled and her breath was ragged.

"You can come out now, little one."

It was the man in the cage. The one who had cast the inferno just moments ago and who had been partially responsible for kidnapping her and murdering her father. She'd never thought to come face to face with him again but...he knew she was there.

She pushed the tablecloth aside and climbed out from under the food cart, stretching her limbs as she did so. She turned to face the mage. His grey flecked hair and smug smile clicked into place with the hazy memories she had of her kidnapping. It was him, all right. But he was trapped now and unable to harm her.

She raised a finger in a crude salute.

Magus Nycol chuckled. "Nice to see you again, young lady. But I assume you didn't sneak in here just to see me."

Shalyn glanced toward the door.

"Oh!" The mage leaned back against the bars on the far side of his cage, seemingly oblivious to the soot they'd been coated in. "Of course. You've been following *him*."

She raised her chin. "No. You don't know anything. The Hooded One will come for you soon and then you'll get it."

"Perhaps." He leaned forward and lowered his voice almost to a whisper. "But he hasn't come for me in hundreds of years. Do you know why?"

Shalyn swallowed. "You're a mage."

"That's right. And just like your hero Draeson, I'm immortal."

Fury rose in Shalyn. "No. You're a murderer. Draeson will kill you. He's just waiting for the king to say so. You'll see." Just as quickly, the fire faded to insecurity. This man was alive and her father was dead. That didn't make sense. Nothing made sense since she'd become an orphan.

"He hasn't killed me yet, has he?" Nycol wrinkled his nose. "So...maybe he won't. We mages stick together, you know."

"Yeah, that's why you're in prison," she snapped. "Because he likes you."

He laughed loudly at that, a rich, open sounding laugh. "You might have a point there." Then he leaned forward, both hands wrapped around bars of the cage on opposite sides of his face. "But tell me this: Does he like you? Does he even notice you exist? I've seen you here many times. You follow him around but I don't think he even sees you. Or am I wrong?"

Shalyn stared at the ground, her chest heavy. The truth was, Draeson never visited and rarely even acknowledged her when she showed up to see what he was doing. Sir Brannon had spoken with her a few times, but the magus hardly at all.

"I don't mean to upset you, child." Nycol's voice was gentle. Kind even, with none of the mocking tone he'd had earlier. "I just know what he's like. It hurts when someone you admire doesn't see the value in you."

Shalyn shook her head and swallowed. "He will. I'll show him. I could be a good assistant. I could help or learn magic or...something..." She trailed off, embarrassed. It all sounded so stupid when she said it out loud. Why would Magus Draeson care about her at all? Nycol was right. There'd been no sign the mage gave a crap about her. He'd rescued her from the kidnappers, sure, but ever since he'd ignored her whenever she was near. Even at the masquerade, he'd thought she was just a nuisance. The thought that he would take the time to teach her magic or let her participate in any way was probably delusional.

She felt the tears well up in her eyes and blinked them away furiously. She had no one else. Not anymore. She would make Draeson see how valuable she could be. She wouldn't stop until he did.

Nycol watched her with kind eyes. "He's a fool if he doesn't see your value, my dear. People are so often blind to what's right under their nose. But I can see how clever and beautiful you are." He slid down the bars and sat cross legged on the stone floor. "You and I both see much more than he does, I think."

Shalyn wiped her cheek. "What do you mean?"

"You and I are honest with ourselves. Most people, when they don't have anyone else to lie to, will still lie to themselves. I don't think you do that. You know what you want and you go after it. I admire that. I admire you."

She sniffed hard and stared at him. "You do?"

"Yeah. I do."

"Why?"

Nycol gestured her to come closer. "I was very much like you when I was younger," he said. "I was forced to raise myself in a lot of ways. I know what it's like to be the only one you can rely on."

Shalyn swallowed the lump in her throat. Her mother had been gone for years and since her father's death she'd been stuck at the orphanage. She had friends there but she didn't want it to be her home. It couldn't be. If Magus Draeson wasn't willing to take her in - or couldn't see the potential for doing so - she'd have to find another way. "How did you do it?" she asked, and her feet took a few hesitant steps towards the cage.

Nycol smiled. "I did what you're trying to do," he said. "I found someone who could teach me magic." He paused, his gaze drilling into her. "I could do that for you."

Shalyn's eyes widened. "I..." There was no point denying she wanted it. She'd given that much away already. But there was little reason to trust this man when the one who had been her rescuer seemed so unreliable. "Why?"

"Because you're lonely. And so am I." Nycol shrugged. "Plus, I have a gift for identifying who has the spark. Not everyone can learn magic. Most will waste their lives trying. You, however...you have it. You could be a powerful mage if you wanted. No one could ever harm you again."

Her feet moved a few more paces toward him of their own accord. Shalyn forced herself to stop. This was a man in prison. He was the definition of untrustworthy and yet he was offering her more than she could have ever dreamed. Power. Magic. Strength. She would do almost anything to have those qualities. Almost.

"I won't let you out," she said. "If that's what you're thinking. I don't even have the key."

Nycol nodded. "Quite right. I don't expect you to. How about this? Go away and think about what I've said. If you think Draeson will make a similar offer, fine. But if you want to truly learn how to keep yourself safe in this world, come back tomorrow and talk to me. Just talk. And we will begin your training. Does that sound fair?"

Shalyn didn't trust herself to answer so she simply turned and ran from the room. It wasn't until she was halfway down the street, surrounded by adults who could ignore or harm her as they chose, that she made her decision. She would return in the morning. Just to talk.

CHAPTER TWENTY-EIGHT

Brannon, Ylani, and Jecksen were ushered from the main throne room, through King Aldan's private audience chamber, and out onto a wide stone porch overlooking a private courtyard garden. The porch held a set of cushioned furniture and a large marble bust of King Aldan's father, King Raldan. A balustrade edged the stone expanse, broken by three wide stairs leading to the garden. A large urn on either side of the stairs held long, colorful poles topped with the pennants of every territory in the kingdom.

The king leaned against the balustrade, sunlight turning the gold of his hair into a halo of light. "So what have you come to tell me today, old friend? We have a mage in custody and a bishop on the run. How much more can there be?"

Brannon gestured to Jecksen to sit on an over-sized velvet armchair. The boy pushed himself so far back into the chair that his feet swung loose above the floor like a much younger, smaller child.

"That's just it," he said. "There is more. And I think it includes a threat to your life."

Aldan sighed. "This again? I can't shut down my royal duties because of a homeless man's delusions and a torn tapestry, Brannon. Even if said homeless man is a murdered war veteran."

"What if it's someone with specialist knowledge of the future?"

The king looked sharply at Ylani. "Ambassador?"

Ylani shook her head. "No, not me."

"Then who?"

She pointed to Jecksen.

"Seriously?"

"The boy has the Instinct," Brannon told him. "Ylani sensed in him. And he was attacked by magic, which makes me inclined to think there's something to it."

Aldan frowned. "Attacked by magic? Are you saying we have another rogue mage running around Alapra?"

"I..." Brannon shrugged. "Honestly, we don't know yet. But maybe. It seems Nycol might not be responsible for all the recent attacks."

The king massaged his temple. "Well that is a

concern. And you think this boy knows something about it?"

"The boy himself, no," Brannon said. "But his father might. According to the boy, Bishop Narayan is his father."

"Really?" Aldan's eyes widened. "That's interesting."

"Not as interesting as the fact that Narayan's abuse of children at the orphanage was apparently an attempt to test *them* for the Instinct as well." A dull ache of nausea sat in Brannon's stomach at the thought of children chained up in that room. The sensation deepened as he saw a flicker of recognition in Aldan's eyes. "You know something."

The king grimaced and shook his head. "Not really. It was a long time ago..."

"Tell me!"

Aldan glanced at Ylani and Jecksen, then gestured to Brannon. "Walk with me."

Brannon followed the king down the stairs and between the bundles of pennants. A few steps into the garden, just beyond earshot of the porch, Aldan paused in front of a wooden bench. Rather than sitting, he gave it a gentle kick with the toe of one foot and hesitated.

"What is it?" Brannon asked. "I won't tell them if you don't want them to know but I think we can trust Ylani."

Aldan gave a weak smile. "I know you do. But I'm held to even stricter guidelines than you when it comes to state secrets." He glanced back to ensure they hadn't been followed, then continued. "This was back in the war. I don't know for certain but there was a rumor that the church and my father had an arrangement."

Brannon frowned. "What do you mean?"

"Let's just say that this Instinct of Ylani's sounds like something I've heard of before. The story goes that the church once had a group of people with such gifts and they reported directly to the king. They were known as the Order of Oracles and they guided kings with secret knowledge and sometimes even could predict the future."

"What do you mean 'once had'? If that was true, they would now report to you, wouldn't they? A group like that would have changed the war entirely!"

"Well, that's the thing. The rumor was the Oracles were a big part of my father's initial strategy and in the early days of the war, we held our own. But then the Oracles and my father had a disagreement and he didn't take it well."

Brannon could well imagine. "Your father didn't appreciate criticism."

Aldan gave a wry chuckle. "Not as a rule, no. The Order disappeared and they were never heard of again."

A chill slid across Brannon's skin. "So then, with no oracles to guide him, he..."

"He was killed. Yes." Aldan shrugged. "It's hard to say if there's any truth to it. I was young at the time and my father kept his cards close to his chest. I had to pick up command with what I had available. But if Bishop Narayan knew about the Conclave. If he's trying to reform it and doing so without my knowledge...we should be ready for anything."

Brannon nodded, slowly turning the information over in his mind. There were so many pieces to this puzzle. Puzzles. He couldn't be sure all the pieces belonged together but there was something that clicked. "The first murdered man," he said quietly. "The General. His real name was Jemiren. Does that sound familiar to you?"

Aldan shook his head. "I'm sorry, no. Should it?"

"A woman who was a childhood friend of his told us he was once part of a special unit attached to the church in some way. She didn't know how. And Master Jordell says he seemed scared to go to the church." He looked up and met the king's eyes. "What if he was part of it? If his unit was connected to the Conclave of Oracles somehow? And he was killed to cover it up?"

"Hooded shit," the king swore. "This is going to bite me in the ass, isn't it?"

Brannon chuckled. "Sorry, but it might. We need to know more and I think this kid might have some answers. At the very least, he might be able to help us find Narayan."

Aldan sighed. "Okay. So what has he foreseen, exactly?"

Brannon clenched and unclenched his fist. "It's hard to say."

"Well, let's ask him." Aldan strode back to the porch and Brannon hurried to keep up. Aldan took the steps in a single stride and looked Jecksen over. "Stand up boy. Tell me what you know."

Jecksen slid off the chair and made an awkward bow, stumbled a step, then straightened up. "I...I don't know what you mean, your majesty."

"This Instinct tells you there's a threat to my life?"

The boy nodded silently.

"What else does it tell you?"

"I don't know, your majesty."

Aldan pursed his lips. "So who is going to kill me?"

Jecksen stared at his feet.

"If you know, tell us," Brannon urged.

The boy's gaze flicked upward and he raised his hand, pointing a finger at Brannon. "It's you." His voice cracked. "You'll kill us all."

Brannon felt a jolt in his gut. This was the same nonsense Narayan had been spouting when confronted by Taran. Like father, like son. Both of them seemed quick to blame whoever was nearest. "I would never..."

Aldan laughed. "Of course not. Want to try again, kid?"

Jecksen opened his mouth, then closed it again. He lowered his hand and stepped back, bumping his calves against the chair.

"It doesn't really work like that." Ylani stepped forward, placing herself between the boy and the king. "Even for the best of us, the Instinct can be hard to interpret or understand. Some people never grasp its use. Jecksen's seems to be a very specific sense. He can identify danger but maybe the exact source of the danger isn't clear. He could be sensing that Brannon is nearby when it happens. Or even just his presence now is confusing him. That doesn't mean the threat isn't real."

"I'm the king, Ylani. There's always some kind of danger around me. I'm going to need more detail than that." The king glanced over Ylani's shoulder at the boy and then back to her. "What about your own talents, Ambassador. Can you provide any more information?"

She shook her head. "I'm sorry, no. It's possible I'll get something later. It usually helps if I'm near the person involved but, as I said, the Instinct is tricky."

Brannon saw the thoughts flicker across his

friend's face. Aldan had a reputation to uphold. He was a war king. A commander. He'd been a good king in peacetime too but he was not a man who hid from danger. Especially when the danger was so ill defined. "At least put a few extra guards on duty, Aldan. For my peace of mind, if nothing else."

Aldan grinned. "I can do that for an old friend."

"Thank you." Brannon glanced across at Ylani. "Perhaps there's something else you could do for me, your majesty."

"Uh-oh," said Aldan. "It makes me nervous when you say 'your majesty'."

Brannon smiled, but he knew it didn't reach his eyes. "Ambassador Ylani has been a valuable ally to my team and to Kalanon as a whole. We can't allow her to be replaced."

"Ah." Aldan turned away. "I should have stopped you after the request for extra guards."

Brannon reached out to touch his friend's shoulder. "Your majesty knows the value of an ally..."

"Brannon." Ylani caught his eye and gave a small shake of her head. "Don't."

He frowned. "Don't you want to stay?"

"Of course I do but it's not up to us." She tilted her head and the brim of her hat cast a shadow over her eyes. "It's not right to make that kind of request of King Aldan."

"I disagree." Brannon folded his arms.

"Kalanon owes you more than one debt."

"I suspect that's part of the problem," Ylani murmured. "If I'm shown favoritism here, why would my own people trust me?"

Brannon swallowed. His mind turned over possible answers. That she didn't need Nilar, she could stay here. That they surely would understand that someone with strong ties in both countries would be the perfect bridge between them. That he didn't want her to leave. Not now. Maybe not ever. Could he say that? Thinking it was strange enough.

"Brannon, you know she's right." This time it was Aldan who rested a hand on Brannon's shoulder. "And even if I wanted to intervene, I have no authority over who the Nilarian government chooses as their representative. Even trying would give them an opening to cause all sorts of difficulties for us. They'd accuse me of trying to influence treaty negotiators and trade deals. What would our people say if Nilarians said we couldn't send your parents as our Ambassadors and had to send someone of their choosing? We'd never stand for it."

Brannon's heart sank. "But you know she's the best person for the job."

Aldan sighed. "I do. But it doesn't matter. This is politics." He gave a respectful nod to Ylani. "I've no doubt at all that the Ambassador will succeed in whatever she and her government choose next for her. We would welcome her in Kalanon again should she visit, but I cannot interfere with the judgement of Nilar or its employment decisions. No matter how much it hurts my friends."

Brannon stuffed his hands in his pockets and clenched them. The sharp edges of Donal the stone mason's medal dug into his palm. He'd taken to carrying it with him as a reminder of the victims of the case but now it was a touchstone of duty. He'd sacrificed a lot to his duty to Kalanon, both during the war and afterward. Now, it seemed a relationship with Ylani would be a casualty as well.

"Thank you, King Aldan." Ylani's voice was soft. "I understand and agree completely."

The edges of the medal pressed even harder in Brannon's hand. He wasn't the only one with a duty to his country. Ylani would never give up on her people either. They would always be pulled in opposite directions. It seemed that even during peace time, the world was too hostile a place to let whatever fragile feelings were between them grow. The political difficulties that were the legacy of war between their countries would always provide a shadow of threat to any relationship they had.

He searched for the right words to respond when Jecksen spoke instead.

"It's now."

Brannon shook himself from his thoughts. "What is?"

"Danger." Jecksen's voice cracked with terror. He flung himself to the ground beside the armchair and shielded his head with his hands. "It's now!"

A familiar whistle sounded over the garden.

Brannon turned to see a wartime memory made real. A hail of arrows streaked toward them.

"Get down!" He flung himself at the gap between Ylani and the king, arms spread to catch them both across the chest as he fell. His weight knocked them both off their feet. Aldan's warrior training kicked in and the king twisted to land safely even as the first arrows passed over them.

Ylani tucked her head into her chest as she landed, protecting her skull but letting out an "Oof" as the air left her lungs on impact.

Brannon tried to hold his own head up, but with his arms caught up in the others, he was unable to catch himself and the point of his chin hit the tiles with a painful crack. He rolled over to watch the arrows fly overhead, keeping Ylani in his sight as he did. "Are you okay?" he whispered.

"Yeah."

"Stay down."

Dozens of red-feathered arrows bounced off the stone wall and clattered to the floor or embedded themselves into the door with rattling thuds like hail.

Brannon rolled the other way and exchanged a look with Aldan. "How could they get so many archers into the palace?"

Aldan shook his head. "It should be impossible."

Should be but clearly wasn't. Brannon touched his chin and saw blood on his fingers. He wiped them on his shirt and looked back toward Jecksen. The boy was sheltered behind the chair, probably the best protected of all of them. If it hadn't been for his warning, they'd likely all be dead. Even now, the longer they sheltered in place, the more chance a stray arrow would find its mark. "We're going to have to crawl. Stay low and try to keep behind something as much as possible. Jecksen, stay there for now. Aldan, I'm going to roll over you before we start moving."

"And put yourself between me and the arrows? This isn't the time for extra heroics, Brannon. You've saved my life once already today."

"Shut up and be king, Aldan. If either you or Ylani get hit, we have a massive incident. I'm expendable."

"You're not..." Aldan started.

"By comparison, I am. Now shush." Brannon edged closer to the king. He'd have to slip over the top of his friend but quickly. The higher from the floor he was, the better target he made. He felt a hand touch his arm and looked back.

"Be careful," Ylani whispered.

Brannon nodded and she withdrew the hand.

He tensed, ready to move but then, as suddenly as it started, the rain of arrows stopped. There was no gradual slowing. The arrows simply ceased, cut off in an instant, with no stragglers at all. He froze, listening for voices, or the twang of bowstrings, rattle of quivers, anything at all. There was nothing.

"Has it stopped?" Ylani sounded shaken but restrained.

Brannon hesitated. No matter how a gang of archers had snuck into the palace, they'd need to escape quickly now that the attack had taken place. "I think so. But stay down just in case. Were you hit?"

"No. I'm fine."

"It would seem you were right about young Jecksen," Aldan murmured.

Brannon crawled forward and risked a peek between balustrades across the garden. "Where were they shooting from? Is that...?"

"Hooded shit," Aldan swore. "That's Claydan's suite over there. Those bastards have my son!" He stood up and ran for the door.

"Aldan!" Brannon shouted. "Get down! You're a target!"

The king ignored him, yanked open the door and disappeared into the audience chamber beyond.

Brannon swore and scrambled after him. As he reached for the doorhandle, he froze, eyes wide with shock. The arrows - the dozens and dozens of redfletched arrows that had poured onto the porch - were all gone. The wood of the door was gouged from their sharp points but the arrows themselves were gone. "What the...?" It wasn't possible. Arrows didn't vanish. But then, people didn't hang with invisible rope or burst into flame for no reason either. "Hooded Blood! It's not archers. It's magic!" He jerked open the door and raced after the king. "Aldan, stop! Stop!"

Aldan ran, unheeding, through the palace corridors that circled the garden courtyard, taking the shortest route to his son's suite that didn't involve an exposed dash through the garden itself. Brannon hurried in his wake, shouting for guards to join them as they went. They reached Claydan's door with a trail of guards stretched out like a comet behind them.

Brannon caught his friend's shoulder and pulled him back. "Let me go first," he said. "Just in case."

Aldan hesitated, then gave a tight nod and stepped back.

Brannon turned the handle and flung the door wide.

The room beyond was an odd mix of palatial luxury and stark functionality. Blue velvet covered the furniture but the extra cushions had been removed and piled up in one corner. A tapestry on the wall had been hacked off and only a rail and a few tattered scraps of fabric clinging to it remained.

A table was pushed up against the wall where the tapestry had been. An array of everyday items lay on the table but each had been modified into a weapon. A hairbrush and comb had handles sharpened into points. A broken wine bottle and been split into shards and twine wrapped around one end of each large piece to create a safe grip. A lute had been smashed and the strings tied to pieces of wood at either end to create garrotes.

Brannon swallowed and stepped into the room, his sword at the ready. Aldan followed, flanked by guards.

Brannon nodded toward the table and its makeshift weapons and raised an eyebrow at the king.

"He still doesn't feel completely safe," Aldan whispered. "It comforts him."

There was no sign of Prince Claydan but the door to the rest of the suite was ajar. Through it, Brannon caught a glimpse of a wide glass door leading to a balcony - the perfect spot for archers to have been shooting across the courtyard.

A thud sounded from the next room.

"Claydan?" Brannon called out.

"In here. We caught him."

"Him? Or them?" Brannon pushed through the doorway, shouldering Aldan back before the king could rush headlong in to check on his son.

Inside, Prince Claydan stood with a dagger at

another man's throat.

Brillen, the released slave, was on the floor. He groaned and pushed himself up onto his hands and knees. He still wore the silk ribbon around his wrist as a bright colored bracelet. "We tried to stop him but he attacked. I'd be dead if it weren't for the prince."

"Be careful," Brannon warned. "He's a mage."

Claydan nudged his prisoner and they both turned.

Brannon gasped. It was Ren.

"Do you know him?" Claydan pressed the tip of his dagger more firmly against Ren's skin.

Brannon nodded. "He's the son of two of the murder victims I'm investigating." He frowned. How had a stone cutter learned such powerful magic? And why would he try to kill the king? "Are you sure that's who was attacking us?"

"Brillen and I were talking in the other room and we heard the arrows." Claydan shook his head slightly. "I don't know how he did it. We found him but he attacked. If you hadn't arrived when you did and distracted him, he would have killed us both and gotten away."

Ren's eyes widened. He glanced toward Brillen and then back to Brannon. "It's a misunderstanding. Please."

Brannon considered putting away his sword but the memories of the arrows and the crushed bodies of Donal and Lira were fresh in his mind. He lifted the point. "If you try anything," he said. "I won't hesitate to use this."

Ren swallowed. "Okay. Can Prince Claydan lower the knife?"

"No," said Claydan and Brannon together.

"Okay."

"I have some questions." Brannon gestured to the guards and they spread themselves around the room, weapons at the ready. If Ren summoned another storm of arrows in this small space, they'd have scant seconds to take him out before they were all killed. "Your Majesty, I recommend you wait in the next room."

"That's my son holding our prisoner," Aldan replied, his voice low. "I'll wait in the doorway but that's as far as I go."

Brannon nodded. He knew his friend well enough to recognize the best compromise he would get. "What are you doing here, Ren? Why did you run from your parents' home?"

Ren swallowed again. "I...I can't say."

"I know about the fake gemstones." Brannon pulled Donal's medal from his pocket and held it out. "You even replaced this one. What did you do with the real gems?"

"I...I can't say that either."

Brannon narrowed his eyes. "Who are you protecting? Why?" The man seemed scared. It was hardly the demeanor Brannon had come to expect from a powerful mage. Yet this was the second time Ren had been found in the exact spot of one of the attacks. It couldn't be a coincidence and it wouldn't be the first time a murderer had hidden behind a visage of innocence and victimhood. He felt the chill hand of fear grip his chest. If Ren chose to use magic, there was almost nothing Brannon could do to stop him.

Ren's gaze flicked around the room, searching their faces, and finally settled on Aldan. "Your Majesty..." He raised his hand toward the king as if to plead for his life but light crackled around his fingers. Magic.

"Look out!" Brillen shouted.

Brannon flung himself between Ren and the king but Prince Claydan was quicker. He drove his dagger deep into the mage's neck. Blood sprayed out across the room in jets.

Ren stared at his hand, eyes wide, and the light died. "I..." He clapped his other hand to his throat but it was too late. Red spilled out over his fingers and he fell to the floor.

"Get the king and prince out of here," Brannon snapped to the guards. They jumped, bundling the royals into the next room. Brannon knelt at Ren's side, pressing his own hand over that of the dying man's at his throat. "You only have a minute," he told him. "I'm sorry. Tell my why you did it. What's your plan?"

Ren blinked at him. His face was white beneath the red stains of blood. "I...but...that's not..." His head slumped and the life went out of his eyes.

"Hooded shit." Brannon lay him flat and removed his hand from Ren's throat. There had never been a chance of saving him with a slash to the jugular. He stared at the blood on his hands. It coated him and spread out across the floor in an unstoppable flood of red. Another life lost to violence and they were no closer to understanding why.

Brannon climbed to his feet and looked back through the doorway to the other room where palace guards surrounded Aldan and Brillen comforted the prince. Claydan's assassin training had served him well - his quick action had stopped a magical attack - but he had taken a young man's life. It was a hard thing to know your reactions could kill. Brannon knew that from experience. Claydan had yet to reconcile his training as a killer with being a peacetime prince.

As Brannon stepped forward, Ylani and Jecksen came into view. Ylani grabbed the boy's shoulders, holding him back from coming into the blood-soaked room. The boy's eyes were round.

"I told you," Jecksen said softly, staring at the dead man. "I told you."

"It's okay." Brannon wanted to reach out to him

but with his hands covered in blood, he kept them to himself and put as much comfort into his voice as he could. "The danger has passed now. We're safe."

Jecksen looked up, his eyes boring into Brannon's. "No," he said. "None of us are safe. It's just beginning."

CHAPTER TWENTY-NINE

Ylani ignored the glares from strangers as she turned away from the public areas of the cathedral and led Jecksen down toward Brother Taran's laboratory in the basement of the Third Alapran Monastery. Her hat and silk gown gave her away as Nilarian and it still pulled attention from regular Kalans going about their day. She might have won the favor of Sir Brannon and, to a degree, the Kalan king, but she would always be an outsider here. And now she'd been recalled and no longer the Ambassador, it seemed there was distrust of her back at home in Nilar as well.

At the door to Taran's lab, a small hand touched her elbow as she reached up to knock.

"I'm not sure I should be doing this," Jecksen said, his voice high and tentative. "My father doesn't like people visiting and he really doesn't like

Brother Taran."

Ylani chose her words carefully. Lying to someone with the Instinct - even as limited a version as Jecksen - could backfire. "We need to learn what he knows about the danger you've been sensing. He'll understand that. We want to keep everyone safe."

He looked at her and chewed his bottom lip in a gesture that mirrored her own thoughtful expression. "Okay," he said at last. "That makes sense, I guess."

It took no time at all to recruit Taran to the task. As Jecksen had pointed out, there was little friendship between him and Bishop Narayan - a situation only enhanced by the bishop's methods for testing children to see if they had the Instinct.

"Um...shouldn't we have brought guards?" Taran asked, as he locked the laboratory door behind him.

Jecksen narrowed his eyes.

Ylani let her toe catch Taran's ankle, then shot a significant look toward the boy. "No need," she said, keeping her tone bright. "We're friendly." The unit of guards Brannon had sent to follow them would be in place around the monastery by now. There was no way Narayan would escape and Ylani's own Instinct convinced her they'd do better if they approached him without them. At least at first. "Lead on, Jecksen. It's fine."

The boy's face softened and he scampered away.

"Slowly!" Ylani hitched her skirt in her fists and hurried to catch up. "It's not a race."

The monastery was a labyrinth of corridors and Ylani would have been lost in moments without her companions. It was an odd mix of familiar and strange - similar in many ways to the churches back in Nilar, but in other ways completely different. There were no silk screens or paper lanterns but the stone walls were painted with religious scenes depicting the lives of the gods. Here, Valdan and the Hooded One fought in the mountains. There, Ahpra wept the River Tilal. But the usual depictions of the gods looking down on their followers and admiring the hats were not present here. That was a distinctly Nilarian tradition. Kalans didn't care what the gods saw when they looked at them.

They followed the boy down a narrow flight of stairs and twisted around a curved corridor. A tapestry at the end covered a doorway to a large storeroom filled with chairs and candlesticks. A thick layer of dust lay over them all.

"These are the old feast chairs," Taran said. "It's a dead end."

"No it isn't." Jecksen scrambled up the first stack of chairs like a mountain goat and scampered across the stacks. "Down here," he said, and dropped out of sight in a heartbeat.

Ylani and Taran exchanged a glance.

"Come on!" Jecksen's disembodied voice travelled back from the pile of chairs.

"I guess we're following." Ylani climbed carefully, following the boy's path until she spotted the gap he'd vanished into. A half-height doorway was hidden behind the piled furniture and Jecksen crouched in the threshold. "It's definitely not a dead end," she called back to Taran.

"What?" The young priest climbed up behind her. "I've never seen that. Where does it go?"

Ylani felt the corners of her mouth twitch upward. "All that Assassin House training and you never found the hidden door under your nose?"

Taran gripped the back of a chair so tight his knuckles paled. "Well, to be fair, I don't come down this way very often."

She chuckled. "Fair enough."

She jumped lightly to the ground, letting her fingers trail down the wall as she went. The stone here was smaller - bricks, rather than hewn stone blocks. This had once been a much larger doorway but had been sealed up. When she crouched to follow Jecksen into the gap, the noticed the rough edges. Someone had smashed through to create this entrance. Perhaps the bishop himself. How long had he known his plans would require a secret lair hidden beneath the monastery? A chill ran through her as she wondered what they would find ahead.

She pushed it aside but it lingered, the sharp taste of Instinct in her mind. When Taran joined them, she leaned in and whispered. "Be ready."

Jecksen fumbled with a lantern just past the opening and a moment later it flared into life.

The room they found themselves in was large and empty. The walls here were painted in a similar way to many of the religious scenes they'd passed in other parts of the monastery but this mural focused not on the gods, but on their worshipers. In particular, a group who wore bright green robes appeared over and over. Ylani found herself drawn to them as she followed Jecksen across the floor toward yet another doorway on the other side of the room. Scene after scene showed the green-robed group against historical scenes - war, coronation, the birth of a king. Somehow the green robes were involved in all these events.

"Does your father come down here often?" Ylani said, her fingers reaching out to touch the mural almost of their own accord. It was cold and paint flakes scraped over her skin like little rough scales.

"Not often." Jecksen shook his head. "It's our secret place but it makes him sad."

She lifted her fingers from the paint with a little shiver. "Me too." There was a chill about the place that sank into her very bones. She wrapped her arms around herself as if pulling the edges of a green monk's cloak closer. As she did so, the Instinct flared and for a moment a man filled her vision.

He was older and wore a creased and dirty military coat of Kalan design. A medal hung on the lapel, the green stone in its center glowing like a tiny star. "Not the church!" The man's eyes were wild and spittle flew from his lips. "You can't make me!" Fire flared from the green gem and the vision burned away.

Ylani stumbled.

Taran reached out to steady her. "Are you okay?"

She blinked, seeing only the room in front of her and her companions. "Yes. I'm fine." As she had told Brannon and the Kalan king, sometimes the Instinct's messages were difficult to understand. There'd be time to examine it later.

The door led to a spiral staircase that descended like a twisted spine to the bowels of the building. With each step the air grew cold and musty. Something about the stone and darkness reminded Ylani of a crypt. Jecksen bounced down the stairs in an excess of youthful energy, the light from his lantern throwing strange shapes on the walls.

"What's down here?"

Neither of her companions answered but at the bottom of the stairs, her feet touched carpet. Jecksen set the lantern on a hook and took a lit taper from it and touched it to the wicks of various iron candelabra, gradually bringing the wide hallway into view. Cobwebs hung from the ceiling like party streamers. Doors ran the length of the hall and enough were open that Ylani could see they were in a dormitory, long abandoned and hidden from the main inhabitants of the monastery. She peered into the first one and saw a green robe strewn across the bed. The monks from the mural upstairs.

She moved toward it, drawn into the room by some inexorable pull. She reached up and brushed the cobwebs out of her way as she reached the robe on the bed and then let her fingers brush over the fabric. Smoke filled her nostrils and forced its way down her throat. A wave of heat washed over her body and the face of the man the Instinct had shown her earlier rose again in her vision. This time he was clean-shaven and his uniform clean and pressed but his eyes...his eyes were haunted.

"Ambassador?" Taran's soft voice cut through the vision and in an instant the heat, smoke, and soldier were gone. He stood in the doorway, his brows pulled together as he regarded her. "Ambassador, the boy says it's this way." He jerked his head back toward the hallway.

"Yes, of course." Ylani lifted her fingers from the dusty green fabric and followed him. She stepped back out into the wide hallway in time to see Jecksen disappear into one of the last rooms. Light already shone from inside the room, adding enough illumination for her to see the door at the very end of the hallway was boarded up with planks nailed in a crisscross pattern.

The sound of a hand striking flesh came from the room and Jecksen yelped.

"Stupid boy!" Bishop Narayan's words were clipped and terse. "I told you not to come here. You could have led them straight to me."

Ylani stepped up to the doorway and paused, letting the light and the doorframe highlight her presence. "We asked him to bring us," she said. "We need to talk to you."

Narayan stared with wide, bloodshot eyes. He was unshaven, dark stubble looking almost like ink marks on white paper against his pale skin. "No! You can't be here!"

Ylani raised her hand toward him. "It's okay. We just want to talk. We understand about Jecksen's gift and want to know what it means."

The bedding was strewn half on the mattress and half on the floor. Several empty bottles were on their sides next to a pile of chicken bones and vegetable scraps. The smell of an unemptied chamber pot was unmistakable. The bishop had been hiding out down here longer than they'd thought. Several sheets of paper were stuck to the wall with lists of crossed-out names on them.

"You believe the king is in danger then?" Narayan's eyes narrowed. "You? A Nilarian?"

"Yes, me." The irony wasn't lost on her. A Nilarian ambassador trying to save the Kalan king. Again. After losing her job for arguably doing just that already. Why did she care what happened in Kalanon? She wouldn't be here much longer if Alyra had her way. But that didn't matter. She did what she did because it was right, because keeping the peace was what was best for both countries, and, if she was truly honest with herself, in a small way because it mattered to Brannon. "You can trust me. Sir Brannon sent me."

The bishop screwed up his face. "But can I trust Sir Brannon? Or him, for that matter." He pointed to Taran, who had stepped into view beside her. "When the oracle saw so much death around them both?"

"Oracle? You mean Jecksen?" Ylani said.

"Or one of the other children you've been testing?" Taran demanded. "They'd likely say anything to stop you torturing them."

Bishop Narayan scowled. "Don't you come in here pretending to be all moral. I've known there was something wrong about you since the moment you arrived at this monastery. With your secret little experiments and the way you have the king wrapped around your little finger. I'll do what I have to do to protect Kalanon from the likes of you."

"The likes of me? I'll have you know I..." Taran

started angrily but trailed off, clearly unwilling to continue. He turned and paced a few steps away. He raised his hand as if to punch the wall but laid it gently on the stone instead. "Kalanon doesn't need protecting from me."

Narayan took advantage of the distraction and lunged forward, shoved Ylani aside, and ran for the exit.

Ylani stumbled, recovered, and reached for the bishop as he passed. Her fingers scraped down the fabric of his robe but closed on nothing. "Wait. Wait!"

"Father!" Jecksen shouted after him.

Narayan hesitated but, as Taran turned back to see what was happening, continued to run. Ylani and Taran pursued him but he reached the door to the spiral staircase a few steps ahead of them. As he crossed the threshold, a fist emerged from the shadows and struck him squarely in the face. The bishop bounced backward, his feet slipping out from under him, and fell like a chopped tree.

An armored figure stepped into the light, the palace guard insignia picked out on his tabard in vibrant purple thread.

"Darnec." Ylani raised an eyebrow. "I was under the impression the guard had agreed to wait for us outside."

"Ambassador," Darnec gave a little bow, a sheepish expression on his face. "Sir Brannon asked me to follow you into the monastery. Just in case I could be of service." He glanced at the unconscious bishop.

"Did he indeed?" Ylani's lips twitched upward. "Well, it seems we found a use for you. I'm glad you're here. Although it might be hard to convince him to talk to us now."

Jecksen ran forward and knelt at the bishop's side. He glared up at Ylani. "You said you wouldn't hurt him."

"He'll be fine," Darnec said. "I didn't hit him that hard."

"I'll ask Sir Brannon to check on him," Ylani said.

"Not Bloodhawk." Jecksen shook his head.

"One of the other physicians then. I promise."

"Help me turn him on his side, lad," Taran told the boy. "I recall Sir Brannon being particular about that when dealing with unconscious people."

As the men fussed over the injured bishop, Ylani felt the tug of her Instinct pulling her away. She let her footsteps take her back toward the room he'd been camped out in, then a few steps further. Her fingers traced over the planks nailed over the boarded-up door. A familiar tingle rippled over her skin. There was something about this place. This door. Open it, the Instinct urged. Look inside.

She closed her eyes and let the Instinct rise within her, an ember at her core fanned into flame.

Flames. A burning conflagration that raged over her in a wash of heat and pain. Screams echoed in her mind as the fire burned flesh. Ylani's fingers clenched on the planks and pulled as she added her own voice to the agonized screams. Splinters dug into her palms as the wood creaked and pulled away. She screamed again and reached for another plank.

Hands grasped her, pulling her back but she fought them.

"Ylani! Ylani. What's wrong?" Taran's voice cut through.

"Help me!" She sobbed, lost in the heat of the flames. "Help me open it."

Taran pulled at the planks with her. Wood and nails screeched as they gave way, then clattered to the ground.

"No!" Shouted Narayan behind them. "Stay out of there!"

Ylani reached for the door handle even as Taran pried the last of the planks away. Her fingers closed around it and the phantom heat of the Instinct flushed out of her into the cool metal. The door creaked open at her touch and light poured in over her shoulder, illuminating the large room beyond.

The place was a ruin.

It smelled like an old fireplace. Furniture was reduced to chunks of charcoal. Soot and ash covered the floor, ceiling, and most of the walls, but for a few patches some quirk of the long dead flames had left bare. It felt like stepping into a crematorium. Flickers of chill ran over Ylani's arms and she knew this was a place of death. Horrible, painful death.

Taran followed her in with the lantern, and blackened piles of soot resolved into shapes. She knew before truly seeing it. They were bodies. Skeletons, mainly. Burned and charred beyond recognition then left without even the kindness of burial. Boarded up where they lay, in a ghastly parody of a crypt.

The Instinct settled inside Ylani, its message no longer an urgent reflection of the pain these victims had endured as they died. Now, it was but a simple, resolute truth: these people had been murdered. She took a long, shuddering breath. "Send for Sir Brannon."

CHAPTER THIRTY

Brannon closed the door behind Ula and turned the key in the lock. Master Jordell was particular about what was allowed in his morgue. Brannon was under no illusions that the old physician would approve of what they were about to do. Very few Kalans understood the Djin people's way with the dead.

"He's over there," he said, unnecessarily. There was only one body in the room. It lay on the preparation table covered in a sheet that did little to hide what it was.

Ula nodded and began to unpack her leather satchel. Candles, little pots of earth, straw, and a bowl. She placed them at various points around the table and lit the candles.

"Is there a risk?" Brannon said. He paused. "I mean, if he's a mage, will the Risen have his powers?"

Ula pursed her lips. "I've not made a Risen wizard before." She glanced around as if expecting Draeson to appear and correct her before continuing. "A kaluki will have access to what the body was so yes, if he is a mage and I don't command the kaluki carefully, it will perhaps use magic and kill us all." She winked. "I be careful."

"Okay then." Brannon nodded and pulled back the sheet to reveal Ren Gifson's face. "Let's do it."

He'd seen Ula perform the Risen ceremony several times before but it still gave him an eerie sense of unease when he felt the brush of wind through the core of his being and Ren's corpse shuddered and sat up. The gash in its throat knitted back together, healing as if it had never been there. "Ruul ka nuk," it said.

"Graa tak nul," Ula replied. "Speak Kalan. And take no action that could harm anyone here."

Ren's eyes narrowed at her, malevolence burning inside them.

Ula snorted. "You are a weak Kaluki. Do not think you are a match for me. Answer our questions and I send you back quickly."

The Risen turned away like a petulant teenager. "Fine."

Brannon stepped forward, unsure, as he often was when facing a Risen, whether to speak as if to Ren or to the being that animated Ren's body and had access to his memories. "Ren...can you answer me as Ren? It will make this easier."

"I *can*," the Risen said, smirking.

Ula snapped in her guttural Djin language.

The Risen straightened up. "I will." He shifted and somehow more perceptively slipped into Ren's mannerisms. Brannon had only met the man twice, yet the change was startling. The otherworldly arrogance of the kaluki slid away and the hint of anxiety masked by bravado of a young man out of his depth soaked into his features. "After all," he said, "I know you will keep me safe, Sir Brannon."

Brannon swallowed and looked away from those reanimated eyes. He should have kept Ren safe. Except it had seemed like Ren was the threat. He had to know. "Are you a mage, Ren? Did you attack the king?"

"A mage? How could I be?" Ren spread his hands palms up. "You know how old I am, who my parents are, and where I've been my whole life. When would I learn magic? How?"

Brannon's stomach dropped. "But we saw magic. Are you saying that was nothing to do with you?"

The Risen shrugged and for a moment it was clear the kaluki was speaking as itself. "I can't access memories close to death but this body doesn't know anything about magic. Until he met you the night of his parents' death, he'd never even seen magic in person."

338

"Hooded shit," Brannon swore. "So he...you...don't know who the attacker was?"

"Nope."

According to Draeson, anyone wanting to become a mage would have to study longer than most human lifespans before they could truly use magic. Their first task was to overcome this limitation and most failed. It was why there were so few mages. None of the people Brannon had seen at the palace were old enough to even come close to being able to master the simplest spell, let alone the kind of magics they'd been subject to. Yet whoever it was had not only attacked the king but pinned it on Ren in a clever act of magical ventriloquism.

"So why were you at the palace?" Brannon asked at last.

"I was hoping to find a client who might protect me."

"Protect you from what?"

"Whoever killed my parents, for starters. And you."

Brannon reached into his pocket, fingers tracing over the edges of the medal and its fake gemstone. "Why would you need protection from me?"

Ren tilted his head and gave him a hard look. "Come on, Sir Brannon. You can't tell me you haven't figured out the scam by now. You took the box from my parents' house. You had to have known."

"The fake gemstones." Brannon nodded. "Was it just you or were your parents in on it as well?"

"They didn't know," Ren said. "They wouldn't have approved. And if it wasn't a huge chunk of marble or basalt, my father wasn't interested."

Brannon scratched at the scar on his cheek. It was possible the murder of the stonemason had been aimed at Ren in retaliation for being sold fake jewels. Donal and Lira could simply have been at the wrong place at the wrong time. "I'll need a list of everyone you sold your counterfeit stones to. It could be that one of them is the mage."

Ren shrugged. "I doubt it. They're mostly well-known figures at court but I'm happy to give you a list."

Brannon took paper, a pen, and ink from a desk in the corner and handed it over to the Risen. He watched over the Risen's shoulder as he jotted down his list of clients. True to his word, most names were Kalan nobles, many of whom had been at the masquerade ball, no doubt displaying their new but fake jewelry. He wondered how many realized they'd been swindled. Brannon himself would never have known the difference if it weren't for the report from an experienced jeweler. The gem in Donal's medal seemed real enough to him.

Brannon frowned and held out the medal he'd been carrying in his pocket. "Why did you replace the stone in your father's medal? You wouldn't have gotten any money from that."

"I didn't!" The young man squinted at it in seemingly genuine surprise and Brannon couldn't tell if it was Ren's shock at being accused of stealing from his father or the Kaluki inside him's surprise that he hadn't done so. "That's not dad's medal. I don't know how he got it. I made that one specially for my employer." He tapped the green gem with his fingertip. "He was very particular about the stone he wanted used. He said he wanted to teach someone a lesson with it."

"How? And who?" Two of the murder victims had been wearing medals when they died. Had one of them been targeted for wearing a fake gem?

"I don't know. He never told me. Just that someone had stuck his nose in where it wasn't wanted." Ren shrugged. "I didn't know if stealing the gem from his medal was the revenge or if there was more to it and, to be honest, I didn't want to know so I didn't ask."

"Who was your employer?" Brannon leaned closer. "What's his name?"

The Risen shook his head. "I didn't ask that either. I just wanted the money so I could do the kind of carvings I wanted to do and not the endless drudgery of building stones that my father spent his life on. Cutting fake gems was just a means to an end so the less involved I got with the criminals I had to deal with, the better. He wasn't from around here and he sometimes wore a hat. That's all I know."

Brannon felt the hairs on his arms raise up. A hat could mean a Nilarian. And the most dangerous Nilarian mixed up in any of this was still the mage they had trapped in the mirror cell. The mage who was supposedly neutralized by the quartz mirrors surrounding him. And yet, somehow, magic was still appearing, still attacking, and still killing people throughout Alapra.

Brannon nodded to Ula. "Put him back. I'm going to speak with Magus Nycol."

He left Ula to unbind the kaluki from Ren's corpse and send it back to its own realm and hurried out into the streets of Alapra on his own. So much of this investigation wasn't making sense. He knew there was something he was missing - some obvious link to tie it all together - but the connections seemed impossible. A mage couldn't send his magic out to attack people without him. Or could he? He paused in the street. Draeson would know. Perhaps he should talk to him first.

He turned to go back when a beggar approached him. "Please sir, do you have any spare coin or food?"

Brannon stared at the man but all he could see was the charred corpse of the General, Jemiren. How many innocent people would die by magic while he struggled to figure out the connections?

The beggar took his hesitation as a refusal. "Okay, have a nice day," he mumbled, shuffling off.

"Wait." Brannon fished a coin from his pocket and pressed it into the man's hand. "Stay safe," he said. "And thank you." He hurried away from the confused man with determination in his stride. With any luck, Draeson would be reinforcing the cell's mirror magic at this time of day and Brannon would question both mages together, but if not, he was determined to get the information he needed no matter what it took. There could be no more homeless heroes burned, or stonemasons crushed, tailors hanged, or children stabbed. The resolve burned in his chest like hot liquor, radiating strength into every part of him. This was the certainty that had kept him alive riding into battle. This was a battle he had to win.

The names of the victims he'd failed to save repeated in Brannon's head as he reached the courthouse complex, a toxic prayer of inadequacy he couldn't shut down. He fingered the medal in his pocket, feeling the hard edges of the fake gemstone, cold against his skin. His thumb ran over the pin at the back, feeling the sharpness of the point like an ineffectual tiny sword. He hardly ever wore his own medals but somehow the fraudulence of this one seemed appropriate for his state of mind. He took it out and pinned it to his chest with a bitter laugh. A fake.

Alyra Jalin, the Nilarian envoy, was arguing with a guard on the steps. Her hat was wide brimmed and overflowing with feathers and ribbons. When she caught sight of Brannon, she broke away from the conversation and called out to him. "Sir Bloodhawk! Perhaps you can explain to this idiot that barring a prisoner's lawyer from visiting looks like an abuse of rights and could be read as Kalanon reneging on peace treaty agreements. We have acted in good faith returning our prisoners. Now you won't even let me visit yours?"

"Nycol isn't a prisoner of war, Envoy," Brannon pointed out. "He's a murderer. But you're welcome to come in while I question him."

The young guard cleared his throat awkwardly. "I'm sorry sir, but Magus Draeson is renewing the spell at the moment. He's asked not to be disturbed."

"You see?" Alyra gestured to the guard. "This is unacceptable. You may have convinced my predecessor to go along with whatever Kalanon wants, but you'll find I work very differently to Ylani. This sort of thing will not be tolerated. You, of all people, should understand that the peace between our two nations is a delicate thing. Brutality of the kind you might be used to dishing out on the battlefield is not going to be allowed going forward."

Brannon clenched his fists. He knew what most Nilarians thought of him. He was the monster they scared their children with. "Bloodhawk will slaughter everyone you love if you don't behave." The war had made monsters of everyone and him more than most. Still, it stung to have those expectations thrown in his face without provocation.

He forced his jaw to unclench. "There is no brutality and you'll see that in just a few minutes. Nycol is being held and questioned but that is all." Despite the man being responsible for many deaths and kidnappings. Possibly more than Brannon could yet explain. "Your patience is appreciated."

"Well it better be." Alyra's lips were drawn tight. "Unless you want another war on your hands."

Another war. Another slaughter. How many more people would die? Worse, how many would Brannon have to kill? The fear that haunted his nightmares rose up inside him. Usually he could crush it down, contain it. He knew how to prevent a war now. He was older, smarter, and more capable. He was solving the strange crimes that could lead to misunderstandings between countries. Except now, today, he wasn't. He'd failed. He couldn't explain it and the threat of things escalating was here. Stronger. Especially now Ylani had been replaced by Alyra. That was his fault too. Alyra could set off a chain of events that would bring disaster to them all if she convinced her government Kalanon was acting in bad faith. His throat was dry and he swallowed, struggling to moisten it. What was wrong with him? Somehow, he had to find a way to stop war. Stop the killing. If he didn't, everyone was at risk. The king, Ylani, this guard in front of him, who was barely more than a boy but would absolutely be called back to battle. Everyone. This was the legacy of being Bloodhawk. He would lead them all to their death. Battle would once more become his life.

Alyra yelped, the high-pitched sound dragging Brannon out of his emotional spiral. She raised a hand to her face and her fingers came away red with blood from a small cut across her cheek. "What?"

Brannon stared. There was no sign of what had cut her.

Then the guard screamed. Bloody gashes opened up in his arm, across his chest, and on his thigh. He fell to his knees.

Another attack.

"Run!" Brannon yelled. "Get inside!" He reached to help the guard to his feet but a long deep slash opened across the young man's throat. Arterial blood sprayed across Brannon's chest and painted the stairs crimson. "No!"

Alyra screamed.

Brannon pushed her through the door and pulled it closed behind them. He leaned against the door, willing whatever power had killed yet another victim to withdraw. When no more cuts appeared on either Alyra or himself, he opened his eyes. Nycol watched from the center of his cell, his head tilted slightly to one side. Draeson stood beside one of the mirror panels, a gentle glow pouring from his hands into the glass. They both looked surprised by the intrusion.

"How did you do that?" Brannon strode to the edge of the cage, his fingers itching to reach through and wring answers from the mage's throat.

"Brannon!" Draeson's urgent warning was sharp but somehow distant. "Keep back!"

"Do what?" Nycol asked with a sickly-sweet smile smeared across his lips.

Brannon trembled, just beyond reach. His fingers clenched and unclenched on the hilt of his sword. "You killed that man out there. With magic. How?"

"You're losing your mind, Bloodhawk." Nycol snorted and folded his arms. "I did no such thing."

"Brannon," Draeson said softly. "Magic can't reach out of this cell. You know that. It wasn't him."

Brannon shook his head. "It has to be him. There's no one else who could have done it. No one is old enough to be a mage. I'm sorry, Draeson but there has to be a way for him to reach past your protections."

"This is ridiculous," Alyra said. "For all I

know, it was you. You're the one with the reputation for bloodshed. People say you move too quickly to be seen in battle. You attacked me and then you killed the guard to cover it and you're blaming my client!"

"Oh shut up!" Brannon crushed the sword hilt with his palm, feeling the metal cutting into his hand. "That's nonsense and you know it. This was magic." He released the sword and pointed an accusing finger from one mage to the other. "I know some spells can be set off remotely. That's what we did with the river in the war. That has to be what's happening here. One of you needs to explain it!"

Draeson reached out as if to sooth him but Brannon pulled away. "A trigger has a shelf-life, Brannon," the mage said softly. "Nycol's been in here too long to manage that. I'm sorry, but it wasn't him."

Brannon let his arm fall to his side. It had been his last desperate shot at an explanation. These magical attacks were just too random. Too insane. Too unexplainable.

"You seem...not yourself, old son," Nycol said. "Are you sure Alyra isn't right? Perhaps it was you and you've just...lost your mind. Forgotten. Battle-haze or something. I hear that happens to soldiers sometimes. And you're the most soldiery of soldiers, are you not?"

The room contracted around Brannon. The air

was hot and oppressive, smothering him as he tried to breathe. He felt trapped. Trapped in the room, in the conversation, in the web of deceit and impossibility that was this case. Trapped in the inevitability of war returning to claim him. It was too much. His fingers itched for his sword again but to draw it now would do nothing but prove himself the monster Alyra and Nycol claimed him to be.

"I..." He had nothing to say. No further ideas. No further questions. As he ran from the room, Brannon realized he was lost. Lost and afraid.

CHAPTER THIRTY-ONE

Draeson felt a tug as he watched Brannon leave. His friend was clearly in distress and part of Draeson wanted to run after him and reassure him. Another part wondered when he'd started thinking of Brannon as a friend. Draeson believed he'd given up on friendships. They were inevitably short lived compared to a mage's lifespan. But then, he'd been tempted by all kinds of relationships recently. It seemed even mages couldn't stay happy alone forever.

Friend or not, there was no question of Draeson following until he'd finished the daily recharge of the containment spell. As he'd promised Brannon, there was no way the mage could reach his magic beyond the mirrors but the containment would collapse if he didn't reinforce it every day. Even now, he could feel hairline fractures in the magic that told him he'd waited as long as was safe. He touched the edge of the silvered mirror surface and let the tingling sensation of the spell speak to him.

Alyra ignored Brannon's exit and hurried to the cage. "Are you okay?"

"I'm fine." Nycol barely looked at her, his eyes distant and thoughtful. "Did you bring what I asked?"

"Yes."

"Keep behind the line," Draeson told her, pouring the last bit of power into the mirror spell before straightening up.

Alyra huffed. "He's not going to hurt his lawyer, Magus Draeson. As far as I can tell, he's been a model prisoner and you have very little evidence against him."

Draeson tied off the magic and poked it with his senses. Strong enough for another day at least. "Then you know nothing," he said. "Which was clear as soon as you started poking your nose where it doesn't belong. You can't even begin to grasp how dangerous this man is."

Alyra glared but Nycol spoke before she could frame a reply. "You old flatterer. Have you thought more about my proposal?"

Draeson snorted. "I barely thought of you at all," he lied. "None of us do. You're lucky we don't forget your existence entirely and let you starve."

"Oh, but that would make you a bad guy,

Draeson. And you are just *so* judgmental of all the necessary bad things I've done in my life that I know you couldn't possibly do anything bad yourself, right?"

"I've not murdered people and kidnapped their children, if that's what you mean," Draeson pointed out. "So, yeah, I'm a bit judgmental about that."

"What evidence-" Alyra began but Draeson shushed her. She bristled. "Who do you think you're talking to?"

Draeson met her gaze with hard eyes, letting his full age seep into his expression. Foolish people sometimes assumed his youthful appearance meant a youthful mind or sense of authority. Draeson didn't like foolish people. Wind whipped at his clothing and furniture rattled as he let his power swirl around him. His skin tingled as the dragon tattoo slithered from behind his ear and peered out from his cheek to hiss at the woman who had angered its host.

Alyra swallowed and stepped back. She caught herself and stiffened, her back rigid as she faced him, tight lipped.

Nycol, of course, was not so easily intimidated. "When you're done showing off, perhaps you can explain to me how you used magic to drown thousands of people and yet I'm the bad guy."

"That was war!" Draeson let the magic dissipate. "And well you know it. I protected my country. That is all."

Nycol raised an eyebrow. "Is it?"

"What's that supposed to mean?"

Nycol shrugged slowly. "I don't know. You say you were just protecting your country but then why use a spell trigger? It would have been safer to activate the spell yourself. But you made someone else do it, from what Sir Brannon says. Maybe even the Bloodhawk himself. He'd killed a lot of people already at that point so I suppose a half army more wouldn't weigh on him too much but why do it? Unless you were up to something else?"

Draeson clenched and unclenched his fists. Nycol was just needling him. There was no way anyone could know. He curled his lip in carefully constructed sarcasm. "Would you like me to find my diary? Perhaps we could go through my entire wartime schedule just for your entertainment."

Nycol laughed but there was no humor in it. "No, I think the official version would bore us both. But there is one thing you could clarify for me." He stepped forward and gripped the bars of his cage, staring through the gap, directly into Draeson's face. "Exactly how long did you wait before using all that death energy to make yourself young again?"

Draeson felt the blood drain from his face. His mouth worked silently.

"So it's true," Nycol whispered. "Well well. And you criticized me for taking the occasional body here and there. Hypocrite!"

Draeson's throat was suddenly scratch and dry. He coughed to clear it. "I don't know what you're talking about. And neither do you. Whatever you're thinking is wrong." He forced himself to meet the other mage's eyes, unblinking, chin raised.

"What *are* you thinking?" Alyra leaned forward, almost but not quite daring to step back into the space she'd vacated.

"I'm thinking," Nycol began slowly, watching Draeson through narrowed eyes. "That my old friend here stored the death energy from all those Nilarian soldiers he murdered in the river to rewind the aging process and make himself young again. Maybe even keep himself young permanently."

Draeson fought the trembling that threatened to overtake his body. He kept his face rigid as stone.

"Is that possible?" Alyra spoke with a quiet awe.

"Not for a mage who preaches against death magic and wizardry," Nycol pointed out. "The energy required would be astronomical. The only way to do it would be to capture the energy released by a lot of deaths. Thousands, I'd say. Wouldn't you, Draeson?"

Draeson said nothing.

"When someone is killed before their time, it releases energy. That can be used for minor spells or stored in certain stones for later use. It's dangerous, but possible." Nycol shook his head. "So after all your moralizing, Draeson, you're the worst of any of us. A wizard after all. And murdered more people than anyone I've heard of to do it."

"It wasn't murder!" Draeson snapped. "It was war! They were going to die anyway. Should I just let that energy go to waste? You have no idea how it feels to be stuck in a four hundred year old body. You just jump into the next one as soon as you get old. Me, I had to suffer through it all. The arthritis, the weakness, the heartburn. Sure, I didn't die but I was Hooded miserable! So yeah, when I realized we had to kill all those Nilarians to save our country and end the war, I did it. And youth was my reward. But I didn't murder anyone to get this body. I simply took advantage of what had to happen!" He raised a trembling hand to cover his face. "If we could have ended the war any other way, we would have."

"And you'd still be old," Nycol pointed out.

"Yeah. I'd still be old." He could have accepted that. He would have. Much as he'd prefer to deny it, Draeson knew immortality had left him jaded. Brannon often judged him insensitive and uncaring when it came to those around him and in his honest moments, he could admit it. When you lived many lifetimes, it was hard to get worked up about the issues of those who would, from his perspective, be gone soon. But that didn't mean he devalued life entirely. Murder was not something to be taken lightly.

Power could have a corrupting influence and mages had access to a lot of power. He'd seen it happen with some of his early teachers. They'd treated regular people as insignificant – meaningless. After four hundred years, Draeson could see those attitudes creeping into his own behavior sometimes but he never wanted to slide so far into darkness that he lost sight of who he really was. Binding his life force to the royal line of Kalanon hadn't been just a way to keep him alive. It was also a way to fix certain values into his being permanently. He would always be loyal to Kalanon because there was no other way for him to be. And he would, for as long as possible, cling to the idea that murder for its own sake was wrong. That wasn't to say he hadn't killed. Nor that he wouldn't do it again. But to kill for no greater necessity than his own comfort – that would truly make him a monster.

The night before the flooding of the Tilal, Draeson hadn't slept. Every time he lay down, sweat would pool beneath his body and his heart would race. He'd held the stone in his hand and checked and rechecked the components that would filter the released death energy into that hard little receptacle. When morning came and the Nilarians began to cross, he'd given Brannon the trigger to the ice wall spell and taken the precious stone out of sight. He hadn't wanted anyone to see him cast this spell. Hadn't wanted anyone to ever know. The ache in his heart rivalled the ache in his bones as he readied himself. As the roar of rushing water reached his ears, he opened himself as a channel into the stone. Power rushed through, tainted with death. First a few, then hundreds, thousands. He thought he'd drown in deaths as they poured through him and into the stone. It felt like an eternity but in truth, it was over in a few minutes. Half an army wiped out. More power than any wizard had ever collected pulsing in the stone like captured stars.

He felt dirty and alone.

It'd been years before he could bring himself to actually use the power he'd trapped there. The death magic began to leak from the stone, wreaking havoc on the people and surroundings. Finally, Draeson realized he could wait no longer. The stone was dangerously close to becoming a spectre. It would have to be destroyed. Or used.

"They were still dead either way," he whispered, forgetting for a moment that Alyra and Nycol were listening to his words. "Nothing could bring them back. At least this way something good could come from it. It wouldn't honor them to pour their energy away. And I would never again have the chance to push an illusion spell into the cells of my body with enough force to make them take it on as reality. That's just not possible!"

"So you did it," Nycol whispered. "Reshaped your body into an illusion made real by force."

Beads of sweat broke out on Draeson's brow as the memory of his cells being torn apart and reshaped rippled through his body. It had been pain like nothing else he'd ever felt. But then...bliss. A youthful, muscular self that was everything he'd always wanted to be. The Draeson he should have been all along. He was more than a wrinkled old man, exhausted scholar, and defender of Kalanon. In a younger body, he was a new man and a better mage. Was it worth the cost? The moral part of him said no. A deeper, darker part of him said yes. But no matter which, he knew he had only achieved this because the price was paid anyway. He'd wrestled so hard with taking advantage of the deaths that were about to happen. Looking into Nycol's calculating eyes, he realized he Nilarian mage had no such difficulty.

"Hmmm," Nycol mused. "There seems no reason a similar spell wouldn't solve my difficulties as well."

The words clenched around Draeson's heart like an icy glove. "Even you wouldn't..."

Nycol said nothing.

"You'll never get the chance." Draeson said. He nodded to the mirrors. "If I was ever considering letting you out of that cage, the fact that you'd consider this would stop me."

Nycol chuckled. "There you go again, assuming I'm here because you put me here. I told you already, Draeson. I came to Kalanon to find you. Learn from you. Everything I've done has been a part of that." He shrugged. "I believe I've learned enough. Class dismissed."

Nycol reached through the bars of his cage and grabbed Alyra's arm. The envoy had edged just a fraction too close. He grasped her wrist and pulled her in until her body was pressed up against the bars and her arm was inside with Nycol. She yelped and struggled but he held her fast. "Magus Draeson, meet my niece, Alyra."

Draeson gasped. "No! Alyra, get back!" He lashed out with magic but, with the cage between him and Alyra, the power could not pass through.

Nycol had Alyra's arm held in both hands now. Light poured from the points where their skin touched. The woman's eyes were wide with fear. Draeson ran around the cage, desperate to get to the Nilarian envoy. Nycol threw his head back and screamed.

Draeson hit Alyra at a run, putting every bit of strength and momentum into the shove. Nycol's grip on her broke and she spun away from the cage, her knuckles clipping the bar as she fell so that the metal rang out like a bell.

Nycol's skin was black where he'd touched her. His flesh cracked like burnt pastry and he stumbled back a few steps, and fell to the floor, still and lifeless.

Draeson smothered a surge of what could only be grief. Whatever magic Nycol attempted had backfired massively. Knowing the restrictions of the mirror spell, it was hard to believe Nycol would have risked so much. Whether it had been a spell intended to harm Alyra or simply smash his way out of the cell by force, Draeson couldn't be sure, but the reflected power of it had stripped the world of one of the few people who had lived as long as Draeson himself. The closest he had left to family, in a way. There was no sign of life in that cracked and broken body. Even Alyra's arm seemed to show some signs of redness from having been inside the cell at the time spell was cast.

Draeson grasped the Nilarian envoy by the shoulders. "Alyra, are you okay?"

She turned to face him with a smile. It was not a pleasant smile. "I'm fine," she said, "But I'm not Alyra." She flicked her wrist and a blast of force caught Draeson in the chest, hurling him off his feet.

He struck the ground with a thud. Breath left him in a whoosh, only to be replaced with horror as he scrambled to his feet. He stared at the envoy, then at the broken body of the mage and back again. "Nycol?"

The woman who had been Alyra gave a mocking little bow. "At your service. I told you I could leave when I wanted. I just needed a suitable new body to be far enough inside your little mirror spell for the bridging to take place."

"You murdered her. Right in front of me, you murdered her and stole her body!"

Nycol ran a hand down her body. "I'm a new man. Or, rather, woman. I think I'll make a good envoy, don't you?"

Draeson pulled power into his fingers. The dragon tattoo hissed and he flung lightning across the room at the smug mage.

Nycol thrust one hand out in front of her and the lightning bounced off her palm and smashed into the desk on the other side of the room. "None of that!" She reached into her pocked with her other hand and flung a glittering handful of dust into the air. Magic pushed it across the room in a dangerously swift cloud.

Draeson barely registered the danger before it reached his face and he breathed it in with a gasp.

"Good night lover," said Nycol.

Draeson's world went black.

CHAPTER THIRTY-TWO

Blood slicked the steps. Sunlight almost made it pretty, shiny and red like liquid rubies, but it wasn't. It was a man's life spilled and gone for nothing.

Brannon slammed the door behind him but stopped, staring at the lifeless eyes of the murdered guard. There was no way out other than to walk through the blood. People gathered, pointing and murmuring. He knew without even hearing what they would say. There was the Bloodhawk, standing over a body once again. No matter how long he worked to be a physician or an investigator, he would only ever be remembered as a killer.

Perhaps that's all he was.

Nycol and Draeson both insisted the trapped mage's power could not reach beyond the quartz mirrors. Brannon's fingers twitched toward his sword. They always did when he was threatened. Or in doubt. It was his nature. Why wouldn't he be responsible for yet another death? It seemed obvious. Who would believe magic had cut a man's throat?

The faces in the crowd swam in his vision, mixed with the blood on the stairs so that it seemed they too had blood dripping down them. A single face stood out in that crowd, clean and sharply in focus. His sister, Reanna.

Someone touched his arm. Brannon looked. The city guard had arrived.

"Sir Brannon," the grizzled man said. "What would you like us to do? Should we cordon off the body for your investigation?"

Brannon stared at him. There was nothing to investigate. He'd witnessed the murder himself and seen nothing. "Just clean it up," he said. "Clean it all up."

He turned his back and walked away. Blood stuck to his shoes, leaving a trail of footsteps behind him as the crowd parted to let him through. No one wanted to mess with the Bloodhawk. No one who wanted to live, anyway. He walked with a miasma of death around him that kept others at bay. No one was truly safe from him. No one. He increased his speed and turned a corner, the crowd dissolving behind him into the city.

A cloud passed over the sun and Brannon was grateful for the shade. Somehow it felt good to think the blood on those steps was not so shiny without the sunlight. It made him think perhaps he could hide the truth of what he feared he was and would always be. Hide the blinding reality of being a killer behind the cloud part of him that was a physician.

Footsteps broke through his haze of self-judgement.

"Brannon? Are you okay?" He turned to see Reanna just a little way behind him. She wore the Kesh crest on her lapel like a medal of honor.

He shook his head. "Yeah," he lied. "I'm fine."

"You seem tired." She caught up and matched her pace with his. "Why don't you come home for a bit? To Kesh?"

Brannon shook his head. Kesh hadn't been home for years. Not since Kaila. Reanna knew that.

She changed the subject. "That was quite a mess back there."

He nodded tersely, saying nothing.

"Is that the sort of thing you deal with all the time now? As Master of Investigations, I mean."

"No. Not really." His fist clenched and then unclenched. "I mean, yes. Lately, it is."

"And are you okay with that?"

A street vendor watched them go past, frowning at the blood on Brannon's shoes.

Brannon sighed. "No. Not really."

Reanna touched his shoulder. "Then why do you do it?"

Something inside him trembled. "The king asked me to..."

"Bullshit," his sister interrupted. "That might be part of it but you'd say no to him if you had to."

He imagined the medal of honor was a heavy weight crushing his heart. Bravery and war were things he'd been proud of once. But now... "I'm afraid. I'm so scared I'll have to go back to doing the things I did before. I can't be responsible for that much death again." The fear and guilt rose up to swallow him just like the rushing wave of unleashed river had swallowed thousands of Nilarian soldiers. He could feel the water in his lungs. He could see it filling his vision.

"Brannon!" A touch on his hand snapped the memories away, dragged him from the water and dropped him, damp and shaking, back on the dry street. Ylani squeezed his fingers, peering into his face before she let them go. "You zoned out for a minute," she said.

Reanna's arms were folded and she glared at the ambassador.

Brannon frowned. "Ylani? Where did you come from?"

She straightened her skirt and the feather poking up from her little hat waved at the sky. "I've been looking for you. We have a situation."

"A situation?"

She nodded. "At the monastery. We're going to

need you and Ula to help sort it out."

"He's busy," Reanna said.

Ylani barely glanced at her. "It's important."

Brannon closed his eyes and shook his head against the fog of emotion that still lingered even after the wave of memory had receded. "Can it wait?"

"I don't think so. The bishop has been hiding something serious. We need you."

"You need me?" Brannon heard the bitterness in his own voice but couldn't stop it.

"Yes. Of course we do."

"Really? It doesn't seem like it. You're leaving Kalanon after all." Leaving just like Kaila had done. Both women he'd cared for. Both chose to leave him behind.

Ylani recoiled, hurt in her eyes. "What's that got to do with it?"

"Nothing." Brannon shook himself. He knew he was being ridiculous yet couldn't seem to help it. Ylani had no obligation to him but she'd been an ally and a friend. Maybe more. Lashing out at her was unfair. She wasn't Kaila and he wasn't a heartsick teenager. Whatever emotional muddle he was experiencing wasn't her fault. The fact that he was afraid to lose her and was always surrounded by death wasn't her fault. "I'm sorry."

Her brows drew tighter. "Are you okay? You don't seem like yourself."

"I..." He didn't feel like himself. He hadn't since the prison. For a moment he wondered if Nycol had cast some kind of spell on him but of course he couldn't have. In fact, he'd been feeling off for a couple of days. He rubbed at the medal on his chest. Even wearing this was unlike him. The constant reminder of what he'd been in the war. He'd fought against people like Ylani. Fought Nilarians who had wanted to destroy his country and all that he stood for. And he'd won. "Perhaps I'm more myself," he said. "Perhaps it's just the true version of me that you don't like."

Ylani caught her lip in her teeth for a moment, studying him intently. "I like the true you very much, Brannon," she said at last. "I think you know that."

Brannon's vision had a greenish haze at the edges. It was as if he was watching himself speak. "That's Bloodhawk to you, Nilarian. You'll remember that when you go home."

Ylani went very still. It seemed she didn't even breathe. As if her heart stopped and she was simply ice. "You're right." Her voice was quiet and cold, like a sharp blade. "We don't need you for the investigation. I'll find Ula and we'll see to it ourselves. Goodbye."

Brannon stared. He tried to speak but the words remained in his throat. He swallowed.

Ylani looked past him to Reanna. "Take care of

him, okay?"

"I will."

Ylani turned and walked away.

Brannon's fingers twitched. There was a physical ache in his chest. A connection that was broken. He'd broken it. When he watched her walk away, he was certain he would never see her again. Just like Kaila. But this time he'd done it to himself.

Reanna touched his elbow. "Come with me," she said. "I have someone you need to talk to."

Brannon nodded, wordless. His feet moved stiffly as she guided him. It would be their parents. Reanna had always wanted him to talk to them again. To rebuild the relationship they'd broken when they drove Kaila away. Another relationship broken. Broken relationships and death. They were what he was good at. Good at and scared of. He'd become the thing he feared the most. Talking to his parents wouldn't change that but he didn't have the energy to argue. He let himself be led away and watched Ylani disappear in the distance.

CHAPTER THIRTY-THREE

Ylani found Ula on the street outside the hospital. The Djin woman had her bag of ritual items packed and was heading back to her apartment. Ylani explained the situation and the two made their way to the monastery in silence. Ylani liked Ula. She understood the fish-out-of-water culture shock that living in Kalanon could mean for a foreigner. She'd have liked to talk more to her but the exchange with Brannon played on a loop in her mind instead.

The coldness in his words cut into her like a whip. She smothered the pain of it with a blanket of urgency. She'd learned to do this in the war. A spy had no time to stop and cry in the middle of a mission. She had to continue no matter what and get the job done. This secret in the monastery was, she was certain, every bit as important. There was an urgency about it that filled her with strength and haste. She'd been gone too long already. The Instinct pulsed in her like a rapidly beating heart and every pulse said to hurry.

"Will we not find Sir Brannon before returning?" Ula asked, quickening her own steps to keep up with Ylani.

Ylani shook her head. "He's not coming. He's with his sister." A sister who clearly did not like Nilarians. It would be interested to see how the parents of two such children would manage as ambassadors in her home country. She turned a corner. The spires of the cathedral rose above the city just ahead.

"Has he upset you?" Ula's dark eyes had depths of insight that might rival the Instinct, it seemed.

"He..." Ylani paused. Brannon was the war hero of an enemy land. An ally in peace time, perhaps, but not someone she should have let herself develop feelings for. Not someone whose stupid words spoken in a moment of emotional turmoil should be worth her tears. She forced a smile instead. "You know how families can be. He's going through some issues, I think. Best we leave him to it."

She took the steps of the cathedral two at a time, dodging and weaving between worshipers who pulled back in alarm at the purple-skinned woman trailing in her wake. The beads in Ula's hair sounded like the chimes of tiny bells following her into the foyer and then beyond, to the monastery compound itself. Taran waited at the top of the stairs. He held a small dagger in one hand which he repeatedly tossed and caught in a most un-priestly manner. When he saw the two women approaching, the dagger vanished into one of his sleeves.

"You're back," he said. "Sir Brannon?"

"Not coming. We'll do this ourselves."

Taran nodded and led the way down to the oracles' dormitory. Light from the lanterns flickered over the stone walls. Darnec Raldene stood between Bishop Narayan and the entrance, watching him for any sign of movement. The bishop himself sat slumped against the wall, his face in his hands. If not for the occasional shudder of breath, Ylani might have wondered if he was even still alive. Jecksen was nowhere to be seen. Ylani frowned at Darnec and the young guardsman nodded toward one of the bedrooms. The boy was inside. Ylani was glad. The contents of the room at the end of the hall were not for the eyes of children. Even one plagued by an Instinct that warned endlessly of death.

Ylani took a deep breath before taking Ula's hand. "It's through here. You'll need to see it for yourself."

Narayan lowered his hands and looked up as they passed. "Please don't," he said. "I'll tell you what you need to know. Don't disturb them. Let them rest."

Ylani hesitated. They couldn't trust Narayan to tell the truth. She could trust Ula and her Djin powers. "Look first. Then we'll talk."

As she led the way into the burnt room, Ylani braced herself for any vibes or sensations the Instinct might have in store for her but this time her extra sense was silent. The eerie horror of the room spoke for itself. Soot coated the floor, most of the walls, and the ceiling. The charred remains of what had once been furniture now looked like the blackened bones of some large creature coated in ash. Rising above it was a statue of Ahpra, blackened like the rest, but whole and watching over the chamber. While Ylani had been gone, someone - probably Taran - had set lanterns around the room and the flickering light was like a memory of flames. She could almost hear the screams of the people who had been trapped inside.

Ula followed Ylani in and paced the room, pausing here and there to inhale the scent of old ash and burnt corpses. "Many died here," she said. She pointed. There were charred bodies by the door, who had succumbed to smoke and flame as they fought to escape. There were others crowded around the statue, either praying for rescue or attempting to protect the image of the goddess from harm. A few were at the edges of the room, slumped and broken against the walls. Soot had been wiped away above their bodies to reveal words hastily scrawled.

"So you see," Narayan spoke softly from the doorway. "Even as they died, they wanted us to heed their warnings. I had to listen."

"Warnings?" Ylani lifted one of the lanterns to read what was written. "'Beware the armies of the Queen of the Dead.' 'The spectre comes.' What does that mean?"

Ula ran her fingers over the wall as she read another of the phrases. "This one says, 'The king's priest brings him life but others death.'"

Narayan nodded. "I believe that refers to Brother Taran. The king has taken him under his wing but he can't be trusted. He dabbles in the unnatural."

Taran's voice wafted in from the hallway. "Um, I can still hear you."

Ylani smothered a chuckle at the young priest's reaction but the truth was, as a former Child of Starlight, Taran had indeed brought death to many people. "So these are prophecies? From the Oracles who died here? The ones you've been trying to replace?"

The bishop nodded. "They are."

She looked from him to the writings to the burned and broken bodies. "I understand that they had important messages but the Instinct is hard to interpret. You could have gotten it wrong. They would have gotten it wrong. You hurt people. You hurt children."

Narayan shook his head. "I didn't get it wrong. The Oracles are always right."

Ylani took a deep breath, regretting the scent of old ash as she did so. "What happened here? Who killed them?"

He stared into the distance, watching the long distant flames. "She wouldn't tell me." He blinked and glanced at Ylani. "I assumed it was the Nilarians but I'm not sure anymore."

"We never knew you had such a thing as this." Ylani said. "I'll be honest, if we had...well, we might have tried to put an end to it, that's true. But as far as I know, it wasn't us." She turned in a slow circle, chewing her lower lip. "Ula, it would be better if we could talk to the victims. Or, at least, something with access to their memories. Would you be willing to make a Risen out of a couple of them?"

The Djin woman was kneeling next to one of the charred corpses, almost but not quite touching it. She shook her head. "They are burned. I can do nothing with them. I tried this with the dead man by the hospital and it was very dangerous. But he was freshly dead. These are burned and old dead. There is nothing I can do."

Ylani's heart sank. There was something vitally important here, she knew it. But with only Narayan's patchy and untrustworthy recollections and no chance to question the dead, it was going to be incredibly difficult to figure out what had happened and why the Instinct was chiming in the back of her mind like an insistent little bell.

"I didn't know you couldn't make a Risen from someone who was burned," she murmured. "I'm sorry, Ula. I've dragged you here and made you see this awfulness for nothing."

Ula shrugged. "Is nothing. I see much worse making Risen at home."

Ylani supposed she must. But there she would have been directed by people who knew the limitations of a Djin's power. "I just wish we had someone else we could ask."

"My mother wasn't burned." The small voice made its way into the room from behind Narayan.

The bishop turned and shushed.

"What was that, Jecksen?" Ylani asked.

The boy pushed past his father, his eyes fixed on Ylani, bravely refusing to look at the carnage in which she stood. "My mother was an oracle. And she didn't burn. You could ask her, couldn't you? I think she would want that."

Narayan stared, his face stricken. "No! You mustn't. You never knew your mother, boy. You can't know what she would have wanted. You don't know what this demon-raiser will do to her!"

Jecksen's chin raised, trembling just a little. "You told me she was an oracle and she served Kalanon. She would have wanted to help. She would want people to know what happened to her friends."

The bishop's mouth opened and closed soundlessly.

Ylani took advantage of the moment. "You mother died after the fire?"

He nodded.

"Do you know where she's buried?"

"She's here. That's part of why father hid down here. To be with her." He pointed past the weeping bishop toward one of the dorm rooms beyond. "She's in there."

The boy led the way and the others followed him. Sure enough, one of the rooms had been cleared of all furniture except a large, lacquered coffin resting on a single solid table. An array of vases filled the table space around the coffin, each with a handful of flowers in various stages of decomposition. It'd been some time since anyone had been down here with fresh blooms.

Ylani turned away, her eyes seeking out the Bishop. "You never buried her? Why?"

He stared at the floor, refusing to meet her stare. "If they knew she'd survived...even as long as she did...I couldn't take that risk." His gaze flicked up to Jecksen then back to the floor.

Ylani understood. Whoever had burned the oracles to death might have come for the boy. She shuddered. Would they also come for her? Or her family? She had to know what had gone on here and why. "Taran, I think it would be best if you and Darnec took the bishop and young Jecksen into another room. They don't need to see what happens next."

Narayan nodded. A tear trickled down his cheek.

Jecksen struggled against Taran's hands. "No. I want to see my mother. I want to-"

"No," Taran told him. "You don't."

For the second time that day, Ylani found herself prying apart wood that had been nailed in place to hide the dead. This time, at least, she knew what she would find. When the lid came off the coffin, she stepped back, careful not to breath too deeply. The woman inside was withered and dry. Her skin was drawn tight over her bones, like dirty grey leather, body gaunt and starved of flesh. Her hair, in a macabre irony, lay in thick waves around her head, almost as if it had been placed there in the pretense of life. The bottom of the coffin was coated in a dark substance Ylani preferred not to think about. Thankfully, the dryness seemed to have removed most of the expected smell.

Most of it.

Ylani stepped back, pushing air out of her nostrils in an attempt to clear away the taint of dusty rot.

Ula leaned over and poked the dead woman.

"Good," she said. "Not too damaged for being dead so long. Will make a good Risen with a strong Kaluki."

Ylani swallowed, regretted it, felt her stomach lurch and swallowed again. "Do what you have to do," she whispered, and stepped back to the edge of the room.

She watched as Ula laid out her candles and bowls and little containers of dirt, focusing on the Djin woman's every moment and blocking out the purpose behind them. She'd never expected to encounter Risen when she'd first come to Kalanon but she'd become far more familiar with the process since meeting Ula. That didn't make it any less disturbing. When the rush of magic blew through the room, she felt the tug on her insides that meant a kaluki was searching for a host. The strange wind whooshed into the coffin and curiosity won out over horror. Ylani peeked inside.

The thick substance lining the wooden base liquified and flowed upward, absorbing into the body. Even as she watched, the flesh plumped out and softened, color returning to the skin. The dead woman's limbs twitched and, with a gasp, she sat up.

Healed by the kaluki's power, she looked to be in her thirties, with curly dark hair and dimpled cheeks. She snarled at Ula and spat a string of rough syllables Ylani didn't understand.

Ula was unmoved. "Speak Kalan," she told the Risen. "You are bound and must obey."

The Risen woman curled her upper lip. "Yes. I am bound and must obey." She stood and jumped to the ground, lithe and sure-footed like a mountain goat.

"Do you have access to the memories of the woman whose body you inhabit?" Ula asked.

"I do." The Risen's eyes narrowed and her head tilted to one side as if listening to a distant sound. "And her power. She was a seer. An Oracle of the church, she called it."

Ylani leaned forward. "Yes, that's right. We need to know what happened to her."

The Risen turned a baleful eye on her. "How she died, you mean? I can't access memories from death. Surely you know this."

Ylani nodded. "But before that. What happened to her people?"

Ula held up a hand before the Risen could reply. It will be better if you answer as if you were her," she told the Risen. "Speak as the woman whose face you wear and do no harm with her body or her powers."

A shudder ran through the Risen and her posture shifted. She blinked heavily and when she opened her eyes, Ylani could tell there was something different about her.

"My name is Callana," the Risen said, her voice

soft and entirely lacking the hostility it had held only moments ago. "I'm the High Priestess of the Secret Order of Oracles. How can I help?"

Ylani wasn't sure which was more disturbing - the transformation from desiccated corpse to near-living woman or from kaluki to priestess. She pushed through her discomfort. They needed the answers Callana had. "Am I right in thinking the people who were burned in the other room were also part of your Order of Oracles?"

Callana brushed the dead and dying flowers aside and jumped up to sit on the table, resting her back against her coffin. She flicked her hair. "Yes, that's correct. It's a secret order, known only to the king and a few high-level officials in the church. And now, obviously, to you." She smiled.

Ylani nodded. That was what she expected. "What happened to them. Weren't they protected?"

"They were." Callana sighed. "We had a military unit assigned to our protection. It seemed like a good idea at the time but...it was also our downfall."

"How so?"

The Risen priestess leaned forward suddenly, looking very hard at Ylani. "You have the gift, don't you?"

Ylani hesitated but there was no point trying to hide it from someone who already knew. "Yes. I have the Instinct. Many in my family do."

Callana nodded. "Good. Good. Then perhaps it's best if I show you." She held out her hands. Her fingers were still thin, almost but not quite skeletal, and there was dirt under the nails. "It's all right. The process can't hurt you. You want to share what I know and this will make it easier."

Ylani glanced at Ula.

The Djin woman nodded. "The kaluki is bound to do no harm. Your power is stronger with a Risen here and hers, I think, was always strong. Perhaps we learn more this way."

Information was power, Ylani reminded herself. Every spy knew that. And although she was a spy no longer, every politician, trader, or investigator knew it too. Every aspect of herself valued information and was willing to take a risk to get it.

She reached out and took Callana's hands.

The Risen's fingers were cold. Despite the appearance of life, she was, after all, still dead. They closed around Ylani's own fingers and, in a burst of light, their Instincts flared and merged, flinging her into a vision.

The Reading Room was the heart of the Secret Order of Oracles. The statue of the goddess in the center of the room served not only as a decoration and inspiration but a focus for their power. Ylani saw it as it had been before the flames: filled with color, draperies, lanterns, and men and women meditating as they sought truth with their minds. Their abilities were a gift from the gods, a way to protect their country from harm and the war. While most generals had to rely on information passed to them by word of mouth, those who had access to the Oracles were blessed with information faster and more accurate than any soldier could supply. There had been many times when this meant the difference between a successful defense and being completely overrun by Nilarian forces.

This was how Kalanon had survived the early days of the war. They'd weaponized a holy sect and turned the Instinct into a craft. Even Ylani, for whom the secret knowledge the Instinct provided had always been a powerful advantage, was impressed. Her family could never have turned their power into this kind of systemic process.

"It takes training," Callana's voice spoke in her mind. "We're brought here as children."

The priestess was both in front of Ylani and within her. Or perhaps Ylani was within Callana. It was a confusing mix of seeing the woman as she was when alive and feeling her as well. Somehow her awareness was both in this memory of the past *and* still in the room with Ula.

"This was your life?" she asked quietly. "Waiting for the Instinct to speak to you."

"It was. And we were happy." Callana's voice had warmth borrowed from the memory of her living self. "We served our country and our gods. But that changed."

The vision darkened and the oracles within it huddled closer together. "What changed about it?"

"What we saw and knew became darker, more violent. The longer the war continued, the more we realized Kalanon was losing. The information we shared became less about how to win an encounter and more about how best to escape with the fewest casualties."

The Callana of the past threw back her head and screamed, twitching in the grasp of the Instinct. Other oracles clustered around her, lowering her gently to the ground. Ylani saw tears in the eyes of many of them and knew they'd seen what their High Priestess now saw.

"Then the Instinct showed us what we all dreaded."

A rush of second-hand half-images and sounds jumbled across Ylani's mind as the Instincts of the various oracles fed into hers through Callana. A sword flashed in sunlight. A horse screamed and reared up and the world tipped sideways. Blood sprayed. Arrows thudded, driving her back with the impact. The details blurred together but one overall message was clear, vibrating within her in absolute certainty. "King Raldan will die!"

Yes," Callana agreed. "We all felt it. And where many of our predictions could be used to avoid a fate, this one was inevitable."

"What did...?" Before Ylani could finish the question, her awareness shifted. She was suddenly in a hallway and a young soldier walked alongside her.

"I warned the king," Callana's voice said in her mind.

"Which king? Aldan or his father?"

"Both."

They turned a corner and confronted a large double door, carved and polished to a gleam.

"You're worried about something, Priestess?" The young man beside her paused, his hand on the handle of the door.

She patted his hand. "I'm always worried about something, Jemiren." She frowned. "I'm sorry you're leaving the church."

The soldier shook his head. "You must have misheard, Priestess. It's an honor to be assigned to the Order. I have no intention leaving."

"Oh." Yet she knew he would never return to the church after today. "My mistake."

The door opened onto the throne room. It had been redesigned into a place of war. Tapestries on the walls had been replaced by maps and charts of statistics outlining casualties, food supplies, troops in training, and weaponry reserves. A huge three-dimensional scale model of Kalanon dominated the middle of the room, with army units represented by carved wooden replicas of horses, soldiers, and tents. The king and his son, Prince Aldan, stood over the model, examining it from every angle as if some new development would reveal itself out of the wood and plaster.

They looked up as she entered the room. "High Priestess. I hope you have something that can help us."

"Unfortunately, Your Majesty, it's quite the opposite."

As she outlined what the oracles had foreseen, the prince sank into a chair and the king's face darkened. Ylani could feel the anger building inside of him like steam beneath a boiling pot lid, ready to burst forth in scalding heat.

"How dare you?" he spat at last. "You treacherous witch! After all I've done for you and your kind."

Callana stammered. "Your Majesty, this is not of our doing. We can only tell you what the gods reveal to us."

"The gods or the Nilarians?" He rose to his full height. "Have they bought your allegiance after all? I would have thought the church was above such betrayal."

Prince Aldan reached out, and the light from the lanterns shone in his golden hair. "Father, I'm sure that's not the case. Let the priestess explain. She must have a plan to save you."

Ylani felt Callana's pain. "I'm sorry but I do not. The best I can offer is time for you to prepare yourself and to prepare the kingdom for what must come next."

The king stared at the model battlefield. His hands clenched tight enough that his knuckles were white. "Get out." He said it quietly at first but then he drove his fist into the table and the horses and soldiers jumped with the force of it. "Get out!" he bellowed. "Before I cut out your treacherous tongue! Get out!"

Callana turned and ran.

"The next day, in the Monastery, I felt something bad was coming but I didn't know what." Her voice in Ylani's mind sounded lost, on the verge of tears. "I think maybe I couldn't face what my gift was telling me."

Soldiers pushed into the dorm, swords drawn, and herded everyone towards the reading room. The oracles scrambled, voices loud in protest, but ultimately were pushed on. Elbows pressed into Callana's side as her people crowded closer together to keep away from the blades of the men who had once been there to protect them. One woman stood her ground until the tip of a sword pierced her skin and blood poured onto the floor. Others screamed.

Callana sought a face she knew. "Jemiren! Please, don't do this!"

The young man refused to meet her eye. He

kept his sword extended as if to distance himself from what he was doing. "I'm sorry, Priestess. I have my orders."

She gently pushed the sword blade aside with the palm of her hand. "Jemiren, you know it's wrong!"

"I'm sorry." He pushed her through the door and into the Reading Room with his free hand. "I'm so sorry."

Callana whirled as the door slammed behind her. She drew a long shuddery breath as the Instinct screamed inside her. All around, other oracles hugged themselves, or paced the room, or stood in dazed confusion chanting, "No, no no."

Panic rose inside Ylani like burning vomit. She knew what was coming next. This was the horror she'd felt approaching from the moment she'd descended the stairs to seek out Bishop Narayan. She looked around at the memory and saw realization on the faces of some of the oracles too. One or two of them grabbed pots of ink from the table and began to write on the walls using their fingers as a pen - the last predictions they would ever make. Urgency pulsed through every movement.

Ylani stood, helpless, as the fear in the room grew like a palpable, liquid thing, filling the room, viscous like oil and with a scent much the same. It wasn't until she felt the wetness on her toes that she looked down and realized the awful truth. The soldiers were pouring oil under door and it was slowly covering the floor. She'd seen oil used in battle before, boiling and poured down from city walls or castle battlements or flung in pots with burning fuses to explode on impact. This was slower. Deliberate, unavoidable, and cruel.

"Oh gods. He's going to do it."

"I'm sorry." Jemiren's voice was muffled through the wooden door. "Please forgive me."

Then flames rushed under the door, tracing the path of the oil, and filling the room in a rush of light and sound. And heat.

The intense, burning heat as the room became a furnace and everything burned.

Ylani screamed. Fire lapped at her skin, searing the hair from her arms. Around her, people thrashed about, struggling to escape the flames or beating themselves as they tried to smother the fire that was already consuming their bodies. The statue of Ahpra was a cool white beacon in an inferno and then it too was swallowed by smoke and fire. Scalding soot filled Ylani's lungs. She beat her fists against the wall.

"Let me out! Let me out!" She pulled her hands away from Callana and the connection between their instincts snapped. She fell to the ground, gasping for air. The past was gone and cold but the memory of those flames burned hot and terrible in her mind.

Ula crouched beside her. "You are okay. You are not hurt. You are okay."

Ylani stared at her, almost not believing for a moment. Then she nodded. She wiped her face, half expecting soot instead of tears, and pulled herself unsteadily to her feet. "I could feel it," she said. "I could feel everything she felt. It was horrible."

The Risen Callana nodded. "It was terrible. But I survived," she said. "My gift - my Instinct - led me to a small part of the room that was spared the worst of the flames and I took shelter in a cupboard. But I was badly burned and the smoke damaged my lungs terribly. Somehow I didn't die but..." She shook her head. "I never forgot the screams or the agony. Even when the fire eased, I couldn't escape because the Order's military unit had been ordered to keep us inside and kill anyone who tried to leave."

"Ordered by who?" Ula asked.

"There was only the king and his son who knew what we had predicted and wanted us silenced. I don't know which of them gave the order. All I know is that the people who were supposed to protect us were ordered to kill us. Narayan found me and nursed me back to health." She gave a wistful smile in the direction of the door as if she knew her lover and son were beyond it. "But I was never the same." She touched her chest. "My lungs never fully recovered. I told Narayan what had happened and he kept me hidden and we fell in love. I became pregnant but...I assume I didn't survive the birth. I don't remember my death. Childbirth is a strain and my body, as I said, was quite damaged."

Ylani pressed a hand to her chest. She could feel the ghost of the heat and smoke from Callana's memory and fought the urge the cough. She could only imagine what the priestess had felt living the reality of that injury. "You had a son," she said, forgetting for a moment that it wasn't truly Callana she was speaking to but a Kaluki inhabiting her body and memories. She wanted desperately to introduce this poor woman to the child she'd brought into the world in her last months but she knew it was a bad idea. It would hurt Narayan and Jecksen far more than it would help them to see the woman they loved seemingly returned to them but, in reality, just a puppeteered shadow of herself. She pushed her thoughts onto something else. "What happened to the soldier? Jemiren?"

The Risen shrugged. "I never saw him again and never wanted to. Not after what he did."

Ylani couldn't blame her.

Ula frowned. "Jemiren? That's the man they called the General. Sir Brannon found him. He burned to death too."

"Is that so?" Callana leaned back against her coffin. "Well, I suppose the gods have a sense of justice after all."

Ylani remembered the affection Callana had felt for the man and the sense of betrayal when he'd trapped the oracles and burned them. Justice indeed. "It's strange though, that he would have spent all his life running from what happened here only to die in a similar way."

Ula shrugged. "Maybe justice. Maybe sense of humor."

"Or maybe something else we're not seeing yet," Ylani said. She chewed her bottom lip for a moment. "This is all connected somehow."

"What about the words on the walls?" Ula suggested. "Do they mean anything?"

"Prophecies of a sort," Ylani nodded. "But, as I've said before, the Instinct is subject to interpretation and those messages were written in a moment of extreme stress. We can't say what they relate to. Callana, have you studied them?"

The Risen shook her head. "The room was boarded up and I never wanted to see what was inside. It's a crypt."

Ylani stared through the wall, visualizing the room beyond. A crypt and a murder scene all in one. These were the only people she'd known other than her own family who had the Instinct. It was a huge loss to the world - even if they were Kalans. "Your son seems to have inherited a tiny portion of your gift. He senses danger. He's not very accurate with it though." She smiled, thinking of the number of times the boy had pointed to Brannan or Taran as a threat. Both men were dangerous when appropriate but not in the way Jecksen seemed to think. "Narayan is trying to rebuild the Order around him. It's not working."

"No," said Callana, sadly. "It won't."

Her words had a ring of certainty to them that Ylani recognized. The Instinct had spoken and the message was not one Callana was happy with. Without thinking, Ylani reached out and patted the priestess on the hand. At the touch of her skin, a jolt of merged Instinct spiked through her mind. A flash of words written on the wall, followed by Jecksen and Brannon facing each other. Then the sudden, irrefutable sense of drowning. She struggled for air. This was how the Nilarian soldiers in that last battle had felt in their last moments of life as the river washed over them. The river Brannon had released.

"Oh gods!" Ylani choked, feeling the water bubble in her lungs.

"Gah fo nok!" Ula shouted.

Callana's hand withered beneath Ylani's fingers. She felt the flesh melt away and skin dry to leather. Ylani jerked her hand back. The Kaluki rushed out of the Risen body like a gust of wind blowing open a door in a storm and then it was gone. Callana's corpse clattered to the floor, old and dead once more.

"Ylani?" The concern in Ula's voice was a near tangible thing, thick and warm like a woolen blanket.

Ylani could only feel icy wash of fear. The Instinct had spoken and she *knew*. The whites of her eyes stood out stark and wide and her whole body trembled. "Jecksen was right," she said. "Brannon's going to kill us all!"

CHAPTER THIRTY-FOUR

During the last years of the war, many of the noble houses of Kalanon built townhouses or apartments within the palace grounds of Alapra. The walled perimeter of the grounds was extended to provide a vital second layer of defense in case the city itself was breached. Thankfully, the Nilarian army never got as far as Alapra, but many maintained their accommodation within the palace area still. Brannon's own apartment building was one such place. The Kesh family townhouse was another.

A narrow, three story building, the townhouse stood in a row of similar houses all with balconies that looked in toward the palace on one side and out over the wall on the other, watching the city beyond. Most of the time they stood empty. A few shared servants dusted and cleaned the entire row. They were only in use when members of the noble families that owned them stayed at court and, when that happened, they brought their own staff with them. The windows of the Kesh house glowed with lamplight even though the sun had barely touched the horizon. A brass knocker in the shape of a rose dominated the huge red door. Appropriate, Brannon thought. Pretty to look at but thorny to touch.

"I still don't understand why you don't just live here," his sister said, leading the way. A butler opened the door before she reached the knocker and stood silently aside. "It's your house too."

Brannon said nothing. His small but functional apartment was more a home than this place or the manor back in Kesh would ever be. Had been for many years now. He hadn't been inside either of his family homes since before the war and he wasn't looking forward to it now.

He climbed the steps and followed Reanna into the house, feeling much as if he were riding into battle. His heart raced and he was short of breath. He felt afraid but also, strangely, almost drunk. Foggy. He'd been so young the last time his parents had spoken to him about his relationship with a woman they deemed inappropriate. Times had changed him. No matter that after what he'd said to Ylani he'd likely never see her again, he still wasn't ready to back down. He would never again let his family destroy a chance at happiness. He was perfectly capable of destroying it himself.

The floor and ceiling of the foyer were dark polished wood that gleamed in the lamplight. The wall spaces between sconces were painted with wide stripes of mauve and cream and crowded with portraits of Kesh ancestors silently watching the prodigal son return. A carved coatrack stood to one side of the entryway and a staircase dominated the far end of the room. It curved gently upward into the private parts of the home. Brannon expected to see his parents waiting. They were not.

He turned to Reanna. "So where are we having this conversation?"

She waved to the staircase. "Let's go to the balcony. I had someone prepare drinks."

The upstairs living room was well appointed but mostly just functional, with its main feature being the wide glass doors leading out onto a balcony almost as large as it was. Wicker furniture with plush cushions made the outdoor area a very comfortable space to spend time when the weather was warm. Many a long summer evening was spent looking over the palace gardens with a glass of wine when the family was in residence. The lowering sun gilded the city in shining liquid gold. As he stepped out onto the tiles, a familiar but unexpected figure rose from one of the chairs to greet him.

"Brillen?" Brannon stopped in his tracks. "What are you doing here?"

The former slave raised his hand in greeting.

The silk ribbon was still tied around his wrist like a bracelet.

"I asked him to come," Reanna said, stepping out into the sunset air. "He has first-hand experience of what I want to talk about."

Brannon frowned. "I thought it was our parents who wanted to talk."

"No. I'm the one who wants to talk." She picked up two glasses of chilled wine from a tray next to the chairs and handed one to each man. "I want us to talk *about* our parents. And how we can stop them going through with their insane plans."

Brannon took the glass and sank into one of the wicker chairs. Condensation beaded the side of the glass. He took a sip. "What plans?"

Reanna folded her arms and gave him a stern look. "Brannon you were at the masquerade. You can't tell me you missed the announcement that our parents are going to Nilar."

"As ambassadors for Kalanon, yes. The king announced it."

She rolled her eyes at him. "Well obviously we can't allow it. It's mad!"

"Why?" Brannon tilted his head.

"Why! Why?" His sister's voice took on a shrill quality. "Brannon, it's *Nilar*. I know you don't get along but do you seriously want to see our elderly parents banished to a place like that?"

Brannon took a long sip of the wine. Reanna

had always struggled with the idea that her brother might not see things as she did. "It's not banishment, Re. It's a job. A promotion. They've always wanted something like this. I doubt very much that our opinions about it will make any difference at all."

"To mum and dad, maybe not. But you have the ear of the king."

He laughed. "Not when it comes to those kinds of decisions, I don't. Aldan is his own man."

"Well, convince him. They should be retired at home in comfort at their age. Not dragged off to some foreign nightmare!" Reanna threw up her hands in exasperation. "Brillen, tell him what it's like. Nilar is not the place for any Kalan."

Brillen shifted in his seat and looked from Reanna to Brannon. He grimaced before he spoke, as if the words were distasteful to him. "You know my experience of the place," he said. "It wasn't nice. There wasn't a day went by that I wasn't abused in some way. I saw people I knew literally worked to death hauling coal and ore for Nilarian forges. They dropped in their tracks and we were told to step over their bodies and work faster so they could make more swords to bring back here and kill our countrymen. After the war, those of us who were left were put to work doing all other kinds of manual labor. So many Nilarian men had died in the war that the workforce is utterly depleted. They had us working before dawn and after dusk and there was still more to do. Eventually I was bought by Alyra to be her household slave." He's leaned back and stared out into the darkening sky. "I was there for years, Brannon. The only person who was kind to me was Alyra's uncle."

Brannon swallowed. Brillen's story was likely a glossed over version of what had happened. The anger between Nilarians and Kalans was hot tinder for years after the war. It was no surprise to hear Kalans had been treated badly before being returned. "I don't mean to be insensitive here, but Brillen, you were a prisoner of war. I'm so sorry for what happened to you but your experience of the place is vastly different to how the official ambassadors will be treated."

"How can you be sure?" Reanna snapped. "Are you willing to bet our parents' lives on that?"

"Nothing is ever sure, Re. But we are in a time of peace. We have to trust that both countries want that to continue. We've had a Nilarian ambassador here for some time now and nothing bad has happened to her. We have to trust that the same will be true for our parents."

Reanna snorted. "Yes, well, she has you mooning over her like some mindless puppy. I doubt Nilarian heroes will find our parents quite so attractive."

"Oh, don't be ridiculous," Brannon snapped.

"And don't lash out at me just because I don't share your prejudice and paranoia. I understand Brillen had a horrible time but that doesn't mean our parents will too."

Brillen shook his head slowly. "Typical Bloodhawk," he said. "Other people's lives are expendable to you, aren't they? Even your own family."

"What's that supposed to mean?" Brannon set his glass down on the small table with a thud that made the wine inside it jump. Blood red liquid splashed onto the table and his hand. The tightness that gripped his chest whenever he heard the name Bloodhawk doubled. Even tripled. In Kalanon, his wartime exploits were almost universally praised. Hearing the guilt he felt for what he'd done expressed out loud by someone else burned.

Brillen spread his hands wide in a melodramatic shrug. "I don't know. Maybe exactly what it sounds like. I would never have been taken prisoner if it wasn't for you. Nor would Prince Claydan. Our torture was your fault and you don't seem to have learned your lesson."

Brannon blinked. Guilt for killing thousands of men and women who had only been following orders was something he was familiar with but to be blamed for what the Nilarians or Children of Starlight had done was baffling. "What? My fault? How?"

Brillen snorted. "You don't even remember, do you?"

"Remember what?"

"You made a choice, Brannon. You could have come back and protected the prince and all of us who were with him but you stayed with the king." Brillen's finger stabbed the air and his eyes narrowed. "The *king* had enough protection already! No one was going to get to him. *We* were the ones who needed you and you abandoned us. We spent *years* suffering because you chose to protect Aldan instead of us. Years!"

"I...but..." Brannon stared. Memories tumbled through his mind like an avalanche. "We were under attack. Boxed in. We came for you as soon as we could get away but you were already gone."

"All I hear is you making excuses for your choices, Bloodhawk. I often wondered how you could sleep at night while I lay shackled to a cold stone floor."

Brannon glanced at Reanna. She seemed as shocked by Brillen's accusation as he was. When he looked back, Brillen met his gaze and held it.

"So how do you feel about making those kinds of choices now, Brannon? The ones where you have to choose who to save and who you might let die? Lately, your choices haven't saved anyone."

"Lately?" The word sent a chill down Brannon's spine. He stared at Brillen as if seeing him for the first time. The bitterness in the man was such a contrast to the grateful returned soldier he'd first met.

The ribbon on Brillen's wrist fluttered in the wind. The man hadn't let it go and he clearly hadn't let his resentment go either. This was a very different side of Brillen from the helpful man who'd reported for duty after being released at the masquerade. Who'd been at the stonemason's house when they died. Who'd been in the palace when the king had been attacked. Who had befriended the prince and helped kill Ren before he could explain himself.

Brannon swore. "You've been here all the time. This whole thing. You've been punishing me for letting you be captured? It was *war*. You think I could have saved you but you're wrong."

Brillen sneered. "Finally, the great Sir Brannon starts to see what's in front of him. You *chose* to leave me for the enemy and you think there's no consequences for that? Oh, no, Brannon. I'm back now and you and your king owe me for ruining my life."

"Brillen, innocent people have died. Tell me that wasn't your idea of getting back at me." Brannon held his breath, dreading the answer he feared was coming.

Reanna rubbed her temples. "What are you two talking about?"

Brannon kept his gaze fixed on the returned soldier.

"Not the sum total of it," said Brillen. "But a start."

"Ahpra's Tears!" Reanna backed away a step but Brillen was too fast. He dropped his wine, leapt forward and seized her, a knife suddenly at her throat. She squealed, frozen like a mouse trapped by a cat.

"No!" Brannon reached out but was too far away to stop him.

"Don't move, Brannon," Brillen said. "Or there's another dead body on your conscience."

Brannon held up his hands, fingers spread wide. "I'm not doing anything," he said. He forced himself to look past his sister's terrified face and trembling body. She was usually so capable. It hurt to see her so scared. "I'm just trying to understand."

"Yeah," Brillen snorted. "Like I spent years trying to understand why my life was less valuable than the king's."

"It's not," Brannon said. "Of course, it's not. But you know what war is like. No matter what we do, bad things happen."

"Well, you tell that to the people whose lives you've ended or ruined."

"I'm not the one killing innocent people, Brillen." Brannon kept his voice calm and quiet despite the roiling emotion inside him. It felt like he was drowning in it. He could hardly breathe.

Brillen smirked. "We'll see."

Brannon ran through the possibilities in his mind. Something wasn't right. "You're not a mage though. You're not old enough to have trained."

Brillen wiggled the knife at Reanna's throat. "You think I need magic to finish this?"

"No! No. I just...the murders have all been magical in nature. I don't see how you could do that."

Brillen chuckled. "I met someone while I was in Nilar. I think you know him. Magus Nycol."

"So it's his magic? Even while imprisoned?"

"Not exactly. He gave me a little gift. And I gave it to the others. A special little stone that drags out a person's fears and makes them happen. Isn't that fun?" He nodded toward Brannon's chest. "You're wearing it now."

Brannon stared. He ran his fingers down his chest, feeling the hard edges of the medal. The medal with the fake gemstone. The same kind of medal someone had stolen from the General's burned corpse. The same medal Donal the stonemason had worn when he was crushed to death. The same medal Alissa had been studying when her husband was hanged. The same medal he himself had been wearing when the king had been attacked, when Jecksen had been stabbed, and the prison guard murdered. A medal containing a dangerous magical artifact.

"Oh gods!" His fingers scrabbled at the pin, desperate to detach it from his shirt.

Brillen laughed. "Oh yes, Brannon. You've been investigating yourself all this time. And that's just the start of it."

Brannon jerked the medal away from his chest, feeling the fabric rip as the pin tore free. He threw it as hard as he could. The stone caught the light as it soared over the edge of the balcony, a glowing green comet against the darkening sky.

Brillen watched it disappear. "That won't stop what happens next."

Brannon lifted his chin. "Whatever it is, you won't get away with it."

"Well, that's up to you, I suppose." Brillen moved closer to the edge of the balcony, pulling Reanna along with him, keeping her between him and Brannon. "You'll have another choice to make. Another decision on who to save. I think it's going to be interesting."

Reanna's eyes widened. "Brannon." Her voice cracked. "I have kids, Brannon. Don't you let him hurt me."

Brillen's lip curled. "Ugh. Nothing so pedestrian as you, my dear." He gave her a shove that sent her stumbling across the tiles. She crashed into the small table, knocking it and Brannon's wine glass flying.

Brannon helped her to her feet and when he looked back, Brillen sat on balcony railing. He swung his legs over and, with a wave, dropped out of sight.

Brannon blinked. "Did he...?"

"He'll break his leg," Reanna murmured.

Brannon shook his head. "No, he's up to something."

He drew his sword and took two steps toward the railing. A green glow raised up from the darkness below. It was the glowing stone in the medal. It hovered, floating like a shining dragonfly, just out of reach.

A moment later, two human figures floated up beside it, their clothes whipping in an unfelt wind and crackling power shining around them. Brannon knew mages could lift objects or even people with their magic - Draeson had once lifted him over a fence in pursuit of a suspect - but this was something else. The man, of course, was Brillen, but the woman...

"Alyra?" Brannon gaped. "But you're not a mage either. Ylani knows you!"

The envoy smiled, revealing dimples in her cheeks. "Such a clever boy, Brannon. And you'd be right...except I'm no longer Alyra." She reached out her hand and lightning burst from her fingers. I struck Reanna in the chest and hurled her back, through the glass doors, and into the living room beyond in a hailstorm of broken glass shards. Reanna lay still.

The power that surrounded them unleashed and lightning showered down all over the balcony. Brannon dropped his sword and crouched down, flinging his hands over his head for shelter. Furniture exploded around him as the blasts found their marks and scattered burning splinters like confetti.

When it finally stopped, Brannon looked up.

"I'm going to kill the king," Brillen said quietly. "And Nycol plans to destroy the city. You could probably stop one of us but not both. Once again, the choice is yours, Bloodhawk. This time, who will you choose?"

CHAPTER THIRTY-FIVE

The cold, hard floor of the cell pressed against the muscles of Draeson's body in a dull ache that ran from the back of his neck down to his toes. Awareness slowly filtered into his drowsing mind and, for a nightmare moment, he thought he was back in his old body - the one with four hundred years of aging bearing down on it in an ache that never stopped. He jerked awake and sat up. The movement stretched his youthful muscles and blood rushed back into healthy circulation. The ache slipped away as quickly as a dream. He smiled. Youth truly was wasted on the young. He would never take this body for granted.

He opened his eyes.

Nycol was gone. Draeson had expected that. At least, the Nycol who now occupied Alyra's body was gone. The old Nycol's body remained, a burnt-out husk, dead on the floor next to Draeson.

He was inside the cell.

He looked around and saw his own reflection staring back at him from each of the mirrors that surrounded the bars. There would be no way to use magic to escape. His own trap was being used against him.

He clambered to his feet and tested the door, clinging to the hope that perhaps it was unlocked. It was not. He was trapped. Nycol was free to do whatever he wanted - whatever *she* wanted - and Draeson could do nothing about it.

Horror stabbed deep in his gut. He knew what Nycol wanted. She wanted a way to preserve her body's youth. She wanted death magic on a scale the world had only seen once before. "Hooded shit!" She would murder an entire city to get what she wanted. Everyone would be dead. The king, Brannon, everyone!

"Help!" He heard the terror in his voice as he screamed and hated himself for it. He'd always told himself it didn't matter when people died. They were short lived anyway. Their lives were always going to end. And that was true...to a degree. But death on this scale for nothing but selfish gains was horrendous. Even Draeson himself might not survive it. Certainly if the royal line was wiped out, so too was his immortality. "Help! Somebody! Let me out!" Helpless and without magic or a key to the cell door, he would scream himself hoarse and die screaming if need be. For the first time in centuries, mortality was coming and Draeson didn't know how to fix it.

"Magus?" A small, childish voice spoke from somewhere. For a moment, Draeson thought he'd imagined it but then it came again. "Magus Draeson? Why are you in the cage?"

He grabbed the bars, searching the room for the source of the voice. "Girl? Shalyn? Where are you?"

The door creaked open and Shalyn's head poked through. "I was looking through the keyhole," she said. "One of the guards gets angry with me when I just come in."

"Why are you even here? Are you following me again?" He shook his head. "Actually, never mind. Find the key and let me out."

She slipped into the room and closed door behind her. She kept her eyes on Draeson even as she edged over to the desk and ran her fingers across it, searching for the key to the cell. A moment later, she held up a large iron key, triumphant.

"Good girl. Bring it over to me."

Shalyn hesitated. She kept the key in front of her and waved it back and forth. "Why should I?" she said. "What's in it for me?"

"What?" Draeson thumped his palm into the

bars of the cage. "What sort of stupid question is that? Hurry up!"

"No." Shalyn sat on the desk and crossed her legs under her. "You're stuck and I can let you out but you have to do something for me."

Annoyed and unthinking, Draeson reached out with his magic to try to pluck the key from her fingers. The power ricocheted off the mirror spell and slapped him in the face. He swore. "Fine," he snarled between gritted teeth. "What do you want? Aside from me rescuing you from slavers? Oh wait, I already did that."

Shalyn closed her fingers around the key and leaned forward. "The other mage wanted me to let him go too. He said he could train me to be like you but I didn't trust him. I trust you."

Draeson waited. "Meaning?"

"Teach me!"

He blinked. "Wait...are you saying you want to be a mage?"

"Yes!" There was no doubting the earnest determination in her voice. "And I don't want to be an orphan anymore."

Draeson rubbed his eyes and dragged his hand down his face before taking a deep breath. "Child, there's no magic that can bring your parents back from the dead. There just isn't. And you could spend your whole life studying to be a mage and never become one. Is that what you want?"

"That's not what Magus Nycol said. He said I have the potential and he would teach me." She lifted her chin defiantly. "Maybe I'll just go find him. He's probably a better mage than you are anyway since he got out of the cage and you can't seem to."

"He is not!" Draeson scowled. He was being played by a child and it grated but the truth was, he had little time to spare waiting for someone else to come along. Besides, what if Nycol had told the girl the truth? Nycol had always claimed to have a knack for spotting those who could master magic. If Shalyn was one of them, perhaps this was his opportunity for something resembling a family. Someone who might live as long as he did. It was a very appealing thought. "If I take you on as an apprentice, it won't be easy. It'll be a lot of study and hard work."

"I know." Shalyn jumped down from the desk and took a step closer, bringing the key with her. "Is that a yes?"

"It's a probationary yes. But it's up to you to keep up with the lessons I set you."

"And I live with you, not at the orphanage."

Draeson's head jerked up at that. "Oh what?"

"I don't want to live like an orphan anymore!" she said firmly.

"Fine. Fine. Now hurry up and unlock the door."

"Shake on it." Shalyn stuck her hand out, close enough for him to reach through to shake it while keeping the other hand, containing the key, behind her.

It would be so easy to pull her in and take the key from her, Draeson thought, but he'd given his word. This girl could have been his great great great many more times great grandchild and now here he was stuck with her. But if it worked, perhaps they'd both have found family after all. He shook her hand gently and let it go.

She nodded and stepped up and unlocked the cage.

Draeson pushed the door open with a clang and strode out. "Right, now we need to find Brannon and warn him about what Nycol is up to." He turned and assessed the mirror cage. "Go and fetch a cart. We're going to need to bring whatever we can to give us an edge."

Shalyn snorted. "A cart? Who's going to give me a cart?"

So much for being an obedient child.

He opened his mouth to tell her exactly what he thought of that when a wave of magic washed over him. It flowed from somewhere near the palace and flooded across the city, crashing into every corner like an oncoming tide. He swayed under its impact. So powerful! More than anything he could do.

Shalyn's eyes widened. She felt it too.

The force of it was like a punch to Draeson's gut, leaving him breathless and afraid.

"Oh gods," he gasped. "It's happening. We're too late!"

CHAPTER THIRTY-SIX

The glowing green stone hung in the air between Brillen and Alyra - rather, Nycol in Alyra's body - like a magical bullseye. Part of Brannon wanted to attack the stone itself for the havoc it had wreaked, but that was a trick. The stone was merely the murder weapon. The villains here, the murderers themselves, floated either side of it and drifted slowly further apart, the increasing distance lending emphasis to the choice they'd demanded he make: try to stop one of them while the other killed again.

His friend or his city. The ruler or the people.

A groan from inside the house indicated Reanna, at least, was still alive.

He glanced across the balcony. His sword lay on the floor, out of reach, with burned and broken wicker furniture scattered around it.

"Perhaps he'll do nothing and let us both go," Nycol said, her words containing the mocking tone Brannon was familiar with from the mage but in Alyra's higher, feminine voice. "How disappointing."

Brannon's gaze flicked between them. There was no way he could let either of them go. This was the point of Brillen's plan - to torture him with a choice with no right answer. The mage would be hardest to take down but also would save the most lives. The would-be assassin was going for Brannon's friend and king. He forced a deep breath into his lungs. He knew what Aldan would say. Trading one life for many was part of a leader's job. He also knew he couldn't live with himself if his friend was killed because of what he did next. But then, Aldan was a soldier too.

"Come on, Brannon!" Brillen hurled the words like a school yard bully. "Choose!"

Brannon forced his body into action. He ran for the balcony railing. One step. Two. Three. A leap and his foot landed on the railing and he pushed off, launched into the air towards Nycol. He pulled a dagger from his belt and hurled it at Brillen. It sank into the man's thigh a split second before Brannon himself collided with the levitating mage. He clung to her, wrapping arms and legs around her, pinning her limbs in a desperate attempt to at least hinder her magic casting. Any lingering hope that Nycol's new appearance was an illusion was quickly dispelled. She felt real. This was no illusion.

Nycol gave a loud grunt and all three of them dropped to the ground as the impact broke her concentration and the magic keeping them airborne was broken.

The remaining magic softened the fall slightly but the ground still hit Brannon like a mallet. Nycol landed on top of him and the shock loosened his grip on her. She rolled off of him and onto her feet. He scrambled after her but a blast of wind from her outthrust hand pushed him back and he landed on his backside on the grass.

A few feet away, Brillen swore, pulled the dagger from his thigh, and dropped it to the ground. "You Hooded bastard," he growled. "You'll get yours." He limped in the direction of the palace.

Brannon reached for another weapon but he had none left. He had to let Brillen go and focus his attention on the mage. She was the greater threat. It had taken his entire team to capture Nycol the first time. Now, he had to do it alone.

He stared at her, his mind racing. Surely someone had seen the lightning storm attack on the balcony. Even now, there could be guards coming to investigate the disturbance. Any distraction would help. He had to stall her.

"So what made you team up with Brillen?" he said, pitching his voice loud enough for Brillen to hear as well. "He doesn't seem all that stable."

The soldier ignored him and limped on.

Brannon grimaced. It'd been too much to hope that he could delay them both.

Nycol raised an eyebrow. "That's your question?" she said, gesturing to her new body. "Not this?"

"Alyra has political power and you have magic." Brannon shrugged. "If you're going to steal a body as part of a getaway plan, you could do worse. Is she still in there?" Perhaps Alyra could be an ally. Perhaps.

Nycol shook her head. "Oh no. She's in my old body and quite dead, I'm afraid."

Brannon shut his eyes for a moment. Much as he hadn't particularly liked Alyra, she didn't deserve to die. It was going to be difficult to explain to the Nilarian government. "So she's another in this list of random people you and Brillen have been murdering together. Why?"

"It's kept you and your merry gang on their toes." She chuckled. "Mostly it's just been Brillen getting his revenge on you. Although he did help me out with one or two difficulties. That homeless conspiracy theorist almost ruined my plans for the masquerade. You should check his history - he's a suspicious one all right. Followed me around and even pointed me out to the city guard a couple of times. But he was a good trial run for the memory spectre."

"The what?" Brannon shifted on the grass. He carefully made no effort to stand up but instead edged himself closer to where Brillen had dropped the dagger. "What's a memory spectre?"

"This." She raised her hand and the bravery medal with the glowing green stone floated up in front of her. "This little chunk of broken magic."

Brannon stared at it. He could feel the thing's influence lapping at the edges of his mind. This was what had him feeling fuzzy and fearful of late. He'd been carrying the thing around in his pocket ever since retrieving it from Alissa's store when she'd confirmed the gemstone wasn't a real emerald. Then he'd *worn* it. "What is it? What does it do?"

"Ah." Nycol chuckled, a light and musical sound at odds with her expression. "It's a corruption. They happen sometimes when those dabbling with death magic try to store the power for later use. The stones can twist the magic in unexpected ways and become dangerous. This one...well, this one is at least a little predictable. It makes people's fears come true."

A bark of laughter broke free of Brannon's throat before he could stop it. "What? That's nonsense." But even as he said it, the humor drained from his face. It wasn't nonsense at all.

Nycol watched his expression closely. "There you go," she said. "It starts to make sense now, doesn't it? Burning to death, being crushed, hanging - people have so many fears. Especially in the wake of a war. So many possible ways this pretty little stone could bring about your death or the deaths of those around you. All we needed was to put it in a form people would keep with them. Ren's little gem forgery side-line was perfect for that. And here we go." She flicked her fingers and the medal flew forward, attaching itself to Brannon's shirt. "Tell me, what are you afraid of?"

Brannon brushed at it like a spider but the medal stuck fast. "None of your business," he snarled.

"Oh, come now. We've seen a few of them already. Weren't you just complaining that people were being magically attacked all around you? That's not a coincidence. That's your fears coming true." Nycol stepped closer and crouched down. Her knees spread in a masculine fashion, pulling on the fabric of her skirt, and she rested her elbows on her thighs. For a moment Brannon could see the man she'd been earlier in the day staring out of her new eyes. She wasn't yet used to this new body, yet. There had to be a way to use that to his advantage.

"I...I don't know." He played scared, crawling backwards a step. His fingers closed on the hilt of the dagger Brillen had dropped. He gripped it tight but kept close to the ground, hidden in the grass. "I guess, I'm scared of the war starting again." Truth was a better bluff than a lie. He had to keep her attention on his face, not the knife in his hand. He would have one shot to incapacitate a mage and one shot only.

"Oh please." She sneered. "Nobody wants war. That's a generic fear. Surface level and broad. Nothing. This is a *memory* spectre. It wants something visceral and yours. Something specific. An attack on the king happened because you fear you let him down. An attack on a child happened because you harmed a child. What else is there, Brannon? What wakes you in the night in a cold sweat?"

Brannon swallowed. He remembered the dream that had woken him most recently. The soaked sheets. The suffocation.

She leaned forward, resting one hand on the ground, and reached out with the other to touch the moisture on his forehead. "Yes. There it is. Tell me how it feels."

"Like this." He lunged at her and thrust the dagger up into her stomach, aiming to slide under the ribcage and cut through lungs, heart, and any other essential organs he could reach.

The dagger struck a solid barrier just a fraction above Nycol's body. The blade shattered. The impact rocked Brannon back. Agony shot through his arm, twisted in his elbow, and thudded in his shoulder. The handle dropped from his numb fingers.

"That was rude." Nycol rolled her eyes. "Did you really think I wouldn't be on my guard against you?"

"You're a menace," Brannon told her. "You and your magic stone."

"Oh, Brannon. How right you are. But I have my reasons." She gave a sad smile and stroked her hand down his cheek. "Shall I tell you one of my fears?"

"I don't care," he said.

She continued as if he hadn't spoken. "I'm afraid I won't be able to find a new body when the time comes. It's simple, I know, to be afraid of death - especially when one is immortal as mages are - but there it is. So I came here to find a solution to my fear. And I have one. I'm sorry it means bringing yours to life but, as Brillen would say, I have to choose."

She flicked her fingers at him and Brannon felt invisible bands of force pinning his arms and legs. He strained against them but couldn't move at all.

"What do you want from me, Nycol?"

She sat next to him, looking for all the world like they were a pair of lovers having a picnic on the lawn. "I want your worst moment, Brannon. I want your most fearful memory to come pouring through that stone and wipe out this entire city so that death magic can be soaked right up and make this body young and immortal forever, like what Draeson did when you drowned half our army."

Brannon's eyes widened. He felt the chill of ice against his hand. The ice that held back the River Tilal. The ice he would smash to trigger Draeson's spell. "No."

"My dear, your fear isn't the war. Your fear is doing what you've already done - being the cause of thousands of deaths." Her voice was soft and gentle but every word brought panic flooding into Brannon's chest. A torrent of terror and memory. The screams. The water. The death.

"No!" He struggled for breath, choking. He coughed up what felt like water but there was nothing.

"You fear you'll fail your country and innocent people will pay for your atrocities," Nycol continued. "So many people will drown, Brannon. And it's all your fault."

The stone in the medal on his chest pulsed like a heartbeat. The weird green light flowed out from it in all directions. Brannon tried to scream but he couldn't.

He was drowning.

CHAPTER THIRTY-SEVEN

Taran pulled his king's pass out and let it hang around his neck like a badge as he and Darnec approached the palace gate. Between that and Darnec's uniform, no one challenged them as they ran headlong through the door and into the huge stone building. Servants and guards scattered as they passed. Nobles turned to shoot disapproving glares but said nothing. When they reached the corridor leading to the throne room, Taran felt a tap on his shoulder.

"You go ahead and tell the king what you all learned," Darnec said. "I'll go and put the palace guard on alert. The rest of my team should be here with the Bishop soon."

Taran nodded, still unsure what he was going to say, and knocked on the huge double-doors as Darnec hurried away.

The left of the two opened, seemingly of its own accord and a small voice said "Enter."

Taran stepped inside and peered behind the door. Young Prince Tomidan grinned back at him.

"Brother Taran!" The boy flung his arms around Taran. "Come play with us. We're playing king and courtier."

Taran patted the boy's back awkwardly and looked over his head to take in the room. He hadn't seen the throne room empty before. There were no courtiers, no guards, just a large, empty space dominated by the throne raised on a dais. The throne, however, was not empty. Prince Claydan sat in the king's seat, one leg casually hooked over the arm of the throne and his head resting on his hand.

"Um," Taran said, cocking his head to the side. "Where's the king?"

"Claydan is the king and I'm the courtier," said Tommy.

"We flipped a coin for it," Claydan said.

"He's a good king." Tommy disengaged from Taran and performed a florid bow in the direction of the throne, almost tipping over due to the extra embellishment.

"I'm sure he is." Taran steadied the boy but kept his eyes on his old friend. The Children of Starlight training included sleight of hand. Claydan was more than capable of rigging a coin toss, even for a game. "Are you all stocked up on stardust elixir?"

Claydan nodded. "Of course."

"Good."

"Still no sign that Tommy needs it?" Claydan queried. He shifted so that both feet were on the floor and leaned forward in the throne but made no effort to get up.

"Not that I've seen," Taran said. "Have you seen anything?"

The prince shook his head.

"Okay. And the real king? King Aldan. Where is he?"

Claydan pointed to a door in the side of the room. "Through there. Signing paperwork."

The door led to a large office dominated by a huge wooden desk carved along the sides with an array of animals all sitting at attention, awaiting a command from the owner of the desk. One entire wall was bookshelves filled with histories and law books for quick and easy reference. Another was an enormous map of Kalanon with each territory marked out in a different color and the names and manors of each noble house written in large calligraphy.

Aldan sat behind the desk, pen in hand, and a sheaf of papers thick enough to be a book itself in front of him. He looked up when Taran entered, blinked, and then gestured to the single chair that faced him across the wide desk. "It's not often you visit these days. Is this about Tommy? Or Clay?"

Taran shook his head and eased himself into the chair. "No, your majesty. But it is an urgent matter. We...that is, me, Ambassador Ylani, Prioress Ula, and Darnec Raldene...believe you and perhaps even the city to be in danger."

Aldan set the pen down on the sheaf of papers. "I'm in danger or the city is in danger? Those are two quite different things."

"Yes, Your Majesty." Taran shifted in the chair. "I realize this seems vague but there is good reason for concern."

"Tell me more." The king rested his elbows on the desk, pressed his fingers together against his lips, and rested his chin on his thumbs, listening.

"It stems from the investigation of Bishop Narayan. It seems the boy he has with him is something of an oracle. Gifted. And he may have been correct in his assertion that Sir Brannon is a source of danger. Ambassador Ylani says-"

Aldan raised his hand for silence.

Taran let his voice die.

"Are you telling me," the king said softly, "that you're accusing my oldest friend of launching some kind of attack, based on nothing more than the word of a Nilarian, a child, and a man you yourself told me was a danger to the children in his care?"

"I..." Taran's mouth moved soundlessly. "Um...th-the Instinct."

Aldan rolled his eyes. "Taran, you know I am eternally grateful to you for your service in the past and I will always listen to your concerns. You unmasked an assassination plot against me when we first met and you helped rescue my son. So when you tell me there is danger, I will listen. But you must bring me something more concrete than this. What can I do with what you've told me? It's an unsubstantiated accusation of an even more vague attack. What do you expect me to do?"

"Um...Ylani suggested more guards..."

"Ylani is not king here or even Kalan. Ahpra's Tears, she's not even the ambassador anymore. Alyra Jalin is replacing her."

Taran stared. He hadn't known Ylani was being replaced. He kicked himself for not realizing her word might not be enough for the Kalan king. Yes, she'd helped Kalanon before but she was still an outsider. Still Nilarian. Even when the others arrived, it was going to be a hard sell to convince Aldan to take the threat seriously. Taran himself had trouble believing Brannon would be a danger to the citizens of Alapra.

He was still struggling to find a suitable response when the door opened without knocking.

"Blood and Tears," muttered the king. "Are my guards just letting anyone wander in now?"

Brillen stepped into the room, pushing Prince Tomidan in front of him. The young prince moved stiffly. Brillen kept his hand on the boy's shoulder and nudged the door closed behind him. "The guards are all gone, Your Majesty. Prince Claydan released them." He frowned. "Brother Taran. I didn't expect to see you here. Do we have one of our group meetings today?"

"No." Taran shook his head, puzzled. "Not today." A meeting like that wouldn't have been in the king's office anyway.

"What brings you to see me?" Aldan said. "If you're looking for Claydan..."

Brillen cut him off. "I'm not looking for Claydan. I'm looking for you."

Aldan raised his eyebrows. "Why is that?"

As they spoke, Taran watched Tommy's face. His lip trembled and his body winced under Brillen's touch. The boy was nervous. Scared, even. Taran leaned in his chair and caught a glimpse of something shiny and metallic behind Tommy's back. "Knife!" He jumped to his feet, pointing.

Brillen pulled Tommy closer, forcing the young prince between him and the others like a shield.

Tommy arched his back, pulling his small body as far from the point of the dagger as he could.

Aldan stood and drew his sword. "What is the meaning of this?"

Brillen snarled. "Oh, shut your face!"

Taran turned and grabbed the back of the chair

and, in one smooth movement, spun back, hurling it up at Brillen's head. It flew too high, as he'd intended to avoid hitting Tomidan, but close enough that Brillen let go of the prince to shield his face with his arm.

Tommy ran across the room and hid behind Taran. He cowered behind him, whimpering, much as he had the night his mother had died.

Taran let the knives in his wrist sheaths drop into his hands and shifted into a fighting stance. "Keep back," he warned.

Brillen used his now free hand to draw a sword of his own. He now had a blade in each hand, one long and one short. "I'm not here for you or the boy, Taran. He was just a way in. I'm here for him." He nodded toward the king.

Taran edged forward, blades raised. "Either way, I can't let you."

Brillen scowled. "Don't get in my way."

Taran threw one of the daggers but Brillen swung his own blade and swatted it out of the air. The clash of metal rang loud in the office and the dagger clattered into the bookcase and then onto the floor. One of the books followed it with a dull thud.

Brillen darted around the side of the desk and swung his sword at the king. Taran leapt onto the desk and lunged out with his dagger. Aldan raised his own sword to block and all three blades clanged together.

"Get the guards, Tommy," Aldan said through gritted teeth.

"Don't move, boy," Brillen snarled.

Tommy ran for the door and Brillen lunged for him, swinging the dagger in his left hand like an axe.

Taran slid off the desk, ducked beneath Brillen's extended sword, and slashed his own dagger at the man's thigh, drawing a long line of red and torn fabric to match the blood leaking from a roughly bandaged wound on his other leg.

Brillen screamed.

Taran rolled and came back up on his feet between the soldier and the boy prince.

"I don't know what this is about but you won't win here." Aldan stepped around his desk, sword raised. "There are two of us and you no longer have a hostage."

Brillen sneered. "I don't need a hostage. I don't even need to kill you myself. I just have to watch."

"Watch what?" Taran gestured behind him for Tommy to back away while keeping himself ready for an attack.

"Here it comes."

Pale green light burst through the wall behind him and washed across the room in a wave. The light filled the room in a strange sort of haze and flowed onward.

The air thickened in Taran's throat. He

swallowed to clear it, then coughed. His chest felt heavy. He gasped for air but the thick wet sensation flooded into his lungs. His eyes bulged. He dropped the daggers and thumped his chest, but it did nothing. He was choking. Choking on nothing.

Across the room, King Aldan's face was red and his mouth was making huge gulping motions.

"Taran!" Tomidan's small voice was filled with panic. His eyes were filled with tears and he too was struggling to breathe.

Taran reached for the boy. He'd kept him safe from the monster that killed his mother and rescued him from kidnap by assassins but this...Taran didn't know how to fight against magic that choked like water poured into the lungs. He held Tommy close. The best he could do was protect him against the other threat in the room.

But it seemed Brillen was no longer a threat. The returned slave was doubled over, gasping for breath himself. His face was contorted in an expression of betrayal and rage. "No!" he gasped. "Not me! Nycol, not me too! You promised!" Then he fell to the floor.

That was the last thing Taran saw before the sparks dancing at the edge of his vision went dark and he tumbled into unconsciousness.

CHAPTER THIRTY-EIGHT

Ylani set the pace and Ula hurried to catch up. The Djin woman's bare feet slapped on the cobblestones but Ylani kept her strides long and swift, just short of a run. People in the street saw her face and moved out of her way. The urgency the Instinct had instilled in her burned like a hot coal in her chest. Her thoughts ran through her mind even faster than her steps.

She'd sent Taran and Darnec ahead to warn the king. She was sure they needed Draeson for whatever was coming and he had to be at the prison with Nycol. He had to. She didn't know where else to find him. And then...

"I thought we had to find Brannon," Ula said, skipping a couple of paces to keep by her side. "Will he be with Draeson?"

"No. But I saw Brannon with Reanna Kesh. Draeson will know where she stays and can help us with whatever is coming. And Brannon wouldn't hurt his sister." She hoped.

"What *is* coming?" Ula asked, puffed for breath. "What's he going to do?"

"I don't know. Something bad." It was so frustrating! She could only imagine how Jecksen had coped all this time with such an undefined threat hanging over him. Everything Ylani had learned about Brannon since coming to Kalanon said he was trustworthy. That he wouldn't hurt anyone without a good reason. And yet she was terrified. He was behind something truly horrifying. Every bit of her Instinct screamed at her to run. To get out of Alapra and run as far as she could.

But she wouldn't. She had to find Brannon. She had to help.

A few streets later, she recognized the intersection where she and Brannon fought. The harsh words seemed like another lifetime. How had she missed that something was wrong with him? She pushed the recriminations and memories out of her mind. There would be time to figure out if there had been signs to see later. Right now, she had to get Draeson and get to Brannon.

She turned and headed toward the court complex where the magically reinforced cell containing Nycol was. This late in the day, the street was quiet, just a few people going about their business under the last rays of the sun and the early-lit streetlamps. The steps at the prison had been washed and there was no trace of the blood that had been there earlier in the day. There was nothing to suggest danger.

Then it hit.

A green haze washed through the streets and the impact was profound. People bent over gasping for air. Ylani felt a thickness in her own lungs and breathing became harder, like forcing water in and out of her chest.

"No!" She gripped Ula's arm as the two women fought for air. "This is it!"

The door at the top of the stairs burst open and Draeson stumbled out, struggling for breath, followed by a girl. His eyes were wide and he missed one of the steps and almost fell, catching himself before reaching the cobblestoned streets.

Ylani rushed up to him and helped him stand. "Draeson! Draeson, this is magic!"

He scowled at her. "Of course it's magic!" he gasped.

"Then-" her words were lost as she choked on the watery air invading her lungs. "Fight it!" she coughed out at last.

The look on the ancient mage's face terrified her. "I can't," he said. He waved to the city around them. People everywhere were choking, gasping...drowning, dry and away from water. The spell was everywhere. It was too big. The entire city of Alapra was drowning. Draeson's words were barely above a whisper but they were flooded with despair. "If I had time to prepare, maybe I could shield one or two people but...I can't."

Ylani stared at him in horror. They were going to die. Everyone. The entire city awash with deadly magic and the most powerful mage they knew was helpless against it.

A hand laid on her shoulder, warm and dry and purple with dark tattoos flowing over and around it. The beads in Ula's hair were glowing like colored fireflies. Her eyes were solid agate. "I can."

Ylani stepped back. Her heart pounded in her chest and she struggled for breath as she stared. She'd seen Ula like this before, when she'd been an avatar for the Earth Spirits and had given her and Brannon boosted abilities to deal with Risen. There were no Risen now, but the Djin woman spoke in a low rhythmic chanting, her strange language like a drum beat just out of earshot.

"Don't do it," Draeson gasped. "Mixing magics...unpredictable." He swayed on his feet and the girl tried to steady him. They leaned into each other and both sank slowly to the ground, puffing as if they'd run the length of the city.

Ylani forced her breathing to calm. Slow and deep. But no matter what she did, the sensation of breathing liquid instead of air only grew worse. Stars sparked on the edge of her vision. No, they were dancing around Ula. The lights in her hair flew free and spiraled in the air.

Ylani blinked to clear her vision but the lights weren't just around Ula. They *were* Ula. A transparent version of the Djin shaman, filled with sparkling lights, separated from her body and moved toward Ylani. The transparent Ula leaned in and brushed her lips against Ylani's and sweet, breathable air flowed into her lungs. Ylani breathed deep, then the transparent Ula moved on and breathed into Draeson, then into the girl beside him, then moved on down the street stopping to breathe into every struggling person she met.

Ylani felt a lift of relief but with her next breath, the choking thick sensation of drowning returned.

Another transparent Ula separated and provided another lifesaving breath. So did another. The real Ula was trembling with effort. Sweat ran down her face.

Ylani used the next gifted breath to help her friend to the stairs and sat her down. "Ula, what are these? What are you doing?"

"Air Spirits," Ula said. Her voice was strained. "Helping to breathe." Her head rolled back as yet another of the Air Spirits separated from her avatar self and her dreadlocks fell back revealing a trickle of red from her ear.

"Ula, you're bleeding!" Ylani dabbed at the

blood even as another of the Air Spirit Ulas breathed into her. She dreaded each one leaving her, knowing the choking flood would return to her lungs - but also that every other person in Alapra needed a life-saving breath.

Ula nodded. "Sacrifice. Every bargain has price."

"Hooded elementals," Draeson said. He was back on his feet now, the periodic breaths counteracting the drowning effect of the spell just enough for him to bring out the growl in his voice. "They're dangerous. They'll drain you dry if you keep this up."

Ula shot him a pained smile but it didn't reach her eyes. "Better hurry then, wizard," she said. "Stop the spell and save us all. Or else, when I die, so will all of Alapra."

CHAPTER THIRTY-NINE

The world dimmed with every beat of Brannon's heart, each pulse slower and darker than before. He was drowning. Drowning on dry land, surrounded by the ghosts of Nilarian soldiers he'd killed. With each pulse of darkness they pulled him closer, deeper, colder. He couldn't breathe. Fight as he might, without air, there was no survival.

Nycol's new face filled his vision. She smiled at him. "Everyone's dying because of you, Brannon," she said. "The whole city is drowning and you won't get the chance to atone for it this time."

He fought for breath, fought to think how to stop the drowning. There was no way to swim when the water wasn't real. No way to breathe when the air was thick and liquid in his lungs. The stone pinned to his chest radiated pale green light and his oxygen-starved brain fixated on it. There was something about that stone. He batted at it weakly but it wouldn't budge.

"Uh-uh," Nycol chided. "You and the memory spectre have a bit more work to do."

His lungs were burning. The pain was sharper and hotter with each passing moment. He coughed and gasped but it made no difference. The darkness closed in even longer this time. Soon the pulse would be endless and the pain would stop. Death was only a few pulses away.

The light returned, hazy and speckled, like looking at the world through the translucent shell of a robin's egg. Something rippled in the haze - a figure.

Nycol's voice came as if from the other end of a tunnel. "What are you?"

Brannon squinted, then reached out towards the strange figure. "Ula?"

The physician part of his brain told him he was seeing things. The lack of air was messing with his mind. This Ula was transparent. She was a shape of air and sparkling lights, like a goddess. She wasn't real. She couldn't be real.

Even as he stared at her, she leaned in and pressed her lips to his. They were cool, soft, a brush of wind against his skin.

Air!

Blessed, breathable air flowed from her mouth to his and he gulped it into his starving lungs in long shuddering gasps. The darkness receded and the world fell back into focus.

Nycol stared at them, her head tilted and eyes wide. "I was not expecting that," she said.

The stone pulsed again and as Ula pulled away, the air thickened in his throat once again. "Ula!" Brannon choked, pointing toward the mage's new body. "Help! That's Nycol. We need to stop her."

But Ula, still indistinct and incorporeal, looked past him and glided away. She floated up and over the balcony into his family's townhouse. Brannon looked around and several other ghostly Ula figures floated in the distance, wafting in and out of buildings and pausing to breathe into fallen citizens.

He grabbed for the broken dagger hilt and gripped it in tight fingers. He had only moments before the drowning spell incapacitated him again. He had to do something to defeat Nycol and her spell. He chipped at the medal on his chest with the broken remains of the dagger. Pain and blood blossomed in his chest as the sharp edge slipped off the stone and cut through his shirt and into his skin. He slashed around the medal, cutting the fabric it was attached to and still it wouldn't fall. He grabbed at it and pulled as hard as he could but it would not budge.

"Come on, Brannon," Nycol taunted. "You should know a soldier's weapons are no match for magic. After all, you used magic to drown thousands of Nilarian soldiers."

Brannon launched to his feet and charged at Nycol, shoulder first, hoping a blunt attack might be enough to shock her into loosening her magic. He half expected to shatter like the dagger blade had done but instead his shoulder connected with Nycol's.

"Oof," the mage grunted.

Brannon slashed upward with the broken dagger.

Nycol pushed at him with her magic and both he and the dagger flew backward to land with a thump. What little air he had left in his lungs exited in a whoosh and he gasped invisible water instead. His eyes bulged and his mouth worked like a fish on land.

One of the transparent Ulas appeared and breathed air into him before drifting off. Whatever they were, it seemed they would keep him alive. Just.

Nycol scowled. "I'll have to see what I can do about those things. Hooded air elementals." She made an odd gesture with her hand and a bolt of lightning shot from her palm and wrapped around the Ula figure. Fingers of electricity jumped between the lights within the Air Spirit's insubstantial body and it screamed like the wind in a cyclone and exploded in a shower of sparks.

"No!" Brannon exclaimed.

Nycol grinned. "That's better."

The other Air Spirit Ulas turned and glared at the mage, then drifted on with their task.

Brannon stared after them, watching for signs of injury or distress. How much of the real Ula was in each of these copies? Did destroying one hurt her? How many could be lost before she would no longer be able to recover? He simply didn't know and the fear ate at him. Ula could be dying one piece at a time because of him. Just as he and everyone else in the city drowned piece by piece. "Please don't do that again." He heard himself beg and hated it. "I don't want anyone else to die."

"You can't always get what you want, Brannon." Nycol said, coolly. She paced around him in a circle, thrusting her hands toward the ground with every second step and with each thrust a rod of crackling energy spiked into the earth. When she finished pacing, the rods stretched over the top of him and connected at the highest point, creating a dome of glowing bars of electricity. "Let's see them get through that," she muttered.

Brannon reached out and brushed one of the bars with his fingers. A slap of pain flung his arm back and he clutched it to his chest. Already the borrowed air in his lungs was running out and the drowning sensation returned. Now he was trapped as well. Darkness shimmered on the edge of his vision. On the other side of the glowing bars of lightning, another Ula made of light and air glided up. She peered through at him but the energy of his cage crackled when she came too close and she backed away. Another one approached from the other side, only to be repelled as the first had been.

"They can't help you now," Nycol sneered. "And eventually your little friend will get tired and these elementals will disappear. Nobody's power is limitless."

Brannon tried to bring his face closer to the bars, hoping the Air Ula could reach him but the sharp slap of stung his cheek and sent him reeling again. He coughed and coughed, each time expecting to bring up river water from his lungs but there was nothing. He felt the wave of darkness rising. Any moment the dam would break and it would wash him away.

The memory of drowned corpses rose in his vision. The rush of water and gurgling screams of dying people struggling to swim in armor filled his ears. He grabbed his head in his hands and rocked on his heels even as his own lungs were swamped with liquid.

"It's your fault, Brannon!" The voices of thousands of drowned soldiers echoed in his dying mind. He could no longer tell if they were real or memory. More voices joined in - the people of Alapra who were dying along with him now. "Your fault, Brannon!"

A flash of light burst across the sky and another scream filled the air.

"Brannon. Brannon!" It was only one voice this time. One familiar voice.

"Ylani?" He opened his eyes. The world was blurry. "You came for me?"

The Nilarian ambassador knelt on the grass beside the glowing cage. Behind her was a horse and cart she'd driven right up onto the grass, presumably with Draeson as a passenger. Brannon wondered blearily why the horse was unaffected by the spell that was drowning every human in the city.

"Magus!" Ylani shouted. "He's here! We need to break him out." She leaned back and one of the Air Spirits breathed into her mouth.

"I know," Draeson shouted back. "Working on it."

The Air Spirit began drifting off. Ylani grabbed at it but her arm passed right through. "Don't you dare," she growled. "He needs you!"

Brannon felt his heart pounding against his ribcage. His chest and face were on fire. He turned to see Draeson hurl a ball of lightning at Nycol. The other mage deflected it upward and it sailed toward the stars. Draeson followed it up with another.

Brannon slumped on the ground. His head rolled back and his sight narrowed so that the glowing balls of energy were suns being thrown about by the gods.

"Now, Draeson!" Ylani screamed. "Or he's not going to make it."

Both mages hurled lightning balls and they collided in a spectacular explosion of color. Draeson flung out an arm toward Brannon and the dragon tattoo on his palm roared. The glowing energy bars froze and shattered under the impact of that roar and the air elemental Ula rushed in and pressed herself against Brannon.

He drew a long desperate gasping breath from her. Then another. And another. Then the Ula figure floated away.

Ylani was beside him, touching his face and breathing in short shallow gasps. "Are you okay?"

He nodded, trying to save the air he had before the drowning spell took hold of him again. "My sister..." He pointed toward the house.

"I'll check on her. Ula is going to breathe for everyone as long as she can." Ylani pressed her lips against his forehead. "You need to find a way to stop this." She stood and hurried up the stairs.

Brannon dragged himself to his feet. Something thudded against his chest. He looked down and discovered the circle of fabric he'd cut earlier was loose and hanging by a thread. The glowing medal with its cursed gemstone swung like a pendulum. The magic that had held it in place was gone now that Nycol's attention was taken up with her battle against Draeson but the spell that connected the stone's magic to Brannon's memories and fears was still very much intact. He could feel it feeding on him even as it filled his lungs yet again. The drowning and being rescued by Ula could not go on forever. He had to find a way to stop the spectre's power from using him. Or at least from influencing the rest of the city.

He wrapped his fingers around the medal and tugged it free of his clothes. If only disentangling it from his mind were as easy. He dragged himself toward the two mages. Lightning crackled across the space between them as they flung magic at each other.

"You're not getting away with this, Nycol," Draeson growled. "I won't let you murder an entire city!"

Nycol sneered. "Oh please. There's no fool like an old fool and you were an old fool even when you were young. I've been playing you ever since I arrived in Kalanon. Give up. We're both getting tired and you know I'm going to win. I'm stronger."

"Draeson!" Brannon held up the glowing stone. "We have to destroy this. And contain her!" He had no idea how to do either.

Nycol laughed. "By all means try to destroy the spectre. Any magic you throw at it now will only feed its power. As long as it's connected to a fear memory, nothing will stop it."

"Almost nothing." Draeson raised his hands

and a swirling wind rose up to tear at their clothes. "You had the right idea, Brannon," he said, his voice raised against the rushing wind. "It's all about containment."

At Draeson's gesture, several large flat objects rose up out of the cart he and Ylani had arrived in. They turned in the wind like a giant chandelier and moonlight sparkled silver on the shining surfaces.

"Mirrors?" murmured Brannon in bewilderment. Then it clicked. Mirrors! From the containment spell that had kept Nycol trapped for so long. He turned back to see Nycol frowning. She would know what they were just as he did. Any second she would realize what she needed to do and shatter the mirrors to shards.

He screamed at the top of his voice and ran full speed at the magus.

She turned at this attack and lashed out with whips of power. The first one wrapped around his wrist, burning like fire. The second caught his ankle and jerked it out from under him. Brannon fell and rolled, the strands of fire cutting into his clothes and his flesh, sharp and vicious. His hand clenched on the medal in his hand with such force that it cut into his palm and he felt the metal bend and pop as the gemstone released from the gold setting. Pulses of pain throbbed through Brannon like a heartbeat. He groaned and writhed on the ground, only slightly exaggerating the effects on his body for the sake of putting on a show. He screamed again.

The mirrors levitated into a wide circle, surrounding him and Nycol. They thudded into the ground, standing like reflective doorways to other worlds.

Nycol's head jerked up at the sound. The lashes of power on Brannon's wrist and ankle vanished.

"Oh no, you don't," she snapped. She thrust a palm at one of the mirrors and a gust of wind shoved it back out of the circle and it toppled over to lay flat on the grass. She pulled something from her pocket and raised her hand to her mouth.

Brannon recognized the gesture. "Draeson! Look out!"

Nycol blew the glittering powder into Draeson's face. "And sleep."

Draeson gasped, blinked twice, and slumped to the ground.

"No! Hooded shit!" Brannon dragged himself toward her again but the congealed breath in his lungs choked him. One of the Ula elementals drifted close but he didn't have time to pause for her. He had to stop Nycol and stop her now.

"You still think you can take me on, little man?" Nycol laughed. "I've beaten your mage and my memory spectre is swallowing you whole. What do you have left to use against me?"

The words hit him like a physical blow. She was right. What did he have? Fists and harsh words, bravery in battle and loyalty to Kalanon. These were things that made him a good soldier but a soldier was nothing against magic. And even now the magic that drew on his memories as a soldier was draining him of his strength. There was nothing left. Nycol had won.

He hung his head and felt the water rising over him, swallowing his body whole.

Ylani's voice caught him like a lifeboat and hauled him up out of despair. "Brannon! Catch!"

She stood on the balcony above and tossed his sword down to him. The Nilarian steel blade flashed in the moonlight and spiked into the earth inside incomplete containment circle. It reflected in the surface of the mirror behind it. He stared. Ylani had made this sword for him. She'd given to him as a sign of their friendship and, despite everything he had said to her, she was here, giving him the sword again.

"Fight, Brannon. Fight!"

Brannon picked up the sword, still holding the spectre stone in his other hand. A movement behind the mirror caught his attention. A small figure slipped from shadow to shadow. Shalyn. The girl made her way around the circle toward the fallen mirror.

He raised the sword and turned back to Nycol. "I have this," he said. "And I have people I care about. To save this city I will fight you to my last breath." The stone in his left hand pulsed against his palm.

Nycol shrugged. "Well that last breath isn't far off. Do your worst."

Behind her, Shalyn grasped the edges of the fallen mirror and dragged it back into place. Then she hauled it up into standing position.

Brannon smiled. "I don't have to," he said. "Like I said, I have people with me."

The mirror slotted into position with a sound like a bell and all of the panels in the circle glowed with silver light. The containment spell snapped into place, surrounding them both.

Nycol's eyes widened. "NO!"

Brannon coughed. The last of his air was running out. He held up the glowing stone. "You're trapped and so is the fear spectre. I might drown but the city is safe." He dropped to his knees. The sword fell from numb fingers. Stars danced in his vision again.

Nycol closed the gap between them in a single, gliding stride. She gripped his torn shirt in hard, manicured fingers. The anger in her eyes was a palpable force, almost as suffocating as the spell. "Not safe, Brannon. Only delayed. You haven't saved them. It might take me longer to gather the power I need, is all. If I have to force the spectre on a thousand people in this Hooded city, I will. They'll die in a million different ways instead of all at once. I don't care. I won't be contained here forever. Just long enough to watch you die!" She shook him by the shirt, a low growl in her throat, teeth bared as if ready to take a bite out of his throat.

The world narrowed until all Brannon could see was that mouth and those teeth. The stone pulsed in his hand again and the weight of invisible water pressed down on him. The pressure could crush him while he drowned. Crushed like Donal or burned like the general or hanged like the tailor or drowned like a Nilarian soldier, it didn't matter. Nycol would watch and laugh with that mouth.

Brannon lunged upward and slipped the glowing stone between Nycol's teeth and pushed it as far as he could. Then he slammed the palm of his right hand up under her chin.

Nycol gasped and gave a surprised grunt. Her eyes widened and she grasped at her throat.

Brannon forced the last of his energy into standing. He kept the pressure on her jaw, holding it shut.

Her throat moved in an involuntary swallow.

Brannon's chest relaxed and air rushed into his straining lungs. Fresh, soft, breathable air.

Nycol staggered back and he let her go. Her eyes were wide. "No no no." She retched, trying to bring up the stone, but it was gone. "What have you done?"

"Gave you a taste of your own medicine, I

think." Brannon felt the strength return to his body and clarity to his mind. The spectre's influence was gone. It had found another host to draw from. He picked up his sword. "What did you say your worst fear was? Something about not being able to find a new body?" He stabbed the blade forward in a short, sharp jab. It slid into her gut like butter. "Find one now."

Nycol looked down as he pulled the sword free. Blood poured down her dress. Her face turned pale. "No no no," she repeated. "This can't be happening. This can't be...". She slid to her knees on the grass. "A descendant. I...I need a descendant. I..."

Her eyes turned glassy. A glowing mist emerged from her body and she slumped over on the ground. The mist hovered for a moment, unsure. It approached Brannon, then turned away. It rushed the gap between two of the mirrors but the containment spell held strong. There was nothing to bridge her to the other side. No body to take the magic inside. Nothing to inhabit. When the mist brushed against the surface of the mirror, the silvery material seemed to pull it in. She lingered a moment, like condensation, then she was gone.

CHAPTER FORTY

Brannon luxuriated in deep clear breaths of air. He'd believed he would never breathe freely again. Relief flowed into his veins along with oxygen, filling him with life once more. But it was short lived. The city was saved but the king was still in danger. Brannon wiped his sword and sheathed it. Shalyn jumped up and down, cheering. Ylani emerged from the house, collected the girl, and came to join Brannon.

"Well done," she said. "I knew you could do it."

"We're not done yet," he told her. He crouched next to Draeson's slumbering form and shook him.

Draeson did not rouse.

Shalyn flung herself to her knees next to the mage, her face crumpled. "Is he all right?"

Brannon nodded, frustration bubbling up inside him. Stopping Brillen without Draeson's help was going to be harder. "He's just sleeping. Roll him on his side and keep an eye on him. I'll be back."

"The king," muttered Ylani. "Of course."

Brannon looked at her, words stuck in his throat. She'd come back to help him and to help Kalanon, despite having good reasons to leave them both to their fate. He reached out to touch her but his hand hung in the air, as helpless as his tongue.

Ylani smiled and the words seemed unnecessary. Then she waved her hand at him. "Go," she said. "Save the king!"

"Thank you." He ran.

He ran past scared and shaking people as they climbed to their feet and clung to each other, grateful they could breathe again. He ran past the stunned guards at the palace door who called out asking if they were still under attack. He ran past sobbing servants and courtiers alike, all wondering what had happened and grateful to be alive. There was no time to stop for any of them. Brillen had too much of a head start. He pushed through the doors to the throne room, still running.

Prince Claydan was on his hands and knees in front of the throne, breathing deeply. He looked up when Brannon appeared. "What was that?"

"Another magical attack." Brannon searched the room for any other signs of life. "Where's your father?"

Claydan pointed. "Through there."

Brannon ran toward the antechamber door, drawing his sword as he went.

Claydan's eyes widened. "What are you doing?"

Brannon ignored him, urgency clawing at the inside of his chest.

Inside the office was chaos.

On one side of the room, Taran knelt over prince Tomidan. The young prince was on his side, tears running down his face. Papers from the desk were strewn across the floor and a bottle of ink had smashed, spilling its indigo blood in a pool. A bookshelf had tipped over, forming a barrier across the middle of the room. Brillen and the king faced off amongst the debris, swords drawn and faces severe.

Brannon caught the king's eye and, in an instant, they were back on the battlefield. Fighting together was second nature to them. They'd trained together as young men and fought side by side more times than they could count. They'd saved each other's lives in battle over and over. No matter how much Brillen wanted revenge for one of those times, Brannon had no intention of letting this be any different.

His old friend gave him an almost imperceptible signal. Aldan would distract Brillen by offering an opening and give Brannon a chance to strike. It was risky but a move they'd used many times before and, in tight quarters, they could use it to end this fight fast. Brannon nodded.

Aldan parried and turned, opening up his side.

Brillen saw the opening and moved forward to take advantage.

Aldan danced back as Brillen lunged and Brannon prepared to strike.

Just as Brannon was about to spike his sword forward, a blurr of movement caught the corner of his eye.

"No!" Claydan barreled through the door and collided with Brannon, knocking him off his feet. The two of them tumbled to the floor. "I won't let you hurt my father!"

Brannon's knuckles struck the side of the desk as he fell and his sword flew from his grasp, skittering across the room. He shoved his elbow back into the prince's chest.

Claydan yelped but held on.

"Get off. Get off!" Brannon shouted as he struggled to get back to his feet.

Too late, Aldan turned and brought up his arm to close up his exposure but Brillen's sword was already there. A line of red opened up across the king's forearm and then, as Brannon watched helplessly, the blade sank into his friend's side.

The dull thud of sword on spine sounded loud as a church bell.

Aldan stumbled. His legs gave way beneath

him and he fell, clutching the side of the desk as he went, like a drowning man clinging to a floating branch.

Brillen released his hold on the sword and let it fall with the king. It stuck out of him like a grotesque flagpole, with fluttering blood as the flag. He turned to Brannon. "You made your choice. Enjoy it." He ran for the door.

Brannon pushed the shocked Claydan off and kicked out with his foot. He caught Brillen's ankle and he tripped. Brannon sprang to his feet and shoved his whole weight against Brillen, forcing him into the wall. His face pressed into the map of Kalanon. The image of the River Tilal ran out of his eye.

"You've chosen to be a prisoner again." Brannon pulled Brillen's arm up behind his back, twisting it tight. "I hope you enjoy that."

Claydan scrambled across the floor to his father's side. His eyes were wide and glassy and his face white. "I'm so sorry, father. I'm so sorry! I thought Brannon was the threat. The prophecy said..."

"That doesn't matter now," Brannon told him harshly. "Come and hold Brillen so I can work on Aldan. I might be able to save him."

The prince stared up at him, shocked eyes uncomprehending for a moment, then he nodded. "Yes. Of course." He left his father on the floor and took Brannon's place pinning Brillen against the wall.

Brillen yelped as Claydan wrenched his twisted arm higher up his back.

Brannon ripped the cushion from the toppled chair and pressed it around the blade to stop the bleeding. "You better not die right now, Aldan. It'd just be embarrassing after getting through an entire war." The blood soaked through the cushion fabric faster than he wanted to see. "Taran," he called out, keeping his gaze fixed on the wound. "Wake yourself up and take Tommy to get Master Jordell from the hospital. Fast."

Aldan coughed. "Blood and Tears, Brannon. I'm on a skewer here. Pull out it, would you?"

Brannon shook his head. "Not until Jordell gets here with some equipment. Just to mop up the mess. This wound isn't really that bad."

Aldan snorted. "Yeah, it's barely a scratch." He swallowed and his grin faltered. "Hurts like a bitch though. Except...I can't feel my legs."

Brannon clenched his fists on the cushion. "Nothing to worry about," he lied. "We'll have you all patched up in no time."

"Of course." Aldan's eyelids drooped. "Well, let me know when you're done. And next time someone tries to kill me..." His voice trailed away and he fell silent.

Brannon drew a long, shuddering breath and

stared at his red-stained fingers. His friend's blood was on his hands. Too much blood.

"The king is dead," sneered Brillen. "Long live the king."

Claydan shoved him harder against the wall and drew a dagger from his belt. He pushed the blade through Brillen's temple and into his brain, jerked it out, and stabbed it back again.

The former soldier twitched once and slid to the floor.

Claydan went with him, still stabbing.

Blood and brain matter smeared down the wall.

"Long live Kalan justice," he said.

CHAPTER FORTY-ONE

The king's hospital room was surrounded by security. Brannon passed several guards on the way to visit his friend. Most of the country had no idea Aldan was there at all and those who did were sworn to secrecy. Nobody wanted a panic in the populace at a delicate time politically. An attack on the Kalan king and the death of the Nilarian envoy in the same night was inflammatory to say the least. People were nervous and the king's absence wasn't helping.

Brannon nodded to Darnec as the young man opened the door and let him through.

The king lay in bed, propped up by pillows, with his legs stretched out in front of him. A blanket covered him from the waist down. Aldan was careful not to look at his own legs. He'd been unable to move them since the attack.

Master Jordell hovered near the end of the bed. He set a pin down on a tray next to him. Brannon had seen him use that pin many times before to test sensation in the king's feet. He raised his eyebrow at his old mentor but Master Jordell shook his head. There was no change.

Brannon forced a cheery disposition. "How's our patient today?"

"Grumpy," said Master Jordell. "But healthy."

Aldan snorted. "There's a pad under me to collect my piss. Excuse me for not being a ray of Hooded sunshine."

"At least you're alive," Brannon said, helplessly. "I remember when that was our criteria for a good day."

Aldan gave him a hard look. "My standards have risen since the war." He sighed. "How's Claydan doing at court?"

Brannon scratched at his scar and took a deep breath. "He's doing fine. He's changed a few things but nothing too drastic."

"Good. Good." The king closed his eyes for a moment.

"When do you think you'll be back?"

Aldan opened his eyes again. He looked at Brannon, lids narrowed, then at his physician. "Could we have a moment, Master Jordell?"

"Of course." The old man bowed and left the room.

Aldan pulled himself further up the bed and pushed the pillows until he was fully sitting upright. His legs dragged behind his torso like an afterthought. "What is it, Brannon?"

"Prince Claydan..." His mouth was suddenly dry and he licked his lips in an attempt to moisten them. "There are those who might consider that he has benefited from your injury. And there are reasons to-"

Aldan held up his hand. "You figured out he was the one who slashed my portrait, didn't you?"

Brannon's eyes widened.

"He confessed to me shortly after it happened," Aldan continued. He patted the side of the bed and Brannon sat next to his king. "You don't have children, Brannon, so you can't understand. He's my son. And he was angry and foolish but he's still my son."

Brannon took a deep breath. "He's also the one who stopped me from saving you. Are you sure we can trust him?"

Aldan smiled weakly. "My son," he repeated, patting Brannon on the arm. "So, yes. I trust him. Don't forget, he thought - as did everyone else at that time - that you yourself were the threat."

The room felt colder than when Brannon had first walked in and Aldan's hand burned hot on his skin. Brannon struggled to swallow the emotion that welled up inside him. After weeks in hospital, the physician inside him knew the truth of the king's injury. Aldan was lucky to be alive but he would never walk again. The strong, vibrant man he'd fought with his whole life was physically broken. It remained to see how much of his mental health would break as well. Brannon felt his jaw tremble and he choked over the words but they spilled out anyway. "I'm sorry. I'm so sorry. I should have reached you sooner. I should have realized sooner."

Aldan stilled. His golden hair had dulled in the absence of sunlight but his eyes remained bright. "You shut up," he said, his voice gentle. "I've had reports from everyone involved. I know what you did and what was done to you." He gestured toward his legs. "This is not your fault. You made the right decision. It's the decision I would have made. A king should sacrifice for his people. The fact that you made the right call or figured out anything at all while under the influence of a magical fear-stone-"

"Memory spectre," Brannon corrected ruefully.

"Whatever." Aldan met Brannon's gaze directly. "You're lucky you didn't die yourself and all of Alapra with you. We owe you a debt of thanks. Remember that."

Brannon blinked away the dampness in his eyes and took a long, shuddering breath. He sniffed and nodded. "Thank you."

Aldan shrugged. "You're welcome. Now, do I wish I had dodged that sword a little better? Fuck yes! But here we are."

A bark of laughter burst from Brannon and his friend grinned at him.

"Good," Aldan said. He reached for a stack of papers on a table next to the bed. "And now that's sorted, I have some good news. Your parents have settled into Nilar and report that things are going well." He handed a letter across. "You have my permission to rub your sister's nose in it."

Brannon laughed again, the familiar banter was an intoxicating relief. "Thank you, Your Majesty."

"You're welcome. Now, get out of here and tell my son I'll be back on the throne soon. He's only temporary regent, after all."

"I will." Brannon stood and bowed. "I look forward to seeing you there."

He made his way out past the guards and through the familiar corridors to the waiting room where new patients presented themselves for assessment. It felt like a lifetime ago since he'd last been working here. His training had required many hours under Master Jordell's close supervision checking on the sick and injured as he learned the healer's craft. He missed those days. Being able to help people felt important. Recent events reminded him he had much more to do before the scales of his life would balance.

He poked his head into the office space where a young physician was writing notes. She looked up with a start. "Sir Brannon. What can I do for you?"

Brannon shrugged. "It's been a while since I've helped out around here. I thought I'd see if you could use a hand."

She smiled and nodded. "Always. But I believe there's someone waiting for you already." She gestured toward the waiting room.

Ylani stood, regal as always, in a deep blue silk gown and feathered fedora. Her lower lip was caught in her teeth and she held a sheet of paper in her hand. The Nilarian government seal was visible on the edge.

"Ylani?" Brannon stepped out into the waiting room

She gave a tenuous smile. "Brannon. I was hoping I would find you here."

"What is it?"

Her fingers clenched on the paper and it crumpled in her grasp. "I've been called back to Nilar. And...I'm hoping you'll come with me."

The words echoed in Brannon's mind. "Nilar?" There was no way he'd be welcome there. His presence would be seen only one way. He frowned. "Do you want Brannon or the Bloodhawk?"

Ylani met his eyes and her expression was shadowed by the brim of her hat. "I'm sorry, Brannon. I think I need both."

COMING SOON:

MERCURY'S RETURN

THANKS FOR READING! IF YOU ENJOYED THIS BOOK, PLEASE POST A REVIEW & TELL YOUR FRIENDS.

FOR "BEHIND THE SCENES" STORIES FROM KALANON AND INFORMATION ON UPCOMING RELEASES, JOIN MY MAILING LIST AT WWW.DARIAN-SMITH.COM

AUTHOR'S NOTE

Thank you for taking the time to read my book. I hope you enjoyed reading it as much as I enjoyed creating it.

Please post a review online and tell your friends about this book. Word of mouth makes a huge difference to an author and is greatly appreciated.

If you'd like to read some of my other work or keep up to date with future books, you can check out my website, join my e-mail list, or follow me on Facebook or Twitter.

Website: www.darian-smith.com

Facebook: DarianSmithAuthor

Twitter: @DarianWordSmith

ABOUT THE AUTHOR

Darian Smith lives in Auckland, New Zealand with his wife (who also writes) and their black cat (who doesn't).

By day, he works with people who have neuromuscular conditions such as muscular dystrophy or charcot marie tooth disease. He is also a qualified counsellor/family therapist and can be seen – by those very swift with the pause button – on television shows such as Legend of the Seeker and Spartacus.

For more information about Darian and his upcoming work, please check out his website at www.darian-smith.com.

SHIFTING WORLDS

A collection of short stories by Darian Smith
Foreword by Jennifer Fallon

Drag queens fight zombies.
An immigrant artist hopes love conquers all.
Deep space explorers wrestle with an alien artifact.
A superhero is locked in an insane asylum.
These 16 stories span the worlds of fantasy, sci-fi, and
literary fiction, and cause the characters' worlds to
fundamentally change. Includes several prize winning
stories as well as some that are seen for the first time in
this collection.

*"Never fails to entertain and surprise…this
collection has it all" – Jennifer Fallon*

Excerpt:

There's a moment, just before waking, when I forget
it's gone. I feel the ghost of it on my shoulders, the
warmth inside. It boosts my confidence and makes me
stronger. I am more myself. I am ready to rule the
islands and mould the day to my bidding.

Opening my eyes is a disappointment. My old bones
ache with craving. It's been missing from me for almost
three decades, but I feel it just the same. I'm simply an
old man with his memories and regrets. I had my chance.
I was not worthy.

Get your copy at Amazon.com & selected bookstores.

CURRENTS OF CHANGE
by Darian Smith

A suspenseful novel about magic, secrets, a haunted house, and a touch of romance.

Haunted house. Haunted heart.
When Sara O'Neill goes on the run, she believes the tiny New Zealand town of Kowhiowhio is just the sanctuary she needs. But a dangerous presence haunts her new home, threatening Sara's chance at peace. Can she create a new life while dealing with ghosts from the old?
For local electrician, Nate Adams, parenting his young daughter alone has not been easy. Even with his help, can the house – or Sara's heart – be repaired?
Someone doesn't want an O'Neill in Kowhiowhio.
Sara's return is awakening generations of secrets.
Why has the house never had electricity?
What was the fate of Sara's ancestors?
Can she discover the ghost's story before it's too late?
The truth will set…something…free.

"Well-paced paranormal romance. . . would appeal to readers who like a good ghost story, with a little bit of history and a dash of romance in the mix."
- SQ Mag International Speculative Fiction eZine

"I really enjoyed this book - a light, but interesting read that I didn't want to put down." - The Happy Homemaker

Get your copy at Amazon.com or selected bookstores.

www.ingramcontent.com/pod-product-compliance
Lightning Source LLC
Chambersburg PA
CBHW021118260626
47169CB00005B/1342